THE ORPHANS OF BERLIN

JINA BACARR

B

Boldwood

First published in Great Britain in 2022 by Boldwood Books Ltd. This paperback edition first published in 2023.

I

Copyright © Jina Bacarr, 2022

Cover Design by Colin Thomas

Cover Photography: Alamy, iStock, Shutterstock

A CIP catalogue record for this book is available from the British Library.

Paperback ISBN: 978-1-83533-940-4

Hardback ISBN 978-1-80415-346-8

Ebook ISBN 978-1-80415-350-5

Kindle ISBN 978-1-80415-349-9

Audio CD ISBN 978-1-80415-341-3

MP3 CD ISBN 978-1-80415-342-0

Digital audio download ISBN 978-1-80415-343-7

Large Print ISBN: 978-1-80415-348-2

Boldwood Books Ltd.

23 Bowerdean Street, London, SW6 3TN

www.boldwoodbooks.com

MIX
Paper | Supporting responsible forestry
FSC® C171272

To the brave men and women who risked their lives to save innocent Jewish children from the ravages of Hitler's war machine...

1

CHÂTEAU DE SAINTE-LUCIE-DES-FLEURS, OUTSIDE PARIS, LATE SEPTEMBER 1942

Rachel

It's drizzling rain when the French police storm the château and arrest my two little sisters, dragging them outside kicking and screaming, Leah's spectacles sliding down her nose, Tovah's big white bow in her short hair soggy and droopy. Crouched behind high bushes, I watch in horror from my hiding place when they toss them into an enclosed black truck: what the locals call a *panier à salade* – salad basket.

I can't move, unsure of what to do next.

It's no secret the local gendarmes take orders from the Nazis. Somehow, they found out we're Jewish refugees from Berlin, though we carry French identity cards.

Forged, of course.

My heart pounding, I can't stop my mind from racing through every possible outcome, every horrible thing they could do to my sisters.

Torture? Beatings? Starvation? Abuse? God, no, they're just children, my mind screams.

I should have seen this coming. Last week we had a scare when the Gestapo blocked off streets in the village and rounded up anyone who looked remotely non-Aryan, stuffing them into trucks without even a slit to look through. A man tried to escape and they shot him and left him in the street. We were terrified they'd question why we speak French with an accent, but we fooled the Gestapo, telling them we're from a small town near the Swiss border.

They let us go.

Not this time. I shudder when I think of the smug looks on the gendarmes' faces when they shoved my sisters into the truck. The glee in their eyes, knowing they got what they came for. Innocents they can parade in front of the Nazis to show their worth to the Germans and save their own skins.

I feel a rush of fear that sends me into despair. If I run and beg the police to let my sisters go, they'll arrest me, too. I draw my breath to keep my focus on saving them. I can expect no mercy; I know the drumroll of war drowned out the beating of their hearts years ago.

I tug on the buttons of my sweater, my heart heavy with dread. It's my fault my sisters got arrested. I'm the oldest. I should know better. I was selfish, weak, and now I'm paying the price.

Earlier I went in secret to meet the tall young man with the fierce look in his eyes. We rendezvoused in the gamekeeper's cottage on the château grounds. I was about to tell him my news when we heard the roar of a big truck, gears grinding. We ran outside and saw it racing toward the château, followed by an old French police car. We sneaked back to the main house and by the time we got here, the gendarmes had rammed their way inside the château, shackling my sisters like animals.

My love bade me to stay hidden, then he was off. Risking his own freedom to save them.

I wrap my arms around my swollen middle. I'm careful to keep my condition hidden. I don't want to worry my sisters. I'm nineteen and soon to be a mother. Leah is barely sixteen, her thin body not yet a woman's, and Tovah is a rambunctious thirteen-year-old who jumps like a frog into a pond every time she sees a German. I can't imagine the fear and horror residing in their battered souls at the hands of the Nazis. My sisters depend upon me. It's all my fault because I dared to fall in love with a Resistance fighter.

I wasn't here to protect them.

And now we're paying the price.

What would Mutti and Papa say? I promised them that day at the train station in Berlin we'd never be separated and now look what I've done. How many times have I held Leah and Tovah tight, shivering and praying we'd evade capture whenever the black truck rambled through the village, transporting Jews jammed shoulder to shoulder to the police station.

And… if the rumors are true… to death camps.

I wipe my eyes, my hot tears dissipated by the raindrops, but not my resolve. I'll fight the Nazis tooth and nail to get my sisters back.

An anguished cry catches in my throat. Oh, God, now they're bringing out Hélène, our governess, the pretty Polish girl with the bright red hair… Her dress is torn, her face bruised… What have they done to her? What kind of monster sends a gang of police thugs to arrest three young women?

All I can do is watch from my hiding place, waiting for my man to return. His first instinct was to shoot his way into the château to rescue the girls, but not only is he outnumbered, my sisters could have been caught in the crossfire. Instead, he went around back to see if he could slip inside unnoticed. Then he'd have the element of surprise, evening up the odds. *No*, he said, shaking his head. The château is closed up tight. Still, he didn't give up. He made me promise to stay rooted to the spot while he checked the perimeter for Germans, hoping to scale up the trellis to the first floor and find an open window.

Where is he?

He's been gone *ten... fifteen minutes*.

Thunder rumbles overhead, mixing with the roar of two German motorcycles pulling up not far from where I'm hiding in the thick brush. In summer, the bushes boast beautiful pink roses now turned a sad, ugly brown. Two SS men confer with the French police officer, checking the truck... then with the clicking of heels and raised hands in salutes, they race off on their motorcycles with the truck following and the police car bringing up the rear. They amble down the road in the rain, taking with them their precious cargo and killing my soul.

My sisters are gone... *Will I ever see them again*?

Their anguished cries echo in my head. How can I forget the gendarmes pinning their arms behind their backs? And then the unthinkable... Tovah kicking a policeman when he yanked her arm so hard it twisted at an odd angle.

Then he slapped her.

That got my blood going. Oh, the rage boiling in me that he dared to touch her. A child... *an innocent child*. Even crouched behind the high brush, I could see the reddening flush on her cheek, the fear in her eyes.

And I could do *nothing*.

I swear I will not let their cowardly deed go unpunished. I won't allow these barbarians to get away with hurting my sisters... I *will* come up with a plan, embrace the challenge to set my sisters free.

I could never live with myself otherwise.

How did this happen? We believed we were safe here in France, then the rumble of war and the smell of blood spread over Europe like a dark cloud thick as a saffron fog, hiding the Nazis' ugly deeds, leaving us in limbo and taking refuge in the countryside in an old château.

Until today.

I grit my teeth, my being shaken to the core. I suffer the pain of knowing an informer betrayed us.

Then as silent as a prayer, Wolf is beside me, his breath hot against my neck. 'They're taking your sisters and Hélène to the local police station,' he says, his tone edgy. 'I'll gather my men right away and we'll stage a raid—'

'No.' I lay my hand upon his arm. 'I've seen how ruthless they are. The sadistic cowards will kill my sisters without remorse if you try to break them free. No, we can't let them know we're onto them. It gives us an advantage... and buys us time. There must be another way.'

He heaves out a heavy breath. 'We could keep them under observation until they're transported to a detention camp... then attack the truck...'

'Oh my God...' I whisper, my hand to my throat. I listen to his plan, dangerous and with no guarantee it will work, but what choice do we have?

He holds me tight, calming me down, but I can't stop shaking.

'Nothing will stop me from rescuing your sisters and Hélène,' he whispers, his vow embracing my soul, his words a salve on my wounds.

'I want to believe you... and I do... but I'm afraid, not for myself, but for Leah and Tovah.'

'My brave Rachel, you can't stay here, they'll come back, looking for you. Let me protect you.'

'How?' I ask, deeply moved by his concern.

'I'll hide you in my camp. You'll be safe with my friends, all loyal

members of the Resistance, while we work out a plan to save your
sisters.'

I say nothing. He has no idea I carry his child. If he knew, he'd
make me come with him. He's that way, always has been since that
first day we met when my sisters and I left Berlin with the American woman—

Oh...

An idea begins to spin in my brain like a dreidel twirling round
and round.

Of course... do I dare?

'I *must* get to Paris,' I whisper in German, my brain so scrambled
I forget about speaking French. 'I know someone who can help us.'

'I'll come with you, Rachel.'

I shake my head. 'No, you're on the Gestapo's most-wanted list.
If you're caught...'

He holds me so tight I can't breathe. 'I won't let you go alone.'

'*I must*... There's only one person who can help me rescue Leah
and Tovah... and Hélène.' I clutch my chest, desperation filling me,
driving me to go through with my crazy plan.

'Who?'

I attempt a smile. 'You remember Fräulein Kay Alexander?'

There are other ways to fight than with a pistol, she said. *A word
and a bribe to the right person with allegiance to no one is often more
effective.*

I'm convinced she can help us.

He nods. '*Ja*... the American.'

'She keeps a room at the Hôtel Ritz.' I feel a ripple of hope.
'She'll find a way to save my sisters and Hélène before the Gestapo
sends them to a death camp... and they're lost to me forever.'

2

PARIS, LATE SEPTEMBER 1942

Kay

I walk from the Hôtel Ritz to the movie theater with purpose, swiveling my head right then left, making sure I'm not followed. My teeth chatter on this chilly late afternoon in spite of my fur-lined coat. *Nerves.* I still can't get used to this undercover business.

I sigh. One more job and I'm done.

Then I'll never have to set foot in that damn hotel or see another Nazi again.

I'm not a trained agent. I've never jumped out of an airplane or shot a pistol or learned to be a wireless operator.

I don't even know Morse code.

But I *do* know how to play bridge, order off the menu in flawless French, and how, at dinner parties, to name-drop the most influential people in Philadelphia, Washington DC, Newport. *And* Palm Beach, where Mother and I spend summers. I never thought I'd be grateful for my debutante skills, but it's my position in society, according to my uncle Archibald, that gives me a certain cachet on foreign soil.

Then America entered the war.

Now I'm an enemy alien in the eyes of the Germans, known to the Gestapo as Kay Alexander, daughter of Mrs Herbert George Radwell-Alexander, Philadelphia society's bluest blood. *Heiress to a candy fortune and party girl*, I imagine my official Nazi dossier reads. *Drinks too much, spends too much money on couture clothes and French perfume.*

I smile. If the secret police only knew *why* I indulge in perfume.

My carefree, useless existence makes me the perfect candidate for this clandestine kind of work. Young, beautiful (so I'm told), and with a past that gives me nothing to live for. I came here on a journey to warm that cold, dead feeling that has been lying in my heart since a terrible, wintry night when my world crashed down around me. The nights are the hardest... when I'm alone. Then the pain returns.

I got stuck in Paris when the Germans goose stepped down the Champs-Élysées alongside their tanks, so I did a little spying for the Allies.

Then things got too hot.

With America in the war, Kay, it's too dangerous for you to stay in Paris.

A warning from my dear friend, Gertrud von Arenbeck, Austrian journalist, bon vivant, and member of the Underground. She's meeting me later back at the Ritz. We received disturbing news about the three Landau sisters I brought to Paris from Germany.

I have to get them out of France. There's a push from the Gestapo to find Jewish children hiding in France and the French police aren't wasting any time rounding them up, child by child. I can't use the telephone in my hotel room to warn Hélène at the château where the girls are hiding. The phones are tapped by the Gestapo. Not to mention hotel informants among the staff. Watching, waiting, for a guest to give them suspicion to report them.

I take a seat in the theater before the film starts. I don't pay attention to the name of the picture starring a famous French blonde bombshell. Sylvie something or other. I'm too busy figuring out how my contact will pass along the information.

Earlier I found a ticket to a movie theater, the Gaumont Palace, in my coat pocket after I left the perfume shop on Rue Saint Honoré. My drop-off point if I need to send a message to London, then Washington. Not original, but it works.

Rich American buying perfume to charm the occupiers is what I imagine the shop girls say to one other.

I haven't been at this spying business long, but I've learned to pick up the subtleties of the game. For example, if an agent sees an upside-down horseshoe on a barn, it means there's a message for them.

For me, it's when I see a distinct perfume in the window displayed with a red rose. *Naomie's Dream.* That means I'm needed for a job. Whoever put that ticket in my coat pocket knows I plan to leave Paris tonight and they're desperate enough to take a chance on me getting their information to the right people in London.

I fidget in my seat, observing... An agent never makes the first move... *Wait for the mark to come to you.* Slow, painful minutes pass while the theme music swells and the pretty blonde vamps it up on the silver screen and the audience loves it. Then, out of the corner of my eye, I catch the silhouette of a young woman standing in the aisle. Slim. Confident. She excuses herself as she makes her way past me in the narrow space between the rows of seats. I look up and even in the dim lighting, I recognize the stunning girl in the black coat with the wide braided collar and felt hat from the perfume shop.

I never learned her name.

I wait for what seems like forever, then she gets up and I follow her to the powder room. She slips a folded-up piece of paper through the stall door.

'Get these names to London,' she whispers. 'It's urgent.'

I admit to wonder how she knows I'm leaving France, but I know better than to ask. Then with a strong whiff of a heady rose perfume, she's gone.

I stuff the list of names into my coat pocket and don't let go of it until I get back to my hotel on Place Vendŏme.

I haven't stopped shaking since.

Once I'm back in my room at the Ritz... my home away from home since 1937... I pull off my black kid gloves, then strip off my fur-lined coat, unbutton my blue dress down the front. Next I take off my slip, heart pounding as I grab the tiny sewing kit provided by the hotel. I rip out the black satin inset in the seam in my girdle and get to work, pricking my fingers with the long needle.

'*Main Line girls never flinch when they're in trouble, Kay.*'

Mother. And her laundry list of platitudes that never cease. Ever since I was a little girl in pigtails, she's never let me forget I dance to a different beat because I'm a Philadelphia Main Line blue blood (her words, not mine) and there are 'rules' to follow.

'*They smile, Kay. And for God's sake, don't run to the nearest powder room. Walk like a queen.*'

Like a queen on her way to the guillotine if I'm caught.

I rip off the extra thread with my teeth.

Sloppy stitches, but they'll have to do. I never learned anything remotely domestic at boarding school, but not knowing what I'm doing never stopped me. I got it into my head when I was a kid I had to prove to everyone I'm not a candy princess, but a normal girl.

I've always been on the outside looking in, wanting to belong, so I race into situations shall we say, which is not always smart. Then I get hurt, *really* hurt. Last time, I barely survived.

This time... well, we'll find out, won't we?

Finally, the list is invisible, sewn into my girdle.

Then I grab what jewelry I can from the hidden cubbyhole in a built-in cupboard. I'm amazed at how many concealed places this hotel contains – even secret rooms to hide refugees... or so I've heard.

I smile. The list isn't the only thing I sew into my clothes. I grab two diamond rings, a necklace, a pearl choker set with emeralds (Goering would love to get his hands on that) and stuff them in the fur lining of my coat. Jewels I bought here in Paris before the war. Then I close it up with large stitches. I have to be ready for anything including dealing on the black market for cash if my escape plan goes awry.

What if the plane can't land? *Strong winds... not enough moonlight... flak from enemy aircraft.*

My line of credit is in good standing, but there's no telling when the Germans will concoct a plan to block funds from my Swiss bank. So far, I've had no problem keeping up appearances at the Ritz to allay suspicion from my spying activities, but a girl can't be too careful.

I run out of thread, so I cram a ruby and diamond necklace inside a small music box, a sentimental item I've cherished for years. I bought it in Berlin on a hot summer day... a day when I entered a world I'd only dreamed about, where the perfect family actually existed in my life if only for a little while. A jealous arrow stung my heart because I wanted that so much when I was a kid and here it was. Yet I could only sigh and tuck that dream of having a loving family away, the memory tugging at me now as I stuff the music box into the side pocket of my coat along with a handful of chocolate bars dropped by an RAF pilot with my family name on it.

Radwell's French Chocolates of Philadelphia.

He also dropped a bundle of rifles and pistols with my name *definitely* not on them. *Guns for the brave souls in the Underground fighting the Nazis,* according to Gertrud. I wasn't offended when she didn't offer me a weapon. I have no idea how to load a pistol, much less fire it.

Now to get the hell out of here.

I leave my hotel room, peeking to check no one is in the hallway, and lock the door. Then I race around the corner to the elevator and run smack into an arrogant SS officer on the prowl.

'*Bonsoir, mademoiselle...* have we met before?'

We stand in front of the elevator, facing each other like two comics in a bad vaudeville skit who forgot their lines, neither of us willing to give up center stage. He grins, I scowl... His eyes are curious, his nose more so.

He leans toward me and inhales. 'Enchanting scent. French, of course.'

I don't need this tomcat sniffing me. I've got to get rid of him.

I return the favor, my nose wiggling. 'Stale beer... German, of course.'

'You dare to insult an officer of the Reich?' he demands in a sing-song, squeaky voice.

'I wouldn't dream of it... Lieutenant, is it?'

'*Captain, mademoiselle.*' He clicks his heels. I ignore his show of command.

Instead, I jam my finger on the 'Down' button. I know the type. A weasel in uniform with a sense of entitlement because he wears black jackboots.

I make my play. 'Now if you'll excuse me, *monsieur,* I'm in a hurry,' I answer in French, not daring to breathe lest I pop my girdle. Then I turn my back to him.

Wrong move.

That was one insult too many for the Nazi. The SS officer snarls, then curses in German. I awakened a *Teutonic* sleeping tiger and he's out for blood.

Mine.

3

RACHEL

When I cross the Place Vendôme, I don't expect to see two Nazi sentries in gray-green uniforms and steel helmets standing stiff and rigid guarding the entrance to the Hôtel Ritz. I haven't been to the city since the Occupation began more than two years ago. I'm shocked and disheartened at what I see. German officers sitting at the cafés, smoking, their beady eyes appraising every young Frenchwoman who dares pass their table; swastika flags flying from buildings like bloodied flags of surrender from a city I love; cinemas splashed with welcoming signs in German for Nazi soldiers; Parisians riding bicycles or walking, no motorcars for private citizens. I want to turn and run, disbelief pushing my spirit into a darkening cloud... a once-proud city of light where that light dims a little more each day of Occupation. But I'm desperate and I have nowhere else to turn.

I *must* get a message to Kay Alexander.

I feel confident she's still in the city. She remarked to me on her last visit to the château that the Germans weren't going to interfere with her mission to help us and others like us, that if she could put up with her mother's brash indignations, the Nazis couldn't be much worse. She was joking, of course, or so I thought, but when I looked into her eyes, I saw an exquisite woman dressed so elegantly, like the models in the magazine, *Die Junge Dame*, but hiding a hurtful secret. If it wasn't for the tears shining in her blue eyes, I never would have believed she was in pain. Yet she always has a kind word... and chocolate dropped from the sky by the RAF... to comfort me. I swear she reads my mind when I stare off into space and think about how much I miss Mutti. She gives me a hug and tells me no one can take my mother's place, but if I have any questions now that I'm grown up... about boys... *anything*, she's here for me. That I shouldn't be embarrassed. I swear she blushes and lowers her eyes. I can't hide anything from her... especially how I feel about Wolf. That wasn't the first time she didn't hide her feelings from me. We have a bond, a strong tie formed years ago when I first met her in Berlin. I saw then she'd been hurt in the most awful way and she needed to reclaim her soul from the devil. I think she's been working on that ever since, this striking brunette with a big laugh and the lightest blue eyes I've ever seen.

I'll never forget how her eyes misted up when she promised my parents that day in Berlin at the *Anhalter* train station that we three sisters would never be separated, her hand shaking, clasping her chest.

Her Austrian friend, Gertrud, snapped photos of us four smiling but anxious. Kay kept her word and we three stayed together.

Until now.

I came to Paris by train, paying for my ticket with the paper francs Hélène keeps in a blue glass jar in the kitchen cupboard for incidentals. The gendarmes didn't find it, their noses sniffing out a bottle of wine instead. Smashed glasses. A broken bottle on the terra-cotta tile floor.

I ignore the light drizzle wetting the stone squares on the Place Vendôme. Few pedestrians dare to wander here so I darted between the parked motorcars, praying no one would notice me. I pace up and down, then peek through my long bangs to see if the guards are watching me. *No.* Then why is my stomach rejecting the stale roll I choked down, sending hot bile into my throat? Why am I so afraid? What if the guard gets persnickety and questions the smeared ink on my French identity card where my thumbprint is?

Then I'm done for.

What will happen to my child... a child the Nazis won't hesitate to take from me when it's born. I'm nearly six months pregnant... I think... but so thin I can hide my swollen belly under my coat. Everyone in France is thin with the shortage of food and only the German generals are getting fat.

I don't know what to do. I can't walk boldly up to the hotel entrance. Stone-faced, eyes moving like slits, the soldiers allow only German officers to pass through the revolving doors. Armed with rifles and bayonets, the sentries stand so still they don't seem human.

I'll *never* get past them.

I didn't think this through. I should have, but who knew about the sentries? So, I have two choices. I can wait for the American *mademoiselle* to come *out* of the hotel. Or catch her when she returns. I cling to that notion. *I must.*

I dig my hands deeper into my coat pockets, cradle my palms over my belly, thinking. I feel the baby kick, but it's my wanting that makes it so. It's more like a fluttering. I long for the days that lighten my heart. Days before the Occupation when the kind American woman invited my sisters and me here for tea to celebrate my sixteenth birthday. She knew how much we missed our parents and on my special day, she wanted to make us smile and forget for a while the emptiness that sat heavy in our hearts. Like a lumpy vanilla pudding thickened with too much starch. Not on that day. Kay did everything she could to make us smile. I've never met anyone with a heart so eager to please. I felt like a film star courted and fussed over by the Ritz staff, despite struggling to speak proper French like I belonged here.

Kay said not to worry, that my sisters and I were her special guests... that she hadn't given a birthday party since she was sixteen when she made a lopsided, two-layer chocolate cake for her mother's special day. The society matron sniffed the cake and left for an evening with her lady friends, reminding Kay she *could* have ordered a perfect chocolate cake from *Kaplan's*. What started out as a dream of bonding with her mother ended up with Kay spending the evening alone in her room, blowing out candles, one by one.

I was so taken by her honesty, I grabbed her hand and just held it. Leah and Tovah hugged her, their melancholy faces making her cry, then Kay insisted on no more sad stories and bade the waiter to bring us 'the works'. Laughing and speaking the French *and* English we learned in Jewish school, we feasted on sweet raspberry tarts and vanilla pastry cream in the terrace garden with white tablecloths and fancy silverware. Flowers in big Chinese vases bloomed and waved at us with their petals like saucy chorus girls. We came again to the Ritz on a whimsical gray, fall day and savored hot chocolate flavored with orange zest and warm gingerbread, and buns oozing with cinnamon and butter.

Never knowing that was the beginning of the end.

Glorious days when Kay – she insisted we call her *Kay* instead of Mademoiselle Alexander – smiled at us with tenderness in her heart as we indulged in petit chocolates and licked our fingers, telling us the chocolate made back home in Philadelphia at her family's candy factory was like tasting heaven here on earth.

Milky sweet and creamy dark, she said. *Thick nougat and melty caramel.*

My sisters and I couldn't imagine having all the chocolate you wanted. A paradise in our minds. Yes, we had sweets at home in

Germany and our favorites were the butterscotch hard candies Mutti kept in her cherished crystal candy dish... but chocolate every day?

That was only for rich people.

We found out *how* rich the American *mademoiselle* is when she showed us her room on the fourth floor of the Ritz. A tall fireplace, as well as elegant and feminine white furniture that looked as though it came from a palace. Our mouths dropped open when she told us every room in the hotel had its own bathroom.

We *oohed* and *aahed*, touching the ivory cream silk and blue velvet furniture, and made funny faces in the huge mirror over the mantel. Yes, she's rich. *Very* rich to live at the Ritz. *And* to get us new identity cards on the black market declaring us not to be Jewish but French Catholics.

More importantly, she cares about us like we're her family.

And now I've ruined everything she's done for us with my impulsiveness.

My sisters are in the hands of the Nazis.

I'll never understand why they want to destroy my people. We wish only to live a normal life, observe Shabbat by the warmth of lit candles, make music in our shop and let it rise to the heavens so God may know we haven't forgotten Him... hug our parents who do so much for us... and fall in love.

I pace up and down the Place Vendôme, tap my fingers against my plain navy skirt, white blouse and long sweater under my coat, and then start humming to calm my nerves. A lullaby I wrote for Tovah on *Kristallnacht* when she was nine. The words came from deep in my soul, breaking free like the shards of glass when the Nazis smashed the front window of our music shop, exploding around us when we crept downstairs to see what was happening.

A night of broken glass.

The night is cold
But my hand is warm
Take my hand, little one
Lay your head against my shoulder
And sleep.

Almost four years have passed and now the whole world is at war.

The Nazis fill their bellies like overstuffed geese, swallowing up the continent with their tanks and armies. Haven't they brought enough misery? How can arresting young Jewish girls be of any significance to them?

All I can think about is better days during the last summer of our innocence when we'd get together in the parlor of our home in Berlin. We filled the air with our music, each note sweet and pure. Me on piano singing, Leah strumming her guitar, her round spectacles sliding down her nose, and little Tovah playing her violin like a busy honeybee, her short dark hair bouncing up and down, the starched white bow sitting like a crown upon her head. Mutti would work on the embroidery in her lap, looking up to read my lips since she lost her hearing years ago... and Papa would film us with his prized movie camera. It didn't matter if there was no sound, he said, on the 9.5 mm film. Each in their own way could hear us in their mind.

Even Mutti.

Everything changed in 1935 when I turned twelve and Hitler came up with his race laws barring Jews from doing almost everything. I did what I could to help Mutti; she never spoke of her deafness, but I know she struggled to make a normal life for us.

Summer should have been a time of having fun with my sisters. Instead, shop windows were smeared in red paint with the words 'dirty Jew' and gangs roamed the streets and warned us not to go inside or they'd beat us up.

Now I'm gripped with that same fear. And guilt. Guilt that I wasn't arrested with them.

I draw back into the late afternoon shadow behind a parked motorcar, my mind scrambling. I quiver inside, a rising panic setting me off course. I dare not approach the German soldiers.

Think, do something, find another way inside.

How? Paris has changed since I last came to the Ritz.

I keep humming to calm my nerves, daring to get closer to the entrance, hoping I can peek inside the hotel and, on the off chance, spot Kay in the foyer. I pull back when an elderly Frenchman dressed in a long gray wool overcoat, colorful silk scarf and hat, shows up, complaining he's in a hurry to meet with Goering and his right-hand Gestapo man, poking his cane at the guards and jabbering that he's a duke and he *always* uses the front entrance. He demands to see the colonel in charge and to my surprise, a guard races into the hotel. The Frenchman paces up and down until an officer comes out and they exchange words: '*No, Herr Geller hasn't arrived*' and he sends him around the hotel to the Rue Cambon entrance.

My heart leaps. Of course... I'd forgotten about the rear entrance. We used it when it was raining and we visited the famous shop of Mademoiselle Chanel on Rue Cambon, though Kay prefers the fancy revolving door front entrance, insisting a young lady always makes an entrance where she can be seen.

Are there German guards at the back door? I have to take that chance.

I start to follow him when—

An old, beat-up Renault cuts me off as it pulls up to the front of the hotel with a large Gestapo man in a black trench coat and fedora hanging out the passenger window, bellowing about a flat tire on his Citroën and yelling for them to help him out of this rattrap and not to forget his briefcase.

The guards give him the Hitler salute with outstretched hands, then do as he asks.

Herr Geller, I imagine, as he heads toward me... then I see his face.

My knees go weak and it's all I can do not to cry out.

No, *impossible*... it's him... the Gestapo man from that day in Berlin... so many years ago. I never knew his name. I can't believe it; the shock is so intense I can't move.

He pushes me out of the way with an expletive so crude I want to kick him. But I'm no fool. Did he recognize me? No, I was a kid then. I'm a woman now. Besides, I'm not important to him. I use that to my advantage. Luckily for me no one is about in the afternoon drizzle to give him an excuse to make an example of me for getting in his way.

I keep to the meandering shadows falling from the archways carved into the building façade, darting from one to the next to stay out of sight, a light mist wetting my cheeks, a pesky breeze blowing my long bangs into my eyes. I squint. I should be afraid, watching him shouting orders in German to the guards to stop anyone trying to leave the hotel, but I'm too desperate to think rationally. Then he starts scribbling on a newspaper and looking at his watch. No doubt in my mind it's the same Gestapo man. I can tell by his clipped accent and cold and calculating snarl he's from Berlin.

I gather my courage and move closer to the hotel entrance. The two sentries look straight ahead at the large square, empty of pedestrians venturing out in the gloomy day. I remember when Kay brought us here, a wistful sigh in her voice when she explained how Napoleon erected the bronze column forged from over a thousand enemy cannons. *A sign of war that lingers among the upscale jewelry shops.* Today it shimmers with raindrops glistening like cheap gems.

The only vehicles I see are a line of Nazi-owned Mercedes and Citroëns parked in a precise row. I could hide between the motor-cars again until the Gestapo man leaves and then race toward the hotel rear entrance, but I don't want to make a sudden move.

The man in the trench coat could turn on me in an instant.

Seconds later I gasp with surprise when a big, black touring Mercedes motorcar screeches to a halt and two Nazi soldiers and an officer jump out. The SS man argues in German with the Gestapo man and has no idea I understand every word.

I use the opportunity to move out of the shadows, my heart pounding when I hear them talking about *'arresting the last American woman on the list'*. The Gestapo man doesn't want to show his hand by barging through the entrance with SS men shouting behind him. The SS officer disagrees.

My stomach plummets. *American woman.*

God, does he mean Kay?

I must be sure.

Lips quivering, I hunch my shoulders and inch closer to the Gestapo man bellowing and grunting like a circus ringmaster, his voice loud and clear in the empty square. He neither cares nor attempts to quell his anger.

I hang on to every word.

He orders the officer and his men to follow him to the Rue Cambon entrance, reminding him the Ritz is comprised of two buildings with a long corridor connecting them. He doesn't want to risk the American escaping. The SS officer balks, unhappy with the Gestapo man's impudent orders; he has no intention of using a back entrance.

With their backs to me, they argue like two bullies in a school-yard, disagreeing on how to proceed with the arrest. The Gestapo man yells and the SS officer demands *he* be in charge. He barely gives me a sneer when he turns and struts by me as he and his men enter the hotel on the Vendôme side.

Fuming, the Gestapo man roars like a wild boar as he rips up his newspaper and tosses it to the wind, giving me a few seconds lead on him. I can't hesitate any longer.

What if there are more guards?

The words, '*Herr Geller sent me*' are already forming on my lips in German as I race around to the back of the hotel. I stop, relieved. No guards. *Gut.* I jam through the Rue Cambon entrance and run up the service backstairs, praying I get to Kay before the Gestapo man does.

4

KAY

'*A debutante never sweats.*'

Oh, really, Mother? I'd say if I were back in Philadelphia. Then again, I wouldn't have been hiding intelligence sewn into my tight black satin girdle with the SS breathing down my neck if I were back home. My garters are snapping against the bare skin of my thighs and... more shocking to my prim, conservative mother, I'm in the company of a Nazi officer, most definitely a man *not* on her approved list of suitors.

I grit my teeth.

So why haven't I stopped sweating since I squeezed past the SS man blocking the hotel elevator? Simple. The tension sizzling between us borders on what we call back home a 'pickup' and the Nazi scare tactics I've seen used on the streets on anyone who gets in their way. He makes me nervous even when he tries to be civil, introducing himself with a slight bow and click of his heels as Captain Horst Bauder. By his sunburned face, I'd say he just arrived from the front.

North Africa, I'd guess.

Still, I have a bad feeling something is about to go down in an unpleasant way.

The German swine is unmovable. He hasn't taken his eyes off me since I pressed the 'Down' button, insisting... no, *demanding* I have a cocktail with him.

'*Pardon, monsieur,*' I say in French with a slight smile, 'but you must be tired after a long day of gobbling up countries.'

'I assure you, *mademoiselle*, we officers of the SS are known for our stamina.' He clicks his heels. Again.

'I doubt I could keep up with you.'

'It's my duty,' he boasts, jutting out his chin, 'to show *mademoiselle* how we Germans are improving life here in France.' He leans closer to me and I get a whiff of arrogance along with an overly strong musk. 'I can get you nylons... whiskey... courtesy of the Reich.'

'Can you get me fresh eggs, bread for the poor of Paris?' I dare to ask.

'Our troops must be fed first... the poor can—'

'I know... let them eat cake,' I quip, but it goes over his head. He gives me a hard stare, then goes on and on about how I should be honored to drink with him.

Why, me? Perhaps he thinks I'm a mysterious Frenchwoman. Blue eyes... dark red lipstick, fair skin and deep, dark hair curling over my shoulders.

So I act French.

With my nose up in the air, I open my clutch and pull out my lip rouge. I feel the German's eyes on me, unnerving me, but I don't flinch. I'd never let him see me as a fragile female he can knock around or worse, as someone who will fawn over him because he and his troops occupy the city.

I refresh my lips with color, smacking them together loudly.

And wait.

I'm hoping he'll get tired of my indifference. I'm taller than he is in my high-heeled pumps and cut a womanly figure in the right places. I'm proud to attest to a small waist and slender hips. To think I was once a pudgy teenager, my presence so distasteful to my mother that she shunned me for years. She never tucked me in at nights (*that's what nannies are for, Kay*), read me a bedtime story (ditto for nannies) or held me in her arms and dried my tears when I scraped my knee. A sad time that sits on the edge of my brain, waiting for me to push it over the cliff, but I can't. The trauma remains. Like a thunderstorm that strikes when you least expect it and drenches you with regret.

There's a part of me that's still that shy, little girl.

God help me… if I let her out now, I'm dead.

I push her back down into that secret place in my soul, tap my black suede pump on the carpeting and play with the flimsy veil on my hat, sniffing the scent of superiority emitting from this man. He's no different than the Nazis I've seen cavorting in the hotel's public rooms, some in civilian clothes since they're off duty, speaking French, showing off their Aryan good looks and bad manners, insisting they want to 'fit in'.

I turn, walk back toward my room, but he's two long strides ahead of me and cuts me off, laying his hand on my arm and making me wince, his dark eyebrows crossed in frustration in contrast to his white-toothed smile. He's the very picture of an arrogant Nazi babbling about how it's an honor to drink with an SS officer. I *have* to get rid of him. I try to pull away, conscious of how close he is to me and the secret list sewn into my girdle. He holds on to me for a long moment, letting me know who's in charge before letting me go. I want to kick him in the shins, but I've got too much to lose. I can't shake the queasiness the man evokes in me, especially when I head back to the long hallway and he's next to me, sniffing my perfume.

'I can't get enough of French perfume, *mademoiselle*… especially yours.'

'*Naomie's Dream*. I'll buy you a bottle,' I quip, but he doesn't get the message. Whatever I say, I can't get rid of him.

I sigh. I wonder what my mother, the proper Millicent Radwell-Alexander, would have said if she'd seen me earlier, slinking through the hotel, head down, avoiding Nazi officers heading for the back bar. I can still hear in my head the buzz permeating the lobby, German and French in the air, forced female laughter as a late afternoon sun dropped below the horizon. All around the city, Parisians are grateful another day under the Occupation had ended.

For me, it was just beginning.

I've changed since I ran away from my charmed, socialite life six years ago. I've survived the Occupation without getting caught because according to my uncle, the Nazis are so by the book, they don't believe 'young and pretty women like you, Kay,' are capable of learning their plans.

But my luck ran out when this Boche attached himself to me.

I have to dump him, but how?

What if he gets fresh and forces himself on me at knifepoint? Nazi officers check their side arms at the front kiosk, but that won't stop him if he lives by the *merde* touted by the Party... that he's a member of the 'master race' and a woman is fair game for him to prove what a big man he is.

It's happened to many Frenchwomen, according to Gertrud. We met when I first came to Paris in the mid-1930s, a time when the city overflowed with literary readings, cabarets, and the air was filled with Gershwin and Cole Porter tunes. She's immune to the Nazis or any man's charm. A secret she keeps hidden under her brown and cedar-toned tweed suit, broad shoulder pads, and sensible walking shoes, her bright, green eyes twinkling behind her monocle. She's never without it.

Not my style, but we do have one thing in common.

We both pine for lovers we can't have.

I made mistakes with the man I love that I wish I hadn't... and now he won't talk to me.

Gertrud, on the other hand, is, in the eyes of the Reich, what they call *socially aberrant*. Unlike if she were a man, she's in no danger since women aren't persecuted for their choice of a partner.

Except the woman she loves doesn't know it.

I've never seen Gertrud as happy as when she's with Hélène. I'll never forget the two of them sitting side by side at the American Hospital, rolling bandages, their hands touching as they worked. Gertrud's eyes were shining, but the Polish girl had no idea what was going on in the Austrian's head and I'll never tell.

There are some things only time can change.

I wish I could help her, but after the mess I made with my man, I wouldn't take my own advice. I'll always cherish the memory of his touch and him folding me into his arms, running his hand through my hair, my head resting on his broad chest. I can't think about him now, though I want to.

I know that Gertrud, as forthcoming as she is, is surprisingly shy in the ways of the heart. I admire her for her courage. Rather envious, too, of how she doesn't back away from who she is.

She's a hero in my eyes, a hell of a writer, and an ally.

It was Gertrud who connected me with the fledging French Underground after Paris fell to the Germans in June 1940. A day neither of us will ever forget... the hush over the city made us stop breathing, even the perfume of gardenias that is Paris at twilight dissipated like holy smoke when the bitter wind from the east invaded the city. Since the American embassy formally closed in June 1941, I've been on my own, cut off from receiving assistance from my uncle Archie or the State Department. Though an air of civility still reigns toward Americans, no one knows how long this cloak of neutrality will last. Gertrud's been my lifesaver. Anything I can do for her and her friends, I'm ready.

Which is what got me into this mess.

Hiding a hot list of names in my underwear.

Double agents.

I keep ignoring the German officer grinding his teeth together as he insists I have a drink with him, hoping my aloofness sends him away. I have no doubt the Boche is trolling through the hotel looking for French pastry. By the stringent odor following him, I wouldn't be surprised if he's already gotten a taste with a willing *mamselle* on this floor and is looking for more.

I let out a long sigh, pulling down the veil on my hat to shield my private thoughts from him. I shift my weight, wishing I could scratch the spot where I'm hiding the list of names.

I don't.

'I must *insist* you have that drink with me, *mademoiselle*,' he snarls, breathing heavy, taking my elbow with his gloved hand and giving me a hard squeeze this time to make sure I understand it's an order, not a request. He's tired of the game and that doesn't bode well for me.

Think of an excuse... anything.

'I'm on my way to the American Hospital to roll bandages, *monsieur*.' I broaden my smile, though I quiver inside.

'*Ja, Fräulein*?' Suspicion lurks in his eyes. 'At this hour?'

'Yes,' I lie. 'I hear the Red Cross delivered the fresh linens they so desperately need.'

The SS man sneers. 'Why waste your evening on men too sick to appreciate your stunning beauty, *mademoiselle*, when you have an officer of the Reich at your disposal?'

I fight to keep from lashing out as his eyes settle on me.

Instead, I say, 'Because they need me more than you do.' I smile. I'll never forget the deep, dark pools questioning me like burning coals. Quite a contrast from his cropped blond hair tinted by the desert sun.

I head back to the elevator which, in true Ritz fashion, is still making its way up to the fourth floor from the lobby like a half-filled balloon.

I *could* run down the winding staircase, but this Nazi jerk would follow me and grab my rear before I got past the third floor. He's keeping his distance. For now. I have the feeling he's retreated to plan his next attack on me. A game to him, with my virtue as his objective. There's nothing more dangerous than a lonely German captain with time on his hands and a hunger in his belly for a willing *mademoiselle*.

Before he can press me further, the elevator's grill door opens and the scent of a heavy cinnamon spice mixed with cognac hits my nostrils. A tall, dapper Frenchman smiles when he sees me. Mid-sixties with a practiced smile on that handsome face. He's wearing a long, gray overcoat and scarf. In another era, he'd be adjusting his pompous white wig and rubbing himself against his brocade knickers, then dabbing snuff to his nose with a lace handkerchief.

The Duc de Savaré.

The man has a youthful swagger in spite of his years.

'Ah, Kay, there you are,' he says. 'I was coming to see you.'

'You two are acquainted?' the German asks, surprised.

'Ah, *mais oui*; *mademoiselle* and I go back a long way before the war.'

His sarcasm isn't lost on me.

What's his game?

I pull back, praying he won't try to kiss me on both cheeks. His bite is dangerous; he's like a snake in duke's clothing. Louis-Marcel Valbert is a man I once liked and trusted. A man I developed an affection for when I felt so alone.

A man who deceived me and used me for his own gain.

5

KAY

Louis had me pegged right from the beginning as an easy mark.

I was a naïve, pretty American girl just arrived in Paris, lonely and with a broken heart. I was barely twenty but no longer the debutante of the season – a ruined woman. I fell for his paternal pat on the arm, his charm, his aristocratic sentiment to show me the sights.

Oh, he showed me the sights all right. A clever scheme he used on unsuspecting females to line his pockets.

I still don't trust him, but I'm not about to out him now.

I need him to distract the Nazi officer. Gertrud is waiting for me at the Rue Cambon entrance in her blue-gray motorcar parked in the shadows on the narrow street. Then we'll return to the château to pick up the Landau sisters. The wily journalist bribed a low ranking French official approved by the Nazis to 'borrow' her motorcar from the Germans since they confiscated all the vehicles.

'I heard you left Paris, *monsieur*,' I address the duke, 'when the shooting started.'

Rumor has it Louis fled to the South of France and I assumed to Switzerland.

I was wrong.

'I had business in Lyon which required my attention.' He grins, unashamed.

'Exporting your usual cargo?'

He ignores my innuendo, a reference to the sordid situation he trapped me in, though I let it pass. Paris is a dangerous city for any Frenchman, though I imagine like other aristocrats, he's aligned himself with the Germans.

'Captain, have you heard the latest news from the Unoccupied Zone?' the duke asks, dripping with Gallic charm. 'It would be my pleasure to buy an officer of the Reich a cocktail.'

The SS man snickers, insulted. 'I prefer the company of a beautiful woman, *monsieur.*'

'I have news about the Eastern Front, *monsieur*, you'll want to hear.' He mentions the name of a Nazi general and other gibberish that means nothing to me.

'*Ja?*'

'Hold the elevator, Captain,' the duke says, 'and I'll try to persuade *mademoiselle* to join us.'

The Nazi thinks for a moment, his brain weighing the odds the duke will have better luck than he did trying to convince me to have a drink with him, then steps inside the elevator. I love how that German sneer turns into a mischievous grin, the officer's sunburned, weathered face beaming as he wets his lips with his tongue. He's anticipating sugar in his coffee tonight.

Louis takes me by the elbow out of the captain's earshot, then whispers, 'Get out of Paris, Kay, *now*! You're in danger.'

'From you?' I raise a brow. 'Or is this one of your tricks?'

'I know what you think of me, but take my advice and run down the service back stairs and *don't* look back. I'll keep the captain busy.'

'If you want to help me, Louis, leave me alone.'

'Kay, *listen*... the Gestapo have already arrested several Americans and sent the men to detention camps.' He hesitates, then: 'I hear the women are next.'

I blink. *Can it be true?* No, they wouldn't *dare* arrest an American guest at the Ritz. The management wouldn't allow it. It would be bad for business. Yet I can't take that chance. What if Louis is right and I *am* in danger? He's risking his freedom if the captain figures out his game. I must get out of Paris and pick up the Landau sisters at the Château de Sainte-Lucie-des-Fleurs and get them to safety. I bought the dilapidated château years ago as a refuge for innocent children. Only the sisters and Hélène and a few servants remain there... We placed the other children with families or got them out of France to Spain then Lisbon.

I promised the sisters' parents they'd stay together. I shall never forget the anguish on their faces as they kissed their children goodbye at the Berlin train station while I hustled them along, my own heart breaking at having suffered a similar loss.

Now the sisters and I are on the move again.

I'm determined to get them to America, but that will take more than luck, what with strict immigration laws and national security concerns, making it almost impossible for Jewish refugees from Germany to enter the States. I've heard private relief organizations have had some success, so I'll try that route.

First, I must escape this annoying SS officer. He's poking his head out of the elevator and looking for me. He's not letting me out of his sight. I take out a silver cigarette case from my clutch. I'm careful the captain doesn't see the British Isles engraving. Not a popular design with Hitler's henchmen, but a certain Englishman gifted me with this case and holding it in my hand gives me courage.

I take out a cigarette, fiddle with it, but I don't light it. Theater on my part. I'm stalling. I used to smoke back in my debutante days

– everybody did – but I find it distasteful now. I only have one left, but Gertrud smokes like a sailor on leave and finds cigarettes hard to get. Since women aren't given a ration card to buy tobacco, I procure what I can for her on the black market. Then I trade cigarettes – and chocolate – for intelligence.

I tap the cigarette against the silver case, going over my plan. I'm headed back to the château after I dump this sleazy German Bluebeard *if* the aristocrat can keep the captain busy while I bolt for the back stairs.

There's no guarantee I'll reach the Rue Cambon exit.

I'm about to make my move when the wily duke whispers to the SS officer and then points to a room number, making the German's jaw drop, taking his attention away from me—

The pounding and hustle and breathy sounds of someone in a hurry reaches my ears. I turn to look and see a young woman rounding the corner at the end of the hallway. I'm not the only one who hears her. A door opens and a curious woman wearing a robe and hairnet peers out, then slams it shut.

Louis and the captain pay no attention... the Nazi is getting antsy and stomps out of the elevator, yelling for me to '*macht schnell*', when the grinding of steel and iron grates on my ears and the captain turns and curses, ranting in guttural expletives, while the young woman pulls back into the shadows before I can see her face... and starts humming... *humming* a tune.

Curiosity takes me out of the situation and I move toward her, drawn by the lovely melody... a lullaby. Oh, God, I know that tune. Whispers of steam rising from a hissing train... then the *clickety-clack* of powerful wheels bring the scene back like a shot to my gut.

'*Rachel!*' I whisper loudly. I glimpse her face when she steps forward, her shadow shivering across the floor, her finger to her lips shushing me. Her face is pale, her dark hair twirling wildly around her face like spit curls. Her eyelids flutter, her eyes a sea of dark secrets; the despair in them dismays me.

And there's something else, too. Fear.

'They arrested Leah and Tovah.' A harsh whisper so low only I can hear. 'And Hélène.'

Disbelief floods my brain as I look toward the elevator... Does the duke know? Is this a setup? My blood runs cold in spite of the fur lining in my coat. A chill like I've never felt before... dead, numb. *They're just babies*, my mind screams. I don't have to ask *who* did the disgusting deed, it's the *why* that sends my head spinning, my world turning upside down like spilled wine. Someone betrayed us. Louis? Did his guilty conscience bring him here? I never thought he'd stoop so low to introduce a spy into the château to get revenge on Hélène for spurning him.

I don't have time to unravel this scenario. The pounding of jackboots behind me tells me the time for us to run is now. Together. Yet something holds me back. If we're caught, Rachel faces certain death if they find out she's Jewish.

Think. Act. I'm not conscious of time, so filled with terror am I, that it takes me a few seconds to realize I have only one choice. I'll stall the captain while she escapes... tell him I'll have that drink with him, then head to the powder room and climb out the damn window if I have to.

I motion for Rachel to go back down the stairs. She shakes her head... This is insane. She has no idea the danger she's in. I send her a final plea with my eyes, begging her to go back down the stairs before the captain sets his sights on her.

'*Kay, please!*' she whispers. 'The Gestapo is on their way up here to arrest you—'

What? So it's true.

I spin around and look down the hallway... The elevator has gone, but the SS officer hasn't. Louis is rambling on, stalling, but the arrival of a new female has stirred the captain's interest. If we run now, he'll know we're guilty.

'Who is this pretty *Fräulein*?' he demands, strolling toward me and casting his eye at Rachel.

I pull myself up to my full height to give me courage. 'She's a maid, *monsieur*, come to collect my dirty laundry.' I grab the first thing that comes to me to save our behinds. 'If you'll excuse me...'

He eyes her plain skirt, coat. 'She doesn't look like a maid.'

'The hotel is short-staffed, *monsieur*, and considering the Reich isn't paying *anything* for their rooms here, housekeeping ran out of maid uniforms.'

The captain smirks. Louis laughs.

Rachel holds her ground.

I pray the captain doesn't notice she isn't carrying a large brass ring of keys on her belt and that he's more concerned with me insulting his precious Nazi party. I also hope he doesn't notice her apple cheeks, pink and full, or her rounded tummy... not big, but big enough to make me wonder if she's pregnant.

I shoot her a look. *Are you...?*

She nods.

I can't help but let out a long sigh... The German takes it for something else.

'Enough of your sarcasm, *mademoiselle*. You should be happy we *allow* you to stay here.' He huffs and puffs. 'I shall see you later at the bar.' He clicks his heels, then gives me the salute that turns my stomach. '*Heil Hitler*.'

'*Bonne nuit*,' is all he'll get from me. I can't believe the captain bought the story about my dirty laundry. More likely, he's tired of the game, but that's in my favor.

I again tune in to the clanking sound of the elevator growing louder. The grill door creaks open like a squealing feline. That was rather a quick trip back up to the fourth floor, as if it didn't make any stops. It doesn't occur to me there's a reason for that.

The duke prattles on, keeping the SS captain occupied, while Rachel and I head toward the staff back stairs—

'*Halt, mademoiselle, in the name of the Reich!*' I hear behind me. The harsh command stabs me through the heart. The game has changed. The voice doesn't bear the prissy accent of the SS captain, but a booming, bellowing tone that shakes the walls.

I turn and see a portly Gestapo man in a fedora and black trench coat slam past the SS captain, followed by an SS officer. I'm cornered. I know this Gestapo man. I've seen him hanging around the hotel, observing me, always with a newspaper in his hand, working a crossword puzzle. He heads toward me like a marauding bull.

'*Go, Rachel!*' I whisper low so they can't hear me.

'I can't leave you, *mademoiselle*,' she insists.

'Think of your sisters... and your baby.' The talented sisters are like musical notes in perfect harmony. Without one, the melody goes flat. 'You can't save them if they take you. *Now go!*'

It works. She grabs my hand, squeezes it, then the young Jewish girl heads toward the back stairs when two SS men cut her off at the stairwell.

A soldier grabs her; she screams.

'*Let her go!*' I yell. 'It's me you want.'

'I should take her in for questioning... the staff here are a treasure trove of secrets,' the Gestapo man threatens, eyeing her.

'She's just a child, *monsieur*... a girl from the country,' I plead, stepping forward. 'Since when does the Gestapo interrogate children?'

His eyes narrow. 'Children make good informants, *mademoiselle*, they don't lie.'

'*Please, monsieur*, if anything happened to her, it would lay heavy on my conscience. No telling *what* I may do.' Something in my voice grabs his attention, the undercurrent of a threat to put a kink in his roundup of enemy aliens real.

Finally, he relents. I see the Gestapo man nod. The soldier releases Rachel... She runs so fast down the hallway, she kicks up a breeze while the disgusting Gestapo man blows cigar smoke in my face, then laughs.

'You're the last one on my list of American women to be detained, *mademoiselle*.'

'You can thank me for holding her here, Herr Geller,' boasts Captain Bauder, grabbing me by the upper arm and shaking me so hard I drop the music box onto the carpeting.

It bursts open.

Amid a flash of sparkles, out falls my ruby and diamond necklace.

The Gestapo man goes very still, a deep-seated greed showing in his eyes. He surprises me when he doesn't pick up the jewels.

The captain dances to a different tune.

'So you're a jewel thief, *mademoiselle*. I should have known.' He smirks, then picks up the necklace, holding it under the light. The damn Boche is so proud of himself, I wouldn't be surprised if he insists on keeping it.

'I didn't steal it. It's mine.' I refuse to back down.

'Give me the necklace, Captain... *schnell!*' the Gestapo man yells. 'I'm sure *mademoiselle* won't object if I add it to Herr Goering's collection.'

I was right. The German policeman cares little about the jewels, only his quarry.

Me.

He pockets the necklace, then shoves the lowly captain out of the way and pulls my hands behind my back. He fastens the handcuffs around my wrists. Tight, then tighter until they're so tight, I cry out.

That pleases him.

'You're under arrest, *Mademoiselle Kay Alexander*.'

I'll never forget that beady look in his eyes. Checking me off his list with the delight of a hangman buying a new rope. He gives me no reason for the arrest, but the Gestapo doesn't have to. They're in charge, and with America in the war, the higher-ups in the Party have decided to put us Yanks in our place.

I'm screwed.

I'd protest, but I know better. Somehow I have to get word to Gertrud, pray she can use her Underground contacts to help me... and find that stubborn man I adore, hope he still cares about me enough not to see me hang or get shot. I know I was wrong to lie to him, but so was he. We both kept secrets deep in our hearts.

That's not important now. If the Gestapo finds the list of names sewn into my girdle, I'll be the first debutante starring in her own Mara Hari film. We *know* how that ends. There'll be no one to help Rachel find her sisters. Help her birth her child. I can't abandon them. I won't. They're like family to me.

How did I get into this mess?

It's all my mother's fault.

6

PHILADELPHIA, 1934

Kay

'Your daughter has a pretty face, Mrs Alexander, but she's not thin enough to be a proper Philadelphia debutante.'

I hear a loud groan from Mother as I skid to a stop on the polished marble floor in the hallway and pop another chocolate raspberry cream into my mouth.

So I'm not the pencil-skinny girl in the high society columns cheesing it up for the cameras. I'm content to stay in the background with my books rather than be paraded around like a poodle on a leash. I'm more like a lonely turtle plodding along, avoiding puddles and not getting its feet wet.

The downside is, I eat to tamp down my emotions and loneliness. It doesn't help that my family owns *Radwell's French Chocolates*, a well-respected candy company with soaring profits even in these hard times. It's quite a tale, though Mother would rather forget the less desirable parts of the story.

My eyes fill with tears as I clutch my tome of poems and a box of our best-selling creams to my chest. *Who is this awful person talking about me?*

I tiptoe closer and peek into the library. I recognize this woman from the society columns. Olivia B. Hathaway, a former debutante from... 1927?

'I had no idea your daughter was overweight, Mrs Alexander... until I caught a glimpse of her.'

She was spying on me? How rude.

Miss Hathaway clears her throat. 'I regret I can't take her on as a client.'

'That's ridiculous,' is Mother's quick retort. 'She's the richest girl coming out this year.'

I wouldn't call it a 'coming out'.

I agreed to a family tea in the garden with light refreshments so Mother wouldn't lose face with my father's family. A bunch of stodgy Philadelphia lawyers, except for Uncle Archibald, who works for the State Department.

No photographers, no press.

No eligible bachelors. I'm not interested in marriage.

Miss Hathaway smiles. 'The debutante wheel isn't greased by money, Mrs Alexander, but by beauty. *And* how well-known a girl is.' To prove her point, she flips through the glossy black-and-white society magazine she picks up from the writing desk. 'There's not *one* photo of Miss Kay Alexander in here.'

'Kay has been abroad—'

Miss Hathaway shakes her head. 'Your daughter has been right here in Philadelphia stuffing herself with chocolates.'

'That's absurd.' Mother goes on a rant. 'Kay may be a few pounds overweight, but a good girdle can fix that.' She pauses, thinking, her lips pursing into what I call her turkey gobble. I stare at her, my toes tingling, wondering what comes next. As usual,

Mother never fails to disappoint. 'Put her into one of those reducing girdles that promise to take three inches off the waist and hips.'

Et tu, Mother?

'It will take more than a tight girdle to turn her into a vivacious and charming debutante the press will adore.'

'It can be done,' Mother insists.

'Time is running out... invitations to an event must be sent out at least a month to six weeks in advance. Then there's the decorations, though I don't advise using artificial moonlight and orchids since it's been done—'

Mother raises her hand. 'Yes, yes, I understand. Paid help will take care of the incidentals. It's *your* job to make a debutante out of her. I won't have my daughter dancing on the edge of society when she should be running it.' She leans closer to the young woman, her manner threatening. 'Do I make myself understood?'

To her credit, Miss Hathaway doesn't back down. I almost like her. 'I have other appointments, Mrs Alexander—'

Mother steps forward, barring her from leaving. 'More tea, Miss Hathaway... or a warm brandy?'

'Do I have a choice?'

'No.'

The young woman reluctantly accepts Mother ringing for refreshments, but the twinkle in Miss Hathaway's eye reveals she's up to something. Whatever it is, it can't be good for me. Not when Mother wants to auction me off like a prize filly.

I huddle in the hallway outside the downstairs library, thinking. I ventured into this part of the house (leaving the sanctuary of my room requires a certain skill and creative means to avoid my mother) to return the book of Byron's sonnets and search for something new to read. The inimitable Miss Hathaway must have seen me cutting through the garden to the kitchen before her meeting with Mother.

'It will be your job, Miss Hathaway, to see that Kay is presentable before her "coming out" tea.' Her snarky smile would send even a lizard under a rock. 'My dearest friend, Mrs Shupe, and her daughter, Antoinette, will be in attendance.'

What happened to just the family, Mother?

Miss Hathaway sips her brandy. 'I imagine we *could* cinch her in and shave off a few pounds with the right gown.'

'Good.' Mother nods. 'Kay must look trim and thin by the Charity Ball in December.'

When the ballroom will be filled with young gentlemen with prestigious pedigrees. Harvard. Princeton.

I shake my head. Mother, always the pragmatist. When Pops died with a pipe in his hand and a highball glass in the other, she removed the empty bourbon tumbler but left the pipe. Made him look distinguished, she said. And proper. Her favorite word: proper.

Philadelphia is known for its prudish, aristocratic society and Quaker background.

But having a pudgy debutante in the family?

No, that will never do.

'The ball is three months away, Mrs Alexander. Not to mention the round of parties, teas, and luncheons the debs attend *before* the event. It would be extremely difficult to have her ready in such a short time. Most girls spend an entire year in training.'

'Kay isn't like most girls. She's highly intelligent even if she *is* a disappointment to me.'

What? That hurt. Another groan. This time it's from me.

'Intelligence is the least important commodity, Mrs Alexander, to be a successful debutante. The girl has to *want* it.'

'Then find a way to win her over.' Mother lifts up her bosom, flashing her huge diamond and emerald rings to assert her authority. 'I don't care how you do it, *just do it!*'

'It won't be easy.'

'I'll double your normal rate.'

Mother mentions an amount that makes me gulp. I always knew she was obsessed with her place in society, but this is ridiculous. She's selling me off like a piece of art she regrets buying. What set her off? She didn't get this itch up her rear to make me thin until she got back from Newport. I was content to stay here and it was lovely having the house to myself.

All twenty-seven rooms.

'It's a temping offer, Mrs Alexander, but—'

'I'll *triple* your rate. I assure you, my daughter will take her rightful place in society no matter *how much* it costs me.'

She stomps her foot into the plush Persian carpet so hard, the floor – inlaid with teak squares from Hong Kong – shakes. I swear her voice echoes throughout the winding hallway that runs from one end of the house to the other like a silk road. Surrounded by mulberry trees, the estate sits on twenty-eight acres outside the city in the northeastern section of Philadelphia accessed only by a private entry called McGinty Road named after my great-grandfather.

The locals know the estate as Lilac Hill.

Named after the glorious garden of lilacs surrounding the mansion.

Anyway, the house is a grand old dame in her own right, the sprawling mansion with its French garrets on the third floor adapting to each new generation with a round of renovations to its center dome, hardwood floors, and odd colors painted on the walls (Mother had the bathrooms repainted a warm butternut to add a glow to her skin).

Mrs Herbert George Radwell-Alexander rules the Main Line like it's her personal kingdom. Millicent to her friends, but never *Millie*, she was born with a silver spoon in her mouth coated with chocolate. She was worth millions even before she married my father, an honorable man. *Mr Alexander*, she called him, a banker and ingenious investor. A wonderful man whom I adored growing up. Kind, smart, but not afraid to listen to my ideas when he'd take me to our candy factory on Market Street. I learned the process of chocolate-making over the years until I knew enough that he made me an official 'candy dipper' on the line. My favorite part was dipping hazelnuts into the gooey chocolate. And then eating them.

Glory days.

My mother is a different animal.

The clawing, growling kind wearing a sealskin coat trimmed with a black sable collar. No doubt she was a beauty when she came out in 1914. What they called a Glamour Girl before the Great War, cutting a slender figure in her ankle-length lace and tulle dress, sixteen-button white satin gloves snaking up her slender arms and a diamond tiara affixed with sapphires the color of her eyes reputed to once belong to a Venetian countess.

Still, it's no secret she harbors a pearl-like irritation under her oyster shell regarding our lineage, that she's not descended from a first family of Philadelphia or Virginia (hence the 'arranged' marriage to my father – arranged by her, no doubt), but a carny man from Ireland.

My great-grandfather on my mother's side, William 'Candy Bill' McGinty came over during the potato famine with his mother and two sisters. He was a man loose with his tongue and a song in his heart, selling bottles of medicine to cure '*what ails ya*' to support the family. Bill gave out the candies his mom made. Coconut cream-filled and cinnamon-covered, popular in their South Philly neighborhood. Soon 'Candy Bill' had a successful sweets business going.

Then came the Civil War.

Bill joined up as a Union Soldier and found himself down in New Orleans. There he met a young French Creole woman who introduced him to pralines. When the war ended, he went home to

Philadelphia and joined the ranks of entrepreneurs that flooded the city. He came up with his own version of his mother's cinnamon candies and added traditional Louisiana pralines to the recipe. Bill started his candy company in 1868 and soon expanded into chocolates and creams. He called it *Radwell's French Chocolates* to give it class, leaving behind the McGinty name in the courts.

He built a candy empire I will own outright someday.

Which means I must take my place in society.

Hence the scene playing out in the library for the past several minutes.

Mother and her new hire, the clever Miss Hathaway, go over the payment schedule, then numerous details about her getting my photo (once I lose weight, ugh) into the social columns and fashion magazines along with my daily doings. Mother insists on only 'A' list eligible young men at my table like Tommy Whitworth.

She goes on and on until my ears burn.

I don't get it. Something happened to bring this on. Mother's hen club always meets on Tuesdays. Someone must have ruffled her plumes. I wonder if it had something to do with her luncheon chit-chat with her old rival, Mrs Pearson R. Shupe. The bejeweled grand dame of New York society blew into town last month and took a lease on the Frotheimer Chestnut Hill estate. According to kitchen gossip, they went back to Germany to save their clothing business after the new chancellor put restrictions on Jewish businesses... odd, but what's the danger?

Mother's been in a tizzy ever since. Ranting and raving. '*That rouged harridan won't get the best of me... I'll show her.*' My upcoming eighteenth birthday also set off her alarm bells. I'd hoped she'd pack me off to Palm Beach or Newport and pretend I don't exist. Something she's been good at since I was fourteen when my father died. A man I treasured, a big kid himself though he was a banker, a man who never fit in with Mother's social events but who went along anyway. Faithful to her until the end, but rarely affectionate toward her.

Yet he never failed to hug me when he came home.

Unless Mother was in the room, then he merely nodded in my direction.

As though he had this stoic image to live up to and wanted my mother's approval. This little girl didn't understand why, but when you're a kid you blame yourself. That's when I started retreating into my own world.

Since my father's family is historic Philadelphia and can trace their roots back to the oldest 'coming out' ball circa 1748, I didn't put up a fight when she announced she expected me to do 'something' when I turn eighteen to show respect to Pops' family. So we agreed on a quiet coming out. A formal tea in late September with a menagerie of aging relatives in attendance along with Uncle Archibald and his wife coming in from DC. Old people who won't judge me. Mother agreed. She also invited the Whitworths and their son, Tommy. We grew up together and spent summers in Newport as kids, but he never showed an interest in me.

Mother is convinced she can fix that.

I implored her not to invite any debutantes from this season to save her the embarrassment of no one showing up, but she ignored me. Now I know why. She'd already decided to spin me into gold. I wouldn't be surprised if she's already hired a string quartet and planned a light supper outside.

I hope it rains.

The ordeal will be over sooner.

But I never expected *this*. A full-scale attack on Philadelphia's café society. The presence of this woman (ex-deb turned press secretary) sets off a new slew of problems. I've heard enough. I turn, determined to hide in my room while I come up with an excuse to thwart her plans when—

'There you are, Kay.'

My heavy breathing must have given me away. I hover outside, dreading what comes next.

My execution.

'Don't be shy, dear. Come join us,' Mother chimes like a perfectly-tuned grandfather clock. 'I want you to meet Miss Olivia B. Hathaway.'

'I know who she is.' I glare at her, giving her my best evil queen stare.

Her eyelids flutter. 'You do?'

'Yes. I've seen you in the *Inquirer* on the society pages.'

I'm not the recluse my mother makes me out to be – that all I do is spend my time reading the classics and eating chocolates. I admit to a curiosity about this world of invitations and pretty dresses. I'm aware that 'coming out' is a husband hunt where the little foxes wiggle their tails to attract the hunter who then becomes the hunted. I also know the press grades the debs from A to D.

I know where I fit in.

F.

I'd never tell anyone that. It's safer to stay in my world of fiction where I can be myself.

'You're one of the richest young women in Philadelphia, Kay,' Mother says in her practiced, soothing manner. 'And with that comes responsibility.'

'I *am* responsible. I graduated Miss Agnes Irwin's school at the top of my class where I excelled in French.' I look over at Miss Hathaway, who, by the bored look on her face, is not impressed. All she cares about is getting me skinny... and her fee. 'I intend to get a diplomatic job with Uncle Archibald in Washington.'

'Women don't belong in politics *or* business,' Mother shoots back. 'It's unladylike. *And* takes away from your job as a wife and hostess. You're a Radwell as well as an Alexander and we've been at the front of society since your grandmother Hannah beat out a Vanderbilt for the most eligible bachelor at the Assembly Ball in 1893.'

'I hear the menu hasn't changed since then, Mother.'

She grabs me by the shoulders, her eyes questioning. 'Oh, what am I to do with you, Kay? You show no interest in finding a husband, you go off by yourself whenever I bring up the subject, and Lord knows, you're not part of the popular crowd. What happened to the girl I knew who couldn't wait to grow up and be a debutante?'

'She never existed, Mother.' I hunch my shoulders, struggling with my emotions. I don't care if Miss Hathaway *is* listening. I can't keep it in any more. 'I tried to tell you I feel more comfortable with my books and learning languages, that I want to be part of world affairs like Uncle Archibald, travel and meet interesting people, not giggling girls who can't think beyond their next invitation. But you never listened. You've had your own agenda set for me since the day I was born. So I gave up telling you, merely nodding and going back to my books. Now if you'll excuse me, I'm behind on my reading.'

I walk away from her – I'm not thinking rationally – taking long strides down the hallway to scram out of here. Fast. I want nothing to do with Miss Hathaway and her 'get thin' scheme.

Mother races after me. I've never seen her move so fast, her imported Italian pumps tapping on the floor like an angry woodpecker. Before I can turn the corner and escape into the safe refuge of the kitchen (she never enters any room remotely used by the servants), she grabs me by my jacket and spins me around. I stop, unable to move. The look in her eyes terrifies me. This is the expression of a woman who is desperate. Why? What drives her?

Since we're out of earshot of Miss Hathaway, I'm about to find out.

* * *

For the next twenty minutes, Mother subjects me to a variety of her moods, from anger to sadness to determination, a whirlwind of emotions that exhaust me. That's her ploy. Wear down the enemy to the point where she's so befuddled, so emotionally drained, she'll agree to anything. A complete capitulation to her whims.

'I've never been so embarrassed, Kay, defying me like that in front of that woman. What if she backs out of our deal?'

'She won't. I saw dollar signs in her eyes,' I snap back at her.

'You'd best hope she doesn't. No daughter of mine is going to sit on the sidelines during her debutante year. I'll show Eleanor Shupe she can't usurp me. Imagine that woman thinking she can come back to Philadelphia with her ten-million divorce settlement after dumping that idiot of a husband of hers and take *my* place at the top of the social register.'

I grin. Now I get it. Mrs Pearson R. Shupe didn't just pay Mother a social call. She's back in the saddle again and this is no short-term lease. She's staying in Philadelphia for good and Mother is fit to be hogtied.

'That woman couldn't stop going on at lunch about how her precious daughter received *eighty* invitations to balls and parties,' Mother continues, spewing. 'How she lost count of the young college men wanting to call on her beautiful Antoinette. *Hmph*. She's probably a toad.'

Mother could be right. I remember the girl from school. A tomboy with freckles and glasses we called Toni. But then toads not only turn into princes, but princesses, too.

'*And* she had the *nerve* to tell me I made a wise decision not giving you a public coming out, but to keep it in the family. She insinuated there's something wrong with you, Kay, *my* daughter.'

'There is, Mother. I'm fat.'

She dismisses my frankness.

'I'll show her. You'll be the debutante everybody talks about... the prettiest, smartest, cleverest—' She heaves out a sob and I almost feel sorry for her. I know how important her place in society is to her. She's like a queen bee tending to her flowers, hovering over every social event, believing it's her *duty* to rule. I want to put my arm around her, console her. I don't. I'm afraid I'll get stung. 'I know you won't let me down, Kay.'

Do I see tears in her eyes?

My mother is trying my soul, but she *is* my mother. And in some crazy way, I love her. I just don't understand her. Mother can't let anyone beat her at anything. Especially the debutante game. She suspects Mrs Shupe returned to Philadelphia because she's worried about bringing her daughter out in New York amid the nasty divorce gossip.

Seems there's another woman in their marital mix.

So I'm to bear the brunt of the situation. Trussed up like a holiday turkey and set out on the dinner table for everyone to gawk at. *Laughed at* is more like it.

What's she *doing here?* they'll whisper.

I don't tell my mother I'm not welcome in the young people's crowd because I don't play their games. Drink bourbon and smoke, let the boys 'feel you up'. I want to fall in love, but not because a boy's parents are rich or because he goes to a good school. I want to fall in love because he makes me laugh and my heart beat faster.

And I want to make something of myself.

Which Mother highly disapproves of.

'I don't want to be a clever debutante, Mother, I want to get a job.'

'A *job*?' She chokes on the word. 'I should have stopped your father years ago from filling your head with his silly nonsense.'

'So what if Pops encouraged me to think for myself? The world is changing and women aren't mere chattels. We have the right to vote *and* work.'

'Your *job* is finding a suitable, honorable husband.' She thinks for a moment, sifting through the invitations in her brain as quickly as dominos falling. 'Tommy Whitworth isn't a bad choice. Excellent family... tall... perfect to walk down the aisle with... and top of his class at Princeton.'

'What if I don't want to get married?' There's nothing worse in Mother's eyes than that. Young women who don't find husbands during their 'coming out' end up as governesses or spinsters.

Like Miss Hathaway.

And she's supposed to teach *me* how to find a man?

Mother, of course, doesn't see it my way. She's a product of pre-war sentiment and I get it. It's all she's ever known and I want to forgive her, but her next words cut deep, making that impossible.

'Ever since you disgraced me at St Moritz,' she says, twisting the rings on her fingers, 'you've been nothing but a disappointment.'

I slouch my shoulders, lower my eyes, and struggle to keep the pain, anger and frustration from showing on my face so she doesn't see how deep her words take me down the rabbit hole.

She's not finished. She clenches her fists. 'And a brat.'

Me? A brat?

Was it *my* fault that celebrity photographer followed me and shot pictures of me kissing that boy in the snow?

I told her I was practicing my French on him, true enough, but when he kissed me, I didn't push him away. It was wonderful. I was fifteen and he wasn't much older. His sin?

He was the son of a maid at the hotel and not an Astor or a Mellon.

She's never forgiven me. I thought she'd put away this notion of me coming out in a big way.

I was wrong. *Very wrong.*

'You shall begin your training with Miss Hathaway immediately, Kay.'

My mind is thinking up a million ways to get out of this crazy scheme of hers when she leads me back to the library, arm in arm. A show of unity in her eyes. Whatever I come up with, it won't do any good. She's lost in a world teeming with invitations and white ball gowns, calculating how soon she can marry me off to bolster her position in society.

'Mother, *please*...'

'Give me that box of chocolates.'

'I'm not a child.'

She raises her brow. 'Then stop acting like one. As long as you live under this roof, you'll do as *I* say. The box, please.'

She thrusts her hand out, waiting. Bands of platinum encircle her fingers with large diamonds and emeralds facing away from me. Her hand is large but slender, soft as if she's never done a day of work in her life. She hasn't. And she's proud of it.

I glance over and see Miss Hathaway sitting patiently, sipping brandy, reassured she got the job. She gives me a triumphant smile, like she snagged the prize in the Cracker Jack box.

Me. At *triple* her normal rate.

So it's two against one, is it? We'll see.

I grab the last piece of chocolate before I hand Mother the empty box and smash the candy into my mouth.

This is war.

7

PHILADELPHIA, AUGUST 1934

Kay

Becoming a debutante is torture.

Every minute in the day is filled with some grueling lesson on 'how to deb', including the art of attracting publicity, like acting surprised and bored when the photographers find you shopping for a gown or dining out with 'friends' (people Miss Hathaway introduced me to). You appear cool and calm, flashbulbs go off, then reporters quiz you on who designed your adorable hat and the rumor that you're leading the march at the Black and White Ball.

Amid all this nonsense, you ignore questions about your fortune (around fifteen million dollars according to Mother) and are never photographed with food in your mouth so the reporters can write about your 'pretty face and splendid figure'.

A fantasy world created by the advertisers, newspapers, and charity ball organizers to sell me to the public. A fairy tale.

Except my fortune.

I'm embarrassed to admit it, but I *am* worth that much... and more.

What pains my heart is that I haven't picked up a book to read since we started this *deb experiment*. I didn't realize how much I depend on my daily dose of reading, experiencing life between the pages so I don't have to face the real world.

But about two weeks ago I discovered the one *good* thing about this coming-out fiasco.

Dancing classes.

With Nico Martez. Where I glide over the shiny Cherrywood floors in the arms of this marvelously handsome dance instructor with the smoldering, dark eyes and lips that invite me to lean closer when he tells me to *step... box... step*. The faint smell of cognac on his breath and—

I could go on and on, but I'm late for this morning's romp into Hell with Miss Hathaway. I slept in, dreaming about Nico and praying she lets me out of my cage for my dance lesson. I surprised her with how easily I took to dancing, though she doesn't approve of the flirty looks Nico and I give to each other. Not a day goes by when she doesn't give me a lecture.

'Stay away from Nico Martez, Kay,' Miss Hathaway warns me.

'You hired him.'

'I had no choice. He was the only instructor not booked up.'

I grin. '*Ooh*, lucky for me.'

'Watch out, Kay. I'm warning you, he's trouble.'

'But what trouble?' I sigh as only an eighteen-year-old can with stars in my eyes.

But I'm not a fool.

I did some digging. No one knows much about him except he's a divine dancer.

Since we're in debutante season, he didn't have trouble finding work. There are never enough good dancing partners for us debs in training to practice with.

I've been on cloud nine ever since he arrived on the scene.

I shouldn't have let Miss Hathaway know about my crush on him. Well, she would have guessed anyway after I made such a big stink about taking dancing lessons. I swore I wouldn't learn the Cotillion to impress the young gentlemen... I imagine that's the *last* thing they notice about a girl... then I saw *him*.

Nico is every woman's dream in a tight morning coat bursting at the seams of his wide shoulders. He's from Cuba... the son of a privileged aristocrat... bred on fine red wine and the fiery steps of flamenco... a man determined to forge his own destiny. He left home to make his own way in the world, he told me. I feel so special to be with him, a man in control of his passion but not afraid to show me the blazing desire in his eyes and that dangerous move he does when we're dancing close, grinding his hip into mine.

No Philadelphia boy would ever do that.

Now I can't wait for my daily dancing lesson.

I drag the brush through my dark hair, letting it fall over one eye when I stare into the mirror over the sink in my bathroom. I look pale... but thinner. Hours with Miss Hathaway making me do sit-ups and waist twists and running the perimeter of our estate. Twenty-eight acres. I'm on first-name basis with every squirrel and rabbit that eyes me like I'm a new species invading their terrain.

I don't see how anyone survives this.

The gown fittings, makeup sessions, hair styling, voice coach (if I have to sing 'Row, Row, Row Your Boat' through my nose one more time, I'll scream), and Mother swooning over the invitations coming in, inviting me to tea, supper, the theater, as if they're rare diamonds.

I've received fifty-three. *Not enough*, she says.

Now I'm up before the sun breaks into my bedroom on the third floor of our Main Line home, the long window flung open by Miss Hathaway and her *debutante-by-the-book* attitude.

She's smoking and lets me take a drag.

I suck the nicotine into my lungs, then my eyeballs roll when I blow out the smoke, coughing.

'I don't like it.' I squash the cigarette into a gold-plated ashtray, then push it away. I don't need this. I'm eager to get started and get the morning over with so I can see Nico.

'You'll learn,' she says, lighting another cigarette. 'Watch me.' She sucks in the cigarette with her red lips, gracefully tilting her head back and half-closing her eyes, then blowing out the smoke. 'When I came out, debs didn't smoke or drink. Now it's de rigueur,' she continues, inhaling. 'It will help you control your weight.'

'What about those exercises and carrot sticks you call *lunch*?'

'You've got to lose ten more pounds by your coming out tea. Now it's either grab this cigarette and inhale...' She sucks in her cheeks and blows out a smoke ring. 'Or do twice around the grounds before coffee.'

I try it again. I cough. I hate it, but what have I got to lose? Except those extra pounds. I do it to please her, not my mother.

And Nico.

I admit I pull back when he takes me in his arms, hoping he won't notice the roll of fat around my waist.

As the weeks drag on, I come to like – and respect – Olivia, as she insists I call her. She's not a bad egg. I enjoy her funny stories about how in 1922 she drank champagne out of her slippers and ruined her fifty-dollar shoes, how she danced on a table in a nightclub and she was so drunk, she jumped into the arms of a waiter.

I admit it saddens me to hear how her mother threw herself out of the top floor of their apartment building after her father lost his money in the crash. Olivia supports him in a sanitarium with her deb coaching jobs.

'Do you have a beau?' I ask her on a hot summer day in June as we motor into the city to try on gowns for the charity ball.

She smiles, her gloved hands gripping the wheel. 'Yes, but he's married.'

'How awful.'

'It's better that way. No strings.'

Seems I don't know much about coming out, but I soon learn.

Nobody is what they seem.

* * *

I get used to having my morning cigarette with coffee and dry toast. Then exercising and shopping and sending telegrams to the young men on Mother's 'A' list, imploring them to come (Tommy Whitworth is at the top. No surprise here). Posing for photos, seeing Mother smile when I appear in the society columns; the whole thing is madness, but wonderful. As the days, then the weeks go by, I've never felt so alive, so vibrant... so *thin*.

I suck in my tummy and feel pride when I look in the mirror and see that it's flat... *really flat*. No more belly rolls and even my upper arms are toned.

And Nico and me?

Well, there's a whole lot more than dancing going on between us.

'There you are, my darling Kay.' Nico rushes over to me when I arrive at the dance studio and sweeps me up into his arms. I'm supposed to be exercising on a silly machine and getting a facial, but this is so much more fun. 'I've missed you terribly.' He rolls his 'R's in that sexy voice of his and I melt in his arms.

'What shall we do today?' I tease him, then wiggle my hips. 'After we practice... the tango.'

'Whatever you wish, *mi amor*.'

We do lots of things. Like head to the country for a picnic with Nico driving Mother's ivory-and-black Cadillac Fleetwood or stroll down Market Street to see the Christmas decorations as the holiday season approaches. Then drive to the Jersey Shore to walk on the boardwalk, bundled up close like two happy seagulls and eating saltwater taffy. At night we make the rounds of the clubs to 'practice' dancing.

I've never been so happy.

But it's not perfect. I keep my head down when I'm around Mother, hiding the excitement in my eyes, the tint of passion written on my face. I keep my romantic relationship with Nico a secret from her. We don't take my red roadster to avoid anyone seeing us and reporting back to her. She'd never approve of me dating my dancing instructor... Sure, we hug and kiss, but I'd never do anything more than that.

I'm not *that* foolish.

* * *

I honestly believe I'll die of boredom at my own coming out.

It's dreadful. We have more violinists strumming Cole Porter tunes than we have guests. It *did* rain earlier and we ate the creamed salmon and salty baked ham in the gold room after Mother presented me to our 'guests'. Two elderly aunts I haven't seen since my First Communion, a second cousin related to Mother through her father's side, Pops' two brothers and their wives. Tommy Whitworth *did* show, then left when I ignored him, looking so disappointed I felt guilty (my mother forced him to come). No debs came (no surprise here), and my uncle Archibald showed up late and kept looking at his watch and instructing our butler to buzz him right away if Washington called.

Something about a telegram he received from his contact in Berlin.

I found out from Mother he was waiting for instructions from the higher-ups on the latest fiasco in Germany. I have no idea what upset him so much when the call eventually came. I don't concern myself with anything happening outside Philadelphia except Paris... I've been there twice, once with Mother when we did the Grand Tour when I was fourteen, and during my year abroad in high school to practice my French so I can impress my uncle and persuade him to give me a job.

But that can wait.

All I can think about is how I'd love to go to France on a honeymoon with Nico. I haven't been able to stop thinking about him the entire afternoon and I'm begging the downstairs grandfather clock to strike seven. That's when I can race upstairs and rip off this dress and put on a cute black satin number I bought (against Olivia's wishes, of course) and go meet him at our favorite spot, *Palumbo's Supper Club* in South Philly, as far away from the Main Line as I can get. Mother is so involved with impressing Pops' relatives, she'll never know I'm gone.

I sip my coffee, half-listening as the talk turns to Uncle Archie's important phone call and how serious things are getting over in Europe since the 'government purge' in Berlin. I tune them out. I have no interest in politics so I don't catch much more than 'Hitler's political career was at stake if he didn't.'

Then, as the party is winding down, I gather up my gauzy skirts trimmed with droopy satin ribbons and pearls, smile and curtsy for their wives and daughters who hate me because I'm richer than they are... and thinner. Their envy is a by-product I didn't see coming.

Mother comes over to me.

With a big smile on her face.

My God, the Sphinx has teeth.

'You did well, Kay, I'm pleased.' Mother slips her arm through mine, still smiling, reminding anyone who will listen (meaning the photographers who 'mysteriously' showed up after dinner), this is the same room where she was presented by *her* mother. She sighs heavily and clasps her hand over her heart and someone snaps a photo of us. Before I can flash my newly minted 'deb smile', she kisses me on the cheek, squeezing my arm, and then hugs me so tight I can't breathe.

And my eyes get misty.

If I knew being a deb was all it took to make her hug me, I'd have gone Southern and come out at fourteen like the girls do in Georgia.

I soften toward her, hugging her back. 'I'm so glad you're proud of me.'

'I said I'm pleased,' she grunts. 'Nothing more.'

Then her eyebrows draw together, making the creases in her forehead more pronounced. Her expression says it all. A rebuff. The affection she showed toward me was only for the cameras. And her guests. My heart sinks. How can she be so cruel? Doesn't she see how hungry I am for her love?

I pull back, my cheeks tinting, my ego deflated, as though she threw a custard pie in my face. It's always about *her*. *Her* needs, *her* wants. I'm just a cog on her society wheel that got stuck and needed a swift kick to get it started up again.

When will I learn the woman has no heart?

The clock strikes seven.

I smile, sucking in a deep breath. My coming out is officially over.

I slip away from Mother chatting with her sisters-in-law about the invitations I received to other debutante events which magically number over seventy (really?), while the family indulges in chocolate mousse with dollops of vanilla-yellow cream, rum, and of course, chocolates from the five (or is six?) tiers of *Radwell's French Chocolates* spinning around on a Lazy Susan silver platter.

No one will miss me.

Even Uncle Archibald is too preoccupied on the telephone to notice me racing up the winding stairs.

Still, I can't forget Mother's awful words.

She's pleased with me, but nothing more.

Hands trembling, I change quickly into the black dress and dry my tears before I call for Henry, our chauffeur, to bring round the ivory-and-black Cadillac. I'm going out tonight.

No one can stop me. I did what I promised and 'came out', holding court with Mother until seven... leaving me the whole evening to embrace the most important thing in my life.

I'm off to meet the man I love.

I forget I'm a Philadelphia Main Line debutante... forget my mother is cold-blooded and selfish. Instead, I find the love I so desperately need and want in his arms. Nico adores me and won't reject me when I put my head on his shoulder, ask him to hold me tight and soothe my hurting soul.

Yes, Mother, your little girl is all grown up. My coming out was a success. I'm a woman now and it's time I fulfill a woman's needs.

I'll show her.

You're damn right I will. It's nowhere near midnight.

For this Cinderella, the night is just beginning.

8

BERLIN, 1934

Rachel

Today Mutti had a party for my eleventh birthday, I write in my diary, *but nobody came. Talia and Frieda said they would, but they didn't. And Mollie, my 'best friend', never answered the invitation I sent her.*

I snap the notebook closed, then the tears come. Big, ugly drops running down my round cheeks onto the pretty, green felt cover embossed with my name in gold leaf, a notebook Mutti had made for me. I flop on my bed, punch my pillow filled with goose feathers. Hard. What does it matter? Who cares? I don't. Birthdays are silly. Dumb. For kids. I'm grown up now. Or I will be. A girl is considered an adult in the Jewish religion when she's twelve and I'm only 364 days away.

I dry my tears off the felt cover of my diary with my handkerchief. I'd never tell anyone I'm crying, not even my diary, and that my spirit is broken. What fun is it to blow out the candles on the beautiful butter cake Mutti made by myself?

I pouted all afternoon, watching the big clock in the kitchen ticking away. My little sisters, Leah and Tovah, didn't know what was going on. They're too young to understand how deep it hurts when your best friend abandons you. That's why I'm so glad I have my sisters. They're only eight and five and prattle about like bunnies sniffing spring grass... daring to stick their fingers in the icing when Mutti isn't looking.

They're silly. Goofy.

But they'd never leave me. And I'd never leave them.

Still, I was uncomfortable that Mutti would say something about my friends not showing up when she brought out her cake knife to slice through the creamy layers. I avoided her gaze. I didn't want her to see my eyes stinging red. I was so upset I forgot to make a wish. Then I grabbed the silver fork with the engraved handle that belonged to my grandmother, the fork Mutti lets the 'birthday girl' use on her lovely day. The story is that fork made its way down through the family and was a gift from a rabbi's wife to my great-great-grandmother on her wedding day.

I felt so blessed holding it in my hand. I swear the metal made my fingers tingle.

Like it's magic.

If only it was and I could have my friends here, but ever since I had to leave my regular school, nothing is the same. Mutti says it's because Hitler doesn't like Jewish people and doesn't want us to learn. Papa says not to worry, it won't last. Hitler will realize that we give back to our community more than we take... Mutti disagrees. And so it goes. Back and forth between them until I get a headache because I don't really understand what they're saying.

But not today.

Today I'm the birthday girl and Mutti wants me to feel special.

She gave me the biggest piece of cake with the decorative flowers made from icing clumped together in a big, sugary mound and I ate every bite. A secret family recipe... Vanilla cake with a thick frosting filled with coconut and what she calls 'mocha'. I think that's coffee. It made me feel grown up. The cake was decorated with swirls of buttercream frosting around the edges and pink and yellow roses made of confectioner's sugar whipped up into plump mounds that melt on your tongue. I ate the pink roses and Leah and Tovah shared the yellow ones.

Even the sweet, gooey sugar didn't make me feel better.

I carry such wonderful memories of Talia and Frieda in my heart, the fun we had playing hopscotch, doing puzzles. I admit we haven't been close since we split up after I started attending a different Jewish school when the Nazis decreed they didn't want us in *their* schools any more. They attend a school in another part of the city and they'd have to transfer twice on the tram and who wants to do that with those scary Brownshirts causing fights on the trolley even if Mutti's glorious cake is worth *any* sacrifice? But I know they *would* have come before the Nazis started messing with our lives.

But Mollie not coming?

That I don't understand. She's my *best* friend.

Mollie and I have been close since our first day at school and we had our pictures taken together when we got our *Schultüte*, our long paper cones filled with sweets, pencils, and presents. We traded pencils and I gave her an apple and she gave me an orange. I even shared Mutti's plum cakes with her. It was a good day, the two of us holding hands and skipping all the way home (we live on the same street), singing and believing school was the most wonderful place ever.

Then the Nazis took it away.

I start to cry again. This time, I can't stop the sniffing and sniveling because it hurts so much. I pull up the coverlet on my bed and hide, but Mutti has a sixth sense I'll never understand, as if she knows I'm hurting though she can't hear me crying.

'Rachel, you mustn't cry, child.' She pulls the coverlet off my head and holds me in her arms. Tight. I feel her body shiver; she's worried about me, but I feel warm and safe and it doesn't hurt so much. Then Leah and Tovah gather around my bed, their faces smeared with cake icing, but their eyes dark and sad.

'If you cry, Rachel,' Leah says, grabbing my hand. 'Then I have to cry, too.'

'Me, too.' Tovah makes a face.

I laugh. 'No, no... *bitte*, please, go eat more cake.'

They squeal and run off, leaving me alone with my mother. I'm so lucky to have her; she never scolds me when I get cranky or when I get emotional over the silliest thing.

She straightens the red-and-white plaid ribbons on the ends of my long braids, then kisses me on the forehead like she did when I was a little girl and scraped my knee.

'There now, Rachel. All better?'

'Oh, Mutti, why do I have to grow up?' I face her so she can read my lips. 'Why do things have to change?'

'Well, we girls don't have a formal "coming out" like the boys do,' she says, meaning a boy's bar mitzvah, 'but it's important that you embrace the changes coming as you grow into a woman.'

Oh, *that* talk again. This isn't the first time she's alluded to something mysterious and a bit scary... yet special. God gifted a woman with a special power, she says. The power to give life. I get that funny fluttering in my belly again when she reminds me my body is changing. And next year when I'm twelve, or maybe thirteen, I'll understand.

I'm not sure if I'm ready for that.

Mutti lightens my mood by saying I can light the Shabbat candles tonight, that I don't have to follow tradition and wait until next year when I'm twelve. She and Papa have bought me a pretty candlestick for the occasion.

Really?

Mutti smiles.

Who knows what next year will bring?

I close my eyes and sniff the tall, white candle. I love its waxy smell. So many strange things are happening... things I don't understand, but the familiar act of lighting the candle is a great comfort to me in these upsetting times.

Over the next few days, I hear Mutti and Papa whispering about the difficulties they face going forward with the German labor laws prohibiting Jews from joining the national trade organization. Many Jews in Berlin are losing their jobs and it's their children who are our music students. Papa's a wonderful teacher, so good he could teach at the university, but he loves connecting with his students in our shop, a place of comfort and support, insisting that learning to play an instrument is as much about opening up your mind to the joy of playing as it is about practice.

Mutti reminds him how the Nazi Party encouraged Berliners to boycott Jewish shops last year. It scares me when she talks with Papa about this leader who has declared himself our 'Fuehrer'.

How much more can he do to us? she asks. *Before we know it*, she continues, *the Nazis will take everything*.

Papa shoos away her concerns with a kiss on her nose and a warm hug. Mutti sees the world differently than most people. Because she can't hear, she's more in tune to reading people's faces and sees deep into their eyes. Like, she says, the people down at the grocer's shop, refugees from Poland and Russia not understanding why they can't get kosher meat, that the observant ritual has been banned. They have fear in *their* eyes, she says, wild pulsating fear telling her what happened to them back home, the *pogroms,* she called it, mob violence against Jews that can happen here. In Berlin.

I don't understand it, but from the way Mutti describes it, they must be something horrible.

Could *it happen here?*

My heart skips, frustration washing over me that I didn't get to show Mollie the silky red-and-white plaid ribbons Mutti gave me for my hair. If I'd known she wasn't coming, I would have gone to see her, given her a ribbon for *her* hair.

A week later I find out she and her family left on a train bound for the western border crossing... and then? No one knows for sure, Mutti said... but I heard whispers from the neighbors the whole family escaped to France.

No one knew they were leaving and Mollie couldn't tell me. It must have been awful for her. I feel sad I'll never see her again. Of course, I forgive her, but why did her family leave like that? Are they *that* afraid of the Nazis?

That's when I feel really scared, as though my life is melting away like the tall, white candle I lit for Shabbat. And no matter what I do, what I think, I can't put out the hot flame growing bigger and bigger until it consumes me.

I can't stop time.

Or the Nazis.

9

PHILADELPHIA, 1935

Kay

I've come undone.

There's nothing left of the wild, crazy debutante who danced and partied till dawn, went to so many social events I lost count. I'm wandering through life like a dried-up corsage, its flower petals brittle and crumbling into gray dust, its pink ribbon faded to a mousy brown.

Yet I cling to the deb I was, the girl who fell in love with a man who never let me down when I needed a shoulder to cry on, when Mother's constant ribbing to find a husband seared the skin off my back, leaving me raw and hurting. My body goes into a tailspin thinking about him, his kisses... his body tight against mine. I thought we were a couple, a death-till-you-part duo. I thought I'd be a bride.

And then...

Nico stood me up at *Palumbo's*, the swank nightclub buzzing with cocktails, highballs and the conga, me in a new scarlet lamé dress and my best dancing shoes. Not even a goodbye letter professing his love for me, giving me hope he'd be back.

No, he sent me a telegram and had the nerve to have it delivered while I sat at our favorite table, nursing a sour stomach with a glass of seltzer and nibbling on a cold plate of spaghetti and soggy meatballs.

Waiting. For him.

I must return to Havana... the telegram read. *Fun while it lasted... Nico.*

A gut punch that made me double over in pain. I was already sweating and feeling queasy from what had happened that morning. Mother had launched into another one of her tirades. I can still hear every word echoing in my head, her words now a prophecy come true.

* * *

'I've invited Tommy Whitworth for tea tomorrow, Kay. At four. I expect you to be here on time.' She dawdled about the library, picking up a society magazine and thumbing through it. *'I also expect to see your engagement photo in the next issue.'*

'Tommy and me?'

I like him as a friend and he's been swell escorting me to Mother's charity events to keep her snoopy nose out of my business, helping me maintain my cover since my coming out last year, but I don't want to marry him. He likes his liquor too much.

'After he showed great interest in you at the Charity Ball last December, I made inquiries and his mother informs me the boy is infatuated with you. Why, every event you went to during debutante season, Tommy found a way to be at your table. The press noticed it, too. I could

barely keep up with the clippings of you two in the society columns. You were an immense success, Kay. I'm very pleased.'

Again, she uses the word 'pleased'. Not proud.

She'll never change.

She put down the magazine and picked up her tea, sipping it before adding in a cautious voice, 'However, I saw the pain and yearning in his eyes when he picked you up for the art auction last week. The boy is getting frustrated. His interest in you won't last forever, Kay, and soon there'll be a new crop of debutantes to pick from—'

I cut her off with, 'We're just friends, Mother. Nothing more.'

'Not if I have anything to do with it, Kay.'

* * *

Yes, a prophecy.

She won't give up until I marry him. But I can't do that to Tommy. It's not fair to him when I'm in love with Nico. So I'll go to Havana, find Nico, tell him I don't care if he won't marry me, I want to be with him.

My mind's made up when I leave the club dizzy-headed, head home in a taxi, clammy hands, my senses reeling. I didn't have anything to drink, so why do I feel so strange?

It's after midnight when I slouch through the kitchen entrance around the back of the house, carrying my high-heeled sandals, my stockinged feet tapping on the floor, my brain in high gear making plans to check which ships leave for Cuba—

'It's time we had the "talk", Kay.'

Mother.

I freeze, startled. What's she doing down here? It must be some-thing serious for her to break her own rule and make a visit to the kitchen to find me. Whatever's on her mind, I can't let her see me like this: disheveled, upset. I don't turn around but attempt to keep an even tone in my voice. 'I know about the birds and bees, Mother.'

'I mean *the* talk, Kay... The one that decides your future.'

'Tommy.'

'Yes. The boy graduated from Princeton and was named junior partner at his law firm. You couldn't do better than to catch him in your bonnet.'

'Because his father runs the biggest law firm in Philadelphia and his family has owned homes on the Main Line longer than we have?' I turn to face her. I shouldn't be so hard on Tommy. He *is* smart and handsome and when we were kids, great fun. But he's turned into a typical three-piece Brooks Brothers suit and claimed his spot in the café society drinking club as a bona fide member. 'Tommy is a nice boy,' I say, not bursting Mother's bubble with rumors about his drinking, 'but I don't want to marry him.'

Mother closes ranks on me like a general zeroing in for the kill. 'I've tried to be patient, Kay, but it's been five months since you came out and you've not given him your answer.'

'When will you stop deciding what's good for me?' I protest, dropping my sandals on the stone floor in defiance.

'When you grow up and take your place in society. I won't be here forever and I want to see you married and doing your duty before I die.' She takes a deep breath and pulls the satin belt on her creamy peach robe tighter, each quilted square lined up perfectly. I've not seen her change her bedtime style since I was five. Always a peach satin robe, always perfect, quilted squares. 'Your father must be turning over in his grave, seeing what a mess you've made of my life.'

Again, *her* life. Not mine.

'I'll be twenty next May, Mother, old enough to make my own decisions when I come into my full inheritance.'

'Not if they're stupid ones.'

I'm not sure what makes me lash out so harshly at her, but I can't stop myself. 'I don't intend to end up like you... a dried-up, old apricot with no heart.'

'*Oh!*' She slaps me across the face and my cheek *burns hot*, my emotional core *hotter*. I don't deny I deserved it. 'How *dare* you speak to me in such terms!'

I regret my outburst immediately.

I try to make amends. 'I'm sorry, Mother, I don't like quarreling with you, but ever since you decided I should come out in society, every moment of my life has been planned. You won't let me breathe.'

She smiles down at me. 'That's because you're Kay Alexander, one of the richest women on the Philadelphia Main Line and you have duties. Like finding a suitable husband.'

'Like you did?' I blurt out.

'Herbert George Alexander was a fine man. A banker and clever investor.'

'And he had oil. Barrels and barrels of it. Your marriage wasn't a love match, Mother, but a corporate deal forged by attorneys and signed with a stroke of the pen. No love involved... That would have messed it up.'

She dismisses my remark with a flick of her wrist. 'I don't know what you're talking about.'

'It's no secret you and Pops had separate bedrooms for fifteen years. I don't know when you ever found time to conceive me with your charities and luncheons and committees. And serving on the board of *Radwell's French Chocolates*.'

'Your great-grandfather, Bill McGinty, built up his candy empire from nothing, young woman. It's what made you Debutante of the Year and pays for those sable and mink-lined coats in your closet.'

'Please, Mother, can't this wait? I'm grateful for everything you've done for me, but I'll never be anything in the eyes of the press but a flighty heiress if I don't go out on my own.'

By way of Cuba, but I won't tell her that.

'For your information, Miss Kay Alexander, I did my duty when I came out, then married and subjected myself to an act that made me shiver with disgust so I'd have someone to carry on the Radwell candy tradition. I expect you to do the same and do it quickly before the next debutante season or you'll be wearing black gowns to the balls.'

Meaning I'm stale goods.

Like last season's Christmas chocolates.

I sink down into the big rocking chair that cook sits in to shell peas, the lingering scent of garlic and onions coming off the quilted Dutch padded seat. Somehow, it's comforting to me, calming me down. I used to sneak down here to the kitchen when I was a kid, beg cook for a cookie, and then watch her rock back and forth in this chair. I once told her I wished I had a normal mother, someone who peeled onions and patted me on the head. She gave me a warm smile, then reminded me my mother is Mrs Radwell-Alexander, the queen of the Main Line. She gives a lot of people jobs and security in these hard times. And I should be proud of her.

'You can't change stormy weather, Kay,' she told me, 'but if you're smart, you learn to live with it.'

And I have.

Until now.

I was wrong to say such hurtful words to my mother, but it's been building up in me for so long, riding me like a bad dream that doesn't go away even when you wake up, I couldn't stop myself. True, I don't like how she acts toward me, but she's *my mother* and though she ignores me like I'm a paper doll tacked onto the wallpaper, I had no right to sass her. It's like a strange creature has taken hold of me recently, riding me hard to break free.

I've come undone.

Completely, this time.

I feel so sick, I can't sit here a moment longer. I jump up and head for the servants' toilet and slam the door behind me. I hear Mother calling me, but I can't stop my chest heaving, the vile taste of vomit in my mouth as I bend over the porcelain bowl and retch my guts out. It must be the cheap spaghetti and meatballs rumbling in my stomach, giving me the heaves, the chills.

Food poisoning.

What else can it be?

10

PHILADELPHIA, 1935

Kay

It's a rainy, spring day in May when the silent war between Mother and me comes to a head. I should have seen it coming, but I don't.

Thunder rumbles overhead, shaking the house, but its crackling roar is nothing compared to Mother's loud burst of anger and frustration when she finds me in the dining room sipping chicken soup and chamomile tea to quell my queasy stomach.

She eyes me warily. 'I need to speak with you, Kay.'

'What about, Mother?' I feign innocence, hoping she'll go away. I've been avoiding her, desperate to keep my condition from her. It wasn't food poisoning after all.

I'm pregnant.

The details would read like a racy story in the scandal sheets.

Debutante dumped with bundle of joy on the way.

Nico left me high and dry. No one's seen him at the club. It's as if he disappeared down a manhole. I know he'll come back; he's got to. Till then, I go through the days like a rag doll in search of a toy box to hide in. I can't go to Mother's physician for help and I can't hide my condition under over-sized jumpers forever. I hinted to Mother I want to go to Newport for a few days to see 'old school chums', hoping I can sneak into the village and find a doctor who won't tattle on me.

I don't have to go to such lengths to keep my pregnancy from her. Mother already knows.

'How *could* you humiliate me, Kay, by giving yourself to that gigolo!' she yells, slamming the sliding oak doors shut. She then grabs the closest thing to vent her anger on, smashing the commemorative plates she brought back from England engraved with a royal crest on the floor.

I've never seen her like this, puffing out her cheeks like a bloated goldfish.

'He's *not* a gigolo.' I go on the defensive, refusing to give in to her tirade.

'Isn't he?' she shoots back, her raised brows emphasizing the smug look on her face. She delights in telling me how she sent her spies to watch me when I wouldn't give Tommy Whitworth an answer. 'I suspected you had another beau. But a sleazy dance instructor?' She gulps. 'I nearly fainted when the agency found you slumming in South Philly with that lowbred, Nico Martez.'

My mother threatens to have him prosecuted for seducing me. She does admit I'm not completely to blame. She didn't know until this morning it was Olivia's doing.

'I was shocked to find out that snippy Miss Hathaway paid him to seduce you, insisting it was *my* idea.'

Mother has my full attention now. My senses reel when she relays how the woman admitted she told him to *charm me and release my inner flirt*, but insisted she never instructed Nico to sleep with me.

I didn't have the heart to tell her *I* seduced *Nico*.

It was the night of my coming out at home when Mother and I argued and I felt so useless, so unloved. Nothing I can say now will change my young girl's stupidity into something redeeming or take the guilt off my white debutante shoulders. I did it because I knew then I could never please Mother no matter *what* I did.

So I did what I wanted. Needed.

I seduced Nico in the back of Mother's ivory-and-black Cadillac. I brought a bottle of bourbon... no, it was *two* bottles and we drank until we got so silly, we kept laughing and kissing.

He told me I was beautiful, smart... but we shouldn't do this... I didn't want him to stop and *begged* him to touch me... *everywhere*. I nudged closer to him. He caressed my heart with words of undying love in Spanish when I needed it most... so *bonita*, he said, pretty like a perfect angel with hair as dark as midnight and skin like snow that melted under his touch.

I sailed away on a cloud, away from the pressure of being a debutante... and my mother's daughter.

I gave myself to him that night out of gratitude.

I don't know what I expected afterward, but not this conversation with Mother.

'I had no choice but to send Miss Hathaway packing with an envelope filled with cash,' she admits, 'and the stipulation she leave Philadelphia and ply her trade elsewhere.'

'Of course, Mother, you had no choice.' I push away my teacup and stand up from the table, eager to leave, but she's not finished with me yet.

'How far along are you, Kay?' she demands, grabbing my arm, her eyes shifting toward my hidden belly. It didn't take her more than a blink of an eye to know why I've been tossing up my guts and why I'm so snippy (well, *snippier than usual* in her words).

'Three months... I think.'

No use denying it. I'm relieved to bring it out into the open.

'Don't you know?' Mother asks.

'I'm pretty sure.'

We had sex only once, but my periods have always been irregular and with the stress of debutante season and smoking and drinking... and keeping late hours, I didn't think anything of it when I skipped a month, then two.

It's happened before.

But then I was a virgin.

Now...

'I hired a private detective to dig up dirt on that gigolo,' Mother lashes out, 'and he dug up plenty.'

'How could you?' I ask her. 'I'm in love with Nico.'

'You call lust... love?'

'I hoped you'd understand.'

'*Understand?*' she bellows. 'How could you be so stupid to give yourself to someone not in our crowd? I had such big plans for you, Kay. All these months, we both worked so hard to bring you out, make you the most popular debutante of the season. I can't let you throw it away.'

'I've slept with one man since I came out, not half the rowing team like Toni Shupe.'

'*She's* not pregnant,' comes her fast retort, making me wonder how she knows that.

'You don't get it, Mother. I didn't do it to spite you. I wanted to pick my own friends for once, be in control of my own life. Forget I'm Kay Radwell-Alexander and just be a woman and fall in love. I wanted to have fun and forget who I am.'

'It's *who* you are that attracted that gigolo from New Jersey.'

'Nico is from Havana,' I protest. 'His family originally came from Spain... they're aristocrats—'

She arches her brow. 'He's from the Jersey Shore and his family runs a concession stand on the boardwalk... They sell hot dogs and cotton candy. And lies.'

My mouth drops open in shock. '*You* made him send that telegram, didn't you?'

'He's not a stupid young man. He had no problem taking me up on my offer.'

She explains that he didn't acknowledge the paternity of my baby, but Mother made sure he keeps his mouth shut or she'll see to it he ends up behind bars. It pays to have a judge and a district attorney counted among the family, she finishes with pride.

'How *could* you, Mother?'

'How could I *not* interfere? It's my life, too, that you've ruined.'

'Is that all you care about? What about me? And my baby?'

She isn't ready to answer me. Not yet.

We leave the conversation there. I don't care what she wants. I intend to have my baby and leave Philadelphia and raise my child by myself. I can give her a good home, education, a loving mother, but as my own mother is quick to remind me, I can't give the child a name.

They will always be a bastard.

What a horrible stigma to put on a child.

Of course, no one knows I'm pregnant. People who saw me at the club with Nico aren't Main Line people and Mother's society friends still see us together at *Wanamaker's* for lunch (even though I've gained weight, Mother says everyone will think it's post-deb syndrome). No one pays me much attention, not with the tearoom buzzing about *this* year's debutantes. Everyone assumes Tommy Whitworth and I are waiting to announce our engagement... In their eyes, we're one more successful coupling checked off their list.

I don't know how long she can keep up this pretense, coming up with stories. My baby is due in early February.

At the rate I'm gaining weight, I'll be sporting maternity clothes way before Christmas.

Which is a problem in Mother's eyes.

Over the coming weeks, she hints to her friends we're spending the holidays in London with friends of Uncle Archibald's where she's hoping to snag an invitation to meet the king and queen.

I have no interest in *what* she tells her friends, but I want to have my baby here at Lilac Hill. Then I'll decide where I want to live. I have my own money. Ever since I was eleven, all I've ever heard about is how rich the family is, though I've never seen it on paper. I get a monthly stipend, and my dress bills and whatever else I buy is done on credit, but that will change once I move to Washington. I can't wait to settle down there with my baby. I'll take over my accounts myself. It won't be easy to unravel the various interests I own, but I'm confident I can do it.

Also, I'm thinking of setting up a charity to help other women in my predicament who are not so fortunate: a dream I have to do some good with my money. I never thought I'd end up single and alone, but I'm determined to make the best of it.

Letting out a long, deep sigh, I make my plans.

I'm going to be a mother and she can't stop me.

* * *

Once we clear the air, life in the Philadelphia suburbs becomes tolerable. There is a truce between Mother and me. I get fatter, she gets craftier, and we barely talk to each other.

So it's no wonder I don't pay attention to her flitting around today, arranging yellow roses in a vase and tossing the less-than-perfect blooms into a wastebasket.

She hums and mumbles to herself. This is the first time my

mother seems happy or at least 'normal' since that night back in May when she discovered my affair with Nico.

We are now in the middle of a sizzling July. The big ceiling fans in the house never stop whirling and the ice truck stops at Lilac Hill twice a day to fill the refrigerated boxes so Mother can indulge in iced coffee and cold cuts.

And I can double up on butter pecan ice cream and pickles.

I drive into the village to satisfy my craving, scooping a pickle out of the big barrel with a two-pronged fork at *Kaplan's Country Deli*. Mr Kaplan always has a smile and a pickle for me, thanking me for telling everyone about his shop – I've been coming here since he opened six years ago when he emigrated from Frankfurt, Germany – and how kind everyone is to him and his family.

I tell him that's because *nobody* can beat his pickles.

Mr Kaplan shakes his head and a worrisome sadness fills his eyes. '*Danke, Fräulein* Alexander, but things are not so good in Germany these days.'

'Is your brother ill? His family?' I nibble on the homemade strudel I bought, licking my fingers. Cinnamon and apple. I'm always hungry.

He wipes his hands on his black work apron, then heaves out a sigh. 'The Nazis are trying to destroy our Jewish businesses, *Fräulein*, boycotting them and decreeing that Germans shouldn't buy from us, and if they do, they must be reported and photographed and their names and pictures displayed in magazines.'

'Whose silly idea is that?' I ask.

He smirks. 'The man they call their leader: Herr Hitler.'

'With stupid ideas like that, I imagine this Hitler won't last long.' I buy another pickle to put a smile on his face, but I can't eat it. The storekeeper doesn't notice. Nor does he notice I'm wearing a camel coat in this heat to hide my growing belly.

His heart is heavy today with worry.

'I have tried to convince my brother to come to America, but he thinks like you. That Hitler and his ideas can't last.' He pops my pickles into a white paper bag and hands it to me. 'Enjoy, *Fräulein*, and don't worry about me. I haven't given up. I'm trying to get visas for my brother and his family.'

'You will.'

He nods. 'I pray you're right.'

I give him as big a smile as my rumbling belly will allow, then make a quick exit to the closest empty field where I toss up the strudel into a ring of pink and yellow wildflowers. I hate the awful taste in my mouth afterward, but my morning sickness has nearly subsided, though today is the exception.

I expect the usual snub from Mother when I return from *Kaplan's*, pickles in hand. It's worse. My *Alice in Lilac Land* adventure comes to an end when I overhear her making train reservations on her personal telephone line in the library.

'Yes, that's correct, a private compartment for two occupants... Mrs Royston Smythe and daughter Penelope.'

Penelope?

After she hangs up the phone I make no secret of my presence. 'What game are you playing, Mother?'

'The game of survival, Kay. I won't let you ruin me, so I've made plans.'

Plans?

'I never wanted to hurt you, Mother, but I have to live my life. I don't want to leave Lilac Hill, but I will if I must.' I've been seeing a doctor in New York for prenatal care. Nobody is the wiser.

'When it's time, you'll have your baby in a place where no one knows you. You're showing now and you can't wear that camel coat every minute. Servants whisper, but they know where their bread is buttered and, in the middle of a depression, they're not going to talk.'

'I won't do it.' I'm willing to leave home, but on *my* terms, not hers.

'You will.'

'I'll rent an apartment in the city or in New York. Have my baby there.'

'Then what?'

'I have no illusions about Nico. You were right. He used me, but I want this child. I'll raise the baby on my own.'

'On the stipend I give you every month?' She laughs. 'What do you know about finances? You sign for anything you need, but I pay your bills. You'll end up living in a shanty down by the waterfront with the rest of the refugees.'

'What are you talking about?' I don't like where this is going.

'Your father thought it wise to draw up an ironclad trust agreement to make sure you didn't get your hands on your inheritance until you either married or' – she snickers – 'you turn twenty.'

'That won't be until—'

'Until *after* your baby is born.' She continues making notes. 'I thought it best not to tell you and there was no reason to do so because I assumed you'd be married before you turned of age and then you'd fall nicely into his plans.'

'You mean *your* plans.' I bristle with anger. 'You *can't* take my money from me.'

'I don't need your inheritance, Kay, but I *do* need your cooperation to make this thing go away. Considering the predicament you've put me in, I have no choice.' She folds her notes into a clean, concise rectangle as if she's folding my life the same way. 'Béatrice will pack your bags.'

'Why? Where are we going?' I don't like the triumphant sneer on Mother's face that makes her nose wrinkle up like a boar's snout.

'You shall have your baby at a private facility far enough away from Philadelphia where discretion takes priority over anything else. A place where no one will know your real name.'

'Why?'

'You shall give up all rights to the child.'

'*What?*' I cry out, my ears ringing. 'I won't... *I swear I won't.*'

'You will. I won't have an unwed debutante and her brat living in my house.'

There's that word *brat* again. She says it because she knows it hurts me.

I play my trump card. 'Then I'll marry Tommy Whitworth. I'll ring him up—'

Mother laughs. 'Do you think any Main Line bachelor will have you if you tell him you're pregnant with that gigolo's baby, *hmm*?' She creases her forehead. 'You're soiled goods, daughter, but we can still save your reputation *if* you do what I tell you and place the child up for adoption.'

'*No!*'

She says nothing, merely starts humming some silly tune that unravels my thinking. I don't like it. She's playing on my nerves. For the first time in my life I feel like she's won, gotten exactly what she wanted in a strange way. There's something in her manner that's jaunty, confident. And her eyes swim with secrets that make me afraid when I'm most vulnerable.

I'm cold with fear when I ask her, 'How can you be so cruel, Mother? I know we don't see eye to eye on everything, but this is my baby we're talking about... *your* grandchild.'

'That baby is no grandchild of mine.' She straightens her bosom, adjusts her diamond bracelets on her wrists and lifts her chin. 'We leave at midnight on the *Broadway Limited.*'

Nothing more is said between us.

There's nothing more to say.

Mother hates me.

Not because I had sex with a man not my husband (she'd advocate against *that* if she could), but because my baby isn't the progeny of a match she orchestrated. An heir descendant of a pompous, fat Philadelphia lawyer who can trace his lineage back to the Revolution. In her eyes, what I did is beyond a sin, it's an inexcusable smear on my place in society.

And it must be wiped out before anyone knows it exists.

11

BERLIN, AUTUMN 1935

Rachel

'*Go home, dirty Jew girl.*'

A barrage of pebbles whiz by me, stinging my cheekbone. I touch my face, a fierce bruising already swelling under my fingertips. *Who, why?*

I spin around. BdM girls. *Bund deutscher Mädel.* The Hitler Youth Group for girls. Girls I went to school with before German law prohibited Aryans mixing with Jews. I should have been more careful, but the trio cut me off on a side street not far from the synagogue next to where I go to school. The cutting look in the eyes of the blonde girl with the dirty mouth makes me shudder.

A girl I played ball with, traded pencils with. Helga Dornstadt. Hands on her hips, laughing, strutting around in her uniform, sneering and spitting.

And she expects me to cower like a scared mouse? Really?

She knows me better than that. We used to make mud pies together on rainy days when we lived over on the west side before Papa moved his music shop to Charlottenstrasse. It makes me sad how the Nazi Party has squeezed her brain into a box of hate for Jews.

I'm her latest stooge.

The cold, drizzly day seeps through the thin threads of my sweater, chilling my heart when her two friends, Sigrid and Anna, echo her insults as they toss handfuls of gravel at me, striking me on the shoulders, the back. Yes, it hurts, but more than that I feel queasy in my stomach and my shoulders shake. I'm scared. I know what happens to anyone who gets in the crosshairs of these gangs. I see boys from the Hitler Youth harassing people, beating them with bricks until their noses bleed and I hear the crack of broken bones. So far, I've been spared.

Until today.

The girls must have tailed me from school and then saw me come out of *Seltzi's Candies* next to the linen store Sigrid's father owns. Swinging their long golden plaits over their shoulders, their tongues slick with prejudice, they yelled at me with Helga leading them and showing off her BdM uniform. Brown rucksack jacket, blue skirt and white blouse, her kerchief tied in a saucy knot, while I hunch my shoulders, pulling down my pea green wool sweater with patches sewn on my elbows.

Dirty Jew girl, she called me. The insult cuts me to the core. I shouldn't let her get to me. I should be on my way, keeping mum about their insults like we're warned to do. *If you're smart girls*, my teacher tells us, *you'll keep your heads down when you see these Nazis*. He tells the class they passed silly laws about race and that Jews aren't allowed to marry Aryans

We're no longer regarded as citizens of the Reich.

Mutti says I should still be proud to be Jewish, that God sees us all as equals. Too bad He didn't get His message to this girl I once went on hayrides with, played games with.

It's the history we share that gives me the gumption to say, 'Let me be, Helga, or I'll pin your braids to a dartboard.'

Brave words. I'm tall for my age and stand eye to eye with Helga. I'm twelve, but she's thirteen and thinks she's queen of the streets, patrolling where she knows Jews live.

'How dare *you*, a Jew, talk to *me* like that.'

She spits at me.

Oh... My jaw drops as I wipe the saliva off my cheek, then she takes the advantage and yanks off my felt hat and stomps on it with her heel until it lies in shreds on the street.

Like a dead bird, its wings torn from its body.

I take a deep breath to steady my nerves. 'I can't believe we were ever friends, Helga. You're the most terrible girl *ever*.'

'Yeah?'

'Yeah.'

'I should report you to my brother,' she says. 'He's a troop leader in the Hitler Youth and serves our Fuehrer proudly. He knows how to deal with Jews.'

'Go ahead, report me.' I raise my fists, ready to fight back.

Why am I doing this? Do I want my nose broken? No, it's because Mutti says these girls are bullies and I can't let them see me be weak. We must be strong. What if they come after Leah or Tovah?

I won't let anyone hurt my sisters. *Ever*.

Pulling up my collar against the wind, I fight back tears of anger. I'm seething inside, wanting so bad to fight back. Here? On a public street? Nosy housewives peeking out from behind curtains watch with stoic faces. A policeman on his rounds looks the other way, then turns the corner. And the two girls with Helga – Anna and Sigrid – won't look at me.

I ignore them, then with an 'evil' eye toward Helga, I turn up my nose and head down the alleyway. I don't want a fight.

Pesky raindrops wet my eyelashes. I walk faster, hugging the bag of butterscotch hard candies I scooped out of the big barrel at *Seltzi's* to my chest. Why didn't I listen to Mutti? She warned me to steer clear of my old school chums, telling me German girls are forced to join the BdM, but I never believed *these* girls would do this to me.

They have one purpose.

To harass Jews.

They're not finished with me yet.

'*Hey, Jew girl,*' Helga yells, coming after me. 'What's in your pocket?'

'None of your business.' I turn away, hiding the sheet music for a Cole Porter tune. I love to sing and Papa says if I study real hard, I'll be good enough to sing in festivals. He has no idea I practice singing with the street singers who rally around the courtyard at the end of our street. He'd be angry, telling me I'm 'wasting my voice', but I love to sing, it makes me happy to share my gift, especially when the I see the old people dabbing their eyes with their handkerchiefs, my singing giving them hope and reviving a memory that still tugs at their hearts.

I sing so they won't have to be lonely like Bubbe was after my grandfather died. His mind had gone long before that... That pained her, sitting out their last years with a beloved man who didn't know her, holding his hand. When his hand turned cold, so did hers.

She said me singing the old songs warmed her again.

I never forgot that even after she died.

I miss her and I know Mutti does, too, but it isn't just her passing that makes my mother sad. She gets upset when Papa talks about expanding his business... the Nazis have made it impossible and his dream died. Over and over I hear her telling him we should consider getting out of Germany... that Hitler and his silly race laws are taking everything away from us.

What if they come after our music shop? Mutti says. They've already orchestrated boycotts of Jewish businesses, urging people not to buy from us. But my father fought bravely in the Great War and he believes the government would never turn on the veterans.

What if he's wrong? Look what's happening to me. Here. Now.

I clutch my bag of candy to my chest and grab the sheet music from my pocket.

'Take it from her,' yells Anna.

'Yeah, Jews can't own anything,' says Sigrid, nudging Helga and giggling.

'Anna is right.' Helga snatches the sheet music from my hand before I can stop her. 'It's against the law for scum like you to own anything of value.'

Why is she picking on me?

Yes, I'm Jewish, but we often shared our lunch with each other. Then everything changed when she joined the BdM. She became prejudiced and nasty. That's not what the group stands for. I sneaked a peek at a pamphlet I found in the street. Girls join the BdM to learn to be good wives and mothers. I want to be a mother, too, with all my heart. But I don't want to be mean like Helga... so, in my mind, I'm glad I can't join their stupid organization. I'd hate it.

I'm also scared of it.

'The sheet music is mine,' I tell her, 'give it back.'

'*Ja, Fräulein*, I'll give it back.'

Helga laughs and tears the music sheet in half.

Why? I die inside when she throws it into a puddle. I bend down to pick it up and she kicks me in the rear. I stumble and fall to the pavement then she kicks me again, calling me names. Sigrid spits at me. Then Anna. I want to cry, but I won't. I hold my precious bag of hard candy close to my chest.

I can't let it fall.

Mutti would be so upset. She always keeps a crystal dish filled with hard candies for the students and customers who frequent our neighborhood shop. Jews and Aryans brave enough. They love Papa and always have a kind word for Mutti as they grab a butterscotch disc.

Then Tovah got into a fit during her violin lesson yesterday and ate the last piece so Mutti sent me to buy more. My little sister just turned six and Papa claims she has real talent. *Really, Papa?* The screechy noises she makes with her bow hurt my ears. And Leah's. She's nine. She escaped upstairs to our apartment above the shop to work on her collection of autographs, leaving Mutti and me to put up with Tovah's practice session.

Mutti smiles and encourages her, but she can't hear it at the same pitch we do. My mother lost her hearing years ago when a bomb exploded near her during the Great War. She was on her way home from school and would have died if the explosion had been closer. I adore my mother and her strength. She reads lips and keeps the accounting books for the shop and never asks for anything for herself.

Except that candy dish.

When Bubbe died, the only thing my mother wanted after her brother and his wife picked clean my grandmother's small room was the crystal dish with the dome-like lid. Her fondest memories as a little girl were sneaking candy from that dish.

No more time for dawdling and memories.

I've got to get home and fill up the dish with butterscotch.

Or is that an excuse because I'm afraid to stay and fight these girls?

I cower next to the building, curled up in a fetal position like a wounded puppy. Then I hear Mutti's voice in my head, telling me not to show fear. That she loves me and that's what matters.

I'm going to need her faith in me... These girls aren't finished.

'Get her soap and water, Sigrid,' Helga says in a mocking tone. 'Jews are so dumb, they're good only for washing the pavements.'

That does it.

No one calls me *dumb*.

'Is that so?' I yell, reaching out and grabbing Helga around the ankle, my anger overtaking my reason. Mutti is always getting on me for my 'adventurous spirit'. A dangerous thing in these times, but I don't care. She tore up my lovely sheet music and called me dumb.

I pull hard on her ankle and down she goes. I'm tired of her bullying me.

'*Aargh...*' she cries out, her long plaits flapping over her shoulder. She lands with a thud, the wind knocked out of her but only for a second. She gets on her knees and throws a punch at me, hitting me in the mouth. My teeth rattle in my head. Pain burns through me. I swear I see stars, then taste blood on my lips.

Something takes hold of me then I didn't know I had. Survival instinct. I don't think twice when I swing my bag of candy at her, smacking her above the eye. The paper bag bursts open and—

Candy explodes everywhere. Rolling into the street, the gutter.

'You'll be sorry,' Helga screams.

I smile even if it hurts, smug. She'll have a shiner, but she won't report me. She'd look like a fool.

But I'm no fool.

I run.

Down the street... I look around... Where can I hide? Not the tailor's shop. The German flag says it's Aryan-owned... Then there's the bank. Closed. There was major panic when customers lost faith in financial institutions months ago and withdrew their money... Then past the bookstore. Its windows are empty except for 'approved' literature with swastikas pasted on the covers.

No place to hide.

I jump between two cabbies parked on the street waiting for fares. They honk their horns at me, but I keep going, praying the girls don't follow me, until I make it to our street... my heart pounding, my face damp with sweat.

I burst into our music shop, so scared I don't kiss the mezuzah Papa placed on the doorpost to thank God and invite Him in. The tiny bell on the door swings back and forth on its hook, ringing loudly. I don't see any customers. *Gut.* I head for the back stairs leading to our apartment when—

Mutti grabs me, spins me around. 'Rachel, *you're hurt*... What happened, *mein Kind*?'

I should have known I couldn't get past her. Even if she can't hear the bell ringing, she can feel the vibrations on the wooden floor under her feet.

'It's nothing, Mutti.'

She cups my face. 'You got into a fight.'

'I had to... Those BdM girls called me names.'

I confess to Mutti how Helga humiliated me, called me a *dirty Jew*. I tell her how I fought back and slammed her with the bag of candy. Mutti reads my lips, telling me to slow down. Her eyes darken to a deep ebony that speaks of her worst fear coming true, that violence could so easily touch me, her daughter.

Then Mutti kisses my brow and soothes me, telling me she's never been prouder of me.

Then she hugs me and I feel safe in her arms.

A brief moment of triumph I will treasure always... even when the darkness descends upon our heads like a heavy veil.

When I remember the ominous shadow falling over my mother's face that day, I think she knew then deep in her soul—

The nightmare was just beginning.

12

BETHLEHEM, PENNSYLVANIA, DECEMBER 1935

Kay

I come here every morning, strolling through the succulent garden behind the Catholic hospital for unwed mothers to watch the changing landscape... First, the summer roses filled my nostrils with a rich, vibrant scent that made me heady with joy that all was not lost, that I'd find a way to keep my baby. Then the late summer daffodils rolled the sun over my face like a bolt of yellow silk unfolding, suffocating me under the mantle of duty. In autumn, I crumbled dry, crisp golden-and-orange maple leaves in my palm, mindful that youth fades and summer follies have a price to pay.

Now, in winter, I walk quickly through the garden in my fur-lined coat heavy with snow that has fallen upon my shoulders. Cold and untrusting, I shudder to think what the next weeks will bring as the birth of my child approaches.

Mother is determined I give up my baby. And she won't change her mind.

Unfortunately, what she told me about the trust my father left me is true. I don't come into my full inheritance until I'm twenty.

I'm nineteen.

If I choose to go out on my own, Mother would see to it my credit disappears at *Wanamaker's* and *Gimbel's*. My bank account would be frozen, my red roadster locked in the garage at Lilac Hill, the keys tossed away.

For myself, I don't care. I never liked the Newport life Mother so adores, but I won't subject my child to a freezing room with a broken radiator, spoiled milk, and not enough mush and crushed carrots to nourish her with. (I'm convinced my child is a girl.)

For a while, I held on to the idea I could appeal to my mother's maternal instinct, but that faded when she showed no interest in either me or the child when we checked in. She held little concern about my health... except to toss away my cigarettes, declaring that in spite of the magazine ads with handsome doctors professing they're not harmful, they stain your teeth and *that's* the reason not to smoke.

She introduced herself to the administrator as Mrs Royston Smythe and the woman never battered a lash. It's all a game to these people. They pretend not to know who you are even when presented with a check engraved with your name. A handsome sum that made me blink. Twice.

That the life of a helpless baby is worth so much money just to be born, then forgotten.

Then Mother left and I settled in.

Béatrice packed enough silk dressing gowns and satin bed jackets and ballet-soft slippers to last me while I'm here, along with casual print day dresses and warm sweaters, sensible shoes with laces. A wide brim sunhat. Sunglasses, so no one gets too nosy.

Then, when she wasn't looking, I slipped a white box with a red ribbon tied around it into my suitcase. A special present for my baby I will open on Christmas morning. Then I'll put it away until my child is born.

Here.

In a hospital that's more like a palatial home surrounded by a thick forest, garden, and white fences.

I'd never heard of the Mary T. Vickers Sanitarium before I arrived here. It's touted in discreet circles as a place for young ladies to rest. A spa. A code phrase meaning *it's a home for unwed mothers of the upper class*. Numerous members of society's blue bloods have passed through here over the past thirty years from every part of the country. Each mother-to-be has her own wing where she sees no one but the medical staff, a personal assistant, and family who sneak in at odd hours through a private entrance.

When I take my morning walk, I'm assigned my own section of the massive garden so I don't encounter anyone I shouldn't.

I've never been so lonely.

Until Sister Bridget enters my life. A young nun from the convent next door, a pious place with a religious aura that handles the adoptions. A sanctuary to give unwed mothers peace that they're doing the right thing.

I call it *coercion*, but I don't hold that against her.

Sister Bridget doesn't judge me. Flitting about in a black habit too big for her, she's always adjusting her wimple and her round, black-rimmed spectacles. She talks and talks with a lovely Irish lilt in her voice about the flowers and the bees and how she's here to help me in the name of our Lord.

That God has plans for me and won't abandon me. Or my child.

She's somewhat of a romantic. She didn't want to become a nun, she touts, but according to her parish priest, every Irish family is obliged to produce at least one priest and one nun. Since she's the last girl in a family of eight, the responsibility fell upon her shoulders. No mind, she said, her poor mum is plum worn out from popping out babies and taking in wash, so she's happy not to burden her any more.

'Telegram for you, Miss Smythe... from your mother.'

Sister Bridget finds me in the garden on this Christmas Eve, holding my big belly and counting snowflakes. Or trying to. Anything to take my mind off the impending deadline when I leave here. Alone. Without my child if Mother has her way. I keep holding on to my principles, but in the end, Mother assures me she *will* win.

I won't give up without a fight. I go through different scenarios, like how I'll run off before my due date and get a job. Or when I'm twenty, I'll hire detectives to find my child and offer the new parents the moon to give her back to me. Then I realize how selfish that sounds and I hang my head in shame under the willow tree, shivering when a breeze shakes a rush of fallen snow on to my bare neck.

Penance, Sister Bridget would say, for my sinful thoughts.

Oh, I can't think straight. I'm tired all the time and I'm so big for seven and a half months, I don't how I can go on much longer. I feel bloated and my back aches. I'm getting sharp pains in my groin, as though my child is anxious to be born. I want to see her, hold her. I refuse to accept that after carrying this baby for so long I have to give her up.

There's still a chance. I have a new tactic to try on Mother. If that doesn't work, maybe the convent will take me in.

'What time will she be here?' I ask without opening the telegram.

'Three o'clock.' Sister Bridget blushes, knowing *I* know she reads the telegrams before giving them to me. 'She upset you so the last time she was here. Are you sure you're up to seeing her?'

'I have no choice, Sister. She's paying the bills.'

'Don't seem right a nice girl like you should have a mother like that.'

I smile. She's more inquisitive, or should I say snoopy, than you'd expect for a nun, but that's what I like about her.

And why Mother can't stand her.

* * *

'I'd like to be alone with my daughter, Sister,' Mother says, her sharp eyes watching the young nun like a hawk as she helps me put my feet up on the ottoman and places a pillow behind my back. We're sitting by the fireplace in my sitting room, the roaring flames making the room cozy, the flowery drapes printed with wistful lavender drawn tight, the lighting dim.

The mood is... testy.

Mother blew in here like a witch on a broomstick on Christmas Eve, wearing her favorite sealskin coat and a cone-shaped hat with a trailing veil, striking a haughty pose designed to intimidate.

It doesn't work on the nun.

'She's feeling poorly today, Mrs Smythe; I should stay with her.' Sister Bridget grins, then gets me another pillow.

I lean back in the damask-covered wingback chair, amused at how the sister isn't afraid of my mother. She showed up with a tray of hot tea and cake and stood her ground even when she shooed her away. 'Mother isn't here today to overexcite me, are you?'

Mother grumbles. 'That depends.'

'Oh?'

'On whether or not you sign the adoption papers.'

Short and to the point. I sigh. Nothing's changed. All my life I've obeyed the rules and look where it got me.

Sister Bridget clears her throat. 'Lemon in your tea, Mrs Smythe?'

'No,' Mother answers, loud and clear.

'Cake?' she asks. 'It was made fresh this morning with blueberries from Florida—'

'*No!*'

I have to laugh at how the sister protects me. 'I guarantee you won't win, Mother. Let her stay.'

'I don't know how you put up with such an incorrigible staff. I imagine she's peeped through enough keyholes to know everybody's business,' Mother mumbles. 'However, I haven't changed my position. You're *not* keeping this baby.'

Silence.

Mother's embarrassing frankness doesn't help my courage. We have this same argument every time she comes, spewing her distaste for me having a baby with a 'foreigner' as she deems anyone not born in Philadelphia. God help me, being Cuban and Italian makes Nico a monster in her eyes.

Today she's nastier than usual.

I want to tune her out, but I don't dare, for my baby's sake. We're united in our determination not to let her have her way.

'Do I make myself clear?' Mother says, unbuttoning her sealskin coat.

'You can't force me to give up my child.'

'Can't I? If you don't agree, I'll have you transferred to that wretched unwed mothers home in New Jersey and you can squat with those Jewish women, no doubt in filthy conditions.'

New Jersey? What's she talking about?

It must be one of the 'secret' hospitals for unwed mothers around the Philadelphia area, what with household help often finding themselves unwed and pregnant. I know my mother paid for more than one maid to go to such a place not deemed fit for 'upper classes', though I never heard her spew such prejudice before. Of course, she harbors prejudice against anyone who isn't of her class (whatever that is). What she has against Jewish people, I don't know.

'However clever you think you are, Mother,' I tell her, trying a new tactic, hoping to appeal to her social side, 'nothing is foolproof and someone here *may* talk.'

'They wouldn't dare.' She swishes her veil over her shoulder, confident.

I smirk. 'Wouldn't they?'

Then what?

Her social status would plummet faster than the crash of 1929.

'Wouldn't it be better to welcome the baby into our home and say I adopted the child?' I persist. 'If anyone on staff at the home says otherwise, I'll say I made trips here to visit the child's mother.'

Their word against mine.

Against Mother's, God help them.

My plea falls on deaf ears. She pooh-poohs my idea with a swish of her gloved hand, then returns to her agenda.

'Why haven't you signed the adoption papers?' she snips at me. 'Your due date is getting close.' Terse, accusing, Mother should have been a prosecuting attorney the way she keeps hammering at me. 'The Mother Superior at the children's placement agency would like to put the impending birth of your child down on her calendar as "available".'

'I haven't changed my mind, Mother,' I insist, expressing myself with a whiff of arrogance. 'I'm keeping my baby.'

There's a buzz in my head that makes me feel dizzy, an emotion so gratifying at standing up to her, I ignore the aching in my back. Then the discomfort shifts to my stomach. Nerves.

'You have no choice, daughter. I won't stand for any more delays, is that understood?'

I bite my lip to keep from lashing out at her. I'll not give her the satisfaction.

She stands up, signaling the visit is over. 'I'll be back to see you next week. I expect you'll have done what I asked before then or you're aware of the consequences. You're cut off from any funds.'

She gives me a sneer, buttons up her coat, closes the snaps on her fur-topped galoshes and then leaves without touching her tea or her cake.

Not even a Merry Christmas.

Exhausted, I don't object to Sister Bridget helping me into my nightclothes... a long silk dressing gown with pink rosettes embroidered on the long sleeves and yoke. I'm still having pains like needles shooting through me, but a cup of hot cocoa helps. I try not to complain. Sister Bridget and I have had enough trauma for one day. She tucks me in under the heavy quilt, humming along to the sound of Christmas caroling in the corridor outside my room. I lie back, exhale. The sound is warm and soothing. The staff have been practicing for weeks, and on this holy night, they bring peace to young mothers like me who tread with fear into the unknown.

Sister Bridget sits with me, reclining in the wingback chair with *her* feet up on the ottoman so I don't have to be alone on Christmas Eve. In her usual manner she chitchats about anything on her mind.

'When I was a lass growing up in a brick row house near the river,' she says, 'I remember my mam lighting one candle in the front window to show the way for the Christ Child.'

'How about Santa Claus?' I ponder, remembering the wonderful Christmases we had at Lilac Hill before Pops died. A ten-foot tree with fancy silver, blue and red balls from Germany; plum pudding and roast turkey and English beef; and so many presents I'd give half of them away to the servants' children. I enjoyed seeing their faces lighting up with holiday joy. My mother never noticed. I never received anything personally chosen by her. With Mother, everything is delegated. Even the presents.

She laughs. 'In Mam's eyes, it was the Lord's birthday and He had top billing over the man in the red suit.'

'My father took me to see Santa at *Wanamaker's* when I was growing up.' I sigh, seeing my father, the tall man who was so smart and proper acting like a big kid when Santa asked me what I wanted for Christmas and I said 'a bookstore'. Pops said he'd get me one.

'I saw Santa at *Wanamaker's*, too, miss... Ain't it funny that Santa doesn't care how much money you have? That he's good and kind to all children.'

My mother could learn a lesson from him.

We chat about snowball fights and the smell of glazed cherries and fruit cake baking in the oven and I feel myself drifting off with the caroling whirling around in my head... and a sugar plum fairy or two dancing when—

I jerk awake with a start.

'*Oh, God... argh!*' I groan out loud and twist about in bed, but I'm so big I can't turn over on my side. I try again, but my body is cramped. When I move, the pains in my stomach get so bad my back arches. What time is it? After midnight according to the tiny clock on the nightstand. I don't know how long I slept; hours by the smell of burnt wood coming from the fireplace. The damp night seeps through my robe, its fingers icy and cold, making me shiver.

I look around. I'm alone.

Sister Bridget, dear soul, went to bed.

I feel the urge to go to the bathroom, but I can't drag myself out of bed. My body feels weighed down, like it's buried in wet sand. Still, I feel a tremendous need to push through the pain. I lie still and take deep breaths like the sister taught me. My heart is racing. I'm sweating, face clammy. Am I in early labor? *Is that possible?*

I try again to get out of bed.

I can't.

I grunt and squeeze my legs together to push them over the side of the bed... My hair is plastered to my face, my nightclothes are wet... Did my water break? Another sharp pain. A contraction Sister Bridget warned me about? *You must relax*, she said to prepare me. I can't, which makes my body tenser and the pain worse. It's silly of me, but the more pain I feel, the more my thoughts drift backward to Nico and wonder if he ever thinks about me... Does he know about Mother's plans of adoption for the baby? I doubt it. Mother made it clear to him he had no legal rights regarding the child. If he did, would he have tried to see me? It's a question I haven't dared to think about because I know the answer.

No.

I wouldn't admit it before, but deep inside me, I know his caress was too practiced, his kiss deep and possessive, a man taking not giving. A man with a warm smile and good looks, but vain and cold.

A man I know now who could be bought.

It's at that moment I free myself from his spell, accept the fact this baby and I are on our own and that's okay. We're going to be fine.

I place my hand on my belly to calm us both down when I feel another contraction begin and then a hardening ball in my stomach, a tightening that scares me. Oh, it hurts *so* bad, then it gets better, a little. I must get up, *walk*.

I feel dizzy as I stand up, my arms hurting from pushing myself up when—

Everything blurs in a mad whirl around me and I can't keep my balance. *Ooh*... Before I can stop myself, my body slams onto the floor and I land on my side. I grab my belly to protect my child.

'*Sister Bridget, come quick, I need you!*'

I call out again and again until I hear—

Footsteps coming... closer, then...

'*Oh my God*... Are you hurt, Miss Smythe?'

I look up at her, her face pale like an angel's. 'Help me, *please*, I think my baby's coming...'

She blesses herself. 'You're not due for weeks, but it looks like the Christ Child is bringing us an early Christmas present.'

She places her hand on my abdomen, then checks the small watch attached to the white collar on her habit and counts... She nods, and then places a blanket over me to keep me warm.

'I'll call the doctor.' She smiles wide.

She's gone for a minute, maybe two, but it feels longer as the pain is so horrible.

I scream.

Sister Bridget runs into my room, then grabs my hand and holds it tight as we wait for the doctor and the orderlies to help me onto a gurney.

When they arrive, they race me into the delivery room... and I begin the journey on the longest night of my life.

I'm in labor for hours.

'Push harder, miss... *harder!*'

All night long the pain is gut-wrenching. I hear the doctor and nurses whispering... A gasp, then a second. The physician grunts loudly, then heaves out a breath, then curses. Why? I don't know. No one will tell me anything.

Push, push, they repeat, the nurse's voice choking on the words.

I clench my teeth and bear down for another push, yet I'm fearful when the moment comes and my baby is born they'll take her from me before I have a chance to hold her.

Ah... I feel the baby moving... her tiny body getting into position, she as anxious as I am to enter my world. The exhausting pains come in a rhythmic cycle that ebbs and flows... My heart pounds and my arms ache to hold her close to my breasts.

Another loud gasp.

I don't know if it came from the nurse or the doctor.

Still, they say nothing.

Something is wrong.

My mind replays the events of the night, looking for answers... When I first called out for Sister Bridget, she smiled and raised her eyes upward with joy, humming Christmas carols as they wheeled me into the delivery room.

Then the doctor examined me and the nun's smile faded. A shadow crossed over her face, a worrisome look I've seen in her eyes when there's an empty room down the corridor and no sound of a baby's cry.

A silence that speaks as loudly to me as if all the martyred saints came to cry at my bedside, their sobs echoing in my head.

Something is wrong... but no one will tell me what it is. I pray to God, telling Him how much I want this baby. Then—

'*Push...* I can see the baby's head...' is the last thing I hear before someone puts a gas mask over my face and I pass out.

13

BERLIN, HANUKKAH 1935

Rachel

It's not as if we aren't good Jews because Mutti lets us go see the Christmas tree in the square at the *Weihnachtsmarkt*. The yummy smell of pine and ginger and cloves wafting from the holiday booths and stalls fills us with a joy that transcends whatever path you follow to righteousness. Here we are all children eager to taste every treat we can, sharing and marveling at how much we can eat without getting sick.

What we forget is that anyone could be hiding in the shadows, watching us, waiting to make a move to take away what little freedoms we have left as Jews.

I don't think about that now as I link arms with Leah and Tovah and we skip through the open market. Brisk, cold air fills our lungs and music fills our hearts. We sing a song I wrote about a lost girl rescuing her baby sister after the wicked witch steals her, a song about daisy chains and tears. Lily ponds and hugs. We sing freely without care... We're three happy sisters reveling in winter's bounty and if it happens to include bitesize marzipan potatoes dusted with cinnamon, why shouldn't we enjoy them when Mutti isn't watching us?

It's just our luck when she spies us, giggling and stuffing our mouths, scolding us that we won't have appetites after tonight's lighting of the candle for *real* potatoes... *latkes*, pancakes fried in oil.

We always have room for your latkes, *Mutti*, we say in unison.

She tries to hide her smile, but I know that pleases her. She takes great pride in making Hanukkah for us. Tonight is the fourth night of the Festival of Lights and she's brought us here to the open market to buy powdered sugar for the deep-fried doughnuts we love filled with red jelly.

Later we'll light another candle on a special Menorah, say a blessing and sing a hymn. In Hebrew. We memorized the lyrics, though I'm not sure what the words mean. Papa says it's the words in your heart that count. We're not Orthodox, but Mutti and Papa observe the High Holidays and teach us the stories handed down for thousands of years. It's very solemn but important we honor our traditions. I'm filled with a comfort knowing where I come from, how hard it's been for my people to achieve what we have.

I see Mutti's eyes mist up when we say the blessing each night, her look troubled when she glances at Papa. He's so involved in his music, I don't think he hears the ever louder drumbeat that has Mutti so worried. And me. I've not been the same since my run-in with the BdM girls. Mutti understands and shares with me her fears about what's happening in Germany while Papa is... well, Papa. He sees only the good in people.

Life is like a melody, he's fond of saying. *You can play it sad or happy and I prefer it happy*.

And my sisters? Leah and Tovah are still babies, wanting only to get presents and play games, but I forgive them. Let them stay innocent a while longer. *Alles ist gut*. They have me to protect them.

Still, I pray the Nazis are gone before my sisters are my age.

Singing to myself, I wait for Mutti to buy her sugar near a stall selling candied fruits and honey-coated nuts when the air around me turns sour. Out of the corner of my eye, I see a teenage boy of about sixteen wearing a Hitler Youth uniform slither up behind me. I shiver. Leah and Tovah don't see him... They're too busy counting the clear glass balls on the Christmas tree. I want to grab my sisters and run. I want nothing to do with his kind, but I don't want to draw his attention, especially with Leah and Tovah so distracted. There's no telling what childish thing they'll do.

The boy coughs to get my attention. I stiffen.

What does he want?

'I'd be careful what songs you sing, *Fräulein*,' he says in a harsh whisper that makes my pulse race. 'If it's on the *verboten* list, you could find yourself in a labor camp.'

'I wrote that song,' I protest, my feathers ruffled.

'*Any* song a Jew writes is on the list, *Fräulein*.'

How does he know I'm Jewish?

I turn and study his face... He looks familiar. Piercing blue eyes that see into my soul; a soul stained in his mind with the sin of being Jewish. He's taught not to see otherwise. He's handsome in an artificial way, his lips pulled tight over white teeth, high cheekbones... His uniform is too neat, too perfect. His expression reminds me of a statue. Never changing. He does what he's told whatever the order.

'What do you want from me?' I get bold enough to ask.

'Keep away from my sister... or you'll regret it.'

A threat...

Then I make the connection. I can't believe it. Helga's older brother, Hans. She hasn't given up trying to hurt me and had him follow me. How long has he been observing me? I don't care for myself, but I'm putting Mutti and Leah and Tovah in danger.

I say nothing, but I feel sick. Not from eating too much candy, but from his ugly words. He leans down and hisses at me, his face so close to mine, I can smell the beer on his breath.

Why won't he go away?

Long seconds drag on my nerves while he snaps his fingers in time to a tune he's humming, tapping his foot on the stone cobbles strewn with festive hay. As though he's waiting for me to do something, *anything*, so he can put me in my place.

Breathe… I tell myself. *Let the frosty air fill your lungs so you stay numb to his freakish game.*

If I run, he'll chase me, so I don't. Defying him angers him. In a swift movement that cuts through me like a sharp piece of ice, he jerks my head back, grabbing onto my long braids and pulling me away from the crowd and behind a holiday booth, then calling me a name so vile I squeeze my eyes tight to make it go away.

I go rigid, my heart pounding hard in my chest. I swear it jumps into my throat, choking me. I can't speak… I hear myself spewing guttural sounds, but the words won't come.

I flap my arms around, trying to reach back and grab his hands, get away, but he has a strong grip on my hair and I can't free myself… My head spins and spins… everything is getting blurry… *I need help—*

He laughs and lets me go, disappearing into the crowd, his stern warning messing with my mind. I start wheezing, trying to catch my breath. I hold my hands over my ears for what seems like forever, wanting to block out what he called me.

Jewish whore.

I can't.

Finally, in a dazed stupor, I wander back to the tall Christmas tree, looking over my shoulder, and find my sisters ogling the tree like two happy magpies. A flutter of relief makes my heart skip. They have no idea of the turmoil roiling inside me to keep them... *us*... safe. My emotions are running high as they're wont to do these days. After everything that's happened to me – changing schools and the BdM girls and Helga's mean brother pulling my braids so tight my scalp still burns – these strange feelings make sense. I'm always on edge and I feel... odd. A funny ache in my lower belly that comes and goes.

I put it out of my mind when I catch up to Mutti making her way toward us, pulling Leah and Tovah along like lost puppies. I should tell Mutti what happened, but I can't. She's preoccupied with her shopping as it gets closer to sundown. We'll have to hurry. Tradition dictates we light the candle soon after dark.

We're about to head home when Tovah cries out, '*Look, Mutti! There's Kris Kringle.*'

My little sister points to a jovial man with a white beard reaching down to his big belly. He's wearing a long red robe and a cap trimmed with white fur and he's giving out toys and oranges in front of the Christmas tree.

Mutti doesn't have to read her little girl's lips to know what she wants. 'We have to get back, Tovah, so we can light the Menorah—'

'Please, Mutti, *please*!' Tovah pleads. 'He's giving out oranges.' Even Leah, who is so shy she hardly speaks, begs Mutti to let us join the throng of excited children gathered around Father Christmas.

'I don't know, girls—'

'I'll stay with them, Mutti,' I promise. 'You go ahead and we'll run all the way home so we won't be late.'

Mutti cups my chin. 'My sweet Rachel, always looking out for her sisters, but don't be late.'

With a nod and a smile, I grab my sisters' hands and push through the crowd until we find ourselves bunched together with squealing children hovering around the big Christmas tree, yelling and hoping for an orange. Kris Kringle lets go with a big belly laugh, then reaches into his burlap bag and tosses oranges into the crowd. I catch one and give it to Tovah, then Leah jumps up and, to my surprise, grabs the fruit. I reach up and grab another one.

I grin. Three sisters. Three oranges.

I edge closer to the front of the line, warning Leah and Tovah to stay near, hoping to snag a piece of fruit for Mutti when the wind blows open the jovial man's red robe.

I gasp.

He's wearing black jackboots. I can't believe it.

Kris Kringle is a Nazi.

I stare at the orange. I can't eat it. I toss it away. Then I get *really* angry at the Nazis for ending my childhood.

I will never believe in Father Christmas again.

I look around, praying Leah and Tovah didn't see what I did, but they've disappeared like two fairy imps chasing fireflies. *Ooh...* They never listen. I told them to stay close to me... They didn't.

Where did they go? I've got to find them, but a sharp pain in my groin makes me double over, like I've been kicked in the stomach. It won't go away, a fullness that makes me feel as bloated as a balloon stretched taut and about to burst.

Must be an upset stomach, but I can't stop.

I head down one street then the next, looking for them. Where did they go? I'm two blocks from where I left them near Father Christmas when I'm cut off by a bunch of boys racing past me. They give the Hitler salute to their leader... *Oh, no...* it's Helga's brother. He's holding a large swastika flag over his shoulder, his face cut in stone as he blows his whistle and the boys get into formation. One boy lights a torch, then another, and the whole street glimmers with dancing flames lighting up their faces. They begin singing and goose stepping to a strong, battle rhythm coming from two boys beating on drums.

The crowds gathering on the sidewalks cheer on the exhibition of boys wearing swastika armbands, their caps strapped under their chins, trying to look like men while most of them are still in short pants. What chills me is, these boys may look like toy soldiers on parade, but someday they'll be in Hitler's army... an army Mutti says, that kills Jews.

That's why Helga's brother was hanging around the Christmas market... They planned to make trouble on what should be a holy night for German Christian families. I see now not only Jews have to put up with Herr Hitler's arrogance.

The pounding boots get on my nerves, but I can't stop moving through the crowd, my head bouncing up and down like a rubber ball, searching every face for Leah... Tovah. I've *got* to find them. Mutti will never forgive me... *I'll* never forgive me if something happens to them. What if someone grabbed them... An eerie alarm goes off in my head... the unthinkable flashes before me... blood smeared on their clothes, their cheeks... my fault, *my fault*. My emotions run away with me.

I want to cry; I've *got* to cry.

I don't know why, but all these feelings collide in my head. I need to get away from this mass of glassy-eyed people hypnotized by the spectacle of boys marching. Papa says the Nazis love nighttime spectacles because it gives them power, a strength that's frightening. I stand in the street, the unholy glow from the torches lighting up the sky.

It alarms me.

I gulp in the air, trying to catch my breath when two more boys in Hitler Youth uniforms rush by me, knocking me down. The taller boy asks me if I'm hurt. I shake my head back and forth. I'm so confused. He's a Nazi, but he seems kind. I don't understand how that can be... then it hits me.

He doesn't know I'm Jewish.

It's then I realize I live in one world and he lives in the other.

There's no crossing the line. If you do, you pay the devil's price.

I glance around at the scared faces of the children, their mothers, drawing back to give way to this bunch of rowdy Hitler Youth. Mutti would never have come here if she knew. She's more cautious than ever, not entering a Jewish shop, whether they sell pastry or thread, if she sees an armed Nazi soldier standing outside to discourage anyone from going inside.

And now look at what I've done. She entrusted my sisters' welfare to me and I've made a mess of it.

I won't give up. They were here a moment ago, before I got wound up in my stupid emotions that made cry for no reason. I button my weak moment into my pocket and forge on. My sisters and I are like three taffeta ribbons... Tie us together into a perfect bow and we're strong, the bond unbreakable.

So it is now as I look around for Leah and Tovah. I haunt the pavements, shops closed for the parade, a few parked motorcars... no tram running here... faces in the crowd blurring... I blink, rub my eyes, look again but I don't see them.

I run up one block... then down the next.

I've *got* to find my sisters.

Ten... fifteen minutes later, I see them sitting on a stoop on a quiet street, peeling their oranges, the juicy pulp smeared over their smiling faces. They don't see me and I can't find my voice to call out... My emotions are caught in my throat. Hot tears burn my eyes. I'm so happy to see them safe. I'll never let them out of my sight again.

Ever.

My heart is pounding as I race across the street, my tired body and my confused mind getting the better of me. I trip and stumble, barely keeping my balance. I gasp loudly when I feel something squish out of me, something warm trickling down my thighs, wetting my underwear, my slip... my high socks.

I look down and see blood running down my legs.

Oh my God, it's happened.

What Mutti said would happen... *Soon*, she whispered, planting a kiss on my forehead.

'*Don't be afraid when it comes, Rachel,*' I hear her sweet voice saying in my head. '*It's good. It means you're now a woman.*'

14

BETHLEHEM, PENNSYLVANIA, DECEMBER, 1935

Kay

My baby is dead.

A little girl.

It's four o'clock on Christmas afternoon and I'm in such a state of depression, I wouldn't be surprised if the heavens opened up and swallowed me whole, gathering me up in the massive snowstorm raging all day. Wind howling, tree branches banging on my second-story window like a bony version of the angel Gabriel begging me to stop my ranting, cursing. I won't. *I can't*. I'm so deeply hurting in my heart it's skipping beats, like it can't catch up to the torment tearing me apart.

My baby is dead. My daughter.

I don't take comfort from knowing I was right about having a girl. If anything, it's more debilitating to my exhausted mind. I cry, fret. Slam my fist down on the nightstand next to my bed. Then curl up like a fetus under the heavy quilt and pull it over my head.

The one thing I *won't* do is answer the damn telephone.

Ringing... again. And again. It has to be Mother. No one else knows I'm here, though she prefers to send telegrams to make sure I understand her instructions. Is she calling to listen to me cry? Or to tell me to move on? The hospital administrator must have called her with the horrible news since she's listed as my emergency contact. Why can't she leave me alone? She got what she wanted, didn't she?

No, that's too cruel even for her.

Isn't it?

After twenty minutes and thirty-seven rings (yes, I'm counting, hoping my heartbeat will right itself), I can't take it any more. I grab the plain black phone marred with nail scratches, as if I'm not the only desperate woman who's suffered a melting down of her soul in this room.

'Yes, Mother...' I begin.

'Why didn't you pick up the phone, Kay?' she asks, her words hot and precise. 'It's not like you're busy.'

'I *am* busy... grieving.'

Something you wouldn't know about because Pops was barely in his grave when you took off for Palm Beach for the summer.

'Well, I suppose it's necessary, but be done with it quickly. You need to forget it ever happened.'

'Forget my own child, Mother?' I sputter. '*Never.*'

'You must. For your sake and mine.' She takes a moment. 'One good thing, this whole sordid affair has come to its proper end.' I swear I hear her breathe out a huge sigh of relief, which is overly dramatic even for her. And cuts deep for me. 'I've made plans for you to come home...'

I drop the phone away from my ear. *Plans? When will she stop?*

I won't listen to another word. I can't believe she's so bitter about me wanting a family of my own that she's relieved my child didn't breathe in life for more than twenty minutes.

It hurts deep down in the core of what motherhood is supposed to be. Warm, sensitive feelings and overwhelming love for your child. I'm suffering the excruciating pain of losing my baby, but to Mother, my motherhood experience is a major inconvenience in her life.

Unless something else is at play here.

She wouldn't dare, would she?

I jump up from the bed and pace up and down, holding the phone away from my ear as she jabbers on. Could this be another one of her tricks? To make me believe my baby died so she can give it away for adoption? Wait... I haven't signed the papers, but that won't stop her. She could forge them. I wouldn't put it past her.

'I'll let you know, Kay,' I hear her saying, 'when I'll be there to collect you.'

No, you won't.

'I'll call you back, Mother. And one more thing. I'll *never* forget my baby. Goodbye.'

I slam the phone down.

Grabbing my robe, I sneak down to the nursery barefoot where the newborns lie in their cribs. The cold tiles chill the soles of my feet like I'm walking on ice, but my cheeks are hot, my lips dry. I'll admit to visiting the nursery more than once since I've been here, pining for the day I could gaze upon my own child lying in her tiny crib, wrapped up in everything pink and lavender and wonderful.

The door creaks when I slip through, but no one's about. The nursery holds a dozen infants, but today I count only three babies. I look for my child. Not by name, but by birthdate. I see Baby X1, Baby X2, and Baby X3.

Three beautiful babies cuddled up like furry bunnies in pink or blue bundling (two pink, one blue). I inch closer, straining to read the tags on their cribs with my red bloodshot eyes, puffy from crying.

Baby X1 is a girl born December 22, 1935. Three days ago. *No, not her.*

Baby X2 is a boy born a day later.

Baby X3 is...

I hold my breath, savoring the moment that I'm right and this is my child when—

'I thought I might find you here, Miss Smythe.'

I don't have to turn around to know the hand upon my shoulder belongs to Sister Bridget, the dear soul who held my hand all night until I fell into a fretful sleep.

'I – I thought there might be some mistake and my baby...'

She shakes her head. 'I'm sorry, she's not here.'

'Then where is she?' I cry out, demanding she tell me what they've done with her. It's too cruel, not knowing. I keep asking her, my sanity dissolving on the edge of my brain and leading me to a dark place where there's no turning back.

'These things are taken care of with discretion and with as little pain as possible for the mother.' A weak excuse, as if she's practiced it.

'I don't want the doctor giving me a pep talk. I want to see my baby.'

'She's gone to Heaven, miss.' She takes me by the elbow. 'I'll take you back to your room. You need rest.'

My knees buckle with defeat. Mother may lie to me, but Sister Bridget wouldn't. Why that's so important to me becomes clear. I can't deny it any longer.

My baby is gone.

'God, no...' I sputter, my hand going to my heart as I stagger back and forth, my bare feet tapping on the tiles then the carpeting as we head for the residential wing. A myriad of rambling thoughts

– none of them good – race through my mind, upsetting me more. Have they taken her away? Without letting me say goodbye?

How could they?

Then I get a strange tingle up my spine when I hear the rumble of a motorcar outside...

I race to the long window, no curtain, and peer out. 'Oh...' escapes my lips in a soft sigh. I see a big, black vehicle with a long running board pull up to the back entrance.

A hearse.

They've come for my child.

Before she can stop me, I break away from Sister Bridget and jam though the back entrance outside into the crunchy snow, my feet bare, hair wet and damp to my cheeks, but I feel nothing. I'm numb. I spin around and I see a nurse in her pristine uniform come out of the side entrance across the courtyard. She's close enough for me to see she's holding a wrapped bundle in a white blanket, her head low.

Is it—?

I heave out a heavy breath and a raw, guttural cry erupts from my throat when she gives the bundle to a man in a dark coat and hat pulled down low over his eyes. He nods, places the baby into the back of the vehicle while the nurse bows her head and prays.

They're taking my baby girl away.

I let go with a loud scream... a wail so filled with pain the earth shakes beneath my bare feet. Ice shoots through my veins and rips me apart inside. Why didn't they let me see her, touch her, *anything*? I want to embrace my child, kiss her cheeks and hold her tiny hands in mine. At least once.

I've got to.

I gather up my long nightgown around my waist, then run over the white mantle of snow as though my feet have angel's wings, needing to get to my child... feeling nothing, my legs numb, my mind set on that one purpose. To hold my baby. Know more about her. See the curly wisps of hair on her head... the color of her eyes... Count her tiny fingers and toes.

It doesn't happen. I've been through so much with the long labor and difficult birth, my body fails me. I fall to my knees, sobbing. I'm so close, but so far. The nurse sees me and races back inside to get help. I struggle to get up, then feel something ooze between my legs. I look down. My nightgown is wet and smeared with blood.

I've torn my stitches and started bleeding.

'Miss Smythe!' Sister Bridget cries out, catching up to me and pulling me to my feet.

'They're taking my baby away, Sister... They can't; I want to hold her,' I cry out. I pray to God to let me see my child, but He turns a blind eye to my plight and the long, black automobile races off down the winding driveway and disappears into the deep, green forest.

'She's at peace now,' the sister says, wrapping a blanket around me. 'Come.'

'No, I want to stay here, *please*...' I beg her. 'I'm closer to heaven out here... and to her.'

'You'll catch your death of cold.'

'You don't understand—'

'But I do,' she says, leading me inside the facility and back to my room. The sudden switch from the chill outdoors to the heated room makes me sneeze, then I let go with a long shiver.

Sister Bridget fetches a handkerchief from the bureau drawer and hands it to me.

'Someday,' she says, 'you'll accept that God in His wisdom took your little girl to Him on this holiest of nights to keep her safe.'

'I will *never* accept that.' I blow my nose hard to emphasize my sentiment.

'*Please*, let me help you find your way.' She grabs a fresh night-gown for me from the closet. 'We can pray together—'

'No, I don't want to pray and have you smile at me with sadness in your eyes or listen to the gibberish you spout to make me feel better. They're lies, *all lies*... telling me how blessed I am, that I may feel broken now, but I have a lot to live for. *Nothing* you say will make me ever feel good again.'

'You have to try, miss—'

'I don't want to try. Now, *please*, leave me. I wish to be alone.'

'Of course. If you change your mind—'

'*No!*' I yell. My voice is hard like stone. Out of the corner of my eye I see her bless herself, then tell me she'll send the nurse to check me over. With a wistful sigh and a promise to keep me in her prayers, she gathers the black rayon skirts of her habit and scurries through the door, closing it gently behind her.

I slump down into the wingback chair and bury my head in my hands, sobbing. I didn't mean to be so awful to the sister, but I'm overcome with a downward spiral of depression, sadness, then anger that's bad, *really* bad, and every sarcastic, nasty remark Mother ever made to me comes rolling back into my brain like a mad, crazy tempest forcing me off the path to recovery.

I come unraveled on this cold Christmas Day.

I feel faint. A great whirlpool overcomes me with a dizziness I can't stop. Where did everything go wrong? I worked hard to please Mother, but in the end I was used by a man who could be bought and sold to the highest Main Line bidder: my mother.

Then I lost my baby, something no one could have foreseen. The doctor explained to me that if nature hadn't intervened with my pregnancy and forced me into early labor – in Sister Bridget's mind, he meant God – I would have died. That I was as big as a house because the child growing inside me had a hole in her spine and the nutrients that should have fed the fetus instead entered my body, blowing me up until eventually it would reach my heart and—

I think about this when the nurse bursts into my room, worry on her face, and checks me over, cleaning the area. Then I see relief in her eyes and she assures me I didn't do any damage when I ran out into the snow. I will heal fine.

She closes the door behind her and I'm alone, truly alone for the first time since I found out I was pregnant. I've always had my baby to talk to, laugh with, and make plans with. I know she was listening to me, my silly jokes and my dreams.

But now she's gone.

I roll over on my stomach, sobbing. Not for myself. But for my baby who never had a chance.

* * *

I have to beg the hospital administrator to give me the name of the place where they've taken her. What about a christening for the child? I ask. She deserves a rightful place in heaven. It wasn't a still-birth. She lived for twenty-seven minutes.

Why didn't anyone ask me what my wishes were?

I tell them to christen her 'Marie Jane' before they bury her. A French name I've always loved and my middle name.

I have the bills sent to Mother who, in an act of humanity I will be forever grateful for, doesn't protest. I want to be there when they lay my baby to rest, but Mother makes certain I have no way of leaving the sanitarium.

A stone marker will be placed where my baby lies in peace.

Marie Jane
December 25, 1935
A child never forgotten.

I try to put the pieces back together, but I can't. I wear myself out crying, meandering around the garden all hours of the day and night. I break down every time they want to send me home. I don't eat, barely sleep, lose weight. I spend two weeks in such a state, my wounded soul hopelessly wandering... needing a path, guidance.

And the nightmares... they don't stop.

I dream I'm standing on a steep cliff that tumbles down to black rocks with an angry ocean crashing against the granite. My arms are empty. My bare toes dig into the moist grass, slippery with my tears. I'm convinced I left my baby on the rocks, but the morning fog drifts in front of my eyes and I can't see clearly.

I lean forward to look down, my feet slide... I pull back, just barely. If I lean too far, I'll plunge down to the rocks below.

I keep calling out, '*Mommy's coming!*' but when I do, my voice is drowned out by the sound of the pounding surf below.

I start sobbing, deep heavy sobs, my body shaking uncontrollably and in a final, grand gesture I cry out for help but no one hears me... then my foot slips and I fall... and I'm swallowed up in the grand darkness—

I wake up.

Oh, God, I need to talk to someone, but the hospital staff always change the subject when I try to engage them in conversation. No one wants to help me. They ramble on about how busy they are and that I should talk to my family. That's like asking the devil to send me a Christmas present.

I ask for Sister Bridget. I haven't seen her since they took my baby away. I was so distraught then it didn't sink in when she told me she'd keep me in her prayers, her way of saying goodbye. She only works with expectant mothers, they tell me. Convent rules. In other words, I don't count any more.

I sink lower into depression, praying, *begging* for help, but no one is there. I don't understand a medical system that works so hard to heal my body, but my mind is a sorry mess.

Then, finally God hears me and sends Sister Bridget back to me, smiling, kind.

She's assigned to a new patient, but she's come to see me on her time off with a hot breakfast and an agenda I don't see coming.

15

BETHLEHEM, PENNSYLVANIA, JANUARY 1936

Kay

'Your mother will be here tomorrow to take you home, Miss Smythe,' Sister Bridget announces on this drab, dreary day when even the smell of freshly baked bread on the tray she brings doesn't rouse me from my bed. 'I heard Mother Superior telling the nurse to pack your things.'

'So the mean stepmother is rallying to reclaim her pumpkin.' I shrug my shoulders, resigned to her butting into my life and barely giving me a chance to heal.

'Miss?'

'She was just *pretending* to be the fairy godmother to get Cinderella back into the kitchen.'

'Not so, miss. You're too strong for her to bully you.'

'Me? I can't even get out of bed.' I sit up, sip the coffee she brought. The tone in my voice tells me *and* her I'm out of plays. It's been nothing but sleeping, crying, and utter depression.

Physically, I'm fine, though the doctor said I shouldn't resume sexual activities for several weeks and avoided looking me in the eye. Is he kidding? I'll never let a man get close to me again.

Sister Bridget smiles, folds her hands into her wide black sleeves. 'I'm so sorry for your loss, I truly am.'

'I wanted that baby and now that she's gone, I have nothing to live for.'

In the past I never would have said that, but I see no future any more.

'Of course, you do... you're Kay Alexander, the Radwell candy heiress.'

I smirk. I never doubted she knows who I am.

'So I should spend the rest of my life commuting between Newport and Palm Beach, a spinster in black, eating bonbons?' I slam the coffee cup down. Finally, I've said what's on my mind. It's been eating at me, as I try to figure out where I go from here. A proper Philadelphia marriage is out of the question. The doctor told me I can't have any more children, ending the conversation when I probed him for more information about why my child died. It's a closed book in his eyes... and I imagine the adoption agency doesn't want me searching my medical records and bringing bad publicity down on them.

So now I'm supposed to go home and be a good girl and do what? Slowly lose my mind? Knit tiny yellow slippers with satin bows for babies I'll never have? I overheard my nurse tell the orderly that's what happened to her *last* patient who lost a child at birth.

I don't want to end up like that. I have a sudden longing to walk out of here now and hitch a ride, go somewhere, *anywhere* so I can forget, but I don't have the strength. It's easier to lie here and wallow in my misery.

'You should be ashamed of yourself, Miss Alexander, saying you have nothing to live for,' the sister scolds, 'when there's girls not so fortunate who lose everything. *They* don't go crying to the Lord to take their soul, not with Him having better souls to welcome to Heaven.'

'How would you know?' I shoot back, defensive.

'I – I didn't have it so nice when my baby came.'

'What? You're a nun.'

'Why do you think I'm here? My family didn't want me when I gave birth to a boy on the cold, bare floor of a boarding house, my man dead in an accident before he could marry me.'

'Then that story you told me—'

'Hogwash. I've never told anyone the truth before... but I see no point in keeping my secret if it helps you. You don't know what it's like to grovel for pennies, then see your baby taken from you after he catches some dreadful disease when he's seven months old and dies because you can't afford proper care. But I didn't give up. I joined the convent and came to work here so I can be around life. Not death.'

'Why tell me?'

Sister Bridget takes my hand. 'Because you have so much love in you to give. Always a kind word for me, talking to your baby like she was here already, putting up with...'

'Go on, say it: putting up with Mother.'

She nods. 'You have *everything*, then to hear you talking about ending it all, well, I never figured a rich girl like you for a coward. Guess I was wrong.'

Her words sting.

'But I'll never be a mother,' I protest. 'Never have another child. What else is there for me but a useless life going to charity teas and listening to my mother complain?'

'Someday what happened to you will become a blessing. You can't see it now, nor can I. Not that the pain will ever subside in your heart; it lessens, but it doesn't go away. If God wills it, then He has a purpose. He took your baby for a reason. That you'll have empathy for someone else's child and help them. Someday it will be clear to you.' She grabs me by the shoulders, her laughing Irish eyes shining like fairy dust. 'Now, are you going to mess up His plans? Or go out there and do His work, live your life?'

'I can't go back to that life. To Mother.'

'You don't have to. You could get a job.'

'Me? A job? What would I do?'

'God will show you, but first you must go... tonight.'

'Tonight? Do you think I can do it?'

I get a chill that makes me shiver... not the kind when you're coming down with a cold, but the kind you get when you're strapped into a rollercoaster and the car is making that steady climb up to the top... the anticipation gives you goosebumps... the idea you're about to take off and experience the thrill of flying.

Being free scares me. *Can I really do it?*

'I know you can. This is your only chance. Your mother will be here tomorrow.'

She's right.

I've always known I have to move on, but this is so sudden... and daring. Bold. Indecent, almost. Like skinny dipping. You know you shouldn't, but the temptation is too great to resist.

So I don't.

Before I can think twice about facing the world without the protective bubble I've always known, Sister Bridget helps me pack my things, checks the bus schedule, and gives me twenty-three dollars from the tiny leather pouch attached to her large brown rosary beads. She explains each patient has a 'petty-cash fund' to draw from to pay for extras and this is what's left over from mine. I don't know if I believe her, but with the money I have in my purse, it's enough to give me a start. Then she gives me instructions on how to get to the bus station... It's about a thirty-minute walk from the medical facility.

Before I leave, I hand her the white box tied with the red ribbon from *Wanamaker's*. Inside, I tell her, is a red velvet jumper and white blouse in size 1. For my little girl.

'Here, take this baby outfit, and make another mother happy.'

'God bless you, miss.' She hugs me so tight I can't breathe. 'Where will you go?'

'Not back to Mother and her society teas and demands, and God knows, not to her pushing me into marriage with a rich college boy.'

'You have a plan?'

'No, but I'll think of one.'

'I have faith in you, Kay.'

'My mother doesn't. No matter how old I get, I'll always be her work in progress. Even when I disappoint her, she tries to fix it, but in the end, all she wants to do is control me.'

'You have to stay strong.'

'And pray she doesn't find me. It's not easy to hide when you're a debutante with her face plastered all over the newspapers.'

'You need a disguise.' She whips off her spectacles. 'Take these.'

'Your glasses?'

'They're not real. The hospital administrator makes me wear them so I look older and more sympathetic and the patients will trust me. I'll get another pair.'

'Thank you, Sister.' I adjust the phony specs on my face. 'Clear glass. *Perfect.*'

An hour later, fake glasses perched on my nose and suitcases in hand, I sneak out of the employee entrance to the Mary T. Vickers sanitarium.

Alone.

But the spirit of my child will always walk beside me.

16

PHILADELPHIA, JANUARY 1936

Kay

The 8:20 p.m. special to Downtown Philadelphia is late.

I pace up and down the busy bus station, pulling my hat down over my face, pushing my glasses up on my nose, praying no one recognizes me. Who would expect to find a Philadelphia debutante hiding out in a bus station? Not the sleepy, boozy, motley group of passengers from a stratum of life I've seen only in pictures. Men sleeping off a night of drinking and hiding a flask in their pockets, spinsters knitting, mothers with drooling babies, children fighting with each other.

My heart pings at the sight of a baby in her mother's arms, even more so when her little sister about three asks me if I have any candy. I smile on the outside, but inside I'm crying. I'll never hear those words from my own child.

'Don't pay her no mind, miss,' the mother says with apology. 'She's always wanting sweets.'

'Well, then, let's see what we can find.' I take the little girl's hand and buy her a *Radwell's French Chocolate* bar at the newsstand. *La Belle Josephine*, named after the French empress and a favorite of mine with double milk chocolate wrapped around a light nougat. Meanwhile, I keep looking over my shoulder. I imagine they've discovered I'm gone at the sanitarium. I pull back when I see an official-looking duo arrive and scan the waiting passengers. I bend down and unwrap the chocolate bar for the child, keeping my head low so they can't see my face. It works. They shake their heads and leave.

I relax.

'Here's a chocolate bar with a pretty name for a pretty little girl,' I tell her.

'Oh, that chocolate's too fancy for the likes of us, miss.' The mother shakes her head.

'Nonsense, my treat.'

She nods *thank you* and the little girl bites into the chocolate with glee. Her eyes pop open wide. She claps her hands and dances around, eating the chocolate and getting it all over her happy face, like the sun beamed its light into her eyes.

The mother takes my arm. 'Thank you, miss, she ain't laughed like that in a long time.'

'Me, either.'

I watch the child licking her fingers, and get misty-eyed. It's a different emotion making me sniffle and grab a handkerchief. A sliver of contentment at seeing how a chocolate bar can make a little girl so happy. When her mother admits they didn't have money to buy dinner, I slip two dollars into her baby's blanket when she's not looking. Nothing will take away the pain in my heart over losing my baby, but it's selfish of me not to help others.

It gets me to thinking. That chocolate bar makes the child smile, but it won't fill her belly.

What if *Radwell's* could stuff more nutrients into a candy bar?
I wonder...

When the bus arrives, I help the mother get on board with her children, but there's no empty seat next to them. I take a seat in the back next to a woman chatting about going to see her nieces and nephews in Philly, that she doesn't have children, so she visits her sister's bunch. I smile and change seats. I'd rather sit next to a tipsy, sleeping salesman than dwell on the emptiness in my heart. It hurts too much. I spend the time on the bus thinking, putting together a telegram to send to Mother so she won't worry though she'll have her detectives out looking for me. I'll tell her I'm getting a job. Nothing else.

I'll find something. I speak French fluently, I'm well-read in the classics, and I can ride English sidesaddle. Not exactly the qualifications a girl needs to get a job in this depression, but I've survived in spite of what life has thrown at me. I *will* get something. It can't be that hard.

First, I need somewhere to hang my hat far away from Mother's social circle on Rittenhouse Square. I ask around the bus station when we arrive, but it's the mother with the little girl who sends me to a working-class neighborhood in northeast Philly crammed with boarding houses. The frost of early morning fogs up my glasses and after walking for blocks, I find a place that suits me. Clean-looking, empty glass milk bottles on the stoop, and a tall candle in the window, its bright flame welcoming me like a beacon. Any place like that has to be decent.

The landlady, however, is leery of renting to a single woman with no references.

'Whatever you're running from,' she insists, 'I don't want to know.'

I keep my head down, explaining I'm from out of town and pray my money speaks loud enough to encourage her to give me a chance. She quotes a monthly rate higher than on the sign posted in the foyer. *Two months in advance*, she insists. I give her the money I got from Sister Bridget. She smiles and shows me to a room on the third floor, then lingers in the doorway. The woman isn't done with me yet, watching me unpack and lay dresses down on the bed. She peers closer and crosses her brows when she sees the expensive labels on my clothes, then gives me a strange look.

'Handoffs from my last position.' I give her a weak smile.

Come up with a story, I hear Sister Bridget advising me.

'Oh?' she sneers, hands on her hips.

'I was a ladies' maid in a mansion in Chestnut Hill,' I say, hoping she has no idea what I'm talking about. 'The family moved away... to Paris.' I grin. I'm not sure if she believes me, but when I empty my suitcases and show her I have no liquor or drugs she seems satisfied.

Now to get a job.

I pick out my favorite navy-blue dress with a white collar and cuffs, low-heeled brown lace-up shoes, stockings, no jewelry. My hair is longer than it was during my deb days so it's easy to arrange it in a tight bun with curly wisps on the side. I adjust my spectacles. No makeup. Not even lipstick.

Over the next two weeks, I make the rounds of offices, but without typing skills they won't let me past the front receptionist. I had intended to keep a low profile out of the public eye, but I come to the conclusion the only job open to me is retail.

I can do sales... I've handled enough charity events to know my way around, but I'm leaving myself open to someone recognizing me. I set up a general delivery box to get mail from Mother, hoping she'll keep her hounds off me once she knows I'm safe but out of her control. She sends me terse messages *telling*, not asking, me to come home, which only strengthen my resolve to make it on my own. I keep my location secret by paying a boy ten cents to pick up the mail for me, then hand it to another boy who gets half and races away on his bicycle before the detectives watching the box know what's happening.

Clever, huh? I feel like a spy.

Today's work quest takes me downtown to Market Street. I try *Lit Brothers* and *Strawbridge and Clothier* department stores, but they're not hiring without experience. I skip *John Wanamaker's* since Mother frequents the Crystal Tea Room and is always coercing the manager to give *Radwell's French Chocolates* the prime location in the store instead of what she calls 'that foreign brand', *Camée*.

I'm getting discouraged and my feet are killing me when I wander into *Gimbel's*. The whiff of our minty coconut bonbons, a *Radwell's* top seller for over forty years, draws me to the candy department on the market floor. I ask the salesgirl behind the counter if they're hiring, knowing to say *I have experience selling* even if I don't, but she shakes her head. Still, the familiar candy is a nice pick me up, but I can only afford one *Parisian Snowball*. To think I had as many as I wanted before.

Ah...

I savor the cool mint covered with coconut-flavored fondant when I hear—

'I thought you sold *Camée* French chocolates here,' says the lady behind me, frustrating the clerk who has no idea what she's asking for.

'*Wanamaker's* sells them,' I offer, 'but they're not French, they're made by a Dutch company.' A fact not well-known to the public, but if there's one thing I do have experience in, it's everything chocolate.

The floor manager in his stiff black suit and bowtie overhears us and glares at me. He slides over on the smooth floor to do damage control but the woman cuts him off with—

'Oh, how silly of me,' she coos, waving her long raccoon fur piece in his face. He does his best not to sneeze. 'This is *Gimbel's*.'

'*Camée* chocolates *are* delicious, miss...' I don't say *ma'am*, though the woman is over fifty, knowing Mother's crowd responds more favorably to a youthful salutation. 'But *Radwell's French chocolates do* come from Paris and you can buy them right here at *Gimbel's*.' They're made here in Philadelphia, but if the Dutch company can tell a fib, so can I. I wave a box of our chocolates in her face. 'And you look like a woman who should be strolling down the Rue Saint-Honoré in a red Chanel suit with lace cuffs and enjoying *real* French chocolates.'

She smiles wide and I sell her *three* boxes of *Radwell's French Chocolates* and impress the floor manager with my pitch. He insists I should be working here and I agree.

I get the job.

I fill out the paperwork as Kay McGinty and give the boarding house as my address. The woman in the employee hiring department is satisfied for now, but she warns me President Roosevelt signed a new law and soon I'll need a funny-looking card with my own unique number on it to prove who I am. Not yet. The luck of the McGinty Irish is with me. All I have to do is perform well at this job, pay my rent at the boarding house, keep my nose clean, and when I turn twenty in a few months, I can claim my inheritance.

Then I *do* have a plan. I'm going to Paris.

Till then, I discover I enjoy sharing my knowledge about chocolate with customers... the smooth buttercreams and nougats, nuts and chews, caramels salty and plain, and decadent truffles. *Crèmes* and *dragées*. Soft centers... and candies with a hard shell and soft center.

I also enjoy telling my favorite story to rambunctious children hanging around the candy counter... how chocolate is made bubbling in vats so big you can climb up to the top on the attached ladder and look down at a river of swirling milk chocolate and dream... and if you're swept away by the heavenly chocolate aroma, you can dive in and float on your back on a chocolate sea while you dip your fingers into the melted, sugary goo and lick them clean. A wild exaggeration, but it works. I get the same, rapturous looks on their faces as the look on that little girl's face when she bit into our *La Belle Josephine* milk chocolate bar.

Seeing those kids so excited helps ease the hurt in me. A little.

And fuels my passion to help our company expand.

I've learned a lot since I came to work here. How hard the clerks work pleasing the customers as well as keeping the candy counter well stocked. How the marketing staff is always looking for new products to increase sales. I feel a new pride in *Radwell's French Chocolates*. I want to keep my family's legacy going strong... make Mother proud of me (I haven't given up)... and honor Pops' memory. That wonderful man who introduced me to the world of chocolate when I was a little girl.

It won't be easy.

Our competitors are buying up chocolate factories in Switzerland and coming up with new candy ideas like white chocolate. We're not as big, but we can keep up with them in our own unique way. I intend to buy up or invest in chocolate shops in France, learn their secrets to make *Radwell's French Chocolates* even *more* exclusive for Mother's crowd, but also start a new brand the average consumer can afford.

I don't know exactly what I'm after, but an idea keeps buzzing in my head. Maybe that's what Sister Bridget meant when she said God would show me what I'm meant to do. And I'm going to Paris to do it *without* being under Mother's thumb.

The weeks turn into months... I go to work every day, sell lots of chocolates, and my heart hurts a little less as I ease into my new position and earn a small salary. And the best part is, Mother has no idea where I am.

Who would ever think the Radwell chocolate heiress is working in the candy department at *Gimbel's*?

17

BERLIN, AUGUST 1936

Rachel

For two weeks in August, everyone is primed with excitement, pride for some... distaste for others... but no one can ignore what's happening in Berlin. The roar of the crowd waving red swastika flags at the Olympic opening ceremony, thousands of spectators standing and giving the Nazi salute, the atmosphere wild and frenetic as though they're drunk on beer and stuffing themselves with hot sausages during *Karneval*, carnival.

Meanwhile, we go about our lives facing more restrictions than before. We've lost our citizenship and are regarded as 'subjects of the state' – but we hang on to every radio broadcast, newsreel, and bit of neighborhood gossip as the Nazis attempt to prove to the world *they* are the superior athletes.

Even Helga Dornstadt can't resist getting in on the action.

She struts her Aryan pride on a hot afternoon sticky with heat at the park where I'm sitting on a bench, doodling and writing down words to a song dancing in my head as I'm wont to do. I pretend not to see her coming, hoping she'll pass me by and go on her way. I imagine she's attending the games. If I remember rightly, her father's a government official and has access to tickets, something a Jewish girl like me could never hope for. I wish I could see the track and field games. I always enjoyed them when I went to a mixed school, but I never competed. Even if I wanted to, we're no longer allowed to compete in sports.

'You don't belong here in the park, you dumb Jew girl,' she spouts, hands on her hips. Her two friends, Sigrid and Anna, back her up. 'Why don't you go back to your pigsty?'

I cringe, but I don't look up from my notebook. 'I can sit here if I wish.'

She smirks. 'For now. My father says soon you'll only be allowed to sit on park benches with a 'J' painted on them that say *For Jews only*.'

Would they go that far?

'Leave me alone, Helga... and tell your friends, too.'

'We're on our way to the Olympic Stadium to see the track and field events.'

'Oh?' I feign disinterest.

'An Aryan will win, of course.'

'They wouldn't if they'd allowed the Jewish girl to compete.' What hurts most is that my idol, a German female athlete, can't compete in the high jump competition because she's a Jew. She qualified for the Olympic team, but then she was removed at the last minute, proving what Mutti says, that the Party has its ways of making sure the Fuehrer's wishes are served at any cost.

And we must be careful *not* to get caught in their sticky web.

The bottom line is... no Jews are allowed in the Olympics.

Helga continues her rant. 'No Jew can beat an Aryan.'

'Can't we?' I stare her straight in the eye.

Her two friends egg her on.

'*Show her, Helga, how wrong she is.*'

'*Yeah, show her.*'

'Since you're so smart,' Helga says, 'I challenge you to run against me from here to the fountain over the bridge, the one with the statue holding the big fish.'

That must be more than eight hundred meters.

She grins. 'First one to jump into the fountain wins.'

She's pleased to see the sallow look on my face. Not that I can't beat her, but what will Mutti say if I come home with wet shoes? I think for a moment. She'd say winning is more important, right? Helga thinks she can beat me because I never participated in sports when we were at school together. I had piano or voice lessons every afternoon. She's aware I haven't won any medals or ribbons at *any* sport.

What the German girl *doesn't* know is that Papa makes me run laps every day to increase my lung capacity when I sing. He makes Leah and Tovah run, too, lauding that musicians must be good athletes as well as good 'string pickers' as he's apt to say. My two sisters hold their own, but I'm the best runner.

But here? Now? I'm scared. I've never run against a BdM girl pumped up and ready to beat me at any cost, but I can't *not* accept her challenge.

Even so, I must be insane, stupid, or bold. The answer is, all of the above.

What have I gotten myself into?

The sneer on her face tells me I can't back out now. I stuff my pencil and my notebook into my jumper pocket, then puff up my chest. 'You're on.'

Helga gives the signal to Sigrid to make the call with the two of us lined up next to each other, right foot in front, standing with our noses pointing forward.

'*Ready, set, go!*'

And then somehow I'm running along the dirt path winding around the park, my long plaits whipping about my face, then racing through the grass where the path ends, across the open space toward the old eighteenth-century fountain with Helga right behind me. From shaded trees to clearings, across a bridge flanked by stone lions creaking under our weight, we run. Passers-by don't know why we're running and make way for us, but Helga is wearing her BdM uniform, giving her the advantage. More than one pedestrian blocks my path, slowing me down and making me run around them... then giving Helga the Nazi salute.

And putting me behind.

I jump over a big rock, trying to gain on her, then slip on the grass. I stumble, but I don't go down. My chest is hurting, lungs bursting. I feel my cheeks puff up like a chipmunk's, but Helga is still out ahead of me, looking over her shoulder and laughing.

Don't stop. Keep going.

The wind is blowing in my face, warm and dusty, but I start shivering. Nerves. I can't let her beat me even if these people are *trying* to make me fall. It's not fair. That's when I dig down into myself and I hear Mutti cheering me on, reminding me that *nothing* is fair in our world, but that doesn't mean we give up. We fight harder... and *harder*.

I take deeper breaths, fueled by a resolve to show that BdM girl she can't beat me. I get my second wind, then I fly over the gravel path that reappears around the next turn. I see Helga up ahead, pumping her legs hard, yanking off her scarf and waving it in the air in triumph as she nearly reaches the fountain. She's less than twenty meters from there... the only way I can win is to sprint.

'I beat the Jew!' she shouts to the small crowd gathering around the stone structure.

Not yet, Helga.

I sprint along the path, gravel crunching beneath my feet, my legs aching, but a strong fervor builds inside me to find strength I didn't know I had.

A burst of energy and pure determination not to let this girl beat me sets me on fire, not just for me, but for my sisters and every Jewish girl denied her right to compete in sports. My arms and legs move so fast my long braids hit me in the face like buzzy bees, stinging my cheeks. I keep going... faster... *faster* until I whiz by Helga and reach the fountain first, jumping over the circular marble rim and into the water. It splashes over me, wetting my face, my hair, but it feels so good.

The elixir of victory.

'*I won, Helga.*'

The irate German girl reaches the fountain ten seconds after me, her eyes wide with disbelief. She's out of breath, holding her ribs, her chest.

'Did you?' she insists. 'Look around you, Jew girl.'

People in the park start booing me... mothers with children, businessmen, ladies doing shopping, and two boys in Hitler Youth uniforms.

I don't care about them. I beat her, but how long can I keep up this constant state of having to prove myself because I'm Jewish?

Seeing how these Berliners reacted when Helga yelled out I'm Jewish, I'm more afraid of the Nazis' influence than ever, but I'd never tell my parents that. They already have enough to worry about with Jewish businesses closing every day.

A guilty sigh escapes me. I don't like Helga, but Papa would want me to do the honorable thing. I jump out of the fountain and extend my hand to her. 'It was a good race, *ja*?'

Helga takes a step backward and lashes out at me. 'I'd never shake hands with you. You cheated!'

'Cheated?' I gasp, disbelieving.

'Yes, my father says *all* Jews cheat.'

Then she slaps me on the face. Hard. My ears ring and I struggle not to lose my balance. It's as if the world around me has become a raging torment of fear and hate where *nothing* is fair, taking over everything I do and sapping my good energy and leaving me with great anger. I want to call her names, push her into the fountain.

Don't do anything stupid. Slow down, breathe... like you do before you sing.

I breathe in... then out, pushing away the anger with those practiced breaths I've learned. I see Helga in a new light. She's not so tough with her snotty nose.

She's a pitiful sight.

I put my hand to my burning cheek. I'm a disheveled mess, too; my brown corduroy jumper is torn, my shoes and socks soaking wet... Then I smile. Who cares? I beat her and I won't let her ruin that for me.

'I won the race fair and square and you know it... your friends know it... *everybody* here knows it even if they won't admit it.' I look at her closer. Her eyes are filled with tears she tries to blink back, her lower lip quivering. 'Or are you afraid your Nazi ideals aren't all they're cracked up to be, that you're not supermen... *or* women. That you're human like the rest of us. And in the end, you *will* lose.'

And with that stirring speech erupting from my lips, I take off, leaving her stunned. Words echo in my head that I often hear Mutti say when she's sitting in the parlor, knitting; that the Nazis are evil and bad but the world won't let them win and they *will* lose... we just don't know when.

Today *I* won.

I discovered I can be strong and stand up for myself against this horrible regime that produces such hate, and turns ordinary girls like Helga and her friends into war propaganda machines. To think

I almost lost faith in myself, that I could be shackled by her and people like her. But they're not as tough as they think they are. We're tougher.

I run home, my heart pounding with pride, knowing she's not fast enough to catch me.

I beat a BdM girl, a Nazi.

And I've never felt so good.

18

ABOARD THE QUEEN MARY, AUGUST 1936

Kay

'I demand you get off this ship immediately, Kay. Do I make myself clear?'

'Perfectly, Mother.' I continue to unpack my trunk.

'Well, then?' Mother probes.

'Hadn't you better go ashore?' I pull out gowns, shoes. Casual deck wear. 'We're sailing soon.'

'You wouldn't be on this ship if I'd found you sooner. Imagine *my* daughter working at *Gimbel's* as a lowly salesgirl. I never—'

'No, you *never* would have believed it.'

In the end it wasn't Mother's fancy detectives who found me, but my own talents as a budding chocolatier that exposed me. I was giving my fanciful talk about how a chocolate factory works to schoolchildren when a reporter overheard me and thought it would make a great article for the Sunday paper. He photographed me, found out my name from the floor manager, and published the story under the title: *Once upon a chocolate story time…*

Mother saw the article about 'Kay McGinty and the chocolate tales' and when she realized it was me, she paid me a visit at my candy counter on my last day of work.

I found the scene amusing when I told her I'd already claimed my inheritance (which she knew, but the attorney wouldn't reveal to her where I was), and I was leaving for Paris on the *Queen Mary*. I booked Cabin Class on the new Cunard ship rather than sail on that old tugboat Mother prefers, the *Aquitania*. It ran aground last year at Southampton.

Anyway, I told Mother she was welcome to say *bon voyage* to me aboard ship and have a chat before we sailed. That chat still hasn't ended and she boarded two hours ago. She's been making her pitch for me to come home nonstop, flitting around like a Queen Bee arranging the baskets of flowers overflowing in my cabin.

In spite of her cajoling to get me to cancel my trip, I suspect the flowers came from her, another way to get a mention on the society page whether I sail or not, advertising someone 'very important' is on board. Ever the marketer, Mother also included a big basket of *Radwell's French Chocolates* for me to give out to the ship's stewards and stewardesses.

'You've had your fun, Kay,' she says, sniffing yellow roses, 'now it's time to get down to business.'

She means the marrying business, but I have another idea in mind.

'I'm not settling down, Mother. I'm my own person now. I know what it's like to earn a living and have my freedom. I'm not going back to the way things were.'

'And what's wrong with the way things were?' she bellows so loud a steward pokes his nose inside the open door to my cabin, smiles, then tips his cap and leaves.

'I can't take attending another charity luncheon or planning committee for this year's deb ball.'

'Running away won't help your chances of finding a suitable husband.'

'I'm soiled goods, Mother.'

'No one knows about your dirty laundry and you can be damned sure they never will, especially Tommy Whitworth.'

'Tommy? What does he have to do with this?' I toss down my jewelry box on the bed in my cabin and sapphire and emerald and diamond necklaces spill out onto the heavy pink quilted coverlet.

'The boy's in love with you, Kay.'

'Tommy's more in love with his cognac than me.'

'You'd be lucky if he'd still have you. And *never* admit you're not a virgin. Keep denying it and he'll believe you.'

I arch a brow. Not like Mother to ever mention *anything* about sex. Her hands shake as she arranges the yellow roses and her lower lip quivers. As if she's in pain. I soften toward her.

'Let's not quarrel, Mother, I'm grateful for what you've done for me, but I have to grow up sometime.'

'I suppose you're right. I can't mollycoddle you to the altar if you haven't got a beau.' A heavy sigh. 'Six months in Paris, Kay, and we'll tell everyone you're studying art.'

'I want to work in our candy business.' I stand my ground, my voice clear, concise. It feels good.

'I forbid it.'

I smile, then hang up my fur-lined coat. I'll need it for winters in Paris. I don't intend to come home anytime soon. 'Times are changing, Mother. Customers want new flavors, more exciting candy names, not the tired old ones from the last century. I'm going to Paris to make that happen. I want to be a chocolatier.'

'That's a man's job.'

'I had a long talk with Charley Hanover yesterday.' I called him up and told him my plans to study chocolate making in Paris. 'He's thinking about retiring and offered to show me the ropes when I'm ready.' I have a fond spot for the jolly man with the big, brown eyes swimming with chocolate flecks. He's been our chocolatier since before I was born.

'*Art* is what you'll study,' Mother interrupts, 'and not another word. You can take classes at the Sorbonne – that's acceptable for a girl of your position. When you return, I shall expect you to take up your place at my side in Philadelphia society... and find a husband. Of course, I shall speak to the captain about sitting you at his table during the voyage to take care of you.'

Not much I can do about that. It's common practice for the captain of a ship to take an 'innocent' debutante under his wing on a sea voyage.

She eyes my silver sequin dress. 'I'd prefer you don't wear that dress at the captain's table.'

'Yes, Mother.' Why argue? She'll never know. It's also common practice for a young innocent to pack dull clothes.

I'm anything but innocent. Mother has a habit of forgetting that.

To appease her, I'll sign up for art classes, but I intend to haunt the cabarets and dancehalls to set my heart free and allow my soul to heal, knowing I can never give birth to a child again, or hold a baby in my arms. I'm the sole heir to a candy fortune and I have obligations to make certain that fortune is protected and passed on to the next generation on my father's side. I don't intend to turn over the reins until I'm a very old lady. Till then, I shall live and dance.

And make chocolate.

The ship's horn toots. Time for Mother to leave.

'I'll send you a telegram when I arrive in Paris, Mother.' We say goodbye, touching cheeks.

'From the Ritz, of course.'

'Of course.' I'll send her a telegram from the famous hotel on the Place Vendôme, but I don't expect to stay there where the press will hound me for photographs. The American magazines are filled with candid photographs of ex-debutantes 'doing Paris' and no place is more popular than the Hôtel Ritz.

I see Mother off at the gangplank and return to my cabin, marveling at the beautiful ship with its unique wood paneling, fancy shops, and luxurious amenities. I have every intention of keeping to myself on the voyage.

The last person I expect to find there is Uncle Archibald.

Pacing up and down, pipe in his mouth, wearing a groomed dark suit with pressed creases in his trousers, a man of stature, but today he's not his usual, calm self. He keeps looking out into the corridor to see if anyone is listening.

I nearly drop my drawers when I find out why.

* * *

'I thought your mother would never leave.' He puffs on his pipe and blows out smoke.

'So did I,' I tease him.

'I haven't much time, Kay, so I'll make it quick. The US government is concerned about recent political decrees and events in Germany involving the Nazi Party.'

'I'm not surprised.' I tell him about Mr Kaplan and his pickles and what he told me about his brother in Frankfurt.

'Then I don't have to convince you that what I'm about to ask you to do is not frivolous in nature, but important work.'

My eyes widen. 'Oh?'

'I want you to spy on Hitler.'

I laugh out loud, then do a double take while I take in his request. My uncle must be joking, but he isn't. His brows knit together, his face taking on the fury of a man who knows things that cut deep into his sense of humanity, but he can't reveal what they are. I've never seen him so affected by anything before. His rigid movements and heavy lids that droop reveal to me a man who's spent many sleepless nights alone with his thoughts. Debating whether he should ask his niece to join in the fight. Then again, he's seen how I defied Mother's plan to make me a carbon copy of her. And that, I imagine, is why he's here.

His eyes lock with mine for a long moment and it's not fear that I'll say *no* I see, but fear I'll say *yes*.

That thought chills me.

He grabs a yellow rose, sniffs it, and then sticks it into his lapel.

'You *are* joking about me spying, Uncle Archie,' I toss off to break the tension between us. 'Mother put you up to this, didn't she? Thinking you'll scare me off traveling to Europe and I'll leave the ship before we sail.'

He shakes his head. 'No, Kay, I'm dead serious. The State Department is very interested in Americans like you traveling to Europe, asking them to keep their eyes open and make notes about what you see before you return home.'

He explains further that the US government is requesting me to do them a 'favor', They want me to travel to European capitals as a casual 'observer'. I gather I'm not alone, but one of many American celebrities and wealthy tourists keeping track of what they witness during their travels.

'You'll report to me anything you see that might be of interest in helping the State Department assess what's happening over there,' he continues. 'We believe storm clouds are gathering over Europe.'

'Why me?'

'You're above suspicion, Kay. Young, pretty, and rich.' He goes on to explain that the Germans would never suspect someone like me.

'Of course I'll do it, but why now?'

'The FBI have been monitoring Nazi influence in New York, gathering intelligence on potential threats to our national security, what they're calling the fifth column.'

'What does that mean?'

'They fear that organized groups are emerging and holding rallies, meetings, and gathering sentiment among German immigrants with ties to the Fatherland and families that can be exploited by the Nazis with threats and lies.'

'I'm headed to Paris. There are no Nazis in France.'

'No, but God help us if the German Army ever goes on the move, Kay, and gets through the Maginot Line.'

'Why would they?'

'Hitler and his cronies are up to something. There's talk of Germany annexing Austria, then who knows what's next. We need a contact in Paris who can observe what goes on in the salons and grand hotels where German spies ply their trade.'

From what I gather, the US government wants to keep its nose clean by employing covert observation of Hitler since it's not popular politically for them to get involved. With the introduction of the Nuremberg Race Laws last year declaring that Jews are no longer German citizens and have no rights, certain parties in Washington are concerned about how far Hitler will go with what's becoming known as the Jewish question.

I cock a brow. 'Does my mother know?'

He shakes his head. 'What you do in France is between you and Uncle Sam.'

'Don't bet on it. Mother has eyes in the back of her head.'

'I don't doubt it.'

We talk about his family and how pleased he is I recovered from my exhaustion after my coming out (the State Department doesn't know everything), when a whiff of heavy perfume and arrogance hits my nostrils.

Mother rushes into my cabin out of breath. 'Archibald, *what* are you doing here?' she asks, narrowing her eyes.

'Seeing off my lovely niece.' He winks at me.

'You frightened me, Archie. When the steward told me there was a strange man in my daughter's stateroom, I—'

'I must be going, Millicent... Kay.' He nods, then before Mother can grill him further, he's gone, the final call to go ashore blasting throughout the ship.

'Well, what a relief it was only Archie. For a minute, I thought—'

'You thought what, Mother? That a man might still find me attractive?'

She scowls as she adjusts her hat sitting askew on her head. 'Whatever you think of me, Kay, I know what I'm talking about. When you're in Paris, don't talk to strange men.'

'Yes, Mother,' I repeat for the umpteenth time.

Then with a rattling of her pearls, Mother disembarks the *Queen Mary.* I imagine the society papers will run a picture of me from my coming out in my white debutante dress and the story will read: *The proper Philadelphia matron, Millicent Radwell-Alexander, bid her daughter Kay Alexander bon voyage on the Queen Mary departing for Cherbourg. The popular debutante will study art at the Sorbonne in Paris.*

Art, my foot.

I grab some chocolate bars from the gift basket and ponder my new role as a spy, but not making too much of it. My role as *Radwell's* chocolate ambassadress is the perfect cover for my clandestine activities. I have a moment of mirth when I think about what Mother would do if she knew. Probably call the president of the Cunard Line and have him turn the ship back to New York. It's intriguing to think I'll be part of the diplomatic corps after all. Let

Mother put *that* in her bonnet. Still, I have to be realistic. I'll do my snooping for Uncle Archie, but I doubt I'll turn up anything useful.

I'm going to Paris, not Nazi Germany. I have nothing to fear.

I munch on a *La Belle Josephine* chocolate bar as I go out on deck to watch the ship leave the harbor. I look forward to perusing the chocolate shops in Paris and expanding the *Radwell* brand, but I can't stop thinking about the haunted look on my uncle's face, the deep circles under his eyes, the heavy burden that made him smoke that damn pipe of his overtime.

I have the strangest feeling spying on Herr Hitler may be more dangerous than he's letting on.

19

BERLIN, SEPTEMBER 1936

Rachel

It's not every day a famous violinist comes into my family's music shop to get his instrument repaired. Asa Heisselberg is referred to us from the synagogue where Mutti goes to pray. We're not Orthodox Jews who attend every week, but Mutti goes in respect of her parents who are buried there in the cemetery. She jokes it's the only place quiet enough for her to think, then winks. She loves to tease us about her lack of hearing. I think she does that so we don't see it as a handicap. I remember when we got a new radio, she said at least *she* didn't have to listen to Hitler's long-winded speeches.

I worry about her going to the synagogue alone since the riots last year when a bunch of ruffians in civilian clothes went 'Jew hunting' around the Kurfürstendamm. We found out afterward they were Stormtroopers, their black boots and uniform trousers giving them away.

This morning, with a kiss to my cheek and a smile in her heart, she left for her weekly trek, putting the danger aside. She insists she's been making the trip since her parents passed, first her father then Bubbe, and she's not going to let the Nazis stop her.

Herr Heisselberg said the rabbi introduced them when he came to bid the spiritual leader goodbye... and inquired if he knew where he could get the broken strings on his violin repaired in a hurry. He's leaving for Shanghai since they don't require a visa. It's too dangerous for him to stay in Germany and he's been offered a spot in the orchestra there playing for the ballet at the Metropol Theater.

It's a great honor to have him here with Papa floating around in a dream, grabbing a chair for the great maestro, sending me upstairs to the kitchen to bring tea and cakes. I offer Herr Heisselberg a butterscotch on the way, then call out to Leah and Tovah to stop playing marbles in the back of the shop and to come meet our guest.

Mutti would want me to offer him a piece of vanilla cake with cinnamon filling so I do, then listen to Papa and the maestro talk shop. Papa looks over the instrument and tells him Ulrich will fix it and have it ready in no time. He sends Leah to the workshop in the back to find him.

A quiet man, so nearsighted he can't see beyond his hand without glasses, Ulrich Mueller is a master at his craft and repairs the string instruments in our shop. He's not Jewish and risks alienation or worse from the Nazis because he still works for my father now that it's forbidden for Aryans to work for a Jew. He's a kind man and I like him. So does Papa and he does everything he can to protect him, allowing him to sleep in the storeroom when his wife berates him and locks him out for working for a Jew.

But for today, this moment, for everything that's bad in our lives under Nazi rule, this is a good thing. To have such a famous violinist in our midst brings honor to our shop and a joy to Papa's eyes I haven't seen for a long time. It warms me to observe the two men kibitzing and laughing and humming melodies together.

Leah and Tovah sit on the floor, their legs crossed, listening intently. I notice Leah has her autograph book clutched to her chest. My brows raise when she asks the famous violinist for an autograph... My shy Leah. Will wonders never cease?

I gather up the empty cake plates, sweeping the crumbs into my hand like Mutti does... wondering why she isn't home yet. She needed to spend more time with her parents, I guess, sitting at their grave site, filling them in on their grandbabies' latest exploits as she's wont to do.

I let a tear fall for those dear, kind souls who always had candy and kisses for me.

With lovely thoughts of those times settling in me, I take a seat and join the fun when Papa encourages his guest to play for us. The maestro picks out a violin from the display cabinet, his bow cutting through the air with long, graceful sweeps across the instrument, playing a classical piece by Mendelsohn.

A forbidden piece by the Nazis, but here in our shop with the windows closed, we shut out that world of hurt and prejudice. Here we enjoy a poignant melody that sets me swaying and humming. Papa nods toward Tovah and she grabs her violin and joins him. Then he gives us a nod, too, and Leah and I pick out chords on the guitar and piano and follow along. Papa joins us and it's a lovely moment of uplifting music filling the shop while Ulrich works on the maestro's violin.

I look at the big, round clock on the wall, the late afternoon sun splintering off the metal baroque musical notes framing it. Where did the time go? We've been playing for an hour. Where is Mutti? She's never this late. She should be home by now.

I don't know why, but I've got a bad feeling.

It could be because my mother is a creature of habit and usually by this time, she'd be in the kitchen chopping vegetables or trying to figure out how to make the meager meat rations go farther.

And she isn't.

I see Papa looking at the time as well. His dancing eyes turn dark for a moment, then he finishes the musical piece with the maestro in a flourish. And as if the musical gods timed it, the bell tinkles as the front door opens and in comes Mutti, shoulders hunched, covering her face with her shawl.

'*Mutti!*' we cry out with joy, gathering around her. She nods and then tries to escape, but Papa is no fool. He may wander about the day in a musical fantasy, but he knows when something is wrong with his beloved wife. He takes her in his arms and when he sees what she's hiding, his eyes go very cold and he lets out a word never heard in this house. The maestro is beside himself, trying to help, asking what he can do. Leah and Tovah start crying, even Ulrich stops working on the violin.

As the oldest daughter, it's my job to console my mother... calm my father's anger, but it will take more than words when I see what they did to Mutti. Blood smeared on her right cheek, purplish bruise around her half-shut eye, her lip split. She looks away, ashamed, trying to fix herself up, wiping the blood off her cheek.

The Nazis.

Who else would defile such a kind woman?

Mutti insists everyone calm down, that she was beaten by SS because she couldn't hear their command when she was walking out of the synagogue and they told her to make room on the sidewalk for them. She's not hurt badly, she insists, then tries to smile but her lip hurts too much.

My world spins and I vow that never again will I allow my mother to go out without one of us by her side. I have only to look at her face, the fear in her eyes, to know she agrees, though she'd never admit it to anyone but me. We've always had a special communication between us; it's not that Mutti loves me more, simply that I keep the family together by watching over my little sisters and keeping Papa from forgetting things when she's busy. It's that special look I see now and I'll never forget it... ever. It makes me feel proud that she places so much trust in me.

We say our goodbyes to the maestro, his eyes sad at what he witnessed today. Before he goes, I hear him pleading with my father to leave Berlin. Come to Shanghai. Papa shakes his head *no*. This is our home, he says.

'Think about it, Herr Landau; the music we love is dying in our country. We must make music somewhere else if we are to survive.' Then the maestro pats my father on the shoulder and disappears into the early twilight.

For us it was a day we'll never forget. Playing with the great maestro, watching my little sister Tovah making beautiful music with him on her violin and Leah getting the courage to speak up and ask him for an autograph.

But the day turned dark and piercing, sending such pain into my heart, it will be a long time before I forget it.

Mutti attacked by SS soldiers because she couldn't hear their command.

I've heard rumors the Nazis don't tolerate the physically impaired. I saw it with my own eyes today. But more significantly, it becomes clear to me life in Berlin isn't safe for Jews any more. If my own dear, sweet perfect Mutti can't bow her head in prayer and find peace, then where are we headed? I fear the worst. That never again will we play the classical Jewish artists in such freedom as we've done here today. Herr Heisselberg is right.

It's the day the music died.

20

PARIS, LATE SEPTEMBER 1936

Kay

He's tall, dark, dangerous-looking and keeps staring at me. I should know better than to stare back at him. Encourage him.

I don't.

Like a lovesick fool, I can't take my eyes off him. That distinctive scar slicing his dark right brow in two fascinates me. Where did he get such a precisely-cut wound? A war? No, he's too young to have served in the Great War – no older than mid-twenties, I'd say – and the only conflict I know about these days are skirmishes in Spain.

Is he fresh from there? Could be. He's muscular and broad-shouldered. He's got an aura of seduction in the way he moves... like a tiger on the hunt, watching, waiting for his prey to give up, his looks so attractive to women they drink up his mysterious elixir before realizing such a man comes with consequences. I'm convinced a beautiful cabaret dancer fell under his spell and he fought with her Apache lover over her.

One thing I *do* know: if the devil were an obnoxiously hand-some Frenchman, he would be it.

Now that I've settled that, why *not* flirt with him? I'm sitting at a table in the Café de la Paix on a sunny day bathed in a rose hue, a day right out of the tourist brochure, the smell of maleness ripe on the breeze and provocative to this single woman rediscovering her hormones. Even so, I shiver. I feel guilty reacting to his stare, as though I don't have the right to flirt with a man because I made a horribly bad choice before and it cost me the most precious thing a love affair can bring to a woman.

My baby.

I'll always be childless and I've yet to come to grips with that. The wound in my soul is still raw. Which is why I'm so surprised at my attraction to this stranger.

Again, the guilt. I can't tamp it down.

Sitting in a cane-backed chair under the broad café awning, fanning myself with the square paper menu, I yearn for romance. Two weeks I've been here. Where is the gaiety I've heard about, the excitement, the debonair young men?

Seems I found him.

Is he an artist? He hasn't stopped moving his pencil across the large sketchpad balanced on his lap. What's he drawing? Me? No, he wouldn't be that brazen, would he? I should say something, make him stop looking at me, but I'm lonely for the thrill, the rush you get when you're excited by a look from a man. The feel of his arms around you, holding you close, and you know nothing can hurt you. A fantasy I no longer believe in after my stupid, juvenile romance with a man who was paid to charm me. My ego hasn't recovered, so when this handsome man gives me a second look, well, I can't look away. The stranger is more rugged-looking than the boys I danced with at my deb balls. Hair falling over one eye, he looks up from his sketchpad and tilts his head, continuing to stare at me; the expression on his face is so intense it makes me shiver.

I also feel guilty because my interest in this cavalier doesn't go unnoticed by my companion. A charming aristocrat I befriended soon after I arrived in Paris.

Louis-Marcel Valbert, le Duc de Savaré.

The catch? My admirer is over sixty.

Tall, erect posture. Gray silk morning coat with striped black-and-white cravat tied with precision, he always has a smile and a pink rose for me and a witty story about Paris in the twenties, how *le jazz hot* ruled the nightclubs and women rolled their stockings and bobbed their hair.

The dapper duke is exactly what I needed. A companion *and* an escort *without* consequences. Our relationship is strictly platonic and we both like it that way. He flirts because it's expected of him... I flirt back knowing that's as far as it goes. He's lonely for the 'old days' when he ruled the cabarets and had a pretty *mamselle* on his arm.

And me? I need someone I can trust.

He found me wandering around the *Gare Saint-Lazare* when my train arrived from Cherbourg, inquiring in French where I could find a cheap hotel. I checked my luggage at the train station and I've yet to send Mother her promised telegram from the Hôtel Ritz. She thinks I'm staying at the hotel on Place Vendôme, but I'm not interested in being feted and cajoled by hotel staff. I wasn't ready to announce to the social Parisian scene that Kay Alexander of the Philadelphia Radwell-Alexanders is in town and find myself swamped with invitations for fancy dinners and literary salons.

I need to heal. Alone.

Still, I found it strange an aristocrat would bother with an American tourist and tried to discourage him, but he said it was his duty as a Frenchman.

Really? I didn't believe him, but he said it in such a charming manner, I let it pass.

He has no idea who I am and I'm not telling, not because Mother told me not to talk to strange men, but because I don't want the publicity, the questions from the press about why I'm here in Paris. I'll never forget how they hounded a famous New York debutante for weeks, then splashed her photos all over a major news magazine... including her drinking at a not-so-classy dive in Montmartre. So I concocted a story right out of the novels I read. I told the duke I'm a dancer and my last show closed in Marseilles when the manager ran off with the week's receipts and the lead girl in the show, so I came to Paris for work. I spun such a good tale, even I believed I'm a down-on-my-luck hoofer named Kay McGinty.

It worked for *Gimbel's*, why not Paris?

Besides, I need a new identity if I'm to spy for my uncle. Really, I take it seriously. I embraced Uncle Archie's request because it makes me feel useful. Whether or not I find anything worth reporting about Hitler (Nazi Germany is so far removed from Philadelphia, I doubt Mother and her friends even know who the chancellor is), I want to experience the *real* Paris the same way an artist rushes to paint a field of flowers blowing in the breeze and take in the glorious hues melting under the sun like sweet butter drizzling on your tongue.

Louis (he insists I call him that and not 'Your Grace') flagged down a porter and rattled off an address so quickly it went completely over my head. I craved a hot bath and strong coffee, so I didn't protest when he suggested we share a taxi and dropped me off on the Left Bank at Le Grand Hôtel du Midi, a 'modest but safe establishment for *mademoiselle*'.

Not the accommodations I'm used to, but I find it charming *and* the perfect base of operations for my covert mission. Louis was the perfect gentleman and bid me *adieu*, but not before dropping a hint that he frequented the Café de la Paix every afternoon during the 'green hour' – five o'clock – a drinking custom once popular among the elite.

I smiled and filed that away in my brain, though I preferred to see Paris on my own.

I soon found out that except for a huge fireplace in my third-floor walk-up, the hotel was anything but grand with the bathroom down the hall. But it fits my purpose, giving me the freedom to wander around Paris, dallying about the boulevards and cafés and chocolate shops, camera in hand. I've shot two rolls of film, but I have my doubts about whether the State Department is interested in quaint chocolate shops and the flower market.

I gawked at the Eiffel Tower and the Winged Victory of Samothrace in the Louvre, then spent two days checking the bookshops on the Rue des Saint-Pères, looking for spies lurking in the shadows. I found odd relics of Old Paris. Books on the occult, brooches of staid ladies carved on ivory from the Victorian age, and a mummy. Yes, a real mummy from Cairo the befuddled shopkeeper insisted I needed for my parlor. I couldn't resist having it shipped back to Philadelphia. 'She' will fit in nicely with Mother's bridge club.

Next, I went to the grand market of Les Halles and except for the steamy, hot onion soup, I found nothing to report. Which makes me wonder if this 'war talk' with Germany is just that. Talk. I can't imagine this city under siege. Paris is lovely and peaceful as we head into late September, the chestnut leaves falling across my windowpane in the hotel in a whisper of muted colors.

I also discover why Parisians spend so much time in cafés. They have decent facilities and a warm place to sit. There's no heat in my hotel room (the concierge has yet to show me how to light the fireplace) and the faucet in the communal *toilette* on my floor has no hot water after 11 a.m. Also, back home I had the freedom to go where I wanted. That doesn't hold true here. I've been tossed out of more than one establishment because I didn't have a male escort. A flash of franc notes in a Russian restaurant did nothing to change the mind of the proper maître d' with his S-shaped, stiff black mustache and Cossack white collar.

So I took the duke up on his offer and, although I hadn't intended on seeing Paris with an elderly gentleman, I could have done worse. Louis is well-read, speaks impeccable English and flatters me regarding my French skills. He's good for my ego and makes me feel safe, if not matronly, with a gentle pat on my arm, a peck on the cheek. A platonic affair that suited me until today, when that ache in my belly undulated in an all-too-familiar rhythm I can't ignore.

I sneak another peek at the hatless man in the deep copper leather jacket, shirt collar pulled up, wavy black hair mussed up by the morning breeze, stubble chin. Pencil in hand. He's still watching me, his pencil moving on the large pad he balances on his lap. An empty cup sits next to him with several saucers piled high, indicating he's been here a while.

And that damn pencil hasn't stopped moving.

'Have I told you, *mademoiselle*,' Louis says, sipping his cognac mixed with water, 'you're the most beautiful woman in Paris?'

I dab my mouth with red lip rouge, then snap the gold case shut. 'Yes, Louis... yesterday and the day before that and—'

The duke laughs. 'I'm flattered you allow me to indulge in my fantasy.' He finishes his drink. 'I have a surprise for you, Kay.'

'You've already done enough for me, *monsieur*.'

'Don't deny an old man the opportunity to show you off at my favorite nightclub this evening.'

Oh.

I'm not keen on going to a club. It brings back the sting of my affair with Nico. 'I don't enjoy clubs, Louis. I find them stuffy and boring.'

He gives me a funny look. 'Odd for a dancer.'

I feel my cheeks tint. A faux pas on my part. 'I'm still not over losing my job.'

'I'm sure you'll find this club quite fascinating,' he continues, giving me an inquisitive look. 'It's the only one in Paris with a dance floor *and* a bathing pool.'

I'm cornered. I have little choice but to go with him if I'm to keep up my ruse. I wet my lips, smile big. 'Of course, I shall be delighted to accompany you this evening.'

'*Bon.* Every man there will envy me and no doubt tempt you to leave me.' He casts a wary glance my way.

I smile. 'No man will ever win my heart but you.'

'If only that were true.' He heaves out a deep sigh. 'Then again, I can't woo you with my artistic skills.'

'*Monsieur?*' I ask.

'That gentleman at the corner table grabbing your intention for the past twenty minutes. He's sketching you, *n'est-ce pas?*'

'Is he?' I feign innocence.

'Be careful, *mademoiselle*, you can't trust anyone these days.'

He's right. I can't.

While I've been sitting here daydreaming, I didn't take into consideration what would happen if the artist sells my likeness to a newspaper and someone recognizes me. The society columns back home are filled with the comings and goings of debutantes and if she's a Philadelphia Main Line heiress to boot, the stakes are higher. Someone once said debs are more popular than film stars. I doubt that, though every season 'coming out' parties take up pages and pages in the major magazines. The press *will* find me (they always do) and there goes my privacy. I'll have to face them sometime, but not yet. It's rather fun to get lost in the crowd.

I intend to put an end to his intrusion in my life. *Now*.

Or is it because I'm curious where it will lead if I *do* talk to him?

I straighten my black straw hat with the red cherries dangling on the side, pull my veil down and strut over to this interloper.

'*Pardon, monsieur*,' I say in French, waving my hand around in the air. 'I demand you cease and desist your invasion into my privacy.'

He keeps drawing.

'Put down your pencil, sir... *now*.' I make my pitch in English, losing my patience.

He looks up and shoots me a piercing look I feel down to my toes. 'It's a free country, *mademoiselle*, though with the Nazis breathing down our necks, it won't be for long.'

'And what does *that* mean?'

He grins, ignoring my question. 'Turn to the right so your face catches the sun... then lift your veil.'

'I will not.'

'You'd deny me the pursuit of my art?'

I smirk. 'The art of picking up women? If you came to Paris to study art, why aren't you drawing nude models in a garret over-looking the Seine?'

'Are you applying for the job?'

'You're quite insolent, *monsieur*.'

'No, I'm British. And a good judge of people. Call it the artist's instinct, but I can see into a subject's soul through their eyes, see if it's dented and marked with ugly scars. Like your companion.' He smirks. 'I don't trust him... and neither should you.'

'Jealous?'

'I'm not the type.'

'What type are you?'

'*Pardon, mademoiselle*, but I must finish my drawing.' He puts the finishing touches on his sketch, then sweeps his signature across the bottom with a grand flourish. 'There... it's done.'

'Show me.'

'You won't like it.'

'Try me.'

He grins, then rips the sketch off his notebook and hands it to me, his dark eyes sparkling.

'Oh...' I can scarcely breathe. He's right. I *don't* like it. 'That isn't me... it's – it's a caricature... a nursery rhyme.'

'It *is* you, *mademoiselle*,' he insists, lowering his voice to a place I don't want to go. 'Even if you won't admit it.'

Is it?

He's drawn me as a sophisticated 'Mary had a little lamb' wearing a sexy, low-cut sheath dress, ruffled pantaloons, and a floppy hat. With a droopy daisy. I'm holding a shepherd's staff with a lamb in my arms while a silver fox disguised as a Paris dandy in spats and black top hat looms over me, his white-gloved hands reaching for me. Hands with very large, very long fingers.

It's playful, fun. And gets under my skin.

He's drawn the duke.

I take in a breath, amazed at his artistic skill. The curvy black lines against the white paper are sharp, perfect, capturing not only my wide-eyed expression, but the way I stand and hunch one shoulder as if posing for the camera, then tilt my head back. It's uncanny. And brilliant, a touch of elegance within a fantasy, but spiked with a dose of reality.

It's *too* real.

And it chills me.

'You insult me, *monsieur*. I don't like it. *Or* you.'

I crumple the drawing into a large wad and toss it back at him. To my surprise, he catches it in mid-air, then salutes me before picking up his notepad and disappearing into the melee of pedestrians making their way toward the Place de l'Opéra. Gone without another word. I should follow him, get the drawing back, but I'll never find him in the crowd.

Oh, the insolence of the man.

Should I worry? No, I'll never see him again. But I can't forget him.

I lift my chin and walk back to my chair, my dream unhinged, my flirtation taken to a new level of intimacy. I can't forget how the rugged stranger looked at me.

As if he's seen me naked.

21

KAY

I can smell a reporter a mile away. Burnt cigarettes and cheap cologne mixed with sweat. It's a distinct smell I learned to recognize when I was a deb, overtaking the scent of crisp starch and too much rosewater we debutantes are known for. I should run like hell when the wind blows it my way, protect myself from nosy stares and lewd undertones in the form of questions that seem ripped from every reporter's notebook.

I don't.

I look up from my empty coffee, the female reporter's piercing brown eyes catching mine. That direct stare makes me think of a fairy-tale queen trying to decide whether or not to write the princess out of the last chapter and keep the prince for herself. I never expect to come up against a reporter in tweed wearing a skirt and laced-up sensible shoes and smelling like schnapps and fresh lavender flowers.

And wearing a monocle.

'Won't you introduce me to your latest conquest, Louis?' the woman coos in French, descending upon us like a falcon returning to its perch. With purpose, familiarity.

And do I detect a German accent?

'Don't you have a train to catch, *mademoiselle*, or something more useful to do than snooping?' Louis spits out his distaste for her with a snarl on his lips.

'And miss watching you lay your trap?' She snorts. 'Not on your life.'

Trap? What's she talking about?

Before I can challenge her, this remarkable personage grabs a chair and slides it over to our small round table. The café is crowded, patrons spilling out onto the sidewalk, but that doesn't stop her from pushing her way between a portly gentleman and his newspaper sitting nearby and ordering a coffee from the waiter.

I swear the duke is ready to pop his cork. He pulls his cravat loose and clenches his fist as though he wants to sock her, but restrains himself. Barely. 'I'd prefer you peddle your sleaze somewhere else, *mademoiselle*. I have nothing for your gossip column today.'

'No? You're sitting here with a beautiful woman I've never seen before.'

'*Enough, mademoiselle*. Please leave.'

She ignores him and extends her hand to me. 'Gertrud von Arenbeck, *mademoiselle*. I'm a reporter for *Die Junge Dame*, a magazine for young women. I write a column about fashion, film stars, lifestyle...' She grins wide. 'And gossip.'

I shake her hand. Her grip is strong, firm. '*Enchantée, mademoiselle*,' I answer in French then add how excited I am to be in Paris.

'Ah, you're American,' she asserts in English, surprising me.

'And you're German.'

'Austrian. From Vienna then Berlin, though I prefer Paris to the insanity marching through the streets in Germany.' She takes off her monocle and wipes it clean with her gloved finger. I have the feeling the glass is for effect. 'I left to avoid the Brownshirts mucking up every story I tried to cover only to have SS men come to dominance over the crude Stormtroopers.'

'*Pardon*?' I have no idea what she's talking about, but the combination of fear and anger darkening her light eyes like an obscure night fog tells me these 'SS' men are to be avoided.

'The SS are Hitler's personal guards strutting around in their black uniforms with lightning bolts pinned on their shoulders like ancient thunder gods. I fear they're not born of woman, but the fire and licks of Hades.' She leans in closer and her breath reminds me of sharp spearmint. 'Pray you never meet up with them, *mademoiselle*. They're despicable creatures.'

'You shouldn't poke your nose where you're not wanted, *mademoiselle*,' says the duke.

'This nose has never failed me when it comes to a story, Louis.' She turns back to me. 'I'd like to interview you for my column, *mademoiselle*. It's rare to find an American woman in Paris these days when they're leaving in droves because of the depression back home. I'd like to know what couture houses you've visited. Chanel, Jean Patou, Schiaparelli?'

Oh, no, I don't like this. Any publicity is bad publicity.

'You flatter me, Mademoiselle von Arenbeck. I'm not a tourist. I came to Paris to work.'

'Then you must be a model. Have I seen you in *Vogue*?' She studies me, curious. 'You look familiar.'

'We Americans all look alike,' I say sheepishly. 'With our curious noses poking where we shouldn't... We're too loud, wear flashy clothes.'

She laughs. 'Well put, *mademoiselle*. Then what *do* you do?'

I explain how the show I was dancing in closed, which elicits raised eyebrows from her.

'And I suppose Louis here came to your aid, *n'est-ce pas*?'

'Yes. How did you know?' I give Louis a look that says, *What aren't you telling me?*

He ignores me. 'Well, *mesdemoiselles*, I must be going.' He stands up, tips his hat. 'I have an engagement.'

'With another mark, *monsieur*?' Gertrud boldly asks.

'I resent your false insinuations, Mademoiselle von Arenbeck. If you must know, I'm meeting a buyer. I'm diversifying my interests and selling off several hectares of my château lands.'

My ears perk up. I've always wanted to live in France. I imagine myself buying land from the duke and building a summer house on the property... then I let the idea go. I won't be in Paris long enough to see that happen.

'Strapped for cash, Louis?' Gertrud probes. The anger flooding his eyes and turning them from gray to a deep slate tells me she's right.

I didn't see *that* coming.

'I had no idea you were in financial straits, *monsieur*.'

'Who isn't these days, *mademoiselle*?' He shrugs his shoulders, then kisses my hand. 'I bid you *adieu* until we rendezvous later at the club.' Then with a snarl at the Austrian reporter, he struts off.

His honesty about his state of affairs surprises me. My income in a month would sustain the average French family for years. Unlike many wealthy Main Line families, we haven't lost a dime in the depression. And not because we're sitting on inherited wealth not touched by stock market losses, but candy sales have never been higher. I plan to expand the *Radwell* brand, but it has to be the right candy, something different.

So far, I've come up with nothing.

I can't tell the duke *or* the reporter who I am. I've got to keep a low profile. Life, after all, is merely presenting an illusion and making someone believe it. Even a hard-nosed reporter like Gertrud. My offensive move is to knock the ball into her court. 'Are you an aristocrat, too, *mademoiselle*?' I ask, referring to the 'von' in her name.

She eyes me warily. 'Austria did away with the aristocracy, but my readers find it thrilling to read stories written by a countess.'

'I've met a duke and a countess since I've been in Paris.' I smile. 'I can only imagine what comes next.'

Gertrud grins, then orders a schnapps before tossing the ball back into my court. 'How about a knight in shining armor?'

Strange words from a woman wearing a monocle, tweed, and sensible shoes with perfectly tied laces in a bow. Teutonic precision. She doesn't strike me as the romantic type.

'And why would I need a knight?' I ask.

'Paris can be a wild, dangerous place when the sun goes down, *mademoiselle*, filled with surprises.' She downs her schnapps quickly. 'You'll find that out when you meet the duke later.' She grins. 'Here's a present for you.'

She tosses the crumpled-up drawing of me as a nursery rhyme on the table. 'Max said you were worth checking out, that there might be a story here. We'll see if he was right. *Au revoir, mademoiselle.*'

Then she's off, leaving me with my mouth open to ponder this strange afternoon.

* * *

It's the Parisian version of a debutante ball.

Only this one is set in a nightclub in the Pigalle.

I've waltzed through balls with over two thousand attendees gawking at debs in white dresses, but this evening's soiree is the most interesting array of female flesh for sale I've ever seen. There's one difference: these girls are not the marrying kind. Blondes, brunettes, redheads in long white gowns and wearing black opera gloves sit on the side with the word 'taxi-girl' looming over their heads. Below the bleacher-like level, pretty girls dance with starry-eyed males on the dance floor to a jazzy beat.

What catches my eye are the half a dozen girls wearing skimpy swimming suits diving into a long, rectangular glass tank filled with water. Splashing around like mermaids, laughing and tempting lonely men to watch them through the glass while they undulate underwater in suggestive poses.

I feel like a tiny minnow swimming upstream.

'Beautiful girls everywhere, *mademoiselle*,' Louis boasts, kissing his gloved fingers in a moment of bliss. 'Paris at its best, *n'est-ce pas*?'

I frown. *At its best... or it's loudest?*

I want to plug my ears with newspaper it's so noisy in here, bursting with the warbling of a whiny French singer belting out jazz. Laughter... giggling... glasses clinking – make that breaking – and the thumping feet of zealous dancers on the wooden dance floor.

'Why did you ask me to meet you here, *monsieur*?' I ask.

'I can get you a job here at the club, *mademoiselle*.'

'Doing what? I can't swim,' I lie. I don't like the setup; something isn't right. Maybe Gertrud has a point about this nefarious lothario. He *isn't* to be trusted.

'Ah, but you can dance.' He winks. 'I hear a girl can make 5,000 francs in tips in one night if she's a good... dancer.'

No translation needed.

'And here I thought you wanted to make an honest woman of me.'

'*Alors, mademoiselle*, now you know my secret. I can't afford to keep you for myself.'

'I get it. You get a cut for every girl you bring here.'

'*Mademoiselle*?'

'A kickback. You know, moolah... *dinero*.'

'She means you're a pimp, *monsieur*.'

I turn around. Gertrud. Standing behind me, polishing her monocle with her sleeve and grinning like a Cheshire cat in tweed. *Where did she come from?*

'I beg your pardon, *mademoiselle*,' he protests, refusing to stand and pull out a chair as a courtesy for the intrepid reporter. As I expected, Gertrud waits for no man. She grabs her own chair and plops down.

'Admit it, Louis. You conned our pretty friend here with that aristocrat *merde* you toss off like breadcrumbs to the pigeons.'

Louis snarls. 'It's an honored act for a gentleman of my station, going back to the days of Louis XIV when my ancestor introduced beautiful young women to court.' He kisses my hand. 'I'll introduce you personally to Monsieur Palumet about the job, *mademoiselle*. Wait here... I'll be right back.'

'You're still a pimp, Louis,' Gertrud calls after him, then pokes me in the ribs. 'The pay is rotten, *mademoiselle*, the working conditions unsanitary, and if you're smart, you won't get caught up in the duke's little scheme for you to "date" his friends. You'll end up in harem pants in the Casbah.'

She is kidding, isn't she?

'I don't wear trousers, Gertrud.'

'You will, if you're not careful.' There's a beat as she looks me over. 'I can put in a word for you at Chanel. You're slim and pretty and have class.'

'*Merci, mademoiselle*.' I smile, a secret grin, making me smile at her calling me slim. 'But I have an audition coming up for a show.'

'Suit yourself.' Gertrud scans the crowd, looking for someone. '*Pardon, mademoiselle*, but I've got to interview a beautiful redhead for my column. If you'll excuse me...'

'*Mademoiselle*... Gertrud... wait,' I begin, saying what's on my mind. I can't forget the handsome Englishman, obviously a friend of hers. 'That artist friend of yours, does he frequent the Café de la Paix often?'

Her brow lifts. 'You mean Max?'

'Yes. What do you know about him?'

'Max Hamilton-Jones is a man on the move, an adventurer who thinks nothing of flying into a thunderstorm in that biplane of his if that's what the client wants. Like the Spanish diplomat who hired him to take him to Madrid because his child was ill with pneumonia. Max wouldn't take a franc for the fare. That's the kind of man he is, and I wouldn't have known *that* about him if I didn't have a starry-eyed female source at the Spanish consul who couldn't wait to tell me. Max didn't deny it when I asked him, but he'd never speak to me again if he knew I'd told you that story.'

'What's he doing in Paris?' I ask. 'Besides drawing women.'

'He's a man of secrets, *mademoiselle*. All I know is we met at the *Shakespeare and Company* bookstore when the owner Sylvia Beach showed me his work. He owes allegiance to no one but himself... and me.'

'You?'

'I act as his agent, selling his caricatures to Berlin newspapers and here in Paris for the editorial pages. He's quite good, but you already know that.' She smiles wryly.

'He could be Renoir for all I care. He's the most impertinent man I've ever met and I don't want him drawing me again.' I finish with, 'It's... it's bad for my image as a dancer.'

'Why don't you tell him yourself?' She snickers. 'He's over by the bathing pool, sketching girls.'

I turn and my jaw drops. She's right. It's him. The artist with the scar. And he couldn't have looked more like the devil. And I couldn't have wanted more to sin.

I lift my chest, gather my courage. 'You're right, I'll tell him myself.'

'Hurry before Louis gets back.' She grabs my arm. 'Don't trust that Frenchman. He's a bad apple.'

Then she's off, leaving me no choice but to confront the man that set my heart fluttering. I find myself racing headlong into what I know is danger and not caring one damn bit. No matter how much this lady doth protest, this guy's got my number. I've fallen heads over heels for him. Oh, I won't tell him that and spoil the fun. What's romance without the angst? But I'm not that naïve debutante. I'm smarter now. I want to see what he's made of.

Hero or conman?

Time to find out. Let the games begin...

* * *

'Back for more, *mademoiselle*?'

Heat races through me when I hear that low baritone. Who wouldn't get hot and bothered? I'm in a Paris nightclub known for its decadence and I'm not immune to its dark magic. Beautiful hostesses flirting with men in evening clothes, a band playing, elegant dance floor, *and* a bathing pool filled with pretty girls in skimpy bathing costumes. I've never seen anything like it, even in New York.

I'm more interested in Max Hamilton-Jones sitting off to the side of the bathing pool near the pretty girls splashing each other, trying to catch his eye and flirting with him, his drawing pad filled with sketches of the scantily clad women.

He *is* an amazing caricaturist from what I see on his pad, but he's also a threat to me.

'I'm here to tell you, Mr Hamilton-Jones, I can't allow you to use me as a model. Is that understood?'

'What's it worth to you?' he asks with a smirk-y smile that's not lost on me. 'You're prettier than any girl here. I can get big bucks for a drawing of you.'

I heave out a big breath. I could pay anything he asks, but then I'm made. 'I don't have any money.'

'Too bad.'

Ooh, I'm itching to tell this guy off like Mother would do with a snarly remark and a snap of her fingers. Then I have a terrible thought: *Am I turning into my mother? Demanding everyone do my bidding because I can?*

I shiver at the thought.

'Well, do we have a deal?' I ask.

'What are you offering?'

'I'm implore you as an English gentleman—'

'Who said I was a gentleman?'

'No, that would be too much to hope for.' I sigh. 'Then what *do* you want? And don't say an encounter of the physical kind because contrary to what you think of me because of my relationship with the duke, I'm *not* that kind of girl.'

'I know that. I can see in your eyes who you are. That's why I wanted to draw you... and warn you at the same time.'

'Oh.'

I stammer about, unable to say anything coherent to this man who sees deep into my soul. I want to do more than stare at him as he sketches two girls waving at him.

I make a sound that's full of frustration when I make my next play. 'I appreciate your concern, Mr Hamilton-Jones—'

'Call me Max.'

I nod. 'Max... will you agree not to sketch me?'

'No.'

'Why not?' I say, perturbed.

'Because you're hiding something, Miss McGinty, and that intrigues me. I intend to find out what it is.'

I start to speak when—

'Here's the girl I was telling you about, Max.' Gertrud saunters over to us, accompanied by a tall redhead with long legs, her skimpy white swimsuit showing off a great figure. 'She's agreed to pose for you. Hélène Remy, meet Max Hamilton-Jones, adventurer, artist... and, well, you'll find out. They all do.'

'*Bonsoir, monsieur*,' Hélène says with a charm that makes me jealous.

'*Enchanté*, Hélène,' Max says in his own inimitable style, then looks her over with an approving eye, nods, and turns his drawing pad to a new page.

Forcing myself to remain calm and not say something stupid, I attempt to keep my dignity intact. 'Then we have a deal?'

'We'll continue this conversation another time, Miss McGinty.' Then he dismisses me like a chorus girl. I've never been so humiliated... and hurt. What did I expect? The Englishman is in the habit of flitting from one flower to another with his stinger ready for action.

His drawing pencil.

Why did I ever come up with this stupid idea of pretending to be what I'm not? Now I'm stuck with it and I don't like it.

'*Pardon, mademoiselle*, but *monsieur* wants *me* for his model,' says the redhead in English, pushing out her breasts and striking a pose. 'Now if you'll please remove yourself...'

I don't get it. Why is this wet female coming at me like that?

'I was here first, *mademoiselle*,' I blurt out, stepping in front of the redhead to assuage my bruised ego and blocking Max's view, much to his amusement.

'I don't care if you're Sylvie Martone, *mademoiselle*,' she says, 'you're not on the menu tonight.' She smiles prettily. 'I am.'

'Oh, no?'

'No.' She grins, then she pushes me out of the way with her hip.

My eyes widen. *Really, sister?*

A long moment passes while I take this in, my dander up that this impertinent *mamselle* expects me to let her get away with it. I'm used to being picked on by the press and of course Mother, but no one *ever* laid a hand on me. It makes me feel strangely vulnerable in a way that frightens me. I'm a big talker... and it usually works, but not this time. Also, I don't count out looking like a weak ninny in front of Max and that bothers me even more.

So before I think about the consequences, I push her back, then the redhead grabs me by the hair and yanks on my long, dark tresses.

'We'll see about that, Red,' I sputter in English.

I can't back down now and keep my self-respect.

I grab *her* long, curly red locks and push her backward. I don't know why I feel obsessed with fighting over a man I barely know and who irritates the hell out of me. Female pride, I guess. For the first time in my life, I'm on my own. Nobody in a Paris nightclub filled with pretty girls both wet and dry gives a damn about one hotheaded American brunette with a fragile ego.

Being an heiress isn't going to help me win the catfight.

Red and I shove each other back and forth while the other girls cheer for the wet *mademoiselle* in the swimsuit... while I struggle to keep my footing on the water-soaked platform in heels. Out of the corner of my eye, I see the English artist scribbling madly on his sketchpad, his dark eyes narrowing, that distinctive scar on his right brow stretched taut as he works. I can imagine what he's drawing. Two felines going at each other after the same man.

Oops, that look at the handsome artist costs me.

Red circles me, then ducks when I lunge toward her. I lose my footing and spin around and grab her by the arm and over the side we both go into the bathing pool with a big *splash*.

And a barrage of flashbulbs goes off in my face.

I hit the water hard and sink to the bottom, my long velvet gown pulling me down. I can't breathe, taking in water, but then I feel a pair of strong arms around me, pulling me up. I don't need or want his help. I struggle to free myself from his grip, but he's too strong for me.

We reach the top, me spitting out dirty water and my savior laughing as I struggle against him.

'Let me go,' I demand, beating my fists against his muscular chest. His white shirt pasted to his bronze body and revealing his bulging biceps isn't helping my plight... especially when he carries me up the pool steps in his strong arms. 'I can take care of myself.'

'Can you?' he asks dryly, putting me down.

'Yes. I don't need you or *any* man.'

I hear him grunt loudly when I spin around, his heavy breath hot on my neck. Good. Let him fume. I stomp off and grab my coat from the cloakroom. I hear footsteps behind me and satisfaction makes me glow in spite of my poor, shivering state. He's following me.

But it's only Gertrud throwing a blanket over me. And then getting me into her motorcar.

Max Hamilton-Jones and his notorious notebook are nowhere to be seen.

22

PARIS, NOVEMBER 1936

Kay

I discover soon afterward Gertrud always has an agenda... her precise mind at work like a perfect piece of machinery. She orchestrated that catfight between Hélène and me. The raucous scene in the bathing pool headlined a popular Paris scandal sheet and people talked about it for weeks. How a brunette and a redhead got into it after an argument over a man and it got out of hand, then everyone took sides and it was a mess.

So typically French.

What *wasn't* planned was Max jumping into the pool to save me when Louis told him I couldn't swim. A lie I told and he repeated. That's just the beginning of lies, but let's move on.

After two bottles of schnapps, Gertrud admitted she went after the duke to right a terrible wrong to her heart. Such a tale I've never heard before with its ups and downs, romance and tragedy... retribution and the fall of an aristocrat. According to Gertrud, all these months I was duped by a man who met the Paris trains in search of young women he could 'entice' to entertain lonely gentlemen. A means to his survival in a world he could no longer control with his title and imaginary line of credit. I didn't fall for his phony pitch (I learned the hard way not to trust men, even a duke), but others did. They didn't know where their next meal was coming from and dove headfirst into the life Louis offered them to survive.

A cautionary tale I won't forget.

I wasn't angry with Gertrude for involving me in her little escapade. If anything, it helped me understand the enigmatic Austrian woman when she allowed me to peer into her heart and understand the mystery of romantic attraction and its impact on our souls no matter *who* we love. How Gertrud was so heartbroken after falling for a young woman in the duke's stable, she threatened him with exposure. She could submit the bathing pool story to the scandal sheet as a catfight between two jealous women... or make known the kickbacks he gets for providing girls for the flesh mill.

Sex trafficking.

Setting up a catfight between Hélène and me set the stage for her blackmail scheme to get back at Louis. It worked. He agreed to end his 'recruitment' of girls at the train station, knowing Gertrud would go public with his sordid story if he didn't. It wouldn't bring her friend back, though. She broke down when she told me the girl's body was recovered from the Seine.

I squeezed her hand, a warm gesture to a woman I rarely understand, but I wanted to comfort her. Her sad, tearful eyes thanked me for caring and we never spoke of it again.

Meanwhile, I'm stuck with a new predicament. Pictures of Hélène and me in catfight mode spread out over a Paris scandal sheet with my soggy hair hanging in my eyes, dripping wet in the arms of this gorgeous man, and my velvet gown clinging to every curve of my body. The paper goes after wealthy foreigners having an affair, but on a slow news day they print provocative photos of pretty girls *en déshabillé* to sell papers. Thank God Mother doesn't read French or care about what happens outside her Philly world, but her rival Mrs Shupe *does* and follows the international set, looking for juicy tidbits about her ex-husband. If she gets too snoopy and reads the Paris papers, I've got problems.

Back to the lies. I'm guilty of the first one, lying about not being able to swim.

Next, lie number two.

Max owns this one. He swears he knew nothing about what Gertrud planned, but Hélène was happy to fill me in when we met for a walk in the Tuileries Gardens. The Polish girl was eager to apologize for her part in the bathing pool incident. She's trying to be a model, she said, but I swear there's more to her story than she's telling. I know all too well how to spot when you're hiding something. You laugh too loud, drink too much. And pile on the black mascara to make your lashes so thick and heavy no one can see the pain in your eyes.

We're about the same age; she's thinner than I am, though I'm keeping my weight down. I notice she walks with a slight limp. Why, I don't know. All she told me is that it gives her a distinctive 'walk' that sets her apart when she gets a modeling gig. She admitted Gertrud instructed her to start a row with me to stir things up, then the photographers showed up to take photos.

Which brings us back to the artist.

'Max can be a charmer, *mademoiselle*, and don't I know it,' she said, wrapping her copper penny hair around her finger as we walk. 'Don't get too close or you'll get burned.'

'Spill it, Hélène; what have you got on him?' I hated to be so blunt, but I have feelings for the man and have no intention of getting hurt again.

'He's not a carefree adventurer, but a man on a mission to right a wrong.'

A side of him I hadn't contemplated. 'Go on.'

'How he feels responsible for the death of a young woman. That's all I know and I got that from Gertrud.'

It all makes sense. Gertrud enlisted Max's help to spy on the duke, see if he had any new 'recruits'... innocent girls she could save from his clutches before he sprung his trap.

That's why he was at the Café de la Paix that day and drew the caricature of me.

Only I'm not so innocent.

Lie number three.

My turn. I told Max I was fresh out of high school when I got the gig with a show headed for Marseilles. I let him think I'm a Pennsylvania girl with small town roots.

I like it that way. No pretense, no expectation... and no, I'm not going to let myself fall in love with him. I've got too much to lose. Like my plans to expand our chocolate brand here in France... and help young mothers in need of support so they don't end up like me, forced to give up their babies. *And* saving young women who end up in the oldest profession because they have nowhere to go. It would serve the duke right if I built a summer house on *his* property for my venture.

That doesn't mean I'm not going to flirt with the wild Englishman, get back some of that 'deb spirit' I lost, not mire myself in loneliness. And maybe, *just maybe*, heal my soul. I healed my body, but I can't let go of that ache of losing a child.

Time will help, maybe...

We'll see.

* * *

Over the next few weeks, Max and I come to an agreement. I'll model for him, but with one request. All I ask is that he draws me with different hair, eyes, mouth.

'Why?' he asked. 'What are you running away from?'

I told him my 'Auntie' back home would never approve of me being an artist's model, and since she sends me money every month so I can study French to become a teacher, I want to keep my face out of the newspapers. To my surprise, he agrees.

Yes, I give in.

I pose for him numerous times, his pencil and pen rendering me in his caricatures depicting life in Paris. Strong black lines that say so much with a sweep and a flourish. A slice of life with a twist and a nod. From a dancer at the *Moulin Rouge* to a flower seller to a shop girl.

He's under my skin and I like it. We spend time together in spite of my misgivings about getting involved again. Our arrangement allows me to take baby steps... a way of testing the water before I jump in. Because that water is hot and sizzling. I cannot and will not get burned. Still, my poor aching heart beats faster when I'm near him, yet begs me to walk away and not get involved with a man again. The sad echo of my own voice resounds in my head. Over and over.

Will it ever go away? Or is this my punishment for acting young and stupid to get back at Mother for her hurtful words?

It doesn't change my attraction to him. The man is intense, especially when he's sketching me. I soon discover he's more than a fascinating artist. He flies airplanes and hates Nazis. Why he does either, I don't know... yet... but needless to say, I contact Uncle Archibald when Max lets it slip he's wary of the German Chancellor's recent move into the Rhineland and intends to find out why.

Especially after he flew a client over the French border.

Not your usual café gossip, but we get into a conversation on a rainy afternoon at the Café de la Paix while he's showing me his sketches of Parisian jazz musicians and how the Nazis banned jazz on the radio.

My antennae go up. Here is the perfect excuse to scratch my itch for the Englishman and combine spy business with pleasure. Convince Max to show me firsthand what he observed at the French border. I'm intrigued by what he saw (isn't this what Uncle Archibald asked me to 'observe'?), so I convince him to take me along on his reconnaissance mission. Why not? I'm just another curious tourist who wants to see France from the seat of a biplane. My uncle is leery of me pursuing the lead on my own (we exchange frantic telegrams back and forth), but I convince him Max is a proper British gentleman with royal connections (not true, but he goes for it). I got myself into this spying business and I'm going through with it.

Even if I hate flying.

23

PARIS, NOVEMBER 1936

Kay

With a passionate stirring in my belly for a man I still don't trust, I look down below from the cockpit of a Beechcraft 17 biplane. I see the wide expanse of green forests and then a patchwork quilt of cultivated land. I tear my gaze away from the incredible scenery down below to Max, his hands working the instruments, his attention focused on flying the plane. And grabbing glances out the window. What's he looking for? Whatever it is, it's a needle *not* in a haystack but hidden in a forest of late afternoon green and purplish hues. A thin layer of fog filters the scene with a smokiness that adds to its romanticism.

The small plane dips lower then rolls from side to side.

Oh, I feel sick...

I fold my arms over my stomach, trying not to retch. Not how I planned to spend my date with the handsome man in the pilot's seat next to me.

We took off from Le Bourget Airport outside Paris and the reality of what I'm doing hits home. If Max is right, I'm about to spot my first... and hopefully last... Nazi.

I'm no professional secret operative, but here's what I know.

The facts:

Hitler violated the Versailles Treaty when he occupied the Rhineland back in March with a lot of fanfare. A maneuver that ruffled the plume feathers of France and her Allies, but they did nothing to stop him, according to the man at the controls.

And now the *why*:

Why I'm risking life and limb up here in the clouds, a woman who as a kid had a hard time climbing up the chocolate vat ladder because I'm afraid of heights (my knees wobble every time I put on a pair of high-heeled pumps). According to Max, there's suspicious 'movement' along the border... The Germans are up to something and he's going up for another look. Something about '*I need to make sure before I volunteer*.'

Volunteer for what? What's he up to?

He told me he had a last-minute fare and ferried a client from Paris to Belgium. On the way back to Le Bourget Airport, he noticed unusual ground movement along the border. Officers in Nazi uniforms as well as men wearing topcoats and hats setting up surveying equipment. That intriguing information piqued my interest, though I didn't tell him why, merely that I find this political talk tedious and wouldn't it be fun if he took me up in his plane for a ride? Showed me the sights?

I never mentioned I'm afraid of heights. I don't know what I was thinking, but I'd never forgive myself if I let this opportunity go by and I flubbed my spying job. And, I have to admit, I need to feel useful. I'm still hurting over Mother's barbs about me being a disappointment. So I flirted with this handsome pilot which, I admit, wasn't hard, staring into those smoldering eyes and wiggling my shoulders to get him to take me along.

He eyed me with skepticism, but he agreed.

I wonder, does he think I'm a German spy and trying to trap him? Wouldn't *that* be amusing?

My pulse quickens when he tells me to hold on, his voice low and husky as he banks the plane right, executing a fancy dip of the wing. Then he pulls up the aircraft and we ascend like an eagle soaring, making me nearly lose my breakfast.

Oh, God, why am I doing this? I grip the seat, snagging a nail, but the moment – and the man – are exhilarating.

Rain drizzles on the windshield of *Nellie Blue*, his nickname for the Beechcraft 17, making the windowpane appear liquid. My head swivels around to see as much as I can. I want to close my eyes and pretend we're on the ground, but I can't. I don't want to miss my first look at the Nazis. Frothy angel clouds drift by and when I peek through them, the sweep of the landscape takes me to a place of wonder. I never dreamed I'd be 5,000 feet up in the air with a daring British adventurer.

I had a deb moment when I boarded the silver-blue aircraft that elicited a whistle from him. I pulled up my dress and revealed my legs as I stepped up from the ground to the low wing and then into the cockpit.

I gave him 'that look'.

The look he gave *me* back set my thoughts on a new course I haven't dared to follow since I was involved with... I can't bear to utter his name so I don't. I convince myself I'm smarter now... wiser. However dangerous my thoughts may be, I'd never let Max know I shivered from the touch of his hands on my waist when he hoisted me up on the lower wing. The pilot entered first, but it was obvious I couldn't get on board in a tight dress and heels by myself, so we maneuvered our way inside the cabin at odd angles.

I took my camera out of my coat pocket and stuffed it, along with my clutch, under my seat, pretending to ignore the moment of closeness between us, commenting instead on my shoes slipping on the wing... I saw a spark in his eye.

No, I tell myself, *keep your mind on business*, an opportunity to do the spying job Uncle Archibald asked me to do. Max owes it to me after that stunt he and Gertrud pulled at the Paris nightclub and I ended up getting dunked in the bathing pool.

Dark clouds hover in the sky, giving us cover as Max rolls the aircraft to the left to get a better view of what's below. More woods... farmhouses. He gives me a headset so I can hear him, otherwise it's impossible to carry on a conversation. The metal siding rattles, it's hard to breathe up here, and it's cold in the small plane, making me grateful for my fur-lined coat.

I shift my weight, crossing my legs. Max eyes me suspiciously when my coat falls open revealing the soft, mahogany mink lining.

Embarrassed, I uncross my legs, close my coat. 'It gets cold backstage in winter... ask any chorus girl.'

'You did well for yourself,' he says wryly, raising a brow.

'It was a gift,' is all I say, trying for indifference. I don't want him probing into my past so I said the first thing that came to mind. Now I wish I hadn't. I don't like the way he looks at me.

'You surprise me.'

'I do?' I attempt a smile.

'You don't strike me as the type to accept expensive gifts from men.'

I purse my lips, as there's no easy answer to that, but I'm not prepared for his next words.

'So you must be a thief.'

'Me? A thief?' I take up his challenge. 'You'd never believe the truth.'

He shoots me a bold look. 'Try me.'

His cocky stare makes me uneasy. My cover story is as fragile as an eggshell, cracking a little more with each lie, but my pride won't allow me to let him think the worst of me. I can't tell him the truth, so I come up with the same story I told the landlady in South Philly... but with more drama.

'I worked in a big mansion back home and "saw" too much when I ran into my married employer meeting her lover at a hotel,' I tell him with a straight face. 'Rather than fire me, she paid for my silence with her mink-lined coat and an introduction to a Broadway producer who gave me a job and well, you know the rest.'

Max's retort is not what I expect, his hands gripping the steering wheel. 'That doesn't surprise me. The elite are different from us and play by different rules. In the end, innocent girls like you pay the price.'

I gather he's not fond of rich girls. Which puts a wrinkle in my bonnet. Did a blonde wearing a diamond choker ruffle his feathers? I have no choice but to stick to my out-of-work hoofer story.

You see, I like him. A lot.

He doesn't ask me any more questions, but I don't think he believes me either. Then again, I don't believe he's telling me the whole story when I ask him where he's from.

'I grew up in Northern England near the seaside town of Blackpool.'

'Where did you learn to fly?' I ask. It's my turn to throw the punches.

'I was a kid when I sat in my first plane, dreaming about flying... I got my first job when I was sixteen in a circus as a daredevil pilot and raced planes when I wasn't doing air stunts.'

Then he clams up. He leaves out a lot, like family. Which makes me wonder what he's hiding... A wife? Children? It would pain me to think he's cheating on them, but he hasn't kissed me so it's unfair of me to make that call.

Also, how he can afford what he calls his *Staggerwing* biplane?

I know nothing about aircraft, but the five-seater is well appointed with soft mohair and rich brown leather. There's even a door leading to the baggage compartment. And boy, is this airship fast. From what I see on the instrument panel, we're cruising at over two hundred miles an hour.

Heading for the French border.

And finally, lie number four. This one's on him, too.

He's not flying me here because he wants to show me *la belle France* from the air. I'm his cover story. His insurance in case the Nazis get nosy if we get too close to whatever they're up to and they start shooting at us and we have to land.

Is he kidding about them trying to take down the aircraft?

'If anyone asks,' he says, banking again, steeper this time, the wing tip pointing to a farmhouse and barn with stacks of hay. It's the only structure within miles. 'We eloped and we're on our way to Switzerland for our honeymoon.'

His stories are as good as mine.

Which is why I don't trust him.

I ask him if he's a spy, calling the kettle black, but a good offensive is best. I learned that from Mother. He laughs and tells me *no*.

'If I were a spy, I'd have a better cover story than a broken-down flyer drawing pictures of pretty girls in Paris.' He laughs. 'But I'll let you in on a secret.'

'I'm all ears.'

'I'm heading to Spain to join the fight and fly for the Republican air service.'

All of a sudden, I forget I'm in an airplane. My heart is racing. This is crazy. I'm determined to set my life straight and he's risking his... for what? Thrills, adventure? I've heard about Americans and British flocking to Spain to fight Franco, some with romantic notions about war, others, pilots like Max, for the money. God, he could get killed. Why is that thought making me want to grab him and shake some sense into him?

You're not getting involved, remember?

'Why take up a fight that isn't yours?' I ask, struggling to keep my voice calm. I'm anything but that as he eases up on the controls and takes the aircraft down in a steep roll and my stomach with it.

He clenches his teeth. 'I don't like bullies, especially Nazis.'

He leaves the rest unsaid.

I was wrong about him flying for the money. Which makes me even more curious... and scared for him. I know how emotion can cloud your judgment.

'I don't get the Nazi connection,' I probe him for more information. For Uncle Archie, of course.

'I'd bet *Nellie Blue* Hitler is behind Franco and supplying munitions and aircraft to the Nationalists,' he says, picking up speed as we emerge from a cloud, 'and he's using the fight in Spain as a testing ground for something bigger. I want to see for myself what kind of air power he's got. It'll be useful information if he decides to tramp his jackboots all over Europe.'

I cock a brow. 'He wouldn't dare do that, would he?'

He snickers. 'You haven't seen "der Fuehrer" in action, how he's rallied hundreds of thousands of Germans into believing his preposterous ideas about a super race. I saw it with my own eyes when I ferried Gertrud to Nuremberg last year. I'll never forget it. Nighttime torches burning, battalions of soldiers marching... men and women raising their arms in a salute and shouting "*Sieg Heil*"... cheering him on till their voices gave out.'

I ponder his words. If the Germans *are* backing Franco and playing war games, then what Uncle Archibald insinuated isn't idle gossip. I feel an odd premonition coming on, a whisper in my mind that I can't quite put my finger on, but it's there. I don't want to believe Hitler is a threat to Europe, certainly not to America, but Max's words frighten me.

'I hate to tell you, Max,' I say lightly to break the tension, 'but Spain is in the opposite direction.'

He laughs and dips the plane, following a wide stream winding through the grassland. I hold on to my seat. I'm still reeling from that last maneuver. 'Hang tight; we're crossing over the border into Germany near Karlsruhe.'

'I thought you said Switzerland?'

'That's our story... That and my instruments aren't working properly and put us way off course if anyone questions us later.'

Why would he say that?

I don't have time to ponder that thought when Max executes a fancy stunt, flying low as we come around a high grassy knoll to get a better look at the field covered with high yellow-brown grass.

My jaw drops. I can't believe what I'm seeing.

Trucks, black touring motorcars parked in a row. Lumber piled up in stacks. Laborers pounding posts into the ground with huge hammers. Men in plainclothes along with Nazi officers wearing uniforms with swastika armbands, surveying the land. Tripods fixed with equipment. Tall wooden posts hammered into the ground and spread out in every direction, marking off patches of land.

Max executes a flyby over the group and the loud roar of his powerful motor sets off a barrage of shouts and yells. He cranks open his plate glass window and leans out and waves at them. '*Damn*, there's a whole Nazi crew down there walking around like they're gods.'

'But why? What are they doing?' I ask, getting an eyeful.

'I'm guessing they're building a defense line and erecting obstacles to use for observation.'

Or machine guns, he adds dryly.

My throat tightens. Machine guns? What if the German troops get antsy and cross the border? That doesn't bode well for the French. Or the rest of Europe if Hitler seeks to land grab more territory than the Rhineland.

I also see the glint of the sun striking off the officers' weapons. I crank down the plate glass side window and hang my head out, a dumb move but I want to look closer. Oh, God help us, I see—

Firearms pointed straight up at us.

Max grips the control stick, pulling up fast, sweat beading on his forehead. 'Hold on, Kay, we're going to circle the open field so I can double check the coordinates.'

'I'll take a picture with my camera—'

'*No.* If we're caught, you'll be shot as a spy.'

'*What?*'

Well, I didn't see *that* coming.

My hand shaking, I grab my chest, daring to look out the window at the picture I *didn't* get, trying to memorize every detail... Five, six Nazis, several men in topcoats, hats... I count how many wooden posts I see stuck in the ground... tiny Nazi flags waving from the posts in the breeze... and did I see a Nazi officer give the Hitler salute to a wooden post?

I turn my head to grab my clutch to make notes when a loud *zing* whistles in my ear... Was that... a bullet? *Was it?* The stark reality hits me when *another* bullet strafes the right wing—

My God, they're shooting at us.

I pull back away from the window. I'll never forget the loud pinging sound as the bullet hit the metal. Sheer terror grips me. My heart is in my throat. I didn't sign up for this, but it's too late now. I can see the newspapers back home.

Debutante of 1934 lost on secret mission over France.

No, the State Department would hush it up. The headline would read:

Debutante of 1934 lost in a storm over France.

And no one, not even Mother, would know the truth. Why does that bother me so? Because, even now, I want her to be proud of me?

No, I'm not checking out so she can dismiss me *that* easily.

'*Max!*' I yell out, choking on my own saliva. 'What can I do to help?'

'*Get down, Kay, now!*'

Before I can tuck my head between my legs, Max maneuvers the aircraft so it dips wildly to one side, down... then up... He pulls back on the throttle to decrease speed and the engine misfires and chokes as he moves it forward again. I'm whipped around with such force I feel like my head is on a swivel, jerking my neck.

I scream.

'Are you hit, Kay...?'

I struggle to answer, but my chest is so tight—

'*Dammit, answer me!*'

'*Oh...* I don't think so,' I get the words out in short breaths, choking. I do a quick check. No blood, but my pulse is racing so fast I feel as though I'm going to explode.

'Put your parachute on,' Max orders, his tone grim. He's working the stick to get the aircraft under control, putting his shoulders into it, all his skills coming into play to keep us in the air. 'It's under your seat.'

'*What?*'

'I said, *put it on.*'

'What about you?' I ask, pulling out the chute.

'I don't need it.'

'Oh, I get it. You want to get rid of me.'

A sudden drop in his voice ushers in a new fear in me, that he has something to say but does so with reluctance. 'If I said no, would you believe me?'

I become quiet at his sudden admission that I'm not just the girl in his sketches... something I can't process. Because then I'll have to admit I'm falling hard again for a man and that scares me.

With shaking fingers, I pull the straps of the parachute over the shoulders of my bulky, fur-lined coat. I tighten them but I'm not jumping out of this aircraft, not because I'm terrified of dropping like a dead pigeon, but because I trust him to land this plane. And I want to be with him. I'm getting attached to this man... and I like it. Something I never thought I'd feel again.

I force my breathing to slow, and act calm even if I'm not. 'I'm not jumping. I don't want to get my coat dirty.'

You're making jokes at a time like this? Or is it to hide your feelings so you don't get hurt again?

'Whoever gave you that coat is a lucky man,' he says in a low, husky voice, gripping the control stick tight and pulling it aft. We ascend into the clouds fast and hard at over fifteen hundred feet per minute, he says, away from the mad scramble of Nazis below.

So he didn't believe my story about the coat after all. *Men*. He's jealous, is he? Which puts me in a quandary. I can't tell him I bought this coat for my eighteenth birthday, or rather I charged it to Mother's account at an exclusive Philadelphia furrier. So I say nothing. I squirm in my seat, digging my nails into the leather. This is not the fun flying trip I imagined, looking for Nazis for Uncle Archie but doubting I'd find any. I envisioned myself flirting with my mad adventurer with the talented pencil and... and then what?

I bury that chance of him trusting me with every lie I tell him. Maybe if I told him the truth... no, Mother would never approve of a man like Max. Too wild, unstable... and too dangerous. He's too tempting, that cocky smile seducing a woman to abandon any propriety she has left.

So I stay quiet, yet a naughtier side of me reminds me my mother is three thousand miles away. Why do I feel she's watching me?

Because Mother is the excuse you need not to let yourself feel again, to want a man...

God, I'm heading into a free fall up here in the clouds, getting lightheaded... not thinking straight. Yes, that's it. The air is misty and a light rain covers the windshield. I feel my cheeks. Cold. My fingers, too. I start shivering even in my fur-lined coat. Silence fills the cockpit. My heart pounds and I pray we don't hear the motor of another aircraft coming after us. We're cruising at 8,000 feet and it's getting colder in here.

Max checks his instruments, says we're low on fuel. He's going to land the plane near the farmhouse we saw earlier... get help. He warns me because of the low visibility, we'll be flying blind, making it difficult to know the proximity of the ground.

'There's still time for you to bail out, *mademoiselle.*'

Back to the formalities, are we?

I squeeze my eyes tight. Terror at the thought of flapping my wings like an ostrich chills me. Ostriches don't fly and neither do I.

'I'm staying right here.' I cross my arms. 'With you.'

He nods, and is that a smile I see curve over his lips? 'You don't give a man much choice, do you?'

'No.'

Satisfied he's stuck with me, he works the controls, keeping the aircraft steady and his eyes straight ahead. 'With this low hanging fog, I can't see a thing... We're flying on instinct and instruments, but from my calculations we should be over the target area. *Hold on.*'

He banks the biplane right and we emerge from the clouds so close to the ground I swear I see grass growing.

I brace myself for a hard landing, holding on tight to anything I can grab. I wish I could grab on to him and that ambitious thought costs me. The last thing I remember is seeing the farmhouse dead ahead... Behind it, haystacks.

Max pulls back on the control stick hard and we barely clear the house... then he brings the biplane down on the ground as visibility improves and I see the field ahead and those haystacks again... brakes squealing, wheels spinning... *but we're not decreasing speed...* My God, *we've got to stop... How?*

Then I hear a loud *pop.* Did we blow a tire? The biplane spins around in a circle.

Max works feverishly to bring *Nellie Blue* under control... Round and round we go until the aircraft slams into a haystack and an explosion of spindly, dried grass smacks against the windshield.

I scream and jerk forward... hitting my head on the instrument panel. Oh, the burning pain above my left temple... sharp, then I fall back as we come to a dead stop. Already I feel the swelling under my fingertips when I touch my head, along with a tumultuous ringing in my ears that shuts out everything... except a strong male voice yelling, *Don't you dare die on me,* ma chérie... *hang on... I can't lose you, too.*

I ignore the warning going off in my aching head, the heat warming my cheeks when he holds me close to him. I can barely breathe.

He called me *ma chèrie.*

Then a lovely, soothing darkness washes over me, as though my body is turning into liquid chocolate, smooth and silky and flowing along a path that never ends but goes on and on along a winding road that leads to... *where?*

I don't know.

And then mercifully, I pass out.

But the dream doesn't end because I don't want it to... because then I'd have to face reality and that will bring back the pain. Of falling in love with a man and knowing I can never be a mother, give him children. No man will ever want me. So I make a pact with my unconscious self. That I won't let him make love to me... that it wouldn't be good for either of us.

If only I believed it.

24

PARIS, NOVEMBER 1936

Kay

'Is *madame* dead?' I hear a man say in French with a guttural German accent.

'No, but she's got a nasty bump on her head.'

Max.

My heart skips, a fierce jackhammer pounding in my ears. I fight not to lapse into unconsciousness again. No chance of that. Odiferous, smoky cooking smells fill my nostrils, overwhelming my senses along with the raw, addicting odor of tobacco leaves hanging over my head and the suffocating stench of—

Pigs.

Pigs?

Snorting, grunting, doing what pigs do, pushing out all semblance of normalcy in a world so unfamiliar to me I can't grasp it. I can't believe we're safe inside a farmhouse that dates back a hundred years. I'm grateful to the elderly German couple who didn't attack us with pitchforks. I was barely conscious as Max held me in his arms and banged on their front door wide enough for a cow, asking for help in French. Especially after the Beechcraft barreled through their haystacks. Thank God there was no damage to the aircraft except for bullet holes in the wing. The best news is: the hay scattered everywhere with piles of it hiding the biplane from any German aircraft searching for us.

I'm not surprised the farmer speaks French, living on the border. He clears his throat, hesitates, then: 'She's your wife, *monsieur*?'

'Yes. We eloped and got married in Switzerland to get away from her abusive stepfather.' To make his point, Max spits on the oak floor. 'The man is a beast.'

I don't believe I'm hearing this.

'Oh, how exciting... a new bride.' His wife claps her hands together, then sighs. Her heartfelt enthusiasm makes me feel guilty I'm *not* a bride.

'You must take our sleeping room, *monsieur*,' says the farmer, giving Max a knowing look that elicits a smile from the pilot. A smile that gets my stomach doing flip flops.

'Yes, please.' His wife giggles, then leads us to the room, leaving a tall, lit candle on a small table. 'I will bring you wine and bread and sausages... and foot warmers.'

The farmer shakes his head. 'They don't need foot warmers, *Mama*, they have each other to keep them warm.'

'*Ja, Papa*,' she lapses into German, then laughter and whispers as I hear them scuffle away.

I groan. The raw sounds coming from my throat are nothing compared to the jittery nerves racing through me.

They have each other to keep them warm.

What have I gotten myself into?

My head and body ache so I can't move and I'm alone with a

man who just announced I'm his bride. The lonely woman in me is secretly excited by this predicament.

What I *don't* expect from this adventurer is a paternal move when he gathers me in his arms and cradles me like a child. A warm feeling surges through me; it feels so wonderful to be held, touched by someone who cares about *me*. I hadn't realized how starved I am for such a simple human gesture. I'll cherish this moment for a long time.

We're lying side by side in what appears to be a bed though it's much shorter than what I'm used to (German farmers follow the old tradition and don't lie down flat, Max explains, though how he knows this I'm afraid to ask) with four, no, five pillows to lean against and a big, fluffy feather comforter.

'You had me worried, Kay,' he says with a huskiness in his voice as he cups my face in his hand. It's a sentimental gesture; the deepening lines around his dark eyes speak of worry, not lust.

Oh...

No one's ever worried about me before and I don't know how to react. So I shoot back a sarcastic comeback as a way of protecting my fragile ego.

'Worried about me dying,' I ask, 'or telling them we're *not* married?'

He looks at me curiously, dark hair falling over one eye, hiding that scar I've grown to love. I'm still waiting to hear the story of where he got it. 'I had to tell them something so they'd hide us if the Nazis come looking for us.'

'You think the Nazis would stoop so low as to harm an innocent farmer and his wife?'

'No one is safe in Germany. We're just over the border and from what we saw earlier, the Nazis are up to something. I wouldn't put it past them to go after *anyone* they see as a threat, including us.' He covers me with the comforter stitched together with blue and red and yellow squares. 'Now get some rest. I won't take advantage of you... I promise.'

I didn't realize how much I wanted him to touch me till our bodies made contact. Now I don't want to give up his warmth. His hard muscular chest is a perfect place to cradle my aching head while the rest of me is reacting in a manner that scares me more than the Nazis. I sigh with pent-up desire when he wets a cloth in the white porcelain basin the farmer's wife set down and places it on my forehead, the tips of his fingers brushing my hot cheeks. His scent, his pure masculinity, overwhelm me. I moan. The pain is still there: both the pounding in my head and the ache in my heart.

'How do I know you won't fly off without me?' I challenge him, eyes blazing.

'You don't.' He grins. 'You're beautiful when you're angry, Kay... I should draw you.'

He leans down closer to me and the only thing between us is the wet cloth on my forehead. I lift my head and it slides off and falls onto the floor. I don't make a move to pick it up, neither does he. Instead, he brushes my lips with that mouth of his I've been dying to touch since that first day at the Café de la Paix, then pulls back, groaning.

'Lost your sketchpad... or your nerve?' I whisper, getting flippant because otherwise he'll kiss me or I'll kiss him. Either way, I'm screwed. He makes me want something I can't have. A man of my own who will love me for me, not my money, because, as Mother is apt to remind me, I'm soiled goods.

But not to this man, not at this moment. He sees something in me I don't see in myself and that fascinates me. That I'm not the castoff debutante destined to wear black.

'Draw me as Alice with a bump on her head after she falls down the rabbit hole.'

After falling for you, my handsome pilot.

'I have a better idea... I'll draw you as a sleeping princess awakened with a kiss,' he says, as he grips me by the shoulders and stares deep into my eyes. For a moment I see more of the man, not the mysterious adventurer I'm falling for. A man hurt... like I was. A man hesitant to fall in love again, yet I know he wants to.

I make it easier for him... for both of us.

'I can't, Max—'

'There's someone else.' He wipes the tears falling down my cheeks with his thumb. 'Like I said, Kay, he's a lucky man.'

'No, there's no one else... There was,' I stutter, 'but he used me. I thought I was in love and he... well, he wanted... sex.'

I can't tell him Miss Hathaway paid him to flatter me, seduce me. Again, I'm caught in a lie.

I'm hesitant to continue, but I've kept it in for so long I can't stop.

'There was a child, my baby... a little girl. A sweet innocent who came into this world on Christmas Day and left before she could take more than a few breaths, as if the angels were eager to have her in their midst. I don't understand why they took her, but a wise sister of the cloth told me God had a reason and someday I'd know what that is, that I must draw upon my inner strength till then. I try, Max, really I do,' I stammer, my eyes burning. 'But the pain gets so bad my body contorts into a symphony of hurt I can't control. Like I've turned into a gnarled tree that can no longer bend in the wind. A tree without blossoms. Dried up with cracked bark that peels off more each day until all that's left is raw pulp. A being without feeling. Without purpose. I never understood what it meant to have a broken heart till I lost my baby.' I take a moment, pull myself together, and then look him straight in the eye. 'Then I met you and—'

He pulls me so tightly to his chest I can't breathe. He breathes out my name over and over. 'You're an amazing woman, Kay, so filled with feeling and love, any man would want you in his arms... to make you his. But your wounds are still fresh, your heart too vulnerable. Your soul is not in its proper place, but wandering. Like mine. We're both caught up in our pasts.' He strokes my cheek, then smiles. 'As much as I want you, Kay, the stars are not aligned for us... not tonight.'

He blows out the candle, then holds me tight in his arms in the pitch-black darkness, the farmhouse and its inhabitants settling down... I hear snoring from the farmer and his wife, an occasional grunt from a pig, a cow shuffling its hooves in its stall. And this man and woman spooning in a century-old bed, our bodies so close together we're as one, but still separated because it has to be. He's hurting, too.

One thing keeps going through my mind.

I told him my story, but only part of it. I don't feel strong enough to tell him everything. Who I am... that I'm an heiress to a candy fortune. That I believe it's my duty to use my fortune to help others, that until I met him, I thought I was destined to be the shadowy figure in the background wielding power but never knowing love.

I'm certain he doesn't know. Nobody in Paris is aware of my identity.

And I damn well intend to keep it that way.

For both our sakes.

25

BERLIN, MARCH 1937

Rachel

I am no better than the dirt under Frau Bessler's feet.

She makes that point loud and clear when I push open the creaking door to Mutti's favorite dress and intimates shop and the woman sweeps me back onto the pavement with her large, spindly broom. Sharp bristles scratch my legs, making me wince.

'*Go away, Fräulein.* Jews aren't wanted here.'

She points to a poster in the window.

Where did that come from?

'But, Frau Bessler, my mother has shopped here for years.'

Mutti loves chatting with the owner, Frau Walter, a lovely Jewish woman from Munich, and seeing the latest modes in undergarments from Paris.

Strange... This woman works for her.

I peer inside through the half-opened door, but I don't see Frau Walter. I ask where she is, but the woman scowls, then spits at me.

Her saliva lands on the sidewalk, but her message is clear. She has me pinned as a nuisance and orders me to leave. Again.

'*I* own the shop now, *Fräulein*.' She chuckles. 'And you're not wanted. *Geh weg, schnell!*'

I draw back, unsure what to do next. I came here hoping to ask Frau Walter for advice about how to sew a brassiere for myself. I made a not-very-good one from old stockings with two buttons fastening in the back, but Mutti gave me extra white cotton she has for mending and several spools of thread. Then she sent me to see Frau Walter, a kind woman known for her strudel, a favorite of her husband, Karl, a professor at the university. She also makes delicious Challah, Jewish braided bread, but Mutti said she stopped bringing it to the shop as a treat for customers after someone complained.

Is there no end to the torment?

Crazy thoughts, but life is only getting more difficult with the race laws dictating who is German and who isn't. If you have two or three Jewish grandparents, then you're a full Jew.

What's a half Jew? I wonder. And which half is Jewish? The top or the bottom? It's confusing. More disturbing is what we hear from the neighbors about the Nazis building 'concentration camps' to house anyone who commits a criminal offense.

A disturbing thought tickles my brain...

Frau Walter's husband is Catholic and they enjoy what the Nazis call a 'privileged' mixed marriage because the man is Aryan, but I heard rumors Herr Walter is far from subtle in his lectures about his distaste for Hitler's government and the race laws.

I have a horrible jarring feeling I can't shake.

Something's wrong.

'Where is Frau Walter?' I ask; a subtle fear makes me shiver.

'How would I know?' She slams the door in my face.

I turn to go, shuffling my feet. Mutti will be so sad to hear what happened... and worried. She'd want me to pay Frau Walter a visit and check on her.

I head to a fancier neighborhood where the trams buzz along the electric wire overhead and Nazi flags fly from shops and apartments. Mutti sent me here with her homemade chicken soup when Frau Walter was sick with an awful cold. I enter the building through a door with a glass windowpane, then into the foyer and turn right, find her apartment... number three... then knock on the door several times. I twist my head from side to side, noting her ground floor apartment looks odd and out of sorts. There are dead plants in pots outside her door and a deathly stillness that frightens me.

I sniff. More disturbing; no heavenly smell of apples and cinnamon or egg bread baking coming from her place.

Where is she?

Something's not right. I feel it in my bones... I knock again, *louder*, and put my hand on the door lever and shake it.

'Open up, *please*, it's Rachel, Frau Landau's daughter.'

My mother is good and kind and has that special quality people react to even when their hearts are heavy. It's that magic that induces the woman to unlock her door.

I gasp.

Her short dark hair is damp with sweat and pasted over her pale cheeks; her dark eyes are ringed with black; her lips are tinted blue.

She clenches her fist to her chest, clutching a letter in her hand. 'Rachel, dear child...' Her voice cracks. 'What are you doing here?'

'I went to your shop and... my God, Frau Walter, you look terribly ill. Let me help you.'

She shakes her head and heaves out a deep breath. 'It's Karl.'

'What happened?' I ask. The most awful thoughts swim in my mind, the fierceness in her eyes preparing me for the worst.

'The Gestapo arrested him and sent him to a labor camp two weeks ago.'

Then every thought I had materializes into a grotesque imagining of what the Nazis did to him that has shattered this woman into pieces.

'My Karl... *he's dead.*'

She falls into my arms, sobbing. My knees wobble and I drop my package, but I must be strong. I help her back inside her apartment and she collapses on a plain gray settee in the parlor, shoulders shaking, tears streaming down her face. She keeps muttering about her dear, wonderful husband, moaning with cries of pain that only a loved one knows... and how she's coming to him soon...

It's then I smell gas.

26

PARIS, MARCH 1937

Kay

Today is the day I've dreaded for weeks.

Max races around Paris getting his papers in order to leave for Spain along with his gear – is that a pistol I see in his belt? – and nothing I say can stop him. After what we saw at the French border, he's more determined than ever to get a front row seat at what he calls 'Hitler's warm-up party'.

I don't agree.

The German chancellor wouldn't be that stupid to rile up the French after the losses they suffered in the Great War.

Would he?

I keep my thoughts to myself. One thing I learned from my uncle Archibald: never come between a man and his politics. You always lose.

That's the last thing I want.

And I want Max. We spend days... then weeks in the 'getting to know you' stage. That blissful innocence about each other you carry in your heart that's like dew on a rose. It makes everything seem so fresh, alive. So perfect.

You glide along on a dream, not wanting to wake up. Observing, learning... teasing. And oh, the places we've been to in this romantic city. From riding the hydraulic elevators in the Eiffel Tower to hopping on the carousel nearby with its fairy-tale carriages, we're like two kids playing hooky from life.

Because we are.

Me... finding out who I am with Max at my side.

Him... keeping his secrets.

Taking me up in his plane and doing loops and scaring the life out of me but only, he says, to help me get over my fear of flying.

And of life, he says.

Is it that obvious?

What makes my heart skip madly is cuddling up to this wildly virile man and talking for hours. About art, French cinema... jazz. His bold personality borders on cavalier, protecting me from itinerant raindrops with his coat wrapped around me, or a crass comment from a man on the boulevards. (I'm still not used to the brash openness Frenchmen show an attractive woman.)

I find myself acting like a schoolgirl around him, giggling and being silly, then he grabs his sketchpad and draws me, saying he wants to capture my playful mood. Like a painter capturing sunrise because that's how he sees me. A burst of color that floods his world after so much darkness.

That touches me deeply because when I feel his hands on me, holding me, it's like sunshine on my face. Warm and strong. My insides shimmy with a familiar dance when we're together and the sparkle in his eyes tells me nothing matters but the time we have together.

A sudden sadness ripples under my skin. Paris won't be any fun without him. I've never felt more connected to anyone. It's what sustains me on this last night before he leaves for Spain. Walking along the Seine, we ignore the cold breeze coming off the flowing river. The heat of our bodies keeps us warm, not to mention the slow burn simmering below the surface.

We're not lovers... not yet.

Max doesn't push me. His next words confirm why. Holding me tight to him, he says in a grave tone, 'If I'm right about the Nazis, Kay, I fear for the future of France... then God help us all. That's why I have to go, why I don't make love to you. I don't want to hurt you.' He pauses. 'If I come back...'

I put my fingers to his lips. '*When* you come back...'

I refuse to contemplate anything else.

He smiles. 'When I come back, I hope you'll be waiting for me.'

'I'm not going anywhere... I promise.'

We stop along the quay and, in a long desperate moment to seal what we have in a kiss, Max cups my face in his hands and brings his mouth down on mine, capturing my heart forever in the heat of that kiss. I'll never forget it.

Then in the morning, he's gone.

And life in Paris goes on, but it's different somehow. The things I took for granted back home that are nonexistent here don't bother me any more... like water that merely dribbles out of the faucet when I'm brushing my teeth... or finding a good shoe repair shop... or the ancient telephone in my Left Bank hotel that hangs on a cord from a hook on a wall.

I breeze through it all with a smile... because I've fallen in love.

And as the French say, *c'est magnifique*.

27

BERLIN, MARCH 1937

Rachel

Frau Walter intended to gas herself.

She isn't the first Jewish woman to try to commit suicide rather than be subjected to Nazi cruelty. Some leave notes for their families, while others 'submerge' or go into hiding in plain sight. I've heard the whispers from the parents of Papa's Jewish students as they wait in the shop for their child's music lesson to end, sucking on a butterscotch while Mutti reads their lips.

But here I can do something to stop it.

Holding my coat sleeve to my nose, I turn off the gas on the stove, then open all the windows and let the fresh, cold air inside.

Then Frau Walter begins to talk.

'They sent Karl to work at a labor camp, a prison for political prisoners,' she explains, her face taking on a pinkish hue. She didn't protest when I foiled her plan. I don't think she wanted to end her life, but she was in so much emotional pain, she didn't see a way out. 'A place called Buchenwald.' She heaves out a heavy sigh. 'I'm next.'

'But why? You've said nothing against Hitler.'

'No, but...' Her eyes crinkle up, get misty. 'You've been to my shop?'

'*Ja.*'

'Then you know Frau Bessler owns it now... The local police forced me to sign it over to her and when I asked her for recompense, she informed on me to the state secret police.' Her face crumbles. 'Then I received this.'

She shows me the letter crumpled up in her hand. I recognize the seal of the Gestapo and the Nazi swastika in the upper right corner, similar to what I saw on a letter Mutti and Papa received regarding the names of their employees. She hands me the letter telling her the apartment is no longer hers and she's to vacate immediately.

'Where will I go?' she cries. 'My sister hasn't spoken to me since I married outside the faith. And Karl's mother would be in danger if I ask her for help.'

I think a moment. 'You must leave Berlin and go to your sister in Munich.'

'I can't,' she sobs. 'She hates me.'

I put down my package of cotton and thread on the settee and take her cold hands in mine, then rub them to give her warmth... and courage. 'She'll help you. Whatever happened, she's still your sister and sisters stick together. Why, I'd do anything for Leah and Tovah... even die.'

My voice cracks, because I've put into words what I've always known. I get angry with them, tease them... even play tricks on them, but I adore my sisters. Like Papa says, together we're a harmony of notes coming together in a joyous melody. And nothing can break us.

Not even the Nazis.

Which gives me an idea.

'Come home with me, Frau Walter. Now.'

'What?' Her eyes widen.

'We'll hide you until you can go to your sister in Munich.' I should ask Mutti first, but there's no time. That letter sounds ominous.

'Hide me? Where?'

My brain scrambles... In our apartment upstairs? No. What if the local Polizei pay us a visit? They'll search our living quarters and find her. In the shop? No...

Then it hits me.

Mutti spends her time in her office upstairs in a room hidden by a large nineteenth-century *garderobe*, a wardrobe built back in the days of the Ring clubs when a gang used the shop as a front for their criminal activities. There she keeps the day's receipts in the old safe and balances the books.

It's perfect.

'I know a place, Frau Walter, where you'll be safe.'

She's not convinced. 'What will your parents say?'

'Mutti and Papa will never forgive me if I don't bring you home. Grab your handbag and pack a small bag... and nothing else.'

She nods, then grabs a photo sitting on the mantel. 'I must take the picture of Karl and me on our wedding day.'

'Hurry!' I hear the roar of a motorcar screeching to a halt outside. I jump up and peek through the door – *no one's there* – then sneak out into the foyer. What I see through the beveled glass pane on the door stops my heart. *The Gestapo.* I race back to her apartment. 'Climb out the back window into the alley. I'll stall them.'

'They'll arrest you.' She has her handbag slung over her arm, a hat askew on her head.

I shake my head. 'I have nothing to hide. *Now go!*'

She moves fast into the kitchen and I hear her cranking open the window. Will Mutti think I've lost my mind when I bring Frau Walter home?

I can't back out now. I grab my package of cotton and thread off the settee and then I see—

Oh, no, Frau Walter dropped her wedding photo. I snatch it up and stuff it into my wide jumper pocket, praying she escaped and is on her way. Our music shop is about a thirty-minute walk. They'll never think of looking for her there.

I race out into the hallway after I close the door behind me and head toward the foyer, praying I can slip out before—

A burly Gestapo man in a black trench coat and Fedora bursts through the front entrance. I'm moving so fast, I slam into him, dropping my package... Spools of thread fly everywhere. He crunches them under his big, heavy black shoes and glares at me.

'Do you live here, *Fräulein*?'

'*Nein*. I – I came to deliver a package to Frau Schmidt from the dry goods store,' I lie. Every building has a Frau Schmidt, *ja*? 'But she's not home.'

'A Jewish store?' he demands to know, his look evil and dismissive.

I lift my chin. 'No, Aryan.'

He grunts, dissatisfied he failed to find someone to harass. 'Pick up your mess and clear out, *schnell*!'

He shoves me out of the way, grabbing me by the shoulder with his big, ugly hand. A sharp pain ripples through me, but I refuse to let him see he hurt me. I pick up the spools of thread, but as I bend down, the photo falls out of my pocket. I gasp loudly, my hand going to my mouth. Before I can grab it, the secret policeman snatches it away from me. Smirking.

What's she hiding? I bet he's wondering.

He studies it a moment, snickers, then: 'Your parents?'

I nod. '*Ja*... Lovely couple, aren't they?'

'*Humph...*' is all he says. Again, he failed to find anything incriminating. Herr Walter isn't wearing a yarmulke in the wedding photo since he was a Catholic.

The Gestapo man hands me back the photo and I don't wait for a '*Heil Hitler!*' Instead, I move so fast out of there my long braids slap against my cheeks. I run all the way home. There, I find Mutti consoling a distraught Frau Walter, thinking she got me into trouble. I give her the wedding photo I stuffed into my jumper pocket and she cries out with joy. I make no mention of my run-in with the Gestapo.

Why worry my mother?

We keep Frau Walter hidden in Mutti's secret office upstairs for several days until her friends can make plans for her to go to Munich. She gets word to us that her sister sobbed when she saw her, then hugged her. I was right. Sisters stick together, no matter what.

And the Gestapo man?

The way he looked at me still gives me nightmares. Crossed brows, bloodshot eyes I could see deep into, cruel and without feeling or mercy. He terrifies me. A creature of the devil.

I pray to God I never see him again.

28

PARIS, AUGUST 1937

Kay

Who would imagine a year-old Paris newspaper threatens to end my freedom?

Thanks to Mother's French-speaking snoopy rival Mrs Shupe, her reach extends across the Atlantic. The same day she sees the scandalous story with me *en déshabillé* in the Paris scandal sheet, she books passage on her favorite ship, the *Aquitania*, and hightails it to Cherbourg. I am her greatest fear come true. Yes, we're talking about the bathing pool incident... me soaking wet in the arms of my handsome adventurer.

My dear, wonderful Max.

So much has happened since that night in the German farm-house when I shared my greatest secret with him, and the weeks that followed since he left for Spain. but Mother has arrived and demands my attention.

I kiss her on the cheek when I meet her train at *Gare Saint-Lazare*. As she waves the wrinkled news sheet in my face, my focus flips right away to Max on the front page. I can't help but smile. He comes across so cavalier, scowling at the camera but holding me tight. A surge of heat makes me squeeze my legs together, the memory of him zipping open that special place in my heart where I keep him safe and strong.

As if I can. The man's in a war zone, buzzing over the towns and mountains of Spain in a military plane, trying to rid the country of its dictatorial leader in a fight that lost its bloom for many foreign volunteers after the battle of Guernica. A massacre that destroyed the town and killed innocent women and children.

He's more determined than ever to fight the Nazi 'bullies' he believes are behind Franco.

Of course, I want him home... in Paris. With me.

Where will it lead? I never thought I'd say this, but I look forward to reaching the point in our relationship when we're more like an old married couple who discovered that a sincere friendship has a warmth that's both endearing and necessary in times like these.

Still, I do what I do every day since he left for Spain. I go over how close we've become over the past few weeks, each with our own pain but knowing we're not alone any more. We have each other, our feelings humming in sync like bees making warm honey. It's a healing thing, knowing you're not alone, how a squeeze of the hand or a smirk when you say something even remotely funny takes away that ache that lives within you.

Yet we're just two people in this upside-down world and like Max says, there's a bigger picture at stake here. After what we saw at the French border, he's convinced the Nazis are building a major defensive along the border. I still don't agree it will amount to anything, but I sent a series of telegrams to Uncle Archibald with cryptic messages anyway.

Went sightseeing near Strasbourg... Cousin Helmut is building a new fence.

Helmut is my code word for Hitler.

I suspected my reports would garner interest from the State Department so I wasn't surprised when I received a package at my Left Bank hotel, a *Guidebook to Strasbourg* sent from the *Shakespeare and Company* English bookstore on 12 Rue de l'Odéon inscribed to me with a date... *5 May.* I went to the bookshop on that day and waited until a sandy-haired young man approached me and asked me in English if I'd *seen Cousin Helmut recently? Uncle Archibald is worried about him.*

I said *yes...* and *would you like to have coffee with me?*

His name is Edgar P. Sands and he's originally from Boston, but he's now living in London. Late twenties, baggy suit that needs pressing, but his collar and cuffs are clean. As though he just arrived after a long train ride. I told him everything except the bullets flying at us – I don't want to worry my uncle – while he made detailed notes. Of course, I didn't mention that I've fallen head over heels for my British pilot.

That's my secret.

Before he left, Mr Sands requested I remain in France... He has an assignment for me. In Berlin. I'll travel there as a tourist during the upcoming birthday celebration for the city and keep my eyes open. I'm not to take chances (no spying on Nazi headquarters, he warns), but to observe how the average Berliner is faring under the new Reich, especially the Jewish citizens. The State Department has reason to believe things are far worse than the reports they receive.

Smiling, I agreed. I have no intention of going home. I'm staying here till Max returns. It eats me up inside wondering if he's safe. I haven't heard from him in weeks. (Americans in Paris can have our mail sent to *Shakespeare and Company*.) His last letter came a month after he wrote it. He was piloting an old French two-seater bomber somewhere near the border, when he got into a skirmish with the enemy. *The Spanish Air Force is poorly equipped*, he wrote, *and no match for the new machines*. His aircraft is so damn slow it was a wonder he survived. He wished he had *Nellie Blue* to show them what she could do, but he tucked his biplane in a rented hangar space at Le Bourget while he's gone.

I'll be back in less than six months, he added, *you'll see*.

Every day I go over word for word what we said to each other when I saw him off at the train station.

You take care of yourself, Max.

Worried about me?

Should I be? You're a damned good pilot, even if you try to toss your passengers out at 8,000 feet.

I wanted to protect you, Kay.

Why, Max?

Because you needed protecting. I knew that when I saw you with the duke. I made it my business then to watch out for you.

Who's going to protect me when you're gone? I teased him.

He grinned. That was before I got to know how strong you are... It's that woman I'm coming back to... you can bet on it.

I fiddle with the veil on my hat and a loose cherry sprig snaps off in my hand. The same silly hat I wore that day at the Café de la Paix. I ache for him, a man I've only kissed, my heart splintering into pieces at the thought of him getting killed.

I tuck the ornamental cherry into my jacket pocket. My lucky talisman.

Back to Mother.

I arrived early at *Gare Saint-Lazare*, checked my lipstick and straightened my suit jacket, ready for Mother's inspection. Funny, I feel like that pudgy teen again wanting her approval. Then I think of Max and the closeness we have, what we've gone through together, and I'm determined not to play her game.

Still, when I saw my mother get off the train, I got a pleasant fluttering in my stomach, past arguments forgotten. I missed her. She's dressed to the nines, fox stole draped over her navy-blue suit, her head swiveling, looking for me. She's wearing a wide-brimmed hat with a bejeweled diamond netting that sparkles like silver stars.

Then reality set in.

She's only been in Paris for ten minutes yet she's done nothing but complain about the lack of porters to carry her luggage, how uncivilized the French are since they don't speak English, and for God's sake, she hopes the staff at the Ritz have changed since last time the maid blew a fuse in her room ironing her wrinkled underwear.

It gets worse. Before I can take a breath and tell her I'm happy to see her, she demands I return to Philadelphia and give up this sordid existence of parties and men. (Men? I've only been with Max unless you count the duke.)

She continues a tirade like I've never heard. How people back home gossip about me nonstop... Why I'm not married, why I don't come home to take care of my ailing mother. (She's a star performer when it comes to swooning and convincing the handsome doctor attending to her that she has heart palpitations.)

And people ask: why did I break off my engagement to Tommy Whitworth?

That makes me smile. We were never formally engaged, but that didn't stop Mother from announcing it in hushed whispers at her club. What makes her fume is that she can't stop their wagging tongues.

'Come back home, Kay, and stop fooling around.'

We're walking at a decent pace toward the taxi stand, making our way through the throng of travelers. Two porters she corralled on a smoking break with a fistful of French francs clear the way.

'We'll see, Mother.'

'I won't take no for an answer. It's high time you married.'

I tug on my gloves. Straight to the point, isn't she? No doubt she's here to 'convince' me to go home with her.

'So Tommy Whitworth hasn't hung up his coat and tails?' I ask. Thank God the taxi stand is straight ahead. I want this conversation to end.

She sniffles. 'He's a good catch, Kay... It's time you started a family.'

'That didn't work out so well for me, did it?' I say with an ache in my heart. What also hurts is that she never has a word of comfort for me. I accept it, but it still hurts.

'The doctors aren't gods,' she says, being pragmatic, not motherly. 'They can be wrong. You'll never know if you don't try.'

I pretend to look shocked. 'Like you did? Look what it got you. Me.'

'I said you were a disappointment to me. Now's the time to make it up.'

'I made a mistake, Mother, but I can't spend the rest of my life paying for it just to please you.'

'Enough, Kay. No one knows about the baby, simply that you went abroad to study art. It's time to come home and find a husband.'

'I'm damaged goods, Mother; what Main Line gentleman would want me?'

'Tommy Whitworth knows nothing about the child and he's willing to forgive your indiscretion in Paris if you'll set a date.'

'No.'

She grumbles. 'We'll speak about this later, Kay.' She rubs her forehead. 'I have a headache.' She tips the porters, then motions for them to pile her bags into a waiting taxi. 'Shall we go to the hotel?'

I know why Tommy is so 'forgiving'. He's interested in my fortune. Since the crash of 1929, many families have sons in need of cash to restart their family businesses. Still, she can't let go of what I assume is a thorn in her rosy life and prattles on about how much I upset her by running off to Paris. The breaking point was when Mrs Shupe sent her the popular French newspaper with my photo on the front page and tied it with a red satin ribbon (meaning I'm a scarlet woman?).

Her smug attitude shines through when she tells me there's an upside to the scandal, that the gossip about me pushed the engagement news of Mrs Shupe's daughter, Antoinette, to the lower columns of the society pages where no one will see it.

But, Mother insists, enough is enough and it's high time I come home to Philadelphia and take my place in society.

I ignore her rant, though I'm happy to see her even if she turns me a crazy shade of blue, upsetting my Parisian applecart. We don't talk about the holidays. I barely got through Christmas and the first anniversary of losing my baby. It would have been nice to have her here, but I never broached the subject because I knew it wouldn't happen. Too many parties on the society circuit.

But she's here now and I have to deal with it. Which means introducing her to Gertrud and then Hélène. Better to get it over with since I never know when the intrepid reporter or the Polish girl will stop by the hotel. I'll never forget the shock on their faces when I insisted they lunch with me at the Hôtel Ritz after Max left for Spain.

'I have an announcement to make, Mesdemoiselles,' I said with a big smile as the waiter served our soup.

'You robbed a bank,' Gertrud joked, 'to pay for this lunch.'

'I bet Max proposed,' Hélène sighed.

'No on both counts,' I said wistfully. 'I've taken a room here at the hotel on the Rue Cambon side.'

'Have you gone mad, Kay?' Gertrud dropped her monocle into her vichyssoise.

Then Hélène went on for five minutes in Polish, waving her hands about. No translation needed. She, too, thought I was mad.

'I haven't been honest with either of you,' I admitted with a choke in my voice, 'and I'm sorry.'

Gertrud retrieved her monocle and wiped it with her napkin. 'I always suspected you were hiding something, Kay. You were too polished, too sophisticated.' She pointed to my shoes. 'And no hoofer wears Italian-made shoes.'

I smiled. I should have known I couldn't fool a fashion editor.

'I wanted to keep my identity secret to escape the scrutiny of the press.'

Then I revealed who I am: an heiress to a candy fortune. Gertrud snorted, Hélène jumped up and down in her chair with glee, then they both said, 'We don't hold it against you, Kay,' making me blush with embarrassment for keeping it from them.

'I came to Paris to forget a horrible time in my life,' I continued, 'when I lost the most precious gift in a woman's life.'

They didn't ask... I didn't tell... but we all knew what I meant.

From that day forward a special bond united us.

No longer in hiding, I set about learning everything I could about the world of Parisian chocolates as Kay Alexander from *Radwell's French Chocolates*. I convinced Charley Hanover to delay his retirement and come to Paris to help me meet with shop owners and chocolatiers to expand our candy business into France. I introduced the Philadelphia chocolatier to Gertrud who has contacts with major department stores here in Paris. Next, Charley assembled a team of local candy experts and amazed me by making a deal with a major department store on the Boulevard de la Madeleine – Rue Duphot to carry our product.

We're rebranding our chocolates for the French market under the name *Radwell Paris*.

Mother couldn't be more pleased with our new business venture.

That doesn't mean she's giving up on getting me back home

She rambles on about the Season coming up, the not-to-be-missed social events while I check my wristwatch set in platinum with diamonds. I've never worn it around Max since my mink-lined coat aroused enough suspicion. 'We must be going, Mother, we're meeting a friend for tea in the Ritz tea garden.'

'Not that man in the newspaper photo, I hope.' She wrinkles her nose.

Max.

I think about the man who flew into Nazi territory to gather intelligence, fought to save children in Spain, and who could express more with a few bold strokes of a pencil than anyone I know. In the past I would have denied knowing such a man so as not to upset Mother.

But there are some things you fight for.

'I'm in love with him, Mother,' I say without remorse. 'A daring pilot braver than any man I ever knew, but he's left Paris.'

'I can't say I'm sorry, though he *is* rather handsome, but he's not our kind. He looks more like a hero in your silly romantic novels.'

How would she know?

I smile. 'Max is away fighting a war in Spain.'

'Whatever for?' she asks.

'Freedom, Mother. You've heard about the bombing of Guernica?'

She scoffs. 'No, should I?'

I shake my head, exasperated. Unless it's on the society pages, Mother pays no attention to world events. I fill her in on how the *New York Times* and other papers including one here in Paris ran a story about the devastating bombing of the Basque town occupied mostly by women and children, and how it inspired a painting by Picasso.

'It's on display here at the Paris Expo at the Spanish Pavilion. The artist painted it to show the ravages of war.' I don't elaborate on the sensitive subject matter of the gigantic black-and-white painting that covers the side of a building, the horror it depicts, including a dead child. My own pain is still too raw. I can't imagine losing a baby in wartime, its tiny body ravaged by men's hate and rage. It sickens me.

'We in Philadelphia have nothing to worry about,' Mother insists. 'Roosevelt would *never* get *us* into a war.'

I don't argue with her, nor do I tell her about my spying for Uncle Archibald. I pray she's right and the folks back home never see a Nazi in their backyard. It's not a pretty sight. 'We're having tea with Gertrud von Arenbeck, an Austrian countess from Vienna. You'll adore her as I do.'

'A countess?' She beams. 'Why didn't you say so?'

Mother can't jump into the taxi fast enough. For someone so fiercely proud of her Philadelphia connections that go back to the Revolutionary War, she's an avid British royal watcher. She was disappointed she didn't get an invitation to the coronation in May, but she sent boxes of *Radwell's French Chocolates* to the new king anyway.

She prattles on about how excited she is to meet a real countess. I leave out the details of Gertrud's interesting lifestyle. I hadn't meant to spring Mother on her, but she rang me this morning and said she had to see me.

* * *

We finish up our tea and cakes in the Hôtel Ritz dining room, though I barely taste the delicious apricot cream tart and mixed fruit compote served with Darjeeling tea, Mother's favorite, though she keeps demanding hotter water and more cream on the cakes.

What's so important that Gertrud will sit through a tea service with Mother? The Philadelphia matron plies her with a million questions about her title, her family... *your lineage goes back to Charlemagne? How fascinating... and is there a Count von Arenbeck... no? Husband hunting, are you? Well, you won't get any pointers from my daughter.*

I thought she'd never stop, but Gertrud takes it like a trouper, though I have the feeling she's making mental notes for a future column: *How to ignore your overbearing mother.* I squirm in my chair, trying to read the look on Gertrud's face, her pale lips tight, her fingers fidgeting in her lap. Dread inches up my spine, waiting for the right moment when we can ditch Mother. Finally, the Philadelphia matron tosses down her napkin, I charge the lunch to my room and then suggest we take a stroll down Temptation Walk here in the Hôtel Ritz. Mother lingers behind us, gaping at the gorgeous jewelry in the showcases as Gertrud takes me by the elbow. 'I must speak with you, Kay.' The pained look on her face alarms me. 'Alone.'

'It's Max, isn't it?'

She nods. 'He was shot down near Madrid and taken prisoner.'

My heart hammers wildly. '*God, no*, what happened?' I barely get the words out.

'He was escorting bombers when they were attacked by Luftwaffe fighter aircraft. Max took out three Messerschmitts before he was hit. He parachuted out and escaped being picked up by the enemy by hiding out in a farmhouse.' She closes her eyes a moment to gather her thoughts. 'Then he joined up with the land forces of an International Brigade group consisting of Scottish troops and fought bravely with them until—'

I hold my breath. 'Until what? Tell me, please.'

Gertrud pauses, choosing her words carefully, fear tracking in her eyes for a man she respects and admires. 'They were surrounded by Franco's Nationalist troops... A firsthand report from a volunteer who escaped indicates Max was captured carrying a wounded comrade on his back.'

I have to smile at that, though I'm mired in pain. Why aren't I surprised? The man has guts *and* a heart. One that's broken. Will I ever know why?

'Where is he?' I have to know.

'A prison in Valladolid in central Spain.' Gertrud lights a cigarette, then blows out the smoke before looking me in the eye. 'Don't get your hopes up, Kay, but there's talk of a prisoner exchange.'

My heart soars. 'God, yes... *oh, Max.*'

I can't stop thinking about him. Somewhere in Spain in prison.

Gertrud stubs her cigarette into the sand of a silver-plated ash urn. 'It could be months before we get word.'

I have to be content with that when we rejoin Mother who has the entire Ritz staff under her thumb, demanding the hotel manager personally assist her in the purchase of a ruby ring she fancies and where is her wayward daughter?

I placate my mother by spending the rest of the afternoon taking her shopping along the Rue de Rivoli and Rue Saint-Honoré buying hats and shoes from Chanel and Galeries Lafayette and perfume from the House of Doujan. Mother enjoys showing off Gertrud, calling her '*Countess*' in front of the salesclerks and asks me if I know any more royals. I could introduce her to Louis and watch her long nose wiggle when I tell her he's a duke, but he left for the South of France as any Parisian with a sane mind does in August.

I had something to do with that.

After Gertrud called him out about him trafficking innocent girls, I made him a deal to buy his château.

'Where would a down-on-her-luck dancer get that kind of money?' *Louis sputtered, ordering another cognac at our regular table at the Café de la Paix though it wasn't even noon. '*

'I'm really an heiress.' I sip my coffee, peering over my cup.

'And I'm Louis the Fourteenth,' he joked.

'You could be related to the Sun King; you're cut from the same silk,' I offered, referring to his love of opulence, 'but I assure you, I am Kay Alexander of Philadelphia and I can buy you and your château many times over.'

I'd been giving a lot of thought to my idea of building a summer house here in France. Then it hit me. Why not make an offer to the duke on his château?

He downed the cognac in one gulp. 'No fool like an old fool, n'est-ce pas?' *Then on a serious note, he said, 'What's your offer?'*

'I buy your chateau and the lands for cash and allow you to stay on the grounds in the hunting lodge as long as you give up your nefarious ways, though I imagine it's hard to teach an old duke new tricks.'

'But not impossible.' He smirked. 'Where do I sign?'

I had the paperwork drawn up. I still don't trust him, especially when Gertrud told me he gave up his 'pastime' of meeting the trains for only a few months, but it's not every day a French château comes on the market at a good price. I intend to turn it into a home for unwed mothers no matter *where* they come from and whether or not they can pay. Gertrud supports my venture, but we make no mention of it to Mother. It was hard enough fooling her I was staying at the Ritz (I made a deal with management to pick up my mail there once a week). Now I have a bigger job.

Convince her to come to Berlin with me. She's the perfect cover for my snooping.

I mention to Mother that since she missed the British coronation, I've booked a trip to the German capital where she can get a firsthand look at an even grander celebration not seen for hundreds of years.

'Berlin?' She balks, wrinkling her nose. 'Isn't that all sausages and beer?'

'Berlin has the Kurfürstendamm and *Café Kranzler*, a shopping district with smart new designs and the charming Unter den Linden.' My argument is weak, since the Nazis are pushing the dirndl look this year and pushing *out* Jewish designers.

Then I toss it to Gertrud, suggesting she come along with us to get an American socialite's view of Berlin fashion for her column.

'What do you know about fashion, Kay?' Mother asks, eyeing my pink suit with black trimming and lacy cuffs. 'You dress like a cabaret girl.'

'I meant you, Mother,' I say sweetly.

'I'd enjoy showing you both around Berlin,' Gertrud offers, though I can see her turning over in her mind why am I making this strange request. I smile, not revealing any more than I have to. She knows I have my reasons, even if I can't share them with her. 'I have connections at the exclusive fashion salon of *Schulze-Bibernell*,' she continues. 'They say actresses, nobility, *and* Magda Goebbels shop there.'

'Well, why didn't you say so, Countess?' Mother gives me 'that look' as she's apt to do when she thinks I'm leaving her out. I throw up my hands and feign complete innocence. 'I'll be the envy of my set if you can introduce me to Frau Goebbels. *And* I heard a rumor the Duke and Duchess of Windsor fancy a trip to Berlin soon. It would be a feather in my cap if I beat the royals to it.' She beams her brightest smile. I haven't seen her so upbeat since she arrived in Paris. 'When do we leave?'

29

BERLIN, 19 AUGUST 1937

Rachel

Mutti always said nothing ever riles Papa, that he's the kindest man she's ever met, but that was before the Nazis turned our lives upside down. Today it all comes crashing down, finally. He can't take it any more. Seeing his daughters kicked out of school, banned from shops, losing his students because he's Jewish... and the scathing abuse toward his beloved wife at the synagogue... He only needs one more thing to remind him that no matter how hard he tries, he's failed to keep his family safe, his business secure.

That one thing is a birthday party not with candles... but swastikas.

Berlin is seven-hundred years old today and the Nazi Party can't wait to celebrate the event as a way to rouse national German pride.

Seeing his great city smeared with swastika flags and Hitler salutes makes Papa sick. He was born here in Berlin, fought in the Great War and received the Iron Cross. He believes in goodwill

toward men, but he loses his temper when Leah and Tovah keep
pestering him to let them go watch the parade with the floats and
bands and marching soldiers. Papa forbids it. Jews, naturally, aren't
invited.

I adore my little sisters but they do dumb things. They're not
grown up like me. I agree with Papa when he says it isn't safe for us
to be out on the streets near the Brandenburg Gate with gangs of
Hitler Youth roaming around in packs. What if something happens
to his daughters?

He'd never forgive himself. *Never*.

He's so angry, my wonderful Papa slams the door to the room in
the back where he gives lessons and spends the day playing melancholy music on his violin. He upsets Mutti so much with his
impetuous behavior, refusing to talk it out with her like they
usually do, huddled together like two squirrels gathering nuts, that
she dons her long white apron and pushes aside her accounting
work and bakes bread all day. She's hurt, but she'll never admit it.
And angry. The Nazis have driven a wedge between them and God
knows how she'll reach him to work it out. She has to do something
with her hands besides break pencils in two, while Leah and Tovah
pout and run off to *Seltzi's Candies* to buy chocolate and ice cream.

Leaving me alone in the music shop.

I dust the instruments on display, humming a Gershwin tune
and straightening sheet music. I can handle the shop myself. We've
had few customers since the festival week began. The truth is, we're
hardly busy other than our regular Jewish clientele since they
passed those silly race laws about Jews not being allowed to do
anything. Next, they'll order us to tie our shoelaces in knots not
bows. The last people I expect to see enter our shop are three
women babbling in English.

A thirty-something woman in tweed and wearing a monocle
sniffs around, curious. Her clothes are stylish but she reminds me

of a math professor. An older woman wearing big, diamond rings on her fingers, scowls and complains. Hmm... she must be very rich. I don't like her. Not because she's rich but because she scares me with her roving eye, as if she's looking for something to criticize.

And a tall, beautiful brunette with a big smile directed at me. Her red hat sits at an angle on her head that says she's got a streak of independence that I like. Her black suit and gloves match, and she has a red rose in her lapel, as well as high heels that sparkle in the sunlight like magical slippers. There's something mesmerizing about her smile. I can't stop looking at her. She's the epitome of glamour, the woman I want to be someday.

I have no idea this is the woman who will change my life forever.

* * *

Kay

I can't take Mother's babbling another minute about the incessant August heat, the screaming crowd cheering and giving the Nazi salute along the parade route, and the awful, *awful* stench of marching soldiers parading down Unter den Linden.

What do they call it? *Goose stepping?* Ugh. Berlin is having a birthday for the whole world to see, but the world isn't watching. I noticed few foreign press on hand, but I did see a British news crew filming the parade. I've taken a few pictures to send to Mr Sands in London, but the film crew will do a better job than I can of documenting the Nazi Party's extravaganza parade.

So far, our trip to Berlin has been a bust. We couldn't get close to Goebbels, and I imagine his wife Magda is in Paris so Mother couldn't get the scoop on her. Gertrud tried to make it up to us by escorting us to the Adlon Hotel to see if we could find any dignitaries, but it was filled with drunken SS officers flirting with pretty girls. The fashion salons are closed for the birthday celebration, so Mother can't boast she purchased 'exclusive Berliner fashion'.

And I don't have much to report to Mr Sands.

Except the parade that goes on for hours and hours.

A marching army of soldiers, boys and girls... *Hitler Youth*, Gertrud called them, and floats with oranges, flowers, farm scenes, parade participants wearing native or historical costumes. Not to Mother's taste. She insists it can't compare to Philadelphia's Mummers Parade on Broad Street. She complains her feet hurt and she's thirsty, but that's Mother even when she's having a *good* time. I suggest we look for a café, so we wander off the main boulevard parade route looking for a shop that's open before we stumble across *Landau's Music and Melody Shop* on Charlottenstrasse.

I'm fascinated by the display of sheet music so carefully presented alongside the musical instruments for sale. A violin, trumpet... cello. Sheet music in German, but I see a few pieces in English, mostly Wagner. Not for me. I wonder if they have any Cole Porter.

And then I see the music boxes.

Every size, shape. They remind me of the time Mother bought me a music box when I was a child... or rather, her secretary picked it out for my birthday, but at least Mother signed the card. A ballerina that twirled round and round to a Chopin tune. I loved that music box and wanted to be a dancer until Mother told me Philadelphia Main Line girls do not become ballerinas, they buy the ballet company for a tax write-off.

I put away my tutu after that.

But I've never forgotten that ballerina music box.

'Look at the pretty music boxes.' I point them out to Mother, hoping they will jog her memory of those times when she *tried* to be a parent and soften her up. 'Do you remember the ballerina music box you bought me?'

'Yes, it broke.'

Simple. Direct. No sentiment here, but I'm not giving up.

'Let's go inside and look around.'

'Anything to get out of this heat.' She fans herself with her handkerchief. Monogrammed, of course.

Gertrud's eyebrows raise. 'Are you sure you wish to go inside *this* shop?'

'Yes, why do you ask?'

'It's not displaying the swastika flag over the living quarters upstairs.'

'So?' I say, not understanding

'That means it's not Aryan-owned.'

'Which means what, Gertrud?' I ask, intrigued.

'That Germans... and tourists like us are discouraged from buying anything here because the owner is Jewish.'

I blink, her comment sparking a memory. I remember Mr Kaplan, the pickle shop owner, saying the same thing. His fears about his brother and his family set off a defiance in me.

I smile. 'All the more reason to go inside and buy something *not* Aryan-owned.'

I'm beginning to dislike this Hitler more and more. It was bad enough when I saw with my own eyes his venture to encroach on the French border, but here in Germany the dictator is taking away basic freedoms I've always taken for granted, not that prejudice doesn't exist in Philadelphia.

I grew up unaware of how it runs so rampant in the business world. My father may have been a tough businessman, but he hired a man or woman based on their ability not their religion, even if his 'club' excluded Jews. I know nothing about the Jewish religion, having never been exposed to anyone other than Mother's society crowd. Even when I came out, there were no Jewish girls in the mix, which I now find disturbing.

I realize how sheltered I was before I came to Paris. It gives me the shivers to think I could have ended up like Mother's crowd if I didn't strike out on my own and work at *Gimbel's*. I'd still be wearing blinders to how people *not* on the Main Line live... their problems, their fears, like I see here in Berlin for Jews. I'm embarrassed I didn't see it sooner.

Gertrud smiles. 'You have a brave daughter, Mrs Alexander. Most tourists would shy away from doing anything *verboten* here in Germany.'

'Foolish is more like it. She never listens to me anyway.' My mother adjusts her bosom and her hat, the veil dripping with her perspiration. 'Thank God my ladies auxiliary will never know I visited a Jewish-owned shop.'

'Not unless I tell them,' I shoot back.

'You wouldn't dare, Kay.'

'I would if you're not on your best behavior.'

'Do I have a choice?' she sneers.

'Not if you want to get out of this heat; it's the only shop open on this street.'

'Why did I ever let you talk me into coming to this barbaric country?' She rolls her eyes. 'Shouting and hysterics from the crowd at the parade, sauerkraut at every meal... and the toilet paper reminds me of brown butcher wrapping.'

Gertrud and I exchange humorous looks at my mother's brashness, and I have to admit my Austrian friend has been good enough to put up with Mother. I imagine she's taking notes on everything from my mother's boasting about her trip last year to Monte Carlo aboard a millionaire's yacht to her Newport escapades. She's loud, insolent, and demanding, but she weighs in heavily with the society set not only because of her money, but her unique business savvy to get *Radwell's French Chocolates* into every hotel in Newport and Palm Beach.

And she's a conservative snob. She doesn't approve of Gertrud's short haircut and the wide trousers and smart white silk shirt the Austrian often wears.

She's an aristocrat. Where are her jewels? she asks. *Her couture wardrobe? Her poodle, for God's sake?*

'*She's the artsy type,' I explained, then let it go.*

Gertrud made no secret to me about her past, how she covered the underground clubs in Berlin before the Nazis came to power when the boyish *Garçonne* style was all the rage. I respect her openness and honesty and wouldn't trade our friendship. I also know she's fallen for someone new by how often she polishes her monocle, smiling to herself, though she won't tell me who the girl is. And I won't ask, though I suspect it's Hélène. I've seen how Gertrud sighs when the Polish girl smiles at her, innocent of her interest. I pray my Austrian friend doesn't get hurt. Of course, I'd never tell Mother what's going on. The shock would be too much for her.

'Well, ladies,' I ask, holding the door open. 'Shall we go in?'

* * *

Rachel

'Have you interest in sheet music, *meine Damen*?' I say in English. Slow, precise, like I learned in school. 'I can play American songs for you on the piano.'

I've never seen such a motley trio enter our modest shop. Three ladies chattering in English. I find them totally fascinating, their clothes, stylish hats... their mannerisms, especially the pretty brunette.

'Do you have any songs by Cole Porter?' she asks, looking around. She seems interested in the music boxes Papa imported from France before the Nazis came to power. Very expensive, which is why we haven't sold any.

'*Ja*. I love your American jazz music,' I tell her. I persuaded Papa to order sheet music in English, songs by Gershwin and Cole Porter. 'We learn English in school, so I can read the lyrics.'

I don't tell her I have to keep the music hidden so the local *Polizei* don't see what the Fuehrer claims is 'degenerate music'. How can these beautiful, romantic tunes by Gershwin be called anything but moving and fun? They inspire *me* to write songs, but I never show them to anyone.

'Yes, that would be delightful. Right, Mother?'

She nods toward the older woman wearing the diamond rings, but she merely grumbles.

I sit down at the piano and pull out a favorite tune by Cole Porter, 'Begin the Beguine', from under the piano bench. I have no idea what 'beguine' means, but I love the dramatic tempo of the music; it stirs my heart with its exotic rhythm. I sing it through twice... then lay my hands down on the piano keys. I forgot myself, I was so enchanted with the music. Embarrassed, I lower my eyes... I'm afraid to look up when—

I hear the ladies clapping... well, two of them. The older woman sighs... from boredom?

'That was... how do you say *wonderful*, Gertrud?' asks the brunette.

'*Sie sind wunderbar, Fräulein*,' says the lady with the monocle. She's from Vienna, she says, a reporter for *Die Junge Dame*, and praises me for my excellent English and singing voice.

'Thank you,' I say in English. I let out a big breath. I haven't felt so good in a long time, hearing someone say they like me instead of turning away from me because I'm Jewish.

The brunette asks me to wrap up the sheet music and anything else I have by Cole Porter. I jump at the chance, humming another Porter tune, 'So Easy to Love', when the bell tinkles loudly and the front door bursts open.

Leah and Tovah.

Racing through the shop like two naughty forest imps, laughing and giggling. Munching on chocolate. Hamming it up. Oh, no, they'll ruin everything. The foreign ladies will leave and not buy anything.

'*Leah, Tovah*, we have guests from America and Vienna,' I say in English. 'Say *hello*.' I don't mean to sound stern, but my little sisters can be less than adorable when they eat too much chocolate. This is one of those moments. I ask Tovah to show me what she has in her hand. A round canister filled with chocolate triangles. They're munching on those new chocolate bars *Seltizi's Candies* started selling last year.

'*Hel-lo, meine Damen,*' they say in unison, giggling, then curtsying, their mouths filled with chocolate.

'I must apologize for my sisters,' I say in English, then turn to the lady in tweed, showing her the canister and explaining to her in German they're eating chocolate bars that give them *too much* energy for a cheap price. She nods, then explains to the pretty brunette in English what I said, reading off the ingredients to her. I can't imagine why the pretty brunette looks so interested in a chocolate bar, but she can't stop smiling when I offer her a piece.

Then Leah offers the other *Fräulein her* chocolate and soon we're munching on candy and laughing together like schoolgirls.

Except the grumpy older lady, who pouts and pulls up her veil, wiping her face with a lacy handkerchief.

Mutti comes in to see what the fuss is about, her hair flying about her worried face in wispy strands, her long white apron and cheeks smeared with bread flour. She looks from our guests to her daughters, puzzled. Before I can swallow my chocolate and tell her why we're laughing—

'I'd like a glass of water,' the older woman directs her words toward Mutti who doesn't understand her. Her tone is terse, her sharpness evident when she says, 'Well, why are you standing there, girl?'

Mutti furrows her brow, trying again, but she can't lip read English very well.

Gasping, the older woman turns toward me. 'Your servant is ignoring me. Where did you find such insolent help? I'd fire her if she worked for me.'

I hesitate, not understanding. *Fire her?*

The woman in tweed translates for me, getting my dander up. Really? Customer or not, I won't stand for this woman's meanness. How *dare* she insult Mutti. I can see the hurt in my mother's eyes when the woman waves her handkerchief in her face and gives her a dirty look. She uses the hand signals I learned, telling me to offer the American woman a piece of apple strudel and tea. My mother has too much class to insult the woman.

I don't.

'She's *not* a servant, *meine Frau*, she's my mother and she's deaf,' I lash out. I have no intention of serving that woman tea. She doesn't deserve it, even if Mutti scolds me later. 'She can read lips, but she doesn't understand much English. Now, if you're not interested in purchasing anything, I suggest you leave. I'm sure you'll find the Nazis and their parade more to your liking. They *shoot* anyone who ignores them.'

'Well, I never—' the older woman says, aghast.

'No, Mother,' says the pretty brunette, her cheeks tinting from embarrassment, 'you *never* will understand.'

The beautiful brunette begs me not to think ill of them, that her mother is tired and overwhelmed by the day's events and the loud, bombastic Nazis. Good. She doesn't like them either. That makes me like her even more. She buys every piece of sheet music we have in English and the most expensive music box in the store. I feel myself holding my breath until it hurts, amazement and regret racing through me. Amazement that the brunette had the courage to stand up to this woman with the bad manners and regret for my quick, spiteful words.

I try to make it up to her.

'You've made a wonderful choice with the music box, *Fräulein*.' She saw the carved, mahogany box in the window. 'It's lined with red velvet from 1889 Paris, trimmed in gold with a miniature of a beautiful woman wearing a tiara and' – I open the box – 'it plays a tune by Mendelsohn, forbidden here in Berlin.'

She assures me the secret is safe with her, then requests the sheet music be shipped to the Hôtel Ritz in Paris, but she takes the music box with her.

'*Danke, Fräulein*,' she says warmly. 'When next I return to Berlin, I shall stop by and listen to you sing... What is your name?'

I smile. 'Rachel.'

She nods. 'Rachel... I shan't forget it.'

A kind thought, but I doubt I'll ever see her again.

30

PARIS, 1937

Kay

I avoid bringing up our Berlin trip. I'm anxious for Mother to leave for Cherbourg then New York and back to the Main Line. I've never been so ashamed of my own mother, treating those kind Jewish people like servants and insulting that lovely deaf woman. I can't forget the young teenager, Rachel, how she stood up for her *Mutti*. I envy her having such a fine mother. I can hardly wait to send mine back to Philadelphia.

Meeting the Landau sisters and their mother got me to thinking about those not so fortunate not only in my country, but in other places as well. I didn't meet their father, but I was astonished when Gertrud informed me the family will most likely lose their music shop. Germany isn't a safe place for Jews and things will get worse if more sanctions are put into place.

It saddens my heart to see this family lost in the quagmire of the Nazi Party, but what can I do?

If only there was some way I could use my fortune to help them and others...

When I write to Uncle Archibald and ask his opinion, even he's at a loss to give me an answer. 'The State Department has no intention of getting involved with the actions of the Nazis toward their own citizens,' he writes back.

Only one thing wrong with that statement.

From what Gertrud tells me, Jews are no longer considered German citizens.

Still, I won't give up...

Meanwhile, I wait for word from Max, praying there's a prisoner exchange soon, and deal with my mother. We forego doing the sights in Paris since Mother has been through this drill numerous times. I believe Mother is lonelier than she lets on and, somewhere under that rubber girdle, she has a heart that cries out for love. She's grumpy the last two days of her trip, which makes her more determined to ruin *my* life. I stay strong. I'm different to who I was before. I have Max in my life and whenever I need courage, I think of him. And that funny drawing he made of me. I still have it.

I convince Mother I haven't finished my duties for the *Radwell Paris* launch. It's a lie... I have, but I can't bear to go home until I hear from Max. It's a damp November night when I ask her to come to my room (she has her own suite at the Ritz) for hot coffee and vanilla iced cake and explain to her why I'm not coming back with her to Lilac Hill. That I intend to stay in Paris and work with a chocolate company on an idea I have for a new candy bar.

Yes, the Berlin chocolate inspired me. It was exactly what I'm looking for. I'm eager to tell Charley and have him put together a team of chocolate makers here in Paris to take my idea and get started on it. I can't wait to taste what they come up with.

'Your home is with me, Kay,' Mother insists. 'Why work here in

Paris? We have a factory in Philadelphia. I imagine Charley is itching to come home and hang up his hat.'

'Quite the contrary, Mother, he loves it in Paris. He has at his disposal whatever financial resources he needs for our venture here.' I put down my empty cup. I haven't touched my cake. I'm too excited to eat.

'Your inheritance, of course,' she states flatly. To her, it's a curse because she no longer has control over me.

'I'll put it to good use, Mother, and increase company profits, I guarantee you.'

Radwell's French Chocolates remains a specialty chocolate company, but more important our family assets consist of oil reserves in both Oklahoma *and* Pennsylvania. We can pour money into the company for modernization techniques far into the next century, improving the automatic production lines with new and better machines needed for chocolate production to mold, blend, and wrap.

The Radwell Chocolate Works... works as my great-grandpa loved to boast. The company is doing better than ever, though America is in the middle of a depression. Which is why I want to bring out a chocolate bar for the folks back home wishing they had a chicken in their pot every Sunday.

It also provides the excuse I need to stay in Paris. And wait for Max. I'm not giving him up. He makes my heart sing a happier tune and believe in myself. The only thing that worries me is I haven't been honest with him.

That thought eats at me when I open up the double doors to my small terrace on the fourth floor of the Ritz Hôtel. A sudden cool breeze makes me shiver. Odd, it's a warm night, taunting me. Surely my money won't come between us?

I push that thought out of my mind. I have a job to do: work with Charley Hanover and his team to create an inexpensive candy bar that gives our customer energy and stamina like the chocolate bars I tasted in Berlin. I'll never forget the Landau sisters bouncing around like bunny rabbits on clouds, smiling and adorable until Mother put her foot in her mouth. I wanted to shake her... Did she insult the Jewish girl's mother on purpose? No, she believed her to be a servant and acted her normal self, but when she found out the truth, she didn't apologize. Was she jealous of the closeness the woman shared with her daughter when Rachel stood up for her?

I'll never know.

'And what you are going to call this new concoction?' Mother asks, trying to act vaguely curious, but I see a light behind her hazel eyes as she lifts her teacup to her lips. She's wiggling with delight in her girdle.

She loves to challenge me.

'A tribute to Great-grandpa *Candy Bill*.' I smile. 'McGinty's.'

31

PARIS, MARCH 1938

Kay

I receive the postcard from Max on a rainy, spring morning when I check for mail at *Shakespeare and Company*, the sharply-drawn caricature on the back of the card making my heart soar with a joy I haven't felt in months. The familiar, sweeping black lines show a pilot breaking free from prison... then awakening a sleeping princess with a kiss.

I find great comfort in that simple postcard, that someone cares about me. I've spent my whole life being the Radwell candy heiress with everyone expecting me to marry well and marry rich, that I never thought I'd find a man who likes me for myself. Of course, I have another hurdle to overcome before there can be anything between us – telling Max who I am.

But *that* is for another day.

For now, I'm off to tell Gertrud the news, hoping I'll find her at the Café de la Paix (she doesn't do more than sleep in her room at the Hôtel Meurice) scouting for interesting personages to write about for her column. She warned me the prisoner exchange was a slow process and I went crazy for weeks waiting to hear from Max, stuffing myself with chocolate concoctions I created to dull the pain while searching for the right 'taste' and 'energy boost'.

Chocolate testing isn't all fun and sugary highs, I write to Mother who continues to poo-pooh our new venture. She writes to me frequently since she returned to Philadelphia with not-so-subtle hints to come home and take up my society duties as her daughter. I ignore them. Instead, I write, *It's a daily grind of experimenting with different recipes and ingredients... too bitter... too sweet... too bland...*

She doesn't understand that I love working with Charley and our Paris team to find the *right* recipe for our *McGinty's* chocolate bars. Milk and dark chocolate blended and fortified with French coffee, kola beans, and vitamins.

Fortunately, we found a small chocolate company on the outskirts of Paris willing to produce the test bars and perfect the formula in exchange for exclusive production and distribution rights in France and my company installing modern state-of-the-art equipment to update their operation that hasn't changed in sixty years. After months of testing and retesting, we finally came up with a chocolate bar that fits the bill. We shipped the finished product back home to Philadelphia along with our notes and test results.

Now we wait for our Philadelphia team to do *their* testing. And their market research on John Q. Public. Then we'll know if we have a winner.

I look back down at the postcard in my hands. It's as if the heavens opened up and dropped my favorite British pilot into my lap.

Well, not exactly, but the smell of him is in the air as I sit inside the Café de la Paix out of the rain, staring at his postcard, running my fingertips over it from top to bottom as if I could cast a spell and he'd appear. Outside on the pavements, rain comes down in a steady stream, a blustery wind so typically Parisian begging to get inside and splaying big drops on the large picture window. The wind sounds almost human, getting into my head, and I swear it calls my name.

'Kay, *Kay*!'

I look up from my sorcerer's daydream and know I'm not alone. The air is charged with a sensuality that buzzes and snaps through me. Then I see him... standing outside in the rain, his leather flight jacket glistening with dewy drops, his dark hair plastered to his forehead... hiding that scar I love but not those eyes. Dark and smoldering. And that smile.

'*Max!*' I yell out, jumping out of my chair and racing to the window, my nose smudged up against the glass. I just want to stare at him, take him in... I pray he isn't an illusion. He presses the palm of his hand against the glass and I do the same, the anticipation of our bodies touching intoxicating, like a heady wine.

Finally, I can't take another moment without him and race through the looking glass... the café door... and out into the rain. He grabs me and sweeps me up into his arms.

'*God,* Kay, I've missed you so much.'

'Max, my darling, you *are* real!'

'A slightly beaten-up version, but, yes, I'm real.'

'Max—'

'Don't talk, just let me look at you.'

We stand in the rain, the hunger for each other bursting with need, our eyes asking that silent question: *Have I changed? Do you feel the same as you did?*

I press my body against his and he groans. I want him to love me, but I'm scared, too. Scared of getting hurt.

He reads my mind... as only he can do... and answers me with a deep kiss that makes my knees wobble and a sweet pleasure in my groin explode.

Then he lets go with a moan and his hands tighten around my waist, thrilling me.

'I'd make love to you here in the rain,' he says in a husky voice, 'but—'

'I know. You fly like an eagle, not swim like a duck,' I quip, easing the rising tension for more than a kiss between us. 'Let's go inside where we can talk.'

Huddling together, we order two hot coffees and wrap ourselves in the blanket the waiter brings us. Then we talk. Max tells me when he couldn't find me at my hotel on the Left Bank (I still keep a room there), he knew where to look for me. And if I know anything about the adventurous British pilot, he won't want to talk about what happened to him in Spain. That he'll keep the pain in like I did when I lost my baby.

I can't let him suffer. Yes, I long for him to kiss me, hold me so tight I can't breathe, but I want to help him heal.

Because I love the man.

And this time, no matter what Mother thinks, I'm not going to let him go.

* * *

'You're going *back* to Spain?'

I make a painful, choking sound in the back of my throat, not believing what I'm hearing. I want to cry, but not now. Staring up at this wildly handsome man holding me tight in his arms, I burst out with a question I shouldn't ask, but I do.

'*Why*, Max?' I beg to know. 'You were almost killed, then captured and spent months in prison... Why go back?'

'The job's not done yet, Kay.' His dark eyes smolder with a fierceness I can't fight.

I want to, *oh how I want to*, but I don't.

'The Republicans have new Soviet fighters that can go as fast as *Nellie Blue* with a full load. I can't let those people down, Kay, if you could see the suffering they've endured... scrounging for food, water, hunkered down in caves and bunkers for weeks with no light, air... the children, the babies so scared they don't cry any more...'

I have no comeback for this man who's taller and more hand-some than I remembered. The prodigal pilot is back in Paris. Home from the war in Spain looking tanned and tousled-haired, tired around the eyes, his hard body leaner but more muscular. As if he's been doing hard labor, those magnificent arms strong and grabbing me from behind, picking me up and swinging me around until I'm so dizzy I collapse in his arms.

'An enemy that cruel *must* be beaten,' I whisper. 'Yes, you must return.'

'I knew you'd understand, Kay.'

He cups my chin, reading my face... my lips red and trembling, big, wide eyes still in disbelief, crossed brows angry with the war that did this to him. He lets go with what's in his heart because if he doesn't, he'll kiss me and the pain in him will run deeper and I don't want that, so I say, 'Please, I want to hear.'

He nods, heaves out a big breath and then jumps into it. 'If you could see the horror happening to the Spanish children, see them looking into the eyes of anyone coming near them, terrified because of what they've seen...' he begins, sitting with me and holding my hand at the small round table in the café, its roundness reminding me of a copper sun that turns on its axis, for it was at this table he sat when I saw him drawing me and now it's made its revolution and we're back where we started.

But then we're not. We've both changed even if the sun... I

mean, table, remains the same. I almost wish we *were* back then, sparring with each other, for what he needs to say is sad, and the warmth I felt in his hand has turned cold.

'Tell me, Max, I want to know.' I attempt a gentle smile, but it's forced. I know now there will be no 'us' until he frees his soul from this new grief that lies fresh over the layer of his past still haunting him. Making it heavier... and harder to live with because he has a hole in his heart like I do.

Does that mean he needs me more?

'After I was shot down, after the skies rained bombs filled with fire and smoke, I found my way to a village where I saw a little girl wandering through the rubble in the streets in a daze, her small hands trembling so hard she dropped her doll along the way like a Pied Piper led her... lost without her parents with no warm hand to hold hers, no gentle voice of a mother to comfort her when the air raid sirens went off and the bombers came again and again, flying low, strafing the running women and children with piercing bullets. They fell in the streets like human dominos, quick and fast.'

Words became sighs after that. He's fighting a war where German aircraft kills indiscriminately, where the Republicans put themselves on the front line, man by man, never giving up, fighting for a country with its assets depleted, trucks and motorcars blown up, roads and bridges wrecked, livestock decimated, and rows and rows of houses lying in ruin.

I shiver listening to him speak, the utter devastation boggling my mind.

'How can men do this to each other?' I ask.

'They're not like us, Kay,' he whispers in my ear. 'These Fascists murder anyone against them, eliminate opposition and send inno-cents to die without missing a heartbeat. It's more than greed for power, but a devil-like mentality set upon an innocent people that's cruel and evil... brutal to the point of decadence so black even prayers to God can't get through.'

We remain quiet, each in our own thoughts, our emotions tossing propriety to the winds when I keep pushing his hair out of his eyes, looking at that scar I love, searching for new ones, and he lays his hand upon my knee, our lips so close barely a breath separates us.

I hear a loud gasp... then the smell of rain and schnapps hits my nostrils—

'Max, *thank God*!' Gertrud rushes over to our table, showing up as I knew she would, a big smile on her face. 'It's so good to see you.'

He grins at her. 'You, too, Gertrud. Thanks for taking care of my girl.'

She nods and whispers in my ear that we'll talk later then does something unexpected; she kisses Max on both cheeks, her eyes misty. Yes, she loves him as much as I do. That warms my heart, two sisters-in-arms giving this man the support he needs.

She bids us *Bonne nuit*, then takes off, leaving us alone to find comfort in each other's arms.

I close my eyes, wanting only to cuddle up to this soldier fresh from the front, but something about him awakens a need in me to comfort him in spite of the fire building low in my belly. I've never felt like this before. As lines blur and feelings shift, I realize Max has taken my heart... and I'm not sure I can survive without him.

Max holds me tightly in his arms, the chill of the March breeze playing tag with the swish of the pedestrians moving quickly along the pavements so close to our world but not part of it. We're each floundering in our memories as he runs his hands through my hair. Then he whispers the names of his fallen comrades, one by one, and finally he utters a name with such reverence, I feel an angel touch my shoulder, begging me not to be jealous, but listen when he says—

'I once loved a girl; she was seventeen. Her name was Althea.'

* * *

Every war has its heroes.

Max doesn't see himself like that, but I do. Like most heroes, something in his past triggered a need in him to right a wrong. *Who is this man, really?* I want to know. He joined up to fight the Fascists, he tells me, though it's illegal for British subjects to engage in the civil war that started with Mussolini, then pushed forward with a fierce momentum with Hitler backing Franco.

But his rebellious nature started long before that.

'My father was an aerial daredevil pilot, rarely at home, but I idolized him growing up. He'd take me out to the field and sit me in his plane, show me the controls, tell me to memorize what I saw,' Max begins, revealing to me a story I never dreamed of hearing. 'I found I had a talent for drawing what I saw instead of memorizing it, so I started sketching the pilots in the aerial circus, the spectators, the crews in these wild almost cartoonish drawings. That's when I discovered I have this odd way of bringing out what I see in a person, their traits... their soul.'

'You have a gift, Max... Gertrud saw that in you.'

He nods. 'She found me in the Café de la Paix drawing her and put my talent to good use. She kept me from starving between ferrying jobs.'

'But why come to Paris?' I ask.

'My life turned upside down when my father lived through a bad plane crash and became an alcoholic. Overnight he changed, turning into a bully. He started beating me when I was twelve to beat the shame out of himself for his failures. I took the blows, *anything* rather than see him beat my mother, a kind, pretty French girl he met when he was flying in an air show in Cannes, a local girl enamored by the handsome pilot. He picked her out of the crowd to take a picture with him on the wing of his aircraft. I grew up speaking French... then she died when I was sixteen and there was nothing left for me to stick around for but flying. I begged my father's circus cronies to take me on. I'd already logged hours in the air with my old man, but it wasn't enough. I did every job there was in the aerial circus... run errands, clean planes... I learned to check the engines, the wings, fix the propellers until I could do anything and then I learned how to do aerobatics up there in the sky where I could forget my mother died of a broken heart and loneliness because my father started fooling around with another woman.'

'Oh, Max, how awful for you.'

'I thought I was done with him, but he couldn't let me go. Couldn't bear to see me fly when he couldn't. He'd already killed my mother with his bullying, but I never expected he'd betray me and take the girl I loved from me, too.'

'Althea...' I whisper, my heart clenching.

'Yes.'

'How?' I ask, dreading what I'm about to hear. 'What happened?'

'Althea found me in the hangar one day after my mother died, sitting in a plane that was out of service, its wing damaged, the paint scratched off. I was a broken kid of sixteen, stiff-backed and stoic, never showing the pain inside me. She was fifteen, the daughter of the owner of the airfield, but she had a crush on me. We talked for hours sitting in that old monoplane and when we were done, I kissed her. And she kissed me back. Even when her father found us, she didn't let go of my hand. He lashed out at her, berating her for kissing a cabin boy, that I was a ruffian who'd never amount to anything, like my father, that I wasn't good enough for his daughter. Then he smacked her in the face, knocking her down. I saw red. I couldn't stand by and see him hurt her, so I punched him, but he came back at me with a switchblade. We fought and he cut me above the eye.'

'The scar...' I mutter.

He nods. 'The blood ran down the side of my face, but I disarmed him and grabbed Althea and we ran. He pressed charges against me and I had to swear not to see her again, but we met secretly and I promised I'd protect her from her father. We planned to run away together when she turned eighteen.'

'In England... Blackpool?'

Max lowers his voice and I have the feeling this is the first time he's talked about what happened next. 'Yes, the seaside resort was a booming hub for flying in England since before the Great War... I hear the RAF is taking it over now, but back then commercial air flights had started. Private owners also rented hangar space there and I picked up extra cash ferrying passengers to London. I was nineteen and had my pilot's license, but my father found out we planned to elope and bragged about it in a drunken stupor in the local bar. Althea's father sent his thugs to work me over that morning at the hangar as I readied a biplane to take off. One of them had a pistol.'

'What happened, Max? Tell me, *please*.'

'The thug pointed the gun at me, but Althea tried to shield me with her body... He shot at me but hit her instead and she died in my arms. In spite of my testimony, the shooting was ruled an accident but I was no longer welcome in town.' He heaves out the breath he's been holding. 'I came to Paris to grieve for her and pick up my life and the rest, well, you know the story. I've never forgiven myself. I let Althea down after I promised to protect her from her father. It's my fault she's dead.'

I know better than to refute his guilt... that he hasn't let go. Not yet. I hug him close to me and he curls up in my arms. Something he couldn't do with anyone else. Instead, he threw himself into a fight for freedom as a way of assuaging his pain. War provides the time and place and in a strange way, benefits from that pain suffered in the past.

Such is the story of this man.

Which is why I don't suggest we find refuge in my room at the Ritz. All that fanciness and opulence doesn't seem the right place for him to come to grips with his feelings, and me, well, I've not yet found the courage to share the truth with him. It will come... but not now.

We find refuge in my room on the Left Bank. We lie in each other's arms, a truce between us, cleansed of our pasts but unsure of our future.

For weeks after that revealing night, I want to say, 'Hey, I have a room at the Ritz... The beds are a heck of a lot softer... and the room service ain't bad,' in a flippant manner but I never do. Max is so involved in writing to the relatives of the men still in prison in Spain and the comrades he lost, it seems a selfish endeavor on my part.

I'm afraid my fantasy of him embracing the reality of who I am is dissipating as fast as the tears on my pillow. Where I come from, men like him – bold and brave warriors – don't understand the frivolities of dances and teas, but move about in a world of battles fought and blood spilled.

Which is why I keep convincing myself there's always tomorrow to tell him.

Tomorrow, of course, never comes.

Still, when the moonlight strikes us both at the same time with that undeniable urge and we first make love, we take off our clothes, grab a bottle of wine and two glasses, and then disappear beneath the threadbare sheets in my tiny hotel room on the Left Bank.

It doesn't matter what the sheets are made of; it's pure magic between us.

Then there's a second, then a third night... until the day comes when it's time for Max to go. I kiss him goodbye. Again. My love for him igniting my blood every time I touch him or he brushes his lips with mine, our hearts beating together in a secret code when we make love, but I keep my secret. I don't want to spoil what we have with a little thing like me being an heiress. I know I'm going to regret it, but like a last dance, the ball is over.

Then he's gone.

And I want to curl up and die.

I don't, of course. That would be too easy.

32

BERLIN, 9 NOVEMBER 1938

Rachel

If Heaven is Mutti and Papa tucking us in at night, then Hell is being roused *out* of bed by the sound of shattering glass. It's the most frightening sound I've ever heard and I'll never forget it. Ear-piercing blasts... the heavy breaths of men grunting under the strain of their labor, pounding, ripping... crushing everything, anything they can get their hands on... It's not medieval demons invading our home, but humans filled with hate.

SA men.

They come in the middle of the night, shouting, breaking the front window of our music shop with the butts of their rifles. I creep down the backstairs in my stockinged feet, keeping to the night shadows, then I duck down behind the upright piano, cover my face, my eyes, with my hands. I peek through my fingers and see the soldiers breaking down the door to our shop with a vehemence I will never understand... then I smell burning coming from somewhere.

Like a building is on fire.

Is it happening? The rumors we've feared coming true? That the Nazis won't stop their brutality until every Jewish house, every Jewish-owned business is destroyed?

Why do they hate us so?

I was sitting up, cuddled up in my featherbed with a small lamp for light, scribbling on a notepad, when I heard the first piercing sound of breaking glass. I couldn't sleep, my restless mind not content as I worked on lyrics for a lullaby for Tovah. Music is the only thing that calms her. She's a progeny with the violin, but in the end she's still a little girl. As fragile as the bow she wields and easily broken. She frets so in her bed each night and doesn't understand why she can't play the music she loves, why she can't run freely in the park, when the shouting outside the shop alerted me.

I keep my wits about me when Mutti comes running down the stairs, grab her by the arm and keep her safe with me. She felt it, too, the earth rumbling under her feet. She was in the hidden room she calls her office, going over the books, checking inventory as decreed by a new edict that we sell our music shop to an Aryan for a pittance.

Why destroy the shop if they want it Aryan-owned? To humiliate us?

I'm scared to show myself, but I can't allow my mother to get hurt. I race out from my hiding place, throw my hands up and yell, 'Our shop is Aryan-owned,' I cry out. '*Go away!*'

'Ja, Fräulein?' I get nothing but a sneer from a young SA man, narrowing his eyes and creasing his forehead, his nostrils flaring when he smashes a trumpet against the wall. 'I have my orders. Where is the *Jew* who owns this shop?'

'*I* own it,' I shout back, arrogant and proud. I won't let him hurt my parents. 'Go away or... or...'

'Or what?'

'I shall report you.'

'*Rachel!*'

It's Papa. Half-dressed, he races down the stairs, his face red, his anger toward me fueled by his fear his oldest daughter will pay the price for her foolishness and his lateness. I have no doubt he ordered Mutti back upstairs to stay with Leah and Tovah. I see a blazing rage in his eyes I've never seen before, raw and cutting, exposing a father's greatest fear. He's afraid for me, that the SA man will do to me what I've heard whispered in dark corners. I was stupid to act out, but I don't regret it.

We *have* to stand up to these brutes.

'I am Herr Landau,' Papa says, 'but I no longer own the shop. I – I sold it my assistant, Ulrich Mueller.'

I shall never forget the shock on Ulrich's face when Papa handed him the keys, the faithful worker saying he didn't want this to happen, but I've no doubt Frau Mueller is already spending the profits.

The SA man seems satisfied. '*Gut*. Then we shall leave, but I must bring in one Jew from every house or shop.' He turns to me. '*You, Fräulein*. You're a sassy girl... pretty, too.'

'You don't frighten me,' I shout back, my knees wobbling. Brave words, but the SA man advances toward me, his breathing fast and heavy. Papa explodes, pushing me aside so hard I trip and fall to my knees.

'*Don't touch my daughter*,' he snarls, his teeth bared.

The SA man laughs. 'Lucky for you, Jew, it's the men we want.' He orders the two Brownshirts to arrest Papa, telling him to bring a small bag. He packs nothing but his violin. Mutti comes down the stairs slowly, silent as a ghost, but she's aware something is horribly wrong. She approaches her husband without so much as a nod to the SA man, and reads Papa's lips.

If he has his music, he tells Mutti, planting a kiss on her forehead, *he'll never be alone.*

Mutti lowers her eyes, wanting no trouble. It's then I realize she's more courageous than I, saying nothing to the invaders, to keep her daughters safe. Without a word, she packs dry socks in his violin case and insists he take his veteran's papers with him. *And* his Iron Cross. After they take him away, Mutti calls a prayer vigil for Papa. My sisters, our mother and I sit in a circle, holding hands, a tall candle burning in the middle, each of us taking a turn to talk about Papa, praying our good thoughts will reach God's ears and more importantly, that He will listen.

Leah says Papa is good and kind and never yells at her when she makes a mistake playing chords on her guitar because he says you only learn from your mistakes. Tovah keeps sniffling, trying not to cry because Papa said it's her job as a violinist to make *other* people cry with her music. That makes us smile. I say that Papa reminds me every time I sit down at the piano to practice a difficult piece that I should play the scales first... because doing the familiar makes what seems impossible possible.

Mutti goes last, saying that Papa is a wonderful husband and father and although she can't hear his music in her ears, she hears it in her heart, as she does now, telling us she's certain Papa is this very minute playing his violin and that gives him courage. And we must have courage, too.

We take a few minutes of silence, each in our own thoughts, when Tovah asks why she told Papa to take his medal. Mutti tells us the Iron Cross saved their neighbor when he was ordered to list his assets to the Gestapo and Mutti prepared the books for him. He told her later his veteran status as an officer in the Great War gained him favor and they let him go with only a warning and a small fine. It could work for Papa, too.

It does.

But only after he enchants the Gestapo man in charge with his rendition of Beethoven's 'Violin Concerto No 1 in D Major'. The composer is beloved by Hitler, thankfully for Papa. My father looks tired and worn when he returns two days later, his cheeks sagging, chin ruddy and raw where he placed it on his violin for so many hours and played while the Gestapo processed Jews one after another. But it's his eyes that bother me most, that what he's seen will stay with him always.

'They interrogated the prisoners, beat them while I played,' he tells us, sitting in his favorite chair with his feet up. Mutti makes him drink hot tea while he nibbles on a fresh *Brötchen*. 'They passed me over when they sent the other Jewish men to a place called Dachau because I have my veteran's papers. I only escaped their fate because of my brave wife.'

Mutti smiles at his words, nodding, pleased her idea worked. 'It is *you* who are brave, Papa, daring to play for the Gestapo man. What if he didn't like music?'

They smile at each other like older people do... that shared history of moments good and bad... and frightful like this one. We're thankful we were spared the destruction of everything we have, but only because it's no longer ours.

I want to hug them both and not let them go for I see something different on their faces, their eyes linked in a secret agreement that frightens me more than that night they're calling *Kristallnacht*, the night of broken glass. When thousands of Jewish businesses are ransacked, Jews arrested and killed. Synagogues burned.

And our lives changed forever.

'Papa and I have made a decision,' Mutti says, speaking in a hushed whisper. 'We must get you girls out of Berlin.'

'What?' I pull back, solemn. 'You can't mean that, *please*.'

'Mutti is right, Rachel,' Papa says, holding my hand. His is cold. 'For years we had no choice in our lives... either endorse the Nazi

Party... *never*... or stay silent. We've stayed silent too long. It's time we resist, we fight.'

'Fight the Nazis? *How?*' I ask.

'By sending you and your sisters out of Germany so you can be safe from these monsters.'

'I'm trying to get visas so my girls can go to England or America, Rachel,' Mutti adds, laying her hand on my shoulder. 'So far, I can only get one visa approved. I'll keep trying. You and your sisters must *never* be separated.'

'Mutti's right. There must be a way someone can help us.' Papa smacks his forehead in frustration. 'If only we had relatives in England or America.'

It's then my mind races back to a summer day and an amazing afternoon.

And a woman's kind smile.

I grab Papa's hand, then turn to Mutti so she can read my lips, and say, 'The Nazis can smash windows and rip apart our lives, but they can't destroy us. I know how we can get visas and save Leah and Tovah. All I need is a pen and some paper.'

'*How?*' Mutti begs to know, holding my face in her hands, searching my eyes for an answer she doesn't understand.

I hug them both. 'You'll see.'

Then I start humming 'Begin the Beguine'.

33

PARIS, 1938

Kay

I remain in Paris, reading the newspapers, following the war in Spain, aching every time I see a list of fallen volunteers, my heart skipping until I assure myself his name isn't there. Then word comes from Charley's team back home; their marketing research shows *McGinty's* are a success. People love them... the price, the energy boost, the packaging.

A chocolate bar every kid can love and every parent can afford is our slogan.

I feel good that I'm giving back to a company that's my legacy.

Meanwhile, I pray Max returns soon. I'm worried sick after I read about a major battle going on in Catalonia and the Aragon region with thousands of Republicans dead or wounded. No mention of their air force. Firsthand reports say Republican Spain is split in two.

Then, on a rainy November morning, I get an urgent craving for onion soup. I had a bad dream and can't sleep and no amount of patient sheep counting brings me rest. My mind spins round and round, my gut trying to tell me something I can't grab onto. I can't help but worry about Max. In my dream, I saw his handsome face in front of my eyes, smiling, his pencil moving quickly across the page, sketching, then a fierce wind came along and pulled the drawing from his hand... and he disappeared.

I woke up, drenched in sweat. I've never been so scared. And so hungry. My stomach, as well as my soul, is churning. Chances are, the dream came on because of the troubling war news, but it was so real, I can't let it go.

I dress and take the elevator down to the lobby, mutter '*Bonjour*' to the hotel doorman, chat a moment about the nip in the air and how I'm looking forward to a bowl of hot onion soup, then I start walking. I seek a place where the silverware is bent and the flower pattern on the plates is faded, a way of connecting with *him*. A place like the farmhouse where we first realized we couldn't keep our hands off each other.

To relive those moments, touching... kissing.

I've never wanted anything so much in my life.

It's early, around 4 a.m. when I join the throng at Les Halles, the heart and belly of the Paris markets. The sprawling cast-iron and glass pavilions are teeming with vendors and farmers and cooks bargaining for their food fare for the day. The earthy and fragrant smells of vegetables and strawberries and fresh meat remind me of that farmhouse.

My stomach growls as I head for a small place nearby that serves the best onion soup. I order a bowl, its steamy mist making my nose wiggle with delight, the soul-melty cheese bubbling, thick onions in broth cradling underneath, waiting to be discovered by my eager spoon.

Diving into the soup, I'm at peace, my soul soothed until—

'I must speak to you, Kay... *immediately*.'

I look up. Gertrud is standing before me, her short hair damp, cheeks shining as though she's been running. Her brown eyes dark and troubled.

How did she find me? The doorman, of course.

'What's wrong?' I ask. Then it hits me. 'It's Max, isn't it?' I push the half-eaten bowl of soup away from me. It's cold. Like the chill wrapping around my heart.

'Let's go back to the hotel,' she whispers, putting her arm around me. 'I have news that can't wait.'

* * *

All the way back to the Ritz, I feel the raw cold of a west wind creeping up my spine. Gertrud links her arm through mine, holding me so tight it hurts, as if she's afraid I'll bolt and run. It can't be good news. That tears at my insides. This is *not* the Gertrud I know. The woman who defies society with her lifestyle, more so the Nazis, and makes no bones about it. Like Max, she sees life from a different angle than this Philadelphia-bred girl who lived in books and not real life. And she knows that. She's afraid I can't take it, whatever it is, and that's why she insists we return to the hotel.

We settle in my room and she lights the fireplace, but it does little to quell my fear. I hunch down in an overstuffed chair, cold and tired from worry, but a spark of hope flares in me that the news isn't bad.

But it is.

I listen to her speak, my hands folded in my lap, my heart pounding so wildly I can hear it beating in my ears.

'I have it on very good sources that Max was captured by Italian Fascists who sent him to a monastery prison called San Pedro de

Cardena.' She pauses, takes a breath. 'I debated whether to tell you the rest—'

'Tell me. I want to know.' My voice is cold.

She nods. 'I had a feeling you'd say that. This prison is known for its horrible conditions, where prisoners are beaten and starved... and then...'

'Then what?' I cry out. I jump up out of my chair, raising my fists, clenching them tight. I can't keep in the surging despair raging inside me a moment longer.

She heaves out a deep sigh. 'Then shot by a firing squad.'

My God, Max, no!

It takes a long moment in Hell for her words to sink in. Up to now, I've teetered back and forth between hope and despair, but now I know. And the pain is excruciating. I let go with a sound so horrible and gut-wrenching, for the first time since I lost my baby, I go into hysterics. Tears... screams... sobs... until I collapse in Gertrud's arms and she holds me tight, whispering in German what I assume is a prayer for his soul.

And mine, too.

Strange, but I'll never know whether the dream I had was a spiritual connection with Max, and that somehow our love is so strong he reached out to me one last time. Or if my troubled mind conjured it up as a way of preparing me.

Wherever the dream came from, the truth is my darling Max is dead.

And I can't change that.

* * *

I wander around Paris for days afterward, unable to think, do anything. I haunt the Louvre because it's so big and has so many exhibits. I have this weird notion I can get lost in time... end up in another era or go back to the day I first met Max. That's the only time I smile. The idea pulls at me, however insane it is, and I can't let it go. When it doesn't happen, I wander around Montmartre, leaving my soul at the altar of Sacré-Cœur on the chance it can join Max's because I don't want it any more. I'll never be whole again without him. I avoid the Café de la Paix at all costs... I can't bear to walk by the establishment, much less sit at *our* table.

I'm a hopeless case.

I barely eat.

I either don't sleep for days or crash for hours... When I wake up, I start the process all over again.

What's more amazing to me is how Gertrud doesn't give up on me. She checks on me day and night to the point I become frustrated with her, especially how she keeps ranting that Max never wrote a 'chapel letter'.

What the hell is a chapel letter? I ask her in a rare moment of mental sobriety.

She tells me it's a note written the night before a prisoner's execution. Yet his name appears on the list of the men executed. She's puzzled, her reporter's mind spinning her theory into a million scenarios.

He switched places with a dying prisoner... he bribed the guards, then took a different name... soldiers of fortune often take a nom de guerre... he's ill... he was transferred.

She drives me crazy. Deep down, I want to come out of my stupor because I *want* to believe her... that somehow Max is alive, but after weeks of asking questions, sending messages, *bribing* anybody with information to sell, it's a dead end.

I have to accept the official list posted by the general in charge.

My wonderful Max lies in a mass grave somewhere in Spain.

When I finally come to terms with that, I pick myself up like I did after I lost my child. Gertrud says I'm stronger than I know and

Max would be proud of me. He wouldn't want to see me bleary-eyed and sad-faced, but the vibrant young woman he drew on his sketchpad, the woman he fell in love with.

It's her words that give me the strength to return to the Café de la Paix and sit at our table, doodling on the menu, seeing Max next to me with his sketchpad. Gertrud joins me to pay homage to the British adventurer and Hélène is by her side and cries with me for a man we all loved.

That done, I pull myself together, wash my face, but nothing can cleanse my pain, fix my broken heart. There's nothing left for me here in Paris.

With a heavy hand, I ask the clerk at the Ritz front desk for writing paper to send a telegram. Then I embrace the life I've shunned for so long with its rules and propriety and somehow it seems almost comforting, welcoming me back into the gilded fold where I belong. I have to accept that my affair with Max is but a beautiful moment in time that has no permanent address in the story of my life, only fleeting moments of happiness I will never forget.

I pen a telegram to Mother.

Three simple words.

I'm coming home.

34

NEWPORT, RHODE ISLAND, JANUARY 1939

Kay

I've always enjoyed opening the morning mail. The personal correspondence of invitations, thank yous, and the like that find their way onto my silver breakfast tray. There's something intriguing about slitting open the envelope, like opening a book. You never know what fascinating tale you'll find inside. Unlike a book, what *is* inside the envelope is wholly personal. Addressed to you. From someone you know. Of course, that doesn't guarantee you'll *like* what you find. Or in this case on a cold winter morning, expect your life to flip in a new direction in a moment.

And to think I nearly toss the letter aside.

I sip my coffee, hot and strong, and breathe in the aromatic brew. It's a typical seal-gray day in the coastal town, not much buzz since everyone from the city is in either Palm Beach or St Moritz. The perfect place for me to hide out. No one knows I'm here.

And Mother won't tell anyone.

She's still trying to figure out her next move. When I came home from Paris, she was insistent I take some time to 'find myself'. I had no idea what she was really up to. Around the holidays, she tried her best to cinch me getting engaged to Tommy Whitworth. She put so much into orchestrating it, I felt sorry for her. I told her I couldn't get engaged to Tommy. It's not fair to him, to myself, even Mother. There's no passion between us and he needs more than I can give him.

What he needs is a woman who adores him... and even more so, a woman who can give him the children I can't.

It always comes back to that, doesn't it?

After the failed engagement debacle, I'll never forget the wheels turning in her mind when she accepted the fact I'm not marrying anyone. It was quite amusing.

'You've changed since you returned from Paris, Kay,' Mother said softly, surprising me. 'You're more sophisticated, more confident than Miss Hathaway could have ever achieved, and if I didn't know better, I'd say you're in love.'

I am... I still am after the news about Max came, but I can't tell her that.

So to please her, I take up my old life and go about doing nothing, wondering how much more of 'nothing' I can stand. I need to be useful, not lounge around like a poodle with its permed tail straight up in the air. I asked Uncle Archibald about another assignment for the State Department, but he remained closed-lipped, saying he had nothing at the moment. Which makes me suspicious that things are heating up in Europe.

I'd give anything to be part of the action.

And if I'm honest with myself, it's a way of feeling close to Max, knowing I'm carrying on his work for freedom.

Fretting about my dilemma, I start with the post.

Mother's secretary sends my mail every Saturday, but today's pile is higher than usual. I flip through ten – fifteen invitations I have no intention of answering, then toss the bunch into the wire trash basket when—

I spy an envelope sticking out between two invitations and bearing French stamps.

Postmarked *Paris*.

My heart skips. *Who?* Not Max, that would be asking too much of the stars. Whatever Gertrud speculates about him being alive, it's a long shot. Still, the stars aligned for us once. I can't hope it will ever happen again. I grab the envelope and turn it over.

Hôtel Ritz, 15 Place Vendôme, Paris, France.

I'm disappointed. Most likely the envelope contains a forgotten room service charge, or even a belated Christmas card. It can't be from Gertrud; she resides at the Hôtel Meurice. I smile. I miss her and her interesting observations, how she's predicting Germany won't be content until she swallows up most of Europe after annexing Austria last March. She's smart enough to confine her public remarks to 'girly stuff' *à la* BdM – Hitler Youth for Girls – in her articles. She sent me a translation of her latest piece in *Die Junge Dame*, instructing girls about using feminine hygiene products after exercising and playing sports to control body odor. I make a wry observation of my own, that *everything* about the Nazis smells.

I often wonder what happened to the reports I gave to Mr Sands, if the Germans are still building that defense line along the French border. I can't believe they'd try to cross into France, but after Austria, who knows?

If I know Gertrud, she'll insist I return to Paris to soothe my soul. I'm not ready to deal with Max not being there, but I haven't forgotten my promise to turn the château into a home for unwed mothers.

I intend to wait until spring before I return to France.

I pray by then my self-imposed isolation will give me the peace *and* the will to go forward with my life. I swore I'd never become a charity-logged heiress flitting from one luncheon to another, writing checks to get my picture in the society columns, like adding the winning run on the scoreboard. I don't know why I said that. I don't even like baseball. Or hot dogs and crackerjacks. I feel more at home in a café on the Right Bank sipping strong coffee, betting on the races at Longchamp (I never win), and grabbing a fresh baguette and carting it home under my arm.

God, I miss Paris.

What I'm really saying is, I miss Max. And Gertrud, Hélène. The taxicabs honking, the smell of perfume that enchants your sense of smell at every street corner, the *Bouquinistes* lauding their used books where, if you're patient, you can find a treasure. And the chocolate shops. It gives me a good feeling *Radwell Paris* is doing well and I wonder if the French are ready for *McGinty's*.

I put another log on the fire in the cozy den of the guesthouse. Two bedrooms and maid's quarters. I didn't open up the main house and bring staff up here since the weather is so cold. It's me and a housekeeper I hired from town. Ethel is a matronly woman with a beaming smile and a hefty bosom, a widow with no children, which I imagine is why I hired her. We both suffer from the critical stigma associated with being childless. No one asks why. It wouldn't be good manners.

So we're left to suffer in silence. I'm happy to have her. She's efficient and cooks well, including French cuisine she's proud to say, which sets my compass back to happier days with the smell of her freshly baked croissants and strong coffee every morning. I spend my time listening to the radio and reading the newspapers and the reports coming in on our *McGinty's* launch. The feedback is good and the public loves them. What surprised me was an official letter I received from the US Army inquiring about our chocolate product and could it be modified for the military? If so, they're offering a contract for special chocolate rations for the army.

Strange. We're not at war.

Or is Gertrud onto something?

'Did you see the fancy envelope from the Paris hotel, Miss Alexander?' I hear Ethel calling out as she enters the parlor with more coffee and croissants. I see her eyes twinkle. The mail is the highlight of her day with Mother sending postcards from Palm Beach and her secretary forwarding jewelry catalogs, travel brochures, chocolate gazette news, and social invitations, which I ignore. Mother and her friends pay little or no attention to the newsreels marching across the movie theater screens showing Hitler's Germany annexing Austria or burning synagogues and destroying Jewish businesses. Instead, they fill their gossip cups with stories about Amelia Earhart being officially declared dead, and filming beginning on the famed novel, *Gone with the Wind*, while they eagerly await the announcement of who will play Scarlett O'Hara.

'I imagine it's a room service charge they overlooked, Ethel, or a lost Christmas card. If so, you may have it for your collection.'

I see Ethel's eyes widening with surprise when I slit it open and discover a *second* envelope inside postmarked *Berlin*. It's been opened and sealed again. Strange. Or maybe not. Most likely the Nazis read everybody's mail and then mark it up with swastika rubber stamps.

'It's from Berlin, Ethel,' I tell her, making a note to find last year's card from the Ritz and give it to her. It's the least I can do with the way she puts up with my melancholy.

'Who's it from, miss?'

I look at the return address. *Charlottenstrasse.* 'It's from Rachel Landau, the teenage girl I met back in 1937 when Mother and I toured Berlin.' I smile, remembering the spunky teenager who put Mother in her place. A grand moment if ever there was one.

How did she find me?

Of course, I asked her to send the sheet music to the Hôtel Ritz and she remembered.

Clever girl. I start to read and my heart leaps into my throat.

Dear Miss Alexander,

I write to you in English to say hello and do you remember me? I played the piano and sang for you. I write to you now because I have much fear of what is happening in Berlin to Jewish people. We have survived what they call Kristallnacht... night of broken glass, when the Nazis looted our shop and arrested Papa. He returned to us safe, but Mutti and Papa fear harm will come to my sisters and me if we stay in Berlin.

Do you know a person who can help us get visas to America?

We are three sisters. Rachel, Leah, and Tovah. We are 15, 12, and 9 years of age.

Thank you.

Your friend in music,

Rachel Landau.

I clasp the letter to my breast. A guttural moan rips from me like the sound of a soul lost on its way to Heaven... so close yet so far to redemption. With no one to show it the way. I can't let that happen to the sisters. I barely know this German Jewish family, but I envy their closeness with their parents, the sisters' devotion to each other, especially Rachel.

How she defended her mother still tugs at my heart.

In a strange way that I can't explain, I hear her plea as a personal mission... imagining she were my child and caught up in events so horrific no one should ever have to endure. I feel a duty to help her. More than that, it does my soul good to know I have the means to make a difference to this family. I've heard of *Kristallnacht*, but the coverage by the international press was sporadic. I intend to find out what's going on over there.

I take pen and paper in hand and write:

> Dear Rachel,
>
> How lovely to hear from you. I haven't forgotten our trip to your charming music shop and meeting your mother and two little sisters. I play the music box often and it reminds me of your courage and your love for your mother. You're a brave girl and after your news about what's happening in Germany, I, too, worry about what may come next for you and your family.
>
> I would like to help you.
>
> I shall do what I can to see about getting the proper documents so you and your family can emigrate to America.
>
> I shall write again soon.
>
> Yours also in music,
>
> Kay Alexander

I write to her in English, but I'll have the letter translated into German and send her both. I want her to see my handwriting, embrace my words to her heart as I wrote them, not typewritten words on crackly tissue paper. There's nothing more personal than handwriting, more endearing to someone waiting for an answer to give them hope. I know. I have numerous doodles Max did of me on scraps of paper and menus. And that first drawing of me as Mary and her little lamb.

Every time I look at them, I feel closer to him.

I want Rachel to feel that connection, too, that someone cares about what's happening to her and her family. That her voice is heard and she's not alone.

She has me.

I know what I have to... what I *must* do. Sister Bridget said the day would come when God would make His plan known to me. I never expected He would send me *three* children to save from the evil dragon.

'Pack my bags, Ethel.'

I feel a rush of adrenaline then a twinge of sadness pinching my heart... That cold Christmas morning is forever embedded in me, but now I know what God's plan is. An angel's sweet breath blows in my ear, whispering, *You can do it.*

'Back to Philadelphia?' she asks.

'No, Ethel, I'm going to Washington.' I heave out a sigh. 'I have no idea how, but I'm going to do my damnedest to save three sisters from the Nazis.'

35

WASHINGTON DC, JANUARY 1939

Kay

Getting visas and affidavits for three German Jewish sisters and their parents to enter the United States is downright impossible. I've been in Washington for three days making the rounds of every government office and immigration department, cajoling, *pleading*, but I get nowhere. Some officials recognize me, some don't, but they all have the same answer. *No*. It's a tapestry of red tape, letters, quotas and more red tape woven into a mass of tangled threads. I discover the quota for America for anyone emigrating from Germany is wildly overbooked and it could take well over a year before any openings can be had.

I offer to sponsor the girls, get domestic work visas for the parents and worry about what Mother will say later, but even that doesn't move me any closer to the front of the line. Simply stated, quotas are filled. The end. The US isn't speeding up the immigration process in spite of what's happening to Jews in Germany, which makes me ashamed to carry an American passport.

Finally, I appeal to Uncle Archibald and he tells me even *he* can't make the process move faster, especially since the President recalled the American ambassador in Berlin and a bill to allow refugee children into the United States failed. He suggests I look for another means of transportation to a different country, then try again to get the sisters here under different quota rules.

Like Shanghai.

Shanghai?

I can't send three young girls and their parents to the Far East on their own. I'll have to go with them. We could set up shop in the Raffles Hotel, I tell him, but the idea is no more than a passing moment of humor on what is becoming the most frustrating experience of my life. It's not until I inquire about my mysterious Mr Sands at the British consulate that I find out the British have initiated a program called *Kindertransport*, children's transport, with the first train of Jewish refugee children leaving Berlin last December. Still, that wouldn't bring the sisters here to America. And most likely, they'd be split up if they were sent to England since children are placed in foster homes. I couldn't allow that.

It gets worse. A snobby, bespectacled clerk tells me only *one* child per family can go. The sisters' parents would be devastated if they had to choose.

There must be another way.

I do more digging, contact various Jewish and Christian aid organizations in Washington, and I have tea with a kindly Jewish woman from Austria who informs me she was lucky enough to emigrate to the US because she has a brother here. *But*, she's eager to share, she has a friend in the Jewish community in Vienna who, with the help of Baroness de Rothschild, arranged visas from the

French State Department for a group of six Jewish girls to emigrate to France.

Perhaps I should try that route?

Of course, it's perfect. I have a château outside Paris where the sisters can stay and Gertrud can help me get through the red tape with the German authorities once we have the visas and affidavits. The only snag is getting domestic work visas for their parents. Jewish families often try every consulate from Portugal to Mexico to Uruguay, I'm told, but that means they'd still be separated. Still, I'm so excited I could hug the wonderful lady for her generosity in seeing me. Instead, I send her half a dozen boxes of our best *Radwell's French Chocolates*.

Being a candy heiress has its perks.

Then I send a telegram to Gertrud at the Hotel Meurice and ask her to meet me in Berlin. That the three Landau sisters we met and their parents are in danger and I need her help to save them.

I receive a reply from Gertrud that baffles me:

```
Meet you at Hotel Adlon
Wire me date of your arrival
There's something you need to know
More when you get here
```

I stare at her telegram for a long time, a slight shiver wiggling up my spine. What in God's name does she mean by that?

* * *

Berlin, February 1939

You see Nazis everywhere. You see them on the streets marching. In the cafés and beer halls drinking. You see them watching you. Their dirty, ugly smell sticks to you and no French rose-lavender soap can wash it off. I feel my skin crawl when I enter the Adlon Hotel and I can barely move without rubbing shoulders with the SS. I ignore their stares and lug my suitcases closer to me as I ramble through the lobby, trying to keep a low profile after a long trek from New York on the *Aquitania*. Yes, that old tugboat. It was the only ship I could book a cabin on. I can still hear Mother chortling when she found out.

I pull down my plain black felt hat, no fancy, black-dotted veil to give any illusion I'm a lady of mystery. That might spark the interest of an SS officer. Black wool coat, cotton gloves, plain pumps. No fancy bows or diamond clasps. Nothing to draw attention to myself. I have over five thousand dollars in Reichsmarks and French francs stashed in my bra and around my waist in a money belt as well as a silk pouch strapped to my thigh containing a ruby and diamond necklace and bracelet, should I need to sell them on the black market. I intend to make my plea directly to whatever Nazi emigration department handles the exit permits. If there's one thing I've learned about government officials, they won't take me seriously if they think I'm a flighty heiress.

I'm also carrying a smaller case filled with *McGinty's* chocolate bars.

I'm not above a little bribery. What can they do to me? I'm an American citizen on holiday.

I arrived in Berlin via a circuitous route of trains and rented motorcars after I stopped in Paris. The Baroness de Rothschild was kind enough to see me and when she heard about my plan of using the château, she put me in contact with the French State Department. It took some fancy footwork and an affidavit securing my intention of being financially responsible for the sisters, but they put the paperwork on a fast track.

At times I want to stomp my feet and scream. I ask myself, why isn't anyone else asking questions, trying to help the Jewish people still left in Germany before things get more horrific? I can't forget what Max and I saw along the French border, the defensive line the Nazis were building. What happens when they finish it? I hate to imagine... and if I fail, then three sisters and their parents will be victims of that madman. I can't... and *won't*, allow it. I've become very attached to Rachel these past few weeks through her letters. She writes to me about her songwriting, a lullaby she wrote for Tovah after *Kristallnacht*, about her Mutti doing her best to make a butter cake for her birthday, using carrots for sweetening... Leah needing new glasses (I'll fix that as soon as they leave Germany), and Papa selling his beloved violins to buy food on the black market.

That pains me deeply. And makes me cry. Uncle Archibald said I'm asking for the impossible from the US State Department and asked me why I haven't given up.

I pulled out the last letter I received from Rachel and read it to him:

Dear Miss Alexander,

I pray my letter finds you well. Yes, I am happy to receive your letters. I read them to Mutti and Papa, Leah and Tovah. We all laughed when you told us about the funny gopher who made holes in your mother's lilac garden. I hope she is well.

Things in Berlin are not so good.

Violence by Nazis is everywhere. Windows smashed, pots, dishes on the sidewalk. On our favorite shopping street (Kurfürstendamm) you see ugly cartoons of Jewish people scrawled on

buildings. I do not wish to shock you, but they are painful to see.
Tovah cried. She said they used waterproof ink like she used in
school to color in her book to make bad pictures. Leah found a
kitten with its paw hurt after a Nazi shoved it aside with his rifle,
and I retrieved books floating in the gutter.

We are so sad to see this.

We know you are doing your best to help us and we thank
you. You are kind and good.

Yours in music,

Rachel

When I finished, I saw my uncle wipe away a tear.

So I keep to my mission.

It should be simple to get them out of Germany.

All I need are their passports and exit permits and other incidentals like letters and a physical examination to present to the
consulate in Berlin. They weren't able to help me secure visas for
the parents since they've been inundated with requests, including
over two hundred from a boys' boarding school. I'm hopeful I can
convince them down the line to give me visas for the sisters'
parents. It could take another six months, but we have no choice.
What worries me is, the Nazis are putting more restrictions on Jews.
I pray we still have time.

Then again, a lot can happen in six months.

With my good news under my cap, I'm eager to see Gertrud
again. *And* the Landau family. I wired Gertrud from the ship to
make arrangements for us to meet with them as soon as possible.
And I sent a personal note to Rachel, *not to give up hope.*

I walk up and down the grand hotel staircase, but I don't see
Gertrud. Then again, I'm early. I took an overnight train from Paris
to Berlin, hoping to get a glimpse of what Max and I saw along the

French border. It was dark and I couldn't see anything, but I suffered a bout of nostalgia and sadness riding on that train, and had to tamp down my emotions for this man I loved. I'll never forget that first day at the Café de la Paix and how he smelled like leather and adventure, his eyes drawing me even before his pencil hit the paper. It was madness and innocence bottled up in an explosive cocktail I couldn't get enough of.

I still can't.

I kept the dream going when we stopped to pick up passengers at the border, then crossed into Germany, the *clickety-clack* of the train wheels spinning the memory of him round and round in my mind, him holding me, kissing me... until reality raised its head in the shape of a portly Nazi guard asking to see my 'papers'. He sniffed around my bags like a droopy-eared bloodhound so I offered him a *McGinty's* chocolate bar before he got *too* curious. He finished it one bite, sputtering *sehr gut* and *Heil Hitler* before he was off to the next compartment.

I didn't know whether to be flattered or disgusted.

* * *

Two hours later, I'm still waiting by the black marble elephant fountain in the lobby of the Hotel Adlon when I get the weirdest shiver up and down my spine. Not the creepy kind, like the Nazi on the train staring at my bosom as if he knew I'd stashed money under the lacy cups. More like an impending moment coming on that seems disconnected to reality, like you've done this before, déjà vu if you will. *That* kind.

It hits me when a tall man approaches me, making his way through the crowd of SS men; bellhops in short, gold-buttoned jackets; and hotel staff in stiff black suits. The late afternoon sun shoots through the lobby just then, ricocheting off the huge chandelier and piercing the shield I set up around myself. My mood shifts from travel weary to dreamy when I notice those broad shoulders, dark hair... He's wearing a long, dark gray topcoat, white shirt, no tie, no hat, and for some reason I search for that familiar scar above his right eye because I want to. He reminds me of Max. Just *thinking* about him raises my courage, but here in Nazi territory the rush of seeing the impossible sends my pulse racing. *It can't be him*, but with the sun swooping in through the window, I finally get a clear view of the man.

And that devil swagger I see only in my dreams.

Oh, my God... it *is* him.

He looks surprised, then anxious, then he's at my side in a long stride and a breath away from kissing me. I still can't believe it.

'Max?' I question. '*Max!*'

I ignore the tuxedoed waiter rushing by me with a tray of canapés in his hand, the SS officer with a blonde on his arm headed for ballroom and the faint music of a Viennese waltz, the foreign diplomats sipping highballs at small round tables. I see only my man.

He cups my chin. 'You're more beautiful than ever, Kay.'

'What are you doing here? You're supposed to be—'

'Dead? I'm very much alive, Kay.' He flashes a smile that borders on naughtiness. 'I promised Gertrud I'd wait till she got here, but I can't stand another moment not holding you in my arms.'

'Oh, my darling, they said you were shot by a firing squad.' His topcoat hangs loose on him, but his shoulders are still broad. I want to tell him nothing matters but him being here. With me, that he'll always be the love of my life.

'It's a long story.' He blows his hot breath in my ear and I shiver all over again. 'Let me kiss you first.' He pushes my hat back so he can see me, his hand fisting in my hair and his other hand going around my waist, holding me so tight I can't breathe, the hard look on his face softening when he searches my eyes. Yes, I still see that wild adventurer who wanted me to parachute out of his aircraft to save me, but more so the man who found a way into my battered soul. Now I'm ready to fly with him again anywhere, anytime. I can never have children, but I can be a wife, a lover, a sweetheart, yet I dare not dream he sees me that way. Oh, I want him to, I want to share everything with him. I need him, and I pray that won't be my undoing. Because this time I can't let him go. Which is why I say nothing about who I am... why I'm here, though I assume he knows about our plan to get visas for the sisters and get them out of Berlin, but *how much does he know*?

What did Gertrud tell him?

I push that thought out of my mind. I shan't spoil the joy surging within me when he kisses me long and deep. Every Nazi eye is upon us, and I don't care. Somehow, this man has come back to me, this battle-weary soldier kept for months in a prison, beaten and starved with nothing to eat but canned fish, stale bread, and rotting figs and barely enough water to survive. In hushed whispers, he tells me it wasn't only soldiers and volunteers who were kept in the old abbey, but how the Gestapo used the prison to intern political dissidents and Jews, stripping them of their humanity and dignity. How he saw up close how brutal the Nazis are in wielding power over anyone who crosses them. How the fight is just beginning... and that it will last until every Nazi is beaten.

'I see you two found each other.'

Gertrud hugs us both, the biggest smile on her face. We all talk at once. Tears flow down my face and there is such joy in my heart to be reunited with the two most important people in the world to me. Mother, of course, is in a separate category all her own, especially when she didn't squawk when I told her I was going to Berlin to bring the Landau sisters home. Seems she reads the newspapers after all and was deeply moved by the reports of *Kristallnacht*. Not that she approves or is getting soft, she's quick to remind me, but it's '*our duty as Philadelphians to help those poor people*'.

'Why didn't you tell me Max was alive?' I ask her after Max tears himself away from me... and I reluctantly let him go... to get us a table in the café. I order coffee and cakes. I haven't eaten for hours and he's worried about me, the darling. I look after him with the biggest smile on my face, disbelieving he's here.

'I got the news myself when he showed up at the Café de la Paix over a week ago.'

'Where's Hélène?' I have to ask.

'Waiting for us at my apartment. She's not fond of mixing with the SS.' Gertrud heaves out a heavy sigh. 'I finally got it out of the girl what happened to her in Poland and it makes me want to choke every Nazi bastard in here.' She cocks her eye and puts her monocle back on, a way of composing herself. 'She can hardly wait to see you, Kay.'

'Me, too.' I can guess what happened to Hélène and it reminds me we're all in danger here. Gertrud makes no mention of what stage their relationship is in, but somehow I feel both women have found a solace with each other even if it's not the intimacy Gertrud longs for. Hearing what Hélène suffered in Poland, I understand better the terrible things that have shaped her... and Rachel.

'Did you tell Max... about me?'

'That you're richer than the whole damn Third Reich?' She shakes her head. 'I know better than to get between the two of you. You'll tell him when you're ready, but be careful, Kay. The longer you wait, the longer you'll try to protect him with more lies. After a while even the truth starts to sound like a lie, so you keep covering your tracks. I know this man. He won't leave you. You'll leave him when the guilt becomes too much. I know. It happened to me.'

'The girl in Paris?'

'Yes. Learn from my mistake and tell him.'

'Like you told Hélène?' I probe.

She grins. 'I didn't say I take my own advice.'

'Won't he find out when I check into the hotel?'

'You're staying at my apartment on Matthäikirchstrasse.' She explains she took the apartment near the Tiergarten after Himmler started building 'cottages' for the SS near her home in the exclusive Dahlem neighborhood in southwestern Berlin. 'The less the Gestapo knows about why you're here, the better.'

'Are you sure you have enough room?'

'I have an extra bedroom, *Fräulein McGinty*. How you use it is up to you.'

* * *

I'm lying next to a magnificent man stroking my bare back, telling me how he thought of nothing but me in that prison. It's freezing cold in Gertrud's apartment when our passion cools. I turn up the heat and get back into bed, not ready to face the dawn. We lie in each other's arms, both of us hungry for what we didn't have during those long, lonely months.

And that settled feeling in your heart that comes with a touch of the hand or brush of the lips that means 'I'm here for you'.

How did I ever live without him?

And then, somewhere between the last sigh and the lingering kisses, Max speaks of the miracle that saved him from the firing squad.

'I shivered not from the thought of death claiming me that morning, but the cold. *A man shouldn't have to die with his teeth chattering*, I told the guard as he led me from my cell. A diversion. My eyes darted left then right, looking for a way to escape... over the fence... into the forested woods... then the mountains. I'd rather die running for my life than standing still and letting death claim me like an animal with the fight beaten out of him. Then I thought of you, Kay, looking as fair and pretty as the pink dawn peeking out over the horizon. I stopped, breathed in the memory of you for the last time and was about to make my play when I noticed two men arriving at the prison in a fancy motorcar. For some reason I stopped, watched them get out... then I saw him. A man I knew. I took to yelling and hollering like a wounded bear. It was that moment that saved my life.'

I sit still, listening to him speak about how he escaped when he recognized the Nationalist diplomat as the man he'd ferried from Paris to Madrid, flying him through a storm to get him home to his child sick with pneumonia. The child had lived.

The diplomat never forgot the brave, young Englishman and bribed the guards to look the other way when Max escaped from the prison. He then made it back to Paris by foot, donkey, then finally he hitched a ride with a priest, Father Armand, on his way back to the city to serve the faithful at Sacré-Cœur.

When he heard from the concierge at the hotel on the Left Bank that I had returned to America, he got into a drunken stupor for two weeks. He had no way of finding me. I left no forwarding address... and Gertrud had gone to Germany on a temporary assignment for the magazine. When she returned from Berlin, she found him drowning his sorrows at the Café de la Paix.

And told him I was returning to Paris.

She followed my exploits after I left, checking the wire services. I'm guessing she hoped if Max and I saw each other again, the magic would repeat itself.

It did. We spent the night together entangled in sheets and desire, but today brings back reality. We're not in Paris any more. Running my finger over the scar over Max's right eye (I notice a new one on his cheek from a knife fight with a guard), I accept that our relationship is on hold until we fulfill our mission.

Secure the exit permits for Rachel and her sisters. And her parents. Get them out of Germany.

Before it's too late.

36

BERLIN, FEBRUARY 1939

Kay

I soon discover Nazi officials have a limited vocabulary. *Nein, Fräulein* tops the list.

Fat ones, bald ones... lazy ones, even ones who pick their teeth while you're standing there with your heart in your hand and your hankie wet with tears, begging them to sign off on exit visas for three Jewish sisters. And their parents.

The problem? Their passports are no good.

Why?

According to the authorities, they don't follow the recent edict of having the middle name 'Sara' or 'Israel' added to their given name, a way of identifying them as Jewish, as well as the big red 'J' splashed on the identification page.

Trouble brews for them if we don't fix this, so I arrange a meeting with the Landaus through Gertrud. I'm disheartened at this change of events, just when we were so close, but seeing firsthand the stupidity and hypocrisy of the Nazi regime up close makes me angry. They're hitting too close to home, hurting this family I've taken on as my own. For the first time in my life, I've discovered with the Landaus the joy of being a part of something... They believe in me.

And no one judges me or expects me to be perfect.

Gertrud and I go together and, after kisses and hugs and tears, we sit down to tea and strudel and hammer out what went wrong.

Gertrud translates as the family speaks.

Herr Landau takes the lead, explaining to me in a calm voice, 'When our shop was "sold" to my employee, Herr Mueller, an Aryan, for a token amount, we disappeared from the rolls even though we still lived upstairs.'

I can't believe this outrageous sale took place.

'We had no choice, Papa,' Frau Landau says, laying her hand over her husband's. She squeezes it.

'How did that happen?' I ask, disbelieving.

'We were unaware Frau Mueller went to great lengths to erase us,' the Jewish woman says, serving me another piece of strudel.

'Why would she do that?' I ask.

Frau Landau lowers her eyes, but it's Rachel who speaks up, her voice loud and clear, 'She's jealous and hates Mutti because she's prettier... and a better baker.'

'Now, Rachel...' her mother scolds.

'Fräulein Alexander should know the truth, Mutti, how she conveniently forgot to advise the authorities we were living upstairs. I heard her say our apartment is a *Jewish pigsty* and she called Mutti—'

'*Rachel!*' Frau Landau calls out, her face turning red. 'Please, *Fräulein*, you must forgive my daughter. She's only trying to protect me.'

My eyes mist up. I envy the Jewish woman to have such love from her daughter.

'Where is this Frau Mueller?' I'm tempted to give her a piece of my mind.

'Ulrich... Herr Mueller told me she's visiting relatives near Potsdam,' says Herr Landau. He wrings his hands together and I see a man broken by a system so cruel he doesn't know what to do. According to Rachel, he lives in his world of music.

'Mutti found out what she was up to when the police came to the shop to check the newly-issued identity cards of the occupants living here,' Rachel says. 'She discovered the police never issued us any such documents because of Frau Mueller's meddling.'

'I couldn't let them know I'm deaf,' her mother explains. 'Every day we hear more rumors about how people with disabilities are sent away never to return. I couldn't bear to be separated from my family. Fortunately, Herr Mueller made an awkward excuse to the uniformed Nazi about the "misunderstanding" and Mutti and Papa secured identity cards for us... but not new passports.'

That can take months.

'I fear we'll be tossed out into the streets before then if Frau Mueller has her way,' she finishes.

Rachel perks up. 'So when I received your letters then your telegram saying you were coming to Berlin, *Fräulein*, I told my mother not to worry.' She smiles widely, her eyes shining. 'You're an American, and Americans can do anything.'

I wish I had her confidence. I don't tell them I've run into a snag with procuring visas for her parents, but I'm more determined than ever to make this happen.

Before I leave, I hand out *McGinty's* chocolate bars and never have I seen happier faces.

Then my work begins.

First, the sisters need new photos since they've grown so since their last ones. Aryan photographers won't have anything to do with a Jewish family... but Gertrud knows the right person for the job.

There's only one problem: she's on the Gestapo's watch list.

* * *

Rachel

I've never seen my sisters so giddy.

Leah is prancing around the cramped photography studio in a long velvet cape that hangs on her thin shoulders. Tovah is posing like a little princess on a small footstool wearing rows and rows of fake pearls. Props from the big trunk sitting in the corner. A copy of *Die Junge Dame* lies on a small table next to a teacup and empty plate.

And I'm staring into a camera, smiling.

The first time I've smiled in days.

Click! Flash!

'Beautiful, *Fräulein*! You could be a model,' calls out the woman behind the camera. Tall, her body slender like a pencil, her silver-gray hair pulled up into tight, pointy bun, she moves like a dancer, a long gray robe shimmering around her like a cloud.

And that red lipstick, as dark as black cherries.

Gertrud dropped us off earlier in her motorcar near Wittenbergplatz and arranged for us to have our passport photos taken by a friend of hers, a famous fashion photographer who worked for two decades for *Die Junge Dame* under the name of La Zélie.

Until she was fired.

Her real name is Freeda Grummich, she tells her with a proud smile. 'Call me Freeda.'

And she's Jewish.

I relax, relieved my photo is done. The third shot... *or is it the fourth*? I keep blinking I'm so nervous, trying to get the passport picture right. Not a full-on boring photo, La Zélie insists, but a sophisticated look showing three-quarters of my face.

'*Me*, a model?' I ask, flattered.

'I've photographed girls not *half* as pretty as you, *Fräulein*... *Ah*, I miss those times, the glamour and the excitement.' She sighs. 'But I have more important work to do these days.'

Dangerous work, according to Gertrud.

From her small studio hidden away in an attic on the fifth floor of an apartment building, La Zélie peddles passport photos to any Jew needing one, even if they're in hiding and wanted by the police. I shudder. I can't help it. The panic that has been with me since Kay told us she couldn't get the visas without new passports pricks at my chest. I'm anxious to get this over with.

La Zélie grins. 'Next, your sisters.'

Leah then Tovah have their photos taken, each unique in pose, but La Zélie isn't finished with us.

'One more photo, *meine Fräulein*, to remember me by in these difficult times... You never know what tomorrow will bring.'

I think that a strange thing to say as she groups us together, me standing, Leah to my left, Tovah sitting on the stool.

She taps her forefinger to her chin. 'I need some something pretty for your hair... *Ah*, I have it.' She dives into her trunk and pulls out sprigs of violets made of silk and arranges them in our hair.

And shoots the photo. The three Landau sisters all together. A special photo, she says, for our parents, a moment in time to keep their hearts full in years to come.

Then she scoots us out of the small studio and tells us to come back in an hour. 'I'll have your passport photos ready for you then.' She winks. 'And the fashion shot, too.'

It doesn't take much convincing to get my sisters to go to the nearby KaDeWe department store. Drinking orangeade in paper cones from the wall fountain, we *ooh* and *ahh* over the fancy dresses, jewelry... and the pretty figurines on display. We keep our heads down so no one asks us questions. As Jews, we shouldn't be here, but we're safer inside than on the streets. Nearby, a girl in short pigtails about Tovah's age is having a fit after her mother tells her she can't have the shepherdess figurine.

'What a spoiled girl,' I whisper to Leah, nodding. Tovah is also looking at the knickknack when the girl gets so mad, she knocks it off the shelf. Our eyes bug out at her insolence, but I can't believe it when the salesclerk races over and demands to know *who* broke the figurine.

'*She did it!*' The girl's mother points to Tovah, who's standing close to the girl.

Tovah is so shocked she can't move. And this from a girl who never gets stage fright when she performs in front of customers.

'*Come here, you!*' The salesgirl grabs my little sister by the arm. 'Did you do this?'

Tovah shakes her head back and forth, her big bow in her hair waving in the air like a flag of surrender in the salesclerk's eyes. This is ridiculous. I won't have her treated like this.

'*Take your hands off my sister,*' I say in a firm, strong voice, gritting my teeth. I pull her away from the woman and squeeze Tovah's hand to give her courage. My heart swells when she squeezes back. 'My little sister did *not* break the figurine. And that woman has no right to accuse her.'

I want to yell that her daughter did it, but I have the awful feeling that will make things worse. Already people are staring at us. What if someone recognizes us? We can't take that chance. We're so close to getting our visas.

Nothing must stop us.

The salesclerk pouts, then goes off to get the manager. The mother is smirking, and the girl thumbs her nose at Tovah. I'd like to grab her by her short pigtails and shake her and make her tell the truth—

But I don't.

I hear Mutti's soft but firm voice in my head telling me my sisters' safety is more important than getting revenge. I grab Leah's hand and, holding onto Tovah, we race out of the huge department store and run back to the apartment and run up the five flights of stairs. I keep looking around to check no one is following us.

But more trouble awaits us.

The door is ajar...

'Freeda, *Freeda*!' I call out. No answer.

A cleaning lady sees us and shoos us out. '*Jewish brats*... get out!'

'Where is Freeda... La Zélie?'

She looks smug. 'The Gestapo came and two SS men took her away.'

'Why?' I ask, but I know the answer. Someone informed on her.

'How would I know?' the woman spews. 'Now get out... *schnell*!'

I pay no attention to her ranting and race into the studio. It's bathed in semi-darkness, the joyous light that filled the apartment earlier with a vision into another world now dissipating into a void stilled and ominous.

The light is gone.

And so is the flamboyant photographer.

The SS men ransacked the studio, destroying her camera equipment, tossing items in the trunk onto the floor, smashing everything in the closet she used for a darkroom.

The work of the devil.

A few scattered photos lay on the floor, left behind in haste. I shuffle through them, Leah and Tovah helping me, but we're disappointed. Ours aren't among them.

The sting of hot tears threatens to spill onto my cheeks, our dream dashed by the evil of the Gestapo. I can't let my sisters see me cry. They're looking at me with big eyes, asking me what to do.

'Freeda knew we were coming back,' I tell them, keeping my voice calm, willing my brain to work out the problem like I work out the notes in a song. 'I know she left the photos for us, but where?'

Then I see it.

The copy of *Die Junge Dame* lying on the table with a sprig of violets on top. The SS men ignored it. With hope surging in my chest, I grab the magazine and—

'Leah, Tovah! *Look*...'

Inside, I find our passport photos crisp and perfect. Freeda hid them there before the SS showed up. I imagine she had a premonition her time was limited and she took precautions to help us. Also tucked inside is the photo of Leah, Tovah and me looking like princesses surrounded by a fairy glow, our eyes big and luminous like black pearls, our hair dark and rich against the shimmering backlight.

I sigh, a heavy feeling in my heart that won't go away... I send a prayer to God to help her, give her the courage to endure whatever they do to her. She's strong and smart and meeting her gives me the courage to fight the Nazis. I have a sick feeling this won't be our last encounter with them.

'I told you girls to get out!' yells the landlady, standing in the doorway. 'Or I'll call the police.'

I clasp the magazine close to my chest and grab Tovah's hand with Leah behind me. We can't wait for Gertrud to pick us up... We run all the way home without looking back, the precious photos safe.

I will never forget the day the famous La Zélie photographed us, the Landau sisters. Photos that will save our lives.

If only we could have saved hers.

37

BERLIN, FEBRUARY 1939

Kay

With new photos in hand for the sisters, I act as a 'friend' of the family and the head of the Lilac Hill Quaker Aid Society, presenting their invalidated passports and asking Nazi officials to make new passports *schnell* so I can complete their applications for visas to France. The official ignores me. When I try to bribe him with a roll of Reichsmarks, he takes the money, then threatens to turn me over to the Gestapo.

Gertrud warns me not to protest, but I learned my lesson.

It's going to take ingenuity not dough to get the sisters and their parents those new passports. I haven't even considered how I'm going to get the parents emigration status to France, then get the family to America. In the back of my mind, I consider smuggling them into France, but it hasn't come to that.

Not yet.

Then, on my next trip to update their passports, I become the Parisian wife of their cousin now living in Paris (speaking French with Gertrud translating). I get close to securing the paperwork I need for them to fill out until the complacent German leaves his desk and is replaced by a mean official who refuses my request when I can't produce a marriage certificate showing I'm married to an Aryan.

Finally, I get desperate enough to go theatrical. I head over to the music shop (I sent a message to Gertrud to meet me here) and explain what I have in mind to Herr and Frau Landau and show them via hand signals and my awful singing and dancing that I want to present myself as their daughters' booking agent to get their visas. That I'm taking them on tour and we need those new passports.

They clap and cheer my humorous performance, then Papa takes out his violin to accompany my dancing. Gertrud arrives in time to witness my 'act' and rolls her eyes. She conveys my plan to the Landaus and they keep shaking their heads.

'*Ja*, we understand, Fräulein Alexander,' Herr Landau says, 'but it's too dangerous. It could backfire and the girls will be sent to a labor camp for lying to the police.'

That rattles me to the core. That these loving parents are so afraid of the Nazis, they're not willing to trust me.

Then again, why should they?

It's a daring plan and my butt is on the line, too, but if there's one thing I learned as a debutante, the key to a successful coming out is to be entertaining, give them a show. I know I can make it work. *If*—

Excited, I burst forth with: 'What if we *show* the police what the Landau sisters can do, that they're a legitimate singing act.'

'What if they ask for proof of a tour?' Herr Landau counters.

Good point.

'I'll have Gertrud's contacts draw up a phony contract Warner Brothers would envy.'

I don't know how Gertrud translates that, but it isn't a firm 'no'. The Jewish couple hold hands and whisper to each other while I die inside. Frau Landau nods, then smiles at me. '*Ja*, we agree to your plan... if we can be there, too.'

I know what she's thinking. If the worst happens and the girls are arrested, they'll never see them again.

'Of course,' I say, taking her hand in mine. It's cold. The poor woman is shaking. 'I promise you, Frau Landau, nothing will happen to your daughters.'

For the first time in my life, my money won't buy what I want, but I'm hoping my charm will. The girls' lives depend on it.

* * *

I return two days later to the office of the German police authorities with the three sisters and their parents in tow. Sporting round, dark glasses and a saucy hat, I explain I'm a talent agent from Hollywood and I booked the '*Landau Sisters Trio*' into cafés in Paris. Sitting on the edge of the official's desk with my legs dangling in a provocative manner, I insist we need new passports and exit permits 'pronto' for them to leave the country. Their parents, too, as chaperones.

'I've never heard of the Landau Sisters Trio,' spouts the stodgy official.

'Oh?' I raise my eyebrows. 'They performed during the 700th birthday party for Berlin... Everybody loved them.'

Well, they weren't *at* the celebration, but they did perform that day. For me. At their music shop. I don't remind him Jews weren't invited.

'Goebbels was there,' his secretary adds.

The official taps his pencil, thinking, the name of the propaganda minister putting a different spin on the situation, a point I intend to drive home.

'Rachel, Leah... Tovah, show the official what you can do.' I smile, nodding at Rachel who grins and starts singing a popular German folk song. Leah joins her, strumming on her guitar with Tovah on violin.

Their angelic voices and heart-lifting music fill the air of the stodgy, authoritarian offices, attracting workers and German citizens waiting in the long line to clap and cry. It works. We leave there with three shiny new passports for the sisters.

But not for the German couple I affectionately think of as Mutti and Papa.

According to Nazi rules, they can't leave Germany until they produce a complete list of their assets, bank accounts, and a laundry list of things I don't understand.

Their passports are put on hold until then.

A cloud passes over everyone's faces and I can't stop it. Frau Landau takes my hands in hers, warm with clean, plain nails and a gentle grip, her eyes searching mine to see into my soul, take away the guilt I can't shake.

'You've done what no one else could, *Fräulein*,' she says in German. Gertrud translates for me. 'You saved my girls. No mother can ever ask for more than that. *Danke*. Go in peace... and may God go with you. Papa and I will stay here and guard the nest for the day when they return to us.'

I look at this woman with years lined on her face in upward strokes, laugh lines not frowns. I don't think I've ever seen her frown. I've never seen such courage and yet I wonder if she cries in her pillow at night when her husband is asleep beside her. If she is also living a lie because there's no other way to survive amidst the daily turmoil of being Jewish in a world turned upside down by a madman? Telling herself that someday her girls *will* return and she'll be there to greet them.

Or will we both be lost when that lie takes from us what we love the most?

Time will tell.

I gather together what courage I have left and, with Gertrud at my side, make the rounds of the consulates asking for visas for the girls' parents, but without those new passports, we come up empty.

I'm sick with fear.

If anything happens to them, it's my fault.

* * *

I suffer a case of nerves when I see the swastika painted on the tail of most aircraft landing and taking off at *Tempelhof*. We're sitting ducks in *Nellie Blue* if a crazed Nazi pilot gets his dander up and uses us for target practice.

We're back from Paris after meeting with the French State Department. After the girls had their medical papers stamped numerous times, letters from their parents giving up their custodial rights, more stamps, then their new passports, protocol dictated I put their name on the list for the *Kindertransport* and we wait. We didn't. To speed up the process, Max and I flew to France to get the final stamped paperwork in person, again representing myself as the head of the Lilac Hill Quaker Aid Society. There I made the last-minute decision to change one thing: the French government requires the parents sign over legal guardianship to the Rothschild's foundation. I wasn't sure of the spelling of the long-winded group name, so I asked the Landaus to leave it blank, trusting me to fill it in.

I did.

With my name. Kay Alexander. I'll never forget the hush in the shop when I explained to them the rules, feeling something reverent and good filling a hole in my heart, how this family showed me that strength comes from being there for each other when the chips are down, like Rachel standing up for her mother. I never forgot that hot August day then receiving her letter begging for help, thoughtful, beautiful words overflowing with a young girl's devotion to her sisters. I decided then not to let my life mean nothing. I was determined that such courage would not doused by the flame of that madman Hitler trying to destroy this family.

A family that touched my heart and helped fill the lonely void within me.

I'm proud to say I'm now responsible for these girls until their eighteenth birthdays.

Max parks the biplane in a rented space in the hangar at *Tempelhof* and Gertrud picks up my handsome pilot and me, then we tie everything up in a neat package. I help the sisters pack the one suitcase they're allowed, adding two *McGinty's* chocolate bars for each sister (did I see Tovah sneak her violin into her suitcase when Rachel wasn't looking?) then we'll head to the train station here in Berlin on the March departure date to join the other children leaving for France. Max will fly back to Paris after we leave and meet us at the château.

Gertrud insists Max and I stay at her apartment until then. She and I will accompany them since parents aren't permitted by the Nazis to be escorts. The parents must also sign a document saying they won't use their children living in France as a means of applying for a French visa, which is why I will apply for them myself as domestic help for my château.

I'm not above a bribe when it comes to getting Herr and Frau Landau out of Germany.

* * *

Berlin, March 1939

'I insist you let me pay you, Max, for ferrying Gertrud and me back and forth from Paris.'

'A kiss... or two... will suffice.' Max leans down to brush my lips with his, but I pull back, teasing him. We're cuddled up in bed in Gertrud's apartment... We depart tomorrow for France, the sisters, Gertrud, and me.

'I'm serious, Max. You have no job and you're still healing from your time in prison.'

He sloughs off any lingering effects from his ordeal, but I can see the toll it took on him. He sits by himself, staring into space with his sketchpad in his lap, he pushes away his food... his stomach is still adjusting to nutritious meals... and he cries out in his sleep. Names of fallen comrades. I soothe his brow, but I worry about him. The only time I see him at ease is behind the controls of his biplane.

'Don't worry about me, Kay. I have back payments for my sketches coming to me from the newspapers in Berlin and Paris.' He kisses me and I melt into him, then, 'And I received an offer from a London newspaper to do a series of drawings on what I saw in Spain. *Everything*.' His eyes darken and his nostrils flare when he speaks about the war. Then he smiles, as if he's shown me too much of his pain and tells me to use the money I collected from the ladies of the Lilac Hill Quaker Aid Society to pay for whatever the sisters and their parents need.

Only there is no Lilac Hill Quaker Aid Society.

Just me and my fortune.

I keep my mouth shut and cradle my head into his chest at night when we lay next to each other. Gertrud was right. The lies don't stop... they keep getting bigger.

To think I once said I'd rather be alone than live a lie. That was before I found Max again.

What fools we liars be...

38

BERLIN, MARCH 1939

Rachel

I sit on my suitcase in the waiting room of the train station, shivering in the dampness, a fistful of unhappy butterflies camping in my stomach while I wait my turn for inspection with the surly SS guard. We've been hovering here since dawn, the steam coming out of the engine reminding me of the devil's breath hissing loud in my ears, eager to take my sisters and me far away from everything we love. Mutti, Papa. Our music shop. Singing for them in the parlor, helping Mutti dust the instruments... watching Papa's head nodding up and down while I vocalize the scales. Then sneaking a butterscotch candy from Mutti's crystal dish.

It was too wonderful.

And now we must go.

I don't want to leave home, but my parents insist we're in danger, that several Jewish people on our street have received 'transportation' orders to pack their bags and show up at a designated place for relocation. We could be next.

We have no choice. Leah, Tovah, and I. The train station is thick with smoke... and tears and a cold mist frosting the air. The waiting room overflows with parents and their children clutching one small suitcase. Mostly young children under twelve, but I see a few my age... especially that good-looking boy munching on a chocolate bar watching me. Mischief flickers in the depths of his dark brown eyes... He shows no fear of the Nazis, as if he has nothing to lose. He doesn't look away, but keeps staring, then grinning.

Why me? I'm not so pretty, but he makes me feel like I am. He's taller than the SS guard, a handsome boy with steely-dark eyes. I can't believe he makes me feel guilty for noticing him on the worst day of my life. He smiles, then tips his cap.

No, this isn't right, I must turn away... but not before I notice the deep dimple in his chin.

I sigh.

I return my gaze to the children, parents sobbing... hugging their young ones so tight, they cry out. I feel a pressure pushing down on my chest, the impact of what our parents are feeling hitting me hard... like a fog closing around them so thick they'll never fight their way out, never see their babies again. So they run their fingers over their son's or daughter's face, willing to memory any little trait dear to them... chubby cheeks, long, endearing black lashes... a crooked smile. A wispy curl that never stays in place. Yet the sweet scent of innocence clings to the children. Fidgeting in their parents' grasp, asking for water... a favorite toy. They don't understand, don't know we're going to France or when we'll see our parents again.

If we see them again.

That fear makes every parent choke back tears, stifle the words they want to say... but don't so as not to frighten them.

Don't forget me, mein Kind, *my child, if we never see each other again... don't forget me,* bitte. *Please.*

I can't believe it's happening today after weeks of paperwork and headaches and Mutti kissing the tops of our heads numerous times. One look at her dark, troubled eyes tells me she's feeling the pain of letting us go hard. She's across the room with Leah, trying to get her to talk, say *something*... My sister hasn't spoken for a week. Papa is here with Tovah and me on the other side, doing his best to keep us brave, telling us that he loves us and that we are the music in his life.

We have to stay separate.

Only one parent can say goodbye to a child.

Not on the platform. Here in the waiting room.

Fräulein Gertrud told us the Nazis are very conscious about creating any negative press, which is why they force us to say goodbye inside the waiting room. But we are three sisters; surely the SS guard won't object. Gertrud insists we can't take that chance so we stay on opposite sides. The guards have the power to revoke our transit permits, she's quick to add. I nod, understanding. Along with Fräulein Kay, she will act as our escort. Earlier, the Austrian woman gathered us together on the platform and snapped a photo of us, promising to send a copy to Mutti and Papa. We are so grateful the beautiful American woman came to our rescue. I knew she was special and wish I could make her smile more. She reminds me of a film star in her smart blue suit with white buttons and that fancy coat lined with fur. She looks puzzled for a moment and then she smiles when she sees me.

Can she see into my heart? Know that it's breaking?

I wipe my eyes with my coat sleeve. I can't let her or my sisters see me crying. I'm nearly sixteen and in charge of Leah and Tovah. Mutti is depending on me. I catch her looking at me from across the room, nodding. Leah is holding onto her around the neck, whispering in her ear, knowing she can't hear the words, but the warmth of her breath lights up my mother's heart. She kisses Leah's cheek and for the first time I'm conscious of the grave duty I have to take care of my sisters and be there for them like Mutti is for us. It's a feeling of excitement that wiggles through me from my head to my toes.

That now I'm a woman.

I must act strong like Mutti. And kind. Yes, never forget *kind*. It's the cream in our porridge, the cinnamon in our strudel. That extra something that makes life wonderful.

I peer over my shoulder at Fräulein Kay... She's in deep discussion with the head escort from the French Jewish Aid organization, a heavyset woman with double chins, her round face flushed. And a funny hat with a long feather that keeps getting in her mouth. She checks her list over and over, counting children, making sure we have our manila tags with our number fastened to our coats.

I balked at wearing a number like a child until the surly SS guard yelled in my face, 'No tag, *Jew girl*? Then you stay.'

I steered clear of him after that, but here he is again. Making us open our suitcases and rummaging through them with his black-gloved hands, spewing lewd comments and pulling out items *verboten* to take with us. Money, silver spoons, forks, watches, anything of value.

Then the SS guard sniffs around Tovah's open suitcase like a hawk eyeing an egg in an eagle's nest, his sharp beady eyes catching the sheen of mahogany peeking out from her nightclothes.

Her violin.

'*Mein Gott*, what is this? A violin?' he yells. 'Jews aren't allowed to own anything of value.'

'My daughter is a gifted violinist,' Papa says, attempting a smile. 'She can play for you—'

'Then she can stay in Germany, Jew, and play for our Fuehrer.'

Papa's eyes widen with fear. What the SS man implies means certain death. 'No, you must let her go, *bitte*, please.'

The German smiles wide. 'She can go... but *without* her violin.'

I can't believe the horror on Tovah's face when the SS man grabs her violin and smashes it on the ground, then stomps on it with his jackboot. She's so stunned, she chokes up with disbelief. Mutti cries out, puts her hand to her throat. Papa goes rigid, his musical core so shaken he can't speak, but he must protect his child and reaches out to grab Tovah—

She's too fast for him.

Spitting at the SS man, she grabs her violin bow and runs.

Into the crowd of children lining up at the entrance and ready to board the train. She disappears into the sea of brown and gray winter coats, hanging braids and winter hats, the children squashed together like new puppies snuggled up tight in a litter.

Where... *where is she*?

We're too afraid to move with the eyes of the SS guard upon us, but Fräulein Kay rushes over to intervene. Her friend lays her hand on her arm and shakes her head. Fräulein Kay pulls back, gritting her teeth, ready to spring into action. We watch with horror when the Nazi pulls out his Luger. I swear I'll trip him if he goes after my little sister. He looks left then right, sizing up the onlookers, then thinks better of creating a bigger scene with everyone watching him. Instead, he shouts, '*Heil Hitler*.'

And stomps off.

The train whistle blows. *One, two, three* toots.

Steam billows up, the great engine roaring to life. Everyone rushes to get on to the train, pushing, shoving, more tears. One father is so distraught, he pulls his daughter off the train and hugs her one more time. Another parent grabs her child and takes off, not bearing to let her go. The French escort lady yells for everyone to get on board or be left behind. Mutti's eyes grow wide and she races from child to child, looking for her baby.

'Tovah, *Tovah*!' she screams.

'We've got to find her!' I yell, grabbing Papa's sleeve.

'You and Leah get on the train,' he insists. 'I'll find Tovah.'

'No, Papa, we're not leaving without her.'

'You *must*.'

'*No!*'

I can't believe it when two strong arms grab me and spin me around. 'Your papa's right, you must get on that train. I'll find your little sister.'

It's the tall, handsome boy, his eyes dead serious. His voice is deep and masculine... making me twitch. Compelled to keep staring at him, I hold in my breath, letting go for a moment my fear. He continues holding me, protecting me, saying *I will find her*.

I trust him.

Why, I don't know. His presence has captured me without warning, and again, I get the feeling he's willing to risk anything for freedom... and that he knows the pain of losing someone and wants to help me. Then, as if he, too, feels the strange pull between us neither of us understand, he lets me go and races off before I can catch my breath.

Can he find Tovah?

What follows next is utter chaos. Mutti, Papa... Fräulein Kay and her friend... Leah... me. Racing up and down the platform, getting on the train to look for her... then getting off the train... back into the waiting room... the toilets... behind the train station...

She's not there.

Then a long, final blast shrills in our ears and the train leaves the station, the white steam billowing up in cloud-like bursts, leaving us standing on the platform, holding each other, tears streaming down our faces.

No Tovah.

And no ticket to freedom.

The station clock on the wall ticks away the minutes... thirty... forty-five... then a whole hour since Tovah went missing. In spite of looking *everywhere* for her, she seems to have vanished.

A cold March wind blows through the empty train station and a light drizzle wets the stone platform. The train for France filled with frightened children is long gone, their parents shuffling away like wounded soldiers, nursing their broken hearts.

Abandoned dolls, teddy bears, sit on the benches without their owners.

Chocolate wrappers litter the waiting room floor. Kay handed out *McGinty's* bars to us and the others to make us smile.

I'm not smiling now. I'm reeling from the raw emotion that rips through me no matter how hard I try to stop it. I can't believe the disgusting inhumanity of that SS man toward my little sister. What that monster did was more damaging to Tovah than smashing her violin. He smashed her dream. And that crushes me. It hurts so bad, I want to hold her tight, tell her that no matter how horrible these Nazis are, I refuse to let them beat us.

Yes, the train has left.

But Kay insists we're not finished.

'A plan is hatching in my brain to make this right, Rachel. I'll get you and your sisters safely to France, I promise.'

'What do you mean?' I have to ask.

She shakes her head. 'First we've got to find Tovah, I can't... *won't* believe anything else.'

I leave Mutti and Papa in the waiting room, go back outside and scan the platform. Passengers for the next train are arriving, milling about with no idea of the urgency making my stomach turn.

No sign of Tovah.

I return inside and do my best to console my parents, holding

Mutti's cold hand, speaking in low tones to Papa that they should wait here should Tovah return, while Kay, Gertrud, and Leah keep up the search. I peek outside, looking for the tall boy... hoping he didn't abandon us, remembering his husky and warm voice, his eyes searching mine, wondering, hoping I believed him... a boy who'd grown up fast but hadn't gotten used to the loneliness that came with it.

I lower my eyes and say a silent prayer he finds Tovah, then I tell my parents she couldn't have gone far, but we all know danger lurks on the streets of Berlin. She could have been kidnapped... or run over by a tram. Yet I must keep their hopes up.

We huddle together in silent prayer when—

'*I've found her!*'

I stand up and turn, hoping, praying... not letting go of Mutti... then I tap her hand to draw her attention to the tall young man racing into the waiting room with Tovah in his arms.

My God, did I ever think I would know such a boy?

Dark eyes shining, the big smile that makes me sing. He's the bravest... most wonderful boy ever. He cradles my little sister in his strong arms, her trust in him telling by the way she lays her head against his shoulder. Peaceful... and relieved. I knew I was right about him. He found her. Tearful, dirty face and scraped knees, but she's safe. Mutti couldn't hear his jubilant cry, but she nearly collapses at the most beautiful scene to a mother's eye, then runs to her little girl.

'My baby, *my baby*!'

'Where was she?' I ask this marvelous boy and at that moment his gaze holds me in its grip and I see the joy he feels that he saved my sister. I have the feeling there's more to his story and I want to know it, and him, better.

'I found Tovah under a tree in the park, curled up like a squirrel,' he says, his eyes never leaving mine. 'Crying and clutching her violin bow in her hand.'

Mutti brushes wispy hair out of Tovah's face, whispering to her how much she loves her. Leah is crying, and Papa is beside himself, taking Tovah into his arms and thanking the boy over and over.

He nods, looks at me, smiles... then walks toward the station door.

I gasp.

Where does he think he's going?

I run after him. 'I knew you'd find my sister,' I say, taking his arm. He flinches, but I don't let go. I don't want to be brash, but I can't let him leave. My heart won't let me. 'I don't even know your name.'

'Jacob Wolf Kadin,' he says, 'number 6752, but everyone calls me Wolf.'

'Where are you going, Wolf?' I ask.

He smiles. 'I don't know... the train's gone and—'

'You have no place to go... and no one, am I right?'

He shrugs. '*Ja*, but I'll survive. I always have.'

'No, you're staying here with us. We're not beaten yet. Fräulein Kay is an American and they can do anything.' I grin. 'She promised she'd help us... and you, too.'

He looks surprised. 'I'm an extra burden you don't need.'

'Please stay... *for me*?' I ask. 'You're my hero.'

His smile is thankful and sends a fluttering through me I've never felt before. A longing for something I don't understand... but want to.

'*Ja*,' Wolf says, taking my hand in his. 'I'll stay. For you.'

* * *

Kay

We've just suffered through the worst nightmare, a moment in Hell with that SS guard and Tovah running away, but a strange thing happened. In the midst of the chaos and fear and disappointment, a moment of joy and peace settles upon us.

A holy gathering of a family come together to thank God for bringing their little girl back to them.

My heart soars with hope, threatening to burst as I listen to Rachel singing to Tovah to soothe her while she peeks at the young man next to her, grinning at her.

> *'The night is cold*
> *But my hand is warm*
> *Take my hand, little one*
> *Lay your head against my shoulder*
> *And sleep.'*

I hum along as Gertrud translates. It's a lovely tune and so fitting. Sometimes, when you least expect it, you witness magic. You don't know how, why... or if it will last then go *pouf*! When it happens, you stand back and watch.

Like now.

I feel a tug to my heart when I look at the young Jewish girl and the boy she's smiling at. He swept into her life during a moment of heartache and despair, his determination to find her little sister making his way into her heart. And he's very handsome, too. Any young girl would fall for his charm. The funny thing is, I hope she does. She deserves some happiness in this crazy upside-down world.

And a protector, too.

Yes, I can trust him not to hurt her. It's something in his bold swagger, his watchful eye taking in the situation and acting upon it... and not expecting anything more than a thank you.

He reminds me of Max.

Speaking of my brave, fearless artist... If I can get the German authorities to give their approval, I know how to get the girls to Paris... the young man, too. He gave up his place on the *Kindertransport* to save that little girl. But I must do it fast. I don't trust that SS man. He could have their transit visas revoked for no reason other than pure hatred of the Jewish people. I don't know how a man like that can live with himself. It makes me want to work harder to save these sisters.

My plan?

I'm going to call on *my* hero, Max.

And tell him to fire up *Nellie Blue.* We're going for a ride.

39

BERLIN, MARCH 1939

Kay

It takes us four hours to get clearance to take off from *Tempelhof*, each Nazi official arguing we must go to the next official for *his* stamp, our hearts in our throats. Max is concerned about flying time to Paris. The afternoon light is dimming... our nerves pulled taut. Papers checked and rechecked, Gertrud is at her best communicating the urgency of our trip with Nazi officers. She's stern yet friendly, and she's not above a sly joke or two that make their eyes widen. She drops the right names to the right people, and soon we're ready to go with Gertrud letting go a vigorous '*Heil Hitler!*'

I find that so disturbing.

Yet it's necessary for her to retain her status. It shows me how deeply the Nazi salute affects me, how fully ingrained it is in me to hate these bastards even when we get the proper papers in our hands. I nearly sob with relief, but keep it in, my shoulders shaking. I can't let the children not see me strong. Max either. He's ready to take off for his return flight back to Paris when our *Kinder* entourage races out onto the field, Gertrud at the wheel of her motorcar, honking her horn, the whole atmosphere exploding as we ramble on about what happened at the train station.

He looks glad to see me, the air between us charged when he takes my hand and rubs the back of my neck. It's a moment I wish could last longer, but my heart is hammering and the girls are exhausted. With suitcases stashed in the baggage compartment and the sisters and the boy huddled together in the back passenger seats, we say goodbye to Gertrud with hugs and kisses. She'll return to Paris by train and meet us at the château.

We take off minutes later.

I try to relax while Max takes us home. Strange, I shouldn't think of Paris as home, but I do. It's a noisy trip, loud and turbulent, the biplane shaking. At one point, we drop in an air pocket, causing alarm for the girls, then we fly steady for the rest of the trip, the roar of the engine putting the younger sisters to sleep. When I turn around I notice Rachel and Wolf holding hands. I smile. I see that sparkle in Rachel's eyes that I haven't seen since that first day she sang for me at the music shop.

And it's a lovely thing to see.

* * *

Rachel

'Tell me, Wolf, how did you end up in Berlin on the *Kindertransport*?'

His eyes burn bright with the memory, the turbulent emotion surging through him, making him clench his fists. We've been in the air for hours, saying little, just being with each other, but I feel compelled to ask him before we land. I sense he's been thinking about it by the way he keeps looking behind him at the clouds gathering, sweeping away his past. The late afternoon sunlight coming through the plane's windows picks up the fierceness of his eyes as he begins to speak.

'My family came from Belarus to Vienna then Berlin to escape the pogroms,' he says. 'My father disappeared after *Kristallnacht* and I didn't want to leave my mother in Berlin, but my older brother made me go, changing my birthdate and making me fifteen not sixteen.'

'But you're so much taller than the other boys.'

He smiles. '*Ja*, the German authorities in Berlin questioned me, but I convinced them to let me go.'

'What do you want to do in Paris?' I ask him above the roar of the engine.

'I want to build things,' he says without hesitation. 'Bridges, hotels... a home someday for—'

He leaves the words unsaid, a dream that lives in his heart... and in mine when I fall in love. I take his hands in mine... big strong hands that can build houses and a quick mind to run his own business. For now, that dream is far away, but the most wonderful thing is, he has me to share it with. He's older than I am, but I'm a woman and as Mutti says, we're wiser in the ways of the heart. When we find a man we want to be with, we take it slow. Like Challah baking in the oven. Weave the dough into lovely braids, then watch them expand as the bread bakes. Like love grows between a man and a woman.

I lay my head on his shoulder... Wolf strokes my cheek and it's a moment of contentment that soothes my troubled soul. I want to fall in love, but first, we must get to Paris where we'll be free from the Nazis.

And then?

Then we're in God's hands.

* * *

Kay

With Le Bourget in sight, we're cleared to land. Everyone is safe, our tears have dried, and our hearts are full. Nothing can harm the girls now; they're safe.

What about the other Jewish children left behind?

'Why don't we bring more children to France?' I say, thinking out loud when Max puts *Nellie Blue* down on the runway.

Max grins. 'Why not?'

And the *Kinder Air Transport* is born.

Over the next several weeks, Gertrud and I secure visas, transit permits, and affidavits for fifty-three more children to fly from Berlin to Paris. Not sure how I do it, whether the Nazis are sick of me begging for exit visas and give in to get rid of me; or because I enlist the help of Jewish communal organizations in Germany to make it happen. Both, I imagine. Finally, we're in business. The biplane holds five adults, plenty of room for us to take as many as five children on each flight.

On one trip, I hold a toddler in my arms who sleeps for the entire trip, but I'll never forget the warmth of that little boy close to my chest. I can smell the flowery fragrance of his mother's perfume on his clothes and understand her anguish. I still hurt from losing a child and start to cry softly. I'm sweating by the time we land, my arms numb from holding the little boy, but he's safe. I mumble a prayer that somehow his mother knows.

We keep trying to get more visas, operating out of the château as our base of operations with everyone taking on a job. I make sure our funds don't dry up by obtaining a letter of credit at the *Banque de France*.

I still have my jewels and I'll sell them if I have to, but so far the financial institutions in France are holding their breath to see what Hitler does next after he moves troops into Czechoslovakia. The newspaper *Paris-Midi* is filled with speculation that France will be at war with Germany before the year is over.

Gertrud continues to act as our translator with the German authorities to speed up the paperwork for the Jewish children. Hélène takes on managing the growing household of refugee children, feeding them and getting them clothes. Max keeps *Nellie Blue* gassed up and ready to go to pick up more children. He's amazed at how organized we are and as much as it kills me, I don't contradict him when he says the duke isn't a bad sort after all for allowing us to make a home for the refugee children in his château.

I grit my teeth and move on, chalking up another lie between us.

Ferrying the children from Berlin to France comes to an end when the French government stops giving out visas, fearing war is inevitable. I fall to my knees when I hear the news, devastated. All the good I'm doing is shoved aside like embers from a fire still burning because a few bureaucrats have ice in their veins. *Cowards.* Don't they know we need the *Kinder Air Transport* more than ever? That Jewish children will die if the Nazis get their way. Hitler's already annexed Austria.

What's next? *Poland? Belgium?*

And what about Herr and Frau Landau?

How will I get them out of Germany? I try to keep a positive outlook around the sisters, but anyone who reads the French newspapers knows how serious things are in Berlin. And they're getting worse. Still, I keep up the pretense things will be better because deep down I *want* it to be true. It's the only way I can go on, find peace within myself, and continue my important work with the Jewish children we *have* saved.

Rachel, Leah and Tovah set up games and music lessons for them. The Grand Hall in the old château echoes with young voices lifted up in song, not always on key but always hopeful that there will be no war with Germany and they'll see their parents again. Outside, the children kick the ball around, play tag, even hopscotch.

I notice Rachel spends most of her time with Wolf.

I see the longing looks passing between them, the way their fingertips brush when they walk by each other. She's barely sixteen, too young to fall in love... *or is she?* I was eighteen when I let myself be swayed by romance and found refuge in a man's arms. I'll have to watch them, but Wolf is strong and a hard worker and very protective of the three Landau sisters.

Of course, I say nothing about Rachel's budding romance to her parents when I write to them. The sisters receive letters from the elder Landaus, saying little except they're surviving and hope to join them soon. They still live above the music shop.

They're safe. For now.

I keep trying to secure French domestic work visas for them since we have the transmit permits and papers needed to fly them out of Berlin.

Finally, that day comes on September 1st.

There's the nip of a cold winter in the air when we take off from Le Bourget to fly to Berlin. Max, Gertrud, and me. The sky is clear, not a cloud anywhere, yet I don't have a good feeling about this. When we checked in with the tower, Gertrud heard, '*Germany is up to something... Hold on, the news is coming in now...*'

We've been in the air thirty minutes when Max gets an urgent call on his radio.

'Return to airfield, *Nellie Blue*, over,' I hear the heavily-accented voice over the radio say in English.

'This is *Nellie Blue*,' Max says, 'I read you. What's wrong? Over.'

'Germany has declared war on Poland, then invaded her borders. It's not safe to proceed. Keep your eyes peeled for enemy aircraft. I repeat, return to the airfield immediately. Over.'

For a moment, none of us move, each lost in our own thoughts.

I narrow my eyes, squinting into the sun, trying to see if we're alone up here. Not for long, I imagine. It will be only days before France and England declare war on Germany. Max adds that England fears the Nazis could take Belgium... Her ports are close to the British coast. Then France will join Britain since the two counties made a pact to guarantee Poland's borders.

Max grips the control stick so hard his knuckles turn white. He's a pilot. He'll return to England and get into the fight as soon as they clear him to join the RAF.

Gertrude is breathing heavily. She's now considered an enemy alien in France, but she's a member of the press and will work that angle to stay free. She doesn't want to leave Hélène.

I'm an American and we're not in this war. I should go home to Philadelphia, but I can't. We were so close to getting the girls' Mutti and Papa out of Germany, but now it's too late. I shudder to think what will happen to them. I'll have to break the news to Rachel, Leah and Tovah. They're my responsibility now... like family to me. How ironic that I lost my daughter and now I have three young girls in my care. I swore to their parents I would never let anything happen to them.

And I won't. We're safe in France, thank God.

I look over at my darling. His jaw is set. I can't tell him who I am. Not now. The war won't last long. Surely only a few months... and once again there will be music in the hearts of the three sisters and they'll see their loving parents.

I wish it to be so, but I wonder where we'll be when this war is over.

Will we have interesting stories to tell, scars to show? Or will we reminisce about how we got through the war unscathed?

Will any of us be here at all?

40

CHÂTEAU DE SAINTE-LUCIE-DES-FLEURS, OUTSIDE PARIS, APRIL 1942

Rachel

My hand trembles when I open the Red Cross letter.

A second envelope, thicker in size, also arrived, hand delivered by Kay from Paris, hidden under her wide-brimmed hat in case the SS searched the train passengers. By some miracle the letters came tied together in a bundle with a piece of twine. A thoughtful gesture by a kind soul and for that I am grateful.

Bent, smudged, stamped with strange markings, the letters made their way through various channels before they found their way to Kay at the Hôtel Ritz via the black market in Vichy, France.

I let go with a sigh, remembering with a deep fondness when we'd gather around the table in our music shop in Berlin, a tall white candle burning, the smell of wax mixing with freshly baked bread filling my nostrils as I read her letters to Mutti and Papa. I never thought then how important those letters would become, giving my parents an address to keep in contact with us.

I scan the Red Cross letter... The printed words are in both German and English... but the clear, precise handwriting is in German. The signature startles me.

'It's from Herr Mueller, Kay.'

Ulrich.

Why is *he* writing to me and not my parents?

'The Aryan forced to buy your music shop?' she asks, sipping tea. We gathered together here in the château library to read the letters; her smile turns downward at hearing this information. 'Why?'

'I don't know...'

Staring outside the window with grim emotions welling up in me, I see my sisters playing tag with Hélène, laughing. I didn't tell them about the letters; something held me back. A gut feeling when I saw the Red Cross on the envelope. Mutti and Papa never wrote to me via the international organization. They'd be too scared to seek them out.

Something's wrong.

I read Herr Mueller's message out loud: '*Herr and Frau Landau have decided not to emigrate... more information will follow.*'

I'm puzzled over his message, so is Kay, but it can't be good.

'Open the other letter, Rachel,' she urges me in a soothing voice.

I feel my chest tighten, my heart locking into place every wonderful memory I have of Mutti and Papa as I read the second letter from Herr Mueller. I don't want anything to change those, no matter what it is in the letter.

'*I regret to inform you,*' I translate for Kay as I read, '*that your parents committed suicide rather than be relocated, that is, sent to a labor camp.*'

'*No!*' I shout, standing up and tossing the letter on the floor. 'There has to be a mistake... It's against Jewish law to take your own life. I refuse to believe it.'

'Of course you don't... and neither do I.' Kay takes my hands in hers, trying to calm me down. 'I'll ask Gertrud if she can help... find out what happened, but it may take months.' She bites her lip, knowing the question she must ask. 'What about Leah and Tovah?'

'I have to tell them.' I have a duty; I'm their big sister and I can't let them see me lose control... I can sob my eyes out later. Fighting to steady my breathing, I ask, 'Will you help me, Kay?'

She nods. 'Of course.'

What follows is the worst hour of my life telling my sisters the sorrowful news, holding them close and crying our eyes out together as we struggle through the grief and loss of our beloved Mutti and Papa. Also in the envelope are their *'goodbye* letters' addressed to me, Leah and Tovah. Simple, beautiful words of love and begging us to understand their decision. That they didn't want us to think they died in a concentration camp, alone, shamed, and without each other. They indicate they intend to take their own lives and sink into a sea of calm in the River Spree where they can find peace. According to a postscript added by Herr Mueller, their bodies were never found.

But their shoes were.

Sitting on the embankment.

Afterward, I sit alone for a long time. I refuse to give in to the potent and horrific hatred I have for the Nazis and let it consume me. I shan't let them win. I will go on fighting... I will take care of my little sisters and I will love my man... but I will *never* believe my parents took their own lives.

Never.

* * *

Paris, May 1942
Kay

Rachel's vehement refusal to accept her parents' suicide stays with me for a long time. I grew to love the charming couple as if they were my own parents. True to my word, I speak to Gertrud and she agrees to discreetly check with her contacts in Berlin, but so far, she's found nothing to dispute that the suicide notes aren't real.

I hold off on saying anything to Rachel. Someday, but not now.

Meanwhile, my own life is unraveling. To think a chocolate bar, *my* chocolate bar, does me in with Max.

And the marketing department at *Radwell's French chocolates*.

'Don't try to deny it, Kay, this is you.' Max points to a splashy ad of me on a box of *McGinty's* chocolate bars. He sent me an urgent message via my usual contact at the perfume shop, the House of Doujan on Rue Saint-Honoré, to meet him at my hotel on the Left Bank so we're not seen together. He's here in Paris on an undercover mission for the Foreign Office.

'I won't deny it. It's me. But I can explain—'

'Good. I'd like to know how *your* picture ended up on a shipment of chocolate bars sent to an RAF airfield in southern England.'

He points to an old photo from my deb days the PR department dug up for the ad.

I attempt a smile. 'It's... well, it's complicated.'

I never dreamed the company would send the chocolate bars with my picture on it.

Just my luck Max is in charge of the drop-off.

'All this time the woman I thought was Kay McGinty, the woman I fell in love with... is really Kay Alexander, heiress. And you didn't think to tell me? I don't like being a made a fool of, Kay. I expected more from you.'

He accuses me of lying to him. I can't deny it, and we've been on the outs ever since. I sent him messages through my usual channels to London. I'm hoping to clear things up between us, but so far I've heard nothing from him.

No cryptic messages over *Radio Londres*.

No messages at the perfume shop.

No tall, handsome stranger with a British accent following me and then grabbing a kiss in the alley.

I get it. He hates me and I don't blame him. But after all we've been through, I yearn to see him one last time, even if my heart is broken, aching.

Don't I deserve a goodbye kiss?

I guess not.

41

PARIS, SEPTEMBER 1942

Kay

The Gestapo man has no heart.

I'm drowning in my own sweat in this fur-lined coat, trapped between him and the SS officer near the hotel elevator, wriggling madly to get these handcuffs loose and fighting to keep my dignity intact while he enjoys watching me squirm. Thank God Rachel escaped after I came up with the story about her being a hotel maid. I'd never forgive myself if she fell into Nazi hands. Hollow-cheeked, her body gaunt, but her eyes shining with the beauty of impending motherhood... filling me with a warmth, though fleeting, that I embraced. Then my world turned cold and dark when the secret policeman snapped the handcuffs on me.

And dragged me down the hallway like a stray cat.

But I know my rights.

'I demand you remove these ridiculous cuffs and allow me to pack a bag.'

He grunts and pushes me toward the elevator.

'According to the Geneva Convention of 1929, rule number 65 B...' I shout. There is no such rule, but I doubt he knows that. 'Civilian prisoners are permitted to pack clean underwear and a toothbrush upon arrest.'

Bold, brazen on my part. There's a good chance I won't need clean underwear where I'm going, but I must have hit a nerve with the SS officer because he reminds the Gestapo man every American woman they picked up took a suitcase with her.

He removes the handcuffs, then watches me pack my clothes and boxes of *McGinty's*, working his crossword puzzle and making sarcastic remarks, like *why do American women love their chocolate so much?*

I hate that man.

It gets worse when the cuffs go on again and he parades me down the elevator and through the lobby with my hands behind my back as though I'm a common criminal. How did it come to this? I remember the day when Germany declared war on Poland. I was so naïve I believed it wouldn't last long. That the world wouldn't close their eyes to the dictates of a society where schoolchildren are forced to utter the Nazi salute over a hundred times a day, that such a thing could never happen here in France... or Belgium or the Netherlands.

Yet here we are, three years later and the world is losing the fight.

And so am I.

* * *

Rachel

Hiding behind a large column near the reception area, I have the perfect vantage point when the Gestapo man marches Kay through the hotel lobby toward the revolving doors. Nazi officers, staff... even maids gawk at her, not because only Nazis pass through those doors, but because she's handcuffed with her hands behind her back.

With an SS man following behind her and carrying her suitcase.

The raw power of the scene is made even more dramatic by the luminous glow of this American woman showing no fear in the face of the enemy. Shoulders straight back, chin up, she struts like a French queen before peasants, not giving in to their demands that she cower and beg for mercy. I've never been more proud of her. How she stood up to that horrible Herr Geller, a man I pray rots in Hell.

How her quick thinking saved me, saved my baby.

Moving slowly away from the scene playing out before me, I take a final look at Kay when the Gestapo man drags her out of the hotel and into the black Citroën waiting at the curb. She's never looked more beautiful, more glorious. I struggle to hold back tears, not break down... not until I'm long gone from here.

Then I race out the back entrance and let go of a torrent of emotions, my shoulders shaking with such intensity I sink to my knees. I can't be weak. Not now.

It's my turn to save her.

* * *

Kay

The Gestapo man pushes me into the back seat of his shiny black Citroën then the SS man tosses my suitcase in after me. It bangs against my knee, its sharp edges catching onto my coat and snagging the fabric. That's the least of my problems. Where I'm going strikes a new fear in me.

What if they strip search me?

They'll find the list of names sewn into my girdle and no one, not even my dearest Max will be able to save me then. I've heard the stories about death camps... the horror of Gestapo headquarters on Avenue Foch, where prisoners are tortured by unspeakable means... the torture chamber near the Eiffel Tower where anyone on the Gestapo hit list is tied to a post and executed by firing squad.

I'll end up nothing but a footnote in history that won't even garner a tiny paragraph on the *Philadelphia Inquirer* society page.

A weak smile comes over my lips. It won't bother me, but Mother will be livid. A wry thought at a moment like this, but I wouldn't change anything. I've had more romance and adventure than I ever imagined with Max and Rachel and her family.

God, I'll miss them.

Having put my emotions through every insane scenario, I force myself to latch onto the logical wiring in my brain and keep sharp, *keep fighting*.

Still, I'm not prepared when the black Citroën screeches to a halt, the door opens and the Gestapo man drags me out of the motorcar. We're here. My prison.

I stare at the wrought-iron fence, the ornate buildings. The cages. I want to laugh, then cry.

My God, I can't believe it.

The zoo.

* * *

Bois de Boulogne

I never thought *I'd* end up in what they call the 'monkey house'.

A now empty, large glass-enclosed structure in the *Jardin d'Accli-matation*, what had been a children's amusement park. Whoever decided at Nazi headquarters that rounding up 351 American women and stashing us here in the zoo is either a fool or an idiot or both. I opt for the latter.

Independent, glamorous, studious, literate, adventurous... and plain hopping mad is how I'd describe this motley group of females.

Put me at the top of that list.

The Nazis have the gall to insist they check my identity and when they don't believe I'm an American heiress, I snap back they should read the society columns more often. I get a jolt when a pudgy SS officer reminds the Nazi in charge that the Gestapo picked me up at the Hôtel Ritz trying to smuggle a ruby and diamond necklace out of the hotel. I shoot back, saying I intended to make it a gift to Herr Goering for his collection, but my identity can't be established until they have verification of Herr Geller's report.

Oh, do the Nazis love to play mind games.

Including this bored SS man. Calling me a whore... a cabaret dancer... a spy.

If he only knew...

All the while, the rain comes pouring down, beating against the glass walls.

I refuse to strip when he insists a medical inspection is neces-sary. I stick out my tongue and say '*Ah...*'

If they find the list of names, I won't be held as an enemy alien, but a *résistante* and executed without delay. There's no way I'm going to allow *any* Nazi to look up my girdle.

It seems I won't have to.

Herr Geller arrives at the opportune moment to verify his arrest report of *Mademoiselle Kay Alexander of Philadelphia*, then yells at the incompetent SS officer for dragging him out in the rain away from his dinner at the Ritz which, he regrets, is now cold. Like the SS man is going to be, cold in his grave, if there are any more interruptions. Then, with a snap of his fingers under my nose to startle me, he reminds me not to bribe the guards or I'll find myself at the bottom of the Seine.

I breathe out, giving myself the first round. The Gestapo has no idea what's hidden in my girdle.

With that lovely thought, I'm escorted to the makeshift dormitory on the second floor consisting of lumpy cots, dirty sheets, and a leaky glass roof. There I spend the night with the other American women, each with a story. They're a lively bunch I'll never forget.

And oh, yes, I hand out my entire supply of *McGinty's* chocolate bars, a welcome respite after a dinner of watery soup, soggy potatoes, meatloaf and black bread. Sitting on our cots with rain puddles from the roof dripping in the background, we're a diverse group of American women, including a bookshop owner, society girl, even an ex-actress reputed to work for the Resistance. I'm surprised to find out how curious several women are about my 'coming out' as a debutante, including nuns, French war brides married to Americans, and ladies of the evening. I don't get to spend too much time with them since the most outrageous escape scheme ever from a Nazi detention center takes place two days later.

* * *

Gertrud knows how to contact me. She buys a five-franc admission ticket to the zoo.

I doubt the Germans bothered to come up with a reasonable plan of how they were going to keep American women in tow in a glass-enclosed structure. Rain or shine, mostly rain, Americans love to exercise so we're given the opportunity to take walks in the small garden. I ignore the water sloshing in my wet black pumps. In my hurry, I packed more chocolate bars than essentials and these shoes are all I have. I push that inconvenience out of my mind when, much to my delight, I see Gertrud waving at me over the hedge.

I hear her calling out to meet her over at the double row of gratings, a place where we can talk. Did she get word to Max? He was supposed to pick us up, but I imagine he's still angry with me for lying to him.

Now I find a different kind of problem.

I may never get out of Paris alive.

'How are the children?' I ask, grateful to see my Austrian friend, a light drizzle wetting my coat, but my heart is racing. Nazi soldiers stand guard between us... listening to every word, though I doubt they speak English.

Still, I don't trust them. Neither does Gertrud.

'They're asking for you, Kay,' she says. 'I'm worried about them.'

My heart sinks. They haven't found Leah and Tovah. Or Hélène. Gertrud looks pale, her shoulder pads drooping.

'Tell them I miss them and I love them,' I call back.

'You can tell them yourself. I'll bring them by tomorrow. Teatime. Be ready.'

Then she's off as the drizzle becomes heavier. I take shelter inside the monkey house, my brain spinning.

She's up to something, but what?

* * *

The intrepid Austrian countess is many things. Journalist, bon vivant, Resistance fighter. And when the wind blows right, a straight-backed, Nazi female *Wehrmacht* officer replete with slicked-back short hair, pressed dirty-mustard-colored uniform with the lightning SS insignia on her jacket pocket, swastika patch on her sleeve and cap, and wearing a monocle.

What the Nazi High Command calls a *Wehrmachthelferin*.

Auxiliary helper. Nicknamed 'gray mice' by Parisians.

I remember the first time I saw these German women marching down the Champs-Élysées in formation, young and eager for adventure in the City of Light. Secretaries, telephone operators... and a few become officers.

Gertrud plays that role to perfection.

A bored guard dragged me downstairs earlier from the dormitory and commanded me to wait. Then precisely at teatime, she marches into the makeshift office of operations on the first floor and gives the captain in charge the Nazi salute without so much as a glance at me. I barely notice the Nazi soldier following her. Armed with a rifle, at first I don't recognize the broad-shouldered *soldat* standing at attention off to the side, legs spread, ready to take orders.

Then I get a whiff of motor oil and... *motor oil*?

Max.

He smells like he just got off an aircraft. Of course. He returned to the RAF airfield at Tempsford when I didn't show up at the rendezvous point and then parachuted back into France. How he hooked up with Gertrud I don't know, but they're here trying to save my sorry behind.

It takes me a moment to regroup, another to tamp down the heated emotions roiling inside me. I want to rush into his arms and feel his strength. I need his strength if I'm going to get out of here.

In spite of our differences, he hasn't given up on me. That, in the end, is why I love this man and I'd follow him anywhere.

What happens next is like a Technicolor nightmare that stays with you long after you wake up. I struggle to understand the rapid-fire German Gertrud throws at the bewildered Nazi, a man so tired of females invading his domain, he doesn't need one more.

Especially an overbearing woman with the battle-piercing eyes of a general and the disposition of a tigress sharpening her claws.

I keep my face stoic lest I burst out laughing at this melodrama. Gertrud has an agenda to get me out of here. How she intends to pull it off baffles me, but for the first time since the Nazis occupied Paris, I feel mirth in my bones. I sober up quickly. If this *doesn't* work, my bones will be buried in a makeshift grave in the Bois along with other 'unknowns' who dare to cross the Gestapo.

The Nazi in charge sits at his desk, tapping his fingers on the smooth wood as Gertrud keeps up her diatribe in German. Then he lights a cigarette, offers her one... She refuses though I know she's dying to accept... then she shoves an official-looking document in his face. By her tone, I think... I *hope*... she's demanding my release.

This cat-and-gray-mouse game goes on for several minutes until—

'You're free to go, *mademoiselle*.'

The exhausted captain signs the paper, Gertrud grabs it, then with a snappy '*Heil Hitler*' salute and a satisfied grin, she motions for Max to escort me out of the office.

I've never moved so fast, though my feet are killing me in my wet pumps. I feel Max's presence behind me, then his strong hand at my back leading me upstairs to the dormitory. His familiar touch makes me want things I can't have.

'Max, I—'

'Don't say a word. Just grab your suitcases.' He pauses. 'We can talk about... us... later.'

I nod. The women in the dorm are either asleep or reading and don't look up. They're used to a Nazi guard hanging around, even following them to the bathroom. I pack quickly, then Max escorts me to a side street where Gertrud parked her motorcar.

'How did you pull it off, Gertrud?' I ask, getting in.

'I had our best man in the Underground forge a document requesting *Mademoiselle Alexander's release from internment* signed by the Nazi Ambassador to France. An official way above the captain's pay grade.'

'Thanks, Gertrud.'

'You can thank me later,' she whispers, starting the engine and jamming her foot on the gas pedal. 'Let's get the hell out of here before the captain gets wise and calls the Gestapo.'

42

PARIS, LATE SEPTEMBER 1942

Rachel

I'm not scared... not really. How can I be? Wolf is holding my hand, his warmth rushing through me, protecting me, protecting our baby as we wait outside the police station for Kay and Max and the funny monsieur who calls himself a duke. I find him bombastic and my knees buckle when I'm around him. He's the collaborator I saw at the Hôtel Ritz with the Nazis, the aristocrat who was so friendly with the SS officer, but he's our only chance at seeing my sisters alive again.

I wish we were invisible, Wolf and me, then we could sneak into the police station, unlock the cell door and grab Leah and Tovah. Then we could disappear far away from here. Go anywhere where we can be free from the Nazis. Sometimes I want to go to sleep and wake up and everything will be the way it was... Mutti and Papa alive... my sisters and I playing our music.

But then I wouldn't be carrying my baby.

My little one is like the unique promise of a snowflake falling to earth... no two alike. No two babies are alike. That's why each baby is special. My child is due in December or January... I'm not sure when. I only went to see a doctor last week when I had awful stomach pains; Hélène insisted I go and not take chances. The doctor got suspicious when I didn't understand his awful French jokes... and I couldn't tell him details about the city on my forged identity card where I was born ... then I blurted out that I wished my baby could be born free—

Oh, God, *he's* the one who betrayed us. The balding man in the crumpled white coat must have suspected I wasn't French when I didn't let him inspect my card too closely... and I refused to send my little sisters for a checkup. Their French is far from perfect and could give us away. Local villagers near the château have been arrested for harboring Resistance fighters and Jews lucky enough to escape the roundup last July.

Again, everything is my fault. If my sisters die, I can't live.

'What's wrong?' Wolf holds me tighter because I'm shaking so much I can't stop.

'It's my fault Leah and Tovah are in danger... *it's my fault.*' I start sobbing, ashamed of acting weak, crying, fretting, but I can't stop. What would Mutti say?

Be strong, Rachel. God will help you.

What if God has abandoned me? What then? I clench my fists, the tension making me squeeze my legs together. *What's taking them so long?*

They've been meeting with the local French police for two hours, trying to get my sisters freed. Wolf enlisted the help of his partisan friends and they're stationed in the woods, ready to storm the police station if anything goes wrong.

So we wait.

And wait.

I keep shivering and Wolf holds me closer. The cold October winds come early this year, making my teeth chatter, but I won't leave our vantage point. I've marked every hour since I left the Hôtel Ritz when I panicked and broke down into tears outside the hotel. Gertrud found me and drove me away in her motorcar before the Germans could question me. When I told her what happened, she said she'd take care of it.

And she did.

The Nazis freed Kay and she made us laugh, telling us about the monkey house and the rain and how they pulled it off. She never lost that spirit I love about her to pick herself up and go forward.

I pray they won't be much longer. The fear remains in me that I'll never see my sisters again, hear their voices lifted in song... tease them... watch them grow into young women... and someday also know the joy that lifts me up every day as I await the birth of my baby.

Now they're like wildflowers growing in the field. Sprouting up here... then there. Bending in the wind and kissing the sky with their innocence. I can't let the Nazis take them away from me, but I can't stand waiting like this.

Laying my hand on my rounded belly, I focus on everything that's happened, whispering to the child growing inside me, telling her everything will work out. We just had a delay, a misstep. I won't believe otherwise. We have good, strong people who love us. Wolf, of course, and the British pilot who captured Kay's heart. Max pulled strings and rescheduled the planned pickup for tonight to get us to safety. Leah, Tovah and me... and Hélène. She's a good woman, kind to my sisters and me. I can't forgive myself for getting her involved in this mess. The seedy physician who treated me for stomach pains must have reported her for harboring Jewish children.

I pray to God no harm has come to her.

Minutes tick by... Nothing. My pulse races, my senses sharpening. Not much time left to make our escape. According to Max, the moon is waning and landing a plane and taking off won't be easy, but we have no choice.

If we don't leave tonight, it will be weeks before we can try again.

Then the moment comes as twilight pushes aside the long, gloomy day, like turning a faded old sock inside out and seeing it new again. Kay and Max jam out of the police station... She's protecting Leah, keeping her close and Max is carrying Tovah in his arms. Gertrud and Hélène race out of the building holding hands, followed by the duke, looking very pleased with himself.

'If only Mutti and Papa could see what I'm seeing, Wolf.'

'They can, Rachel,' he says, his breath hot in my ear. 'Now let's get you and your sisters out of France.'

* * *

Kay

I never thought the day would come when I'd kiss the Duc de Savaré on both cheeks. He's a cad, a sycophant, a dandy from another era, and a Nazi sympathizer, but today he's a hero. He saved two innocent Jewish children and a half-Jewish Polish girl from deportation to a concentration camp.

And he did it with a bottle of cognac. Two glasses. And a rat.

At first, I was reluctant to approach the irascible duke, considering his dubious past and involvement with the underbelly of Paris. I didn't know then how low he would go, but in the end it was to our advantage. I found him at the Café de la Paix cavorting with two German girls, 'gray mice', chatting them up with his usual stories of *le jazz hot* and offering to show them a good time.

I rolled my eyes, but said nothing.

He didn't seem surprised to see me and excused himself while we took a walk and I filled him in on my grand adventure at the zoo.

Then I dropped a hint that I had a bit of a problem at the château and needed his help with the local gendarmes... and then casually reminded him that without me, he has no place to live. With that in mind, he couldn't wait to come to my assistance and when I told him what happened to the Landau sisters... and Hélène... he seemed genuinely disturbed.

I swear his mouth quivered and he went pale. He gripped his cane tighter and I swore I could see the wheels turning in his head.

Then...

'I am at your service, *mademoiselle*,' he offered, then kissed my hand. 'Here's my plan to get these girls free...'

I'm still amazed at how he pulled it off. When we arrived at the local police station near the château, I hung back, keeping in the background. After my encounter in the zoo, I can't be too careful. I chatted up the bored guard while Gertrud acted as the Nazi presence, staring down the police captain and, I have to hand it to her, conning him out of his cigarettes. Smoking overtime, she paced up and down, intimidating the police captain who was sweating and tugging on his collar.

Max, still in his German *soldat* uniform, his rifle ready, stood guard at the entrance. No wonder the pudgy police captain shook. He was out of his league when Louis took center stage, opening the bottle of cognac and pouring the chief of the French police a glass, then recounted how he should be ashamed of himself for arresting two innocent children and their nanny. It was a case of mistaken identity, he insisted. These children are guests at his château and the duke would *never* allow a Jew to cross his threshold... his ancestors would haunt the place if he did.

He also implied the chief of police was a frequent client of a *maison close* on Rue de Provence in Paris, supplying the madam with stolen prime cuts of meat and wine intended for the Nazi High Command.

Tsk, tsk. What if the Nazis were to find out the truth? *C'est possible*, the duke hinted, raising his brows.

I caught snippets of his conversation, my ears burning when I heard Louis tout his connections to the *Carlingue*, a French gang that preys on corrupt public officials. It would be a shame if the gang outed him to the Nazis as a rat. A snitch, a loose cannon.

In other words, expendable.

And with that, the police captain ordered the release of the two sisters and Hélène. I couldn't believe our good luck. A battle won without firing a shot.

But we're not free yet.

43

OUTSIDE PARIS, OCTOBER 1942

Kay

We move silently across the moonlit, grassy field, clearing away brush, making a flare path for a landing zone with unlit torches and bicycle lamps, each in our own thoughts. An icy wind blows through the forest surrounding the improvised landing zone. We listen for the Lysander's big engine, then Maxi will flash the Morse code signal they agreed upon. When the pilot responds, we'll have only three... four minutes to get on board.

The Landau sisters, Hélène, and me. A tight fit, but it's been done.

Yet I can't push aside the storm of emotion raging in my soul, my gut telling me I'm not meant to be on that plane. Something else is on my mind.

I don't think about going back to my life in Philadelphia and seeing Mother with her diamond rings sparkling as she checks for dust on the banister, or facing the press in London when word gets out about our daring escape. I don't see myself going back to a world struggling to understand a war that hasn't yet planted its bloody jackboot upon their doorstep. No, instead I see myself fighting alongside this man. Here. In France. I have the perfect cover as an heiress. Above suspicion, isn't that what Uncle Archibald said? Why not exploit it?

But first, we have to clear the air.

'I'm sorry I lied to you, Max, about who I am, but I didn't think you'd understand.' I hug my arms to keep warm.

'You're right, I don't. We're from two different worlds and I don't fit in yours.'

'We both want what's best for the sisters. That's what counts.'

With long strides, he moves ahead of me, knowing I'm right, trying to come to terms with what that means. He accepts me for who I am or—

We never see each other again.

Out of the corner of my eye, I spot the sisters huddled together, waiting, their sad eyes glowing by moonlight, pale faces. Heavy hearts. I'm going to miss them, but it's because of them... and Mutti and Papa and every soul caught up in Hitler's crossfire that makes me swear I can't leave this fight.

'I'm staying in France, Max. We're in this war together. You and me. Partners.'

He spins around, his jaw set. 'I can't let you, Kay. You'll be killed.'

'You can't make me go. I'm not a member of your squadron you can order around.'

If he's surprised by my stance, he doesn't show it. 'Are you sure you know what you're getting into? Smiling at the enemy when it kills you, the taunts from people judging you for that friendly smile, yet never knowing you're working for their freedom.'

'I've never been more certain of anything in my life, Max.' I pause, not holding back how I feel because I'll never get another chance. 'Except how much I love you.'

'You're a crazy American, Kay.'

'And an heiress... Forgive me?'

He heaves out a heavy breath. 'I must be crazy, too, because I can't stop loving you. Not since that first day I saw you.'

'Even if I hand over my girdle to the pilot?' I tease him.

He narrows his eyes. 'What are you up to?'

Laughing, I explain to him about the list of double agents the agent in the perfume shop gave me as we disappear into a cluster of trees and behind the cover of a thick tree trunk. How I sewed it into my girdle. I shiver as I unbutton my dress with nervous fingers, not trying to be coy, but with an urgency that makes my heart race for all the wrong reasons. Making love isn't on my mind, but how to get this damn thing off before the plane lands.

'Need my help?' he whispers, and is that him breathing heavy?

'I could use a hand... or two.' I undo the hooks and eyes at the midriff.

'My pleasure, *mademoiselle*,' he says. 'I promise I won't look.'

'I don't believe you.'

'Seeing you like this in the moonlight is too much for any man, but duty comes first.'

I yank on the talon zipper built into my girdle until it loosens and with his help, I pull down the garment, his strong hands holding me tight, my heart racing. I unhook my garters and down roll my stockings. I hand him my girdle and tell him where the list is hidden so he can relay the information to the pilot. I'd love to overhear *that* conversation.

Still, we're both thinking it's a big gamble, me staying here in Paris, but after the brutality I've seen and the heartache the Nazis have enforced on so many innocents, I have to do my part in this war. I'm in a unique position. They couldn't train an agent to do what I do, knowing my way around in society, name-dropping, the history I have with the Hôtel Ritz, even the jewels and clothes down to my mink-lined coat. I'll be acting as an undercover agent in the Nazi hornet nest in the Ritz, just itching to light their fire and watch them burn.

'I started on this path to gather intelligence to beat the Nazis,' I tell him, 'but I ended up finding so much more. You and the Landau sisters, Gertrud, Hélène—'

The wind stirs as we hear the roar of the engine of the Lysander approaching overhead. Max flashes the signal with his pocket flashlight, the pilot flashes back and we light the torches and turn on the bicycle lamps. The plane lands on the makeshift airstrip less than two hundred yards long. There isn't much time to get the girls on board. Rachel's face drops when I tell her I'm not going, that I have a job to do here. Hélène pulls back, too, announcing she's staying to continue the fight.

'You and your sisters will be safe in England, Rachel,' I tell her, helping her up the fixed ladder on the side of the plane. 'And your baby, too.'

'Oh, Kay, I'm going to miss you so much.'

'You take care of your sisters. I told your parents you'd stay together and you will. And when this war is over, we'll see each other again.'

'Promise, Kay?' she begs, her eyes wide with hope.

Feeling the passion of her plea, I smile. 'Promise.'

* * *

Rachel

I hold on tight to Leah and Tovah, my heart pounding as the pilot turns the plane around and we take off into the wind. I should be happy we're on our way to freedom, but without the people I love, my soul bruised and aching with loneliness.

Mutti, Papa... My heart will not rest until someday I return to Berlin and find out the truth, for I know my parents would never dishonor Jewish law.

Kay... the bravest woman I know. She's an American and they can do anything, *n'est-ce pas*?

Max... a man strong and fearless with the heart of a prince. I'll never forget how he smiles and how protective he is. A handsome hero. Perfect for Kay.

Gertrud... Her road is the hardest. When the Allies win and I know they will, she'll have to prove her loyalty to the cause of freedom.

Hélène. I admire her courage to stay behind with Gertrud. I sense a growing love and friendship between them that grows deeper each day.

And my dearest love. *Wolf*. A boy I met in a train station in Berlin who never once stopped protecting me. He kissed me hard on the mouth before we left Paris, telling me he loved me and then he was off to set explosives on a railroad track to stop a train carrying munitions for the Germans. I didn't tell him I carry his child. I couldn't. His work is so dangerous and requires a clear head. I don't want him to worry about me.

When will I see him again?

When will I see *any* of them again?

When will this war be over?

As the Lysander flies higher and higher above the clouds, I hold my sisters' hands. Leah hasn't spoken a word since we arrived at the makeshift field and Tovah's teeth are chattering. She keeps clenching and unclenching her fingers tight like she does before she picks up her bow to play her violin. She's scared.

I remember what Papa said we should do when we're scared. That we're stronger in harmony.

I put my arm around her, then Leah, and pull them closer, my voice echoing in the small aircraft as I begin to sing, then Leah and Tovah join me.

> *'The night is cold*
> *But my hand is warm*
> *Take my hand, little one*
> *Lay your head against my shoulder*
> *And sleep.'*

And sing we do.
All the way to London.

EPILOGUE
PHILADELPHIA, JULY 1946

Kay

When I arrive home after a long sea voyage on the Liberty ship *SS Marine Perch* from Bremen, Germany, Mother is in bed with a summer cold, her bedclothes pulled up to her chin, but her makeup is on and her fingers are sparkling with her diamond and emerald rings.

Always the proper Philadelphia socialite.

Even when she's got the sniffles.

I think she's vying for attention in her own home, the old faker, demanding the staff bring her hot tea toddies on the hour, according to our butler Seymour who welcomes me warmly.

I'm not sure this is the same house I left.

It's filled with live music and laughter and a little girl's squeals. None of which Mother can compete with, so she's playing the sympathy card.

Lilac Hill is no longer the quiet, stately mansion living in a hushed silence since the Landau sisters took over and the servants love them.

Mother does, too, according to our cook, a robust woman with a South Philly accent she hired after our last one joined the WACs. I sneaked into the kitchen because I brought a special surprise with me and I need a place to hide her. I ask the cook to make tea and does she have any strudel from *Kaplan's*? I want our guest to feel at home.

First, I go to see Mother, who hugs me so tight it brings tears to my eyes. I catch her up on all the news, then it's time for my surprise. I want to wrap my arms around the wonderful sisters and break the news to them no one thought was possible.

I can't wait to see how much Rachel's daughter has grown. I saw her last before her third birthday when I made a quick trip to London.

The little girl was born in England right after Christmas 1942.

Oh, how I wish I could have been there, a way of reliving my own Christmas, but with a happy ending. Since the Landau sisters were part of the original *Kindertransport*, they were welcomed as refugees and stayed in England for the rest of the war with a foster family who was delighted to take them on... and the new baby.

Then I found a theatrical agent with connections to the musical theater and the *Landau Sisters Trio* performed for British and American troops throughout the rest of the war. They were a sensation, Max said, and the boys loved them. It was Max who orchestrated their trip to America aboard the *Queen Mary* on what were called 'war bride voyages' last May. The British-owned ship was only too happy to accommodate the *Landau Sisters Trio* who gave so much to the troops.

I remained in France, determined to show Max I could be a good agent. I became officially sanctioned by the US intelligence agency, the OSS, Office of Strategic Services. I made clandestine trips back to England for debriefings, giving me a chance to check on the sisters and spoil the new baby.

Sadly, from the dispatches I could get my hands on, Wolf was killed in early 1944 when the fighting heated up and his group of Resistance fighters were ambushed by a German patrol.

I don't know if he ever knew he had a daughter.

Gertrud continued to work for the Underground and her relationship with Hélène remained strong until the beautiful Polish girl was arrested by the Gestapo in a small Paris hotel operating a wireless. She was sent to Ravensbrück... Sadly, she died before the camp was liberated.

I continued to work in Paris at the Hôtel Ritz, doing what I do best... creating havoc for the Nazis as a spoiled heiress. The OSS decided I was most valuable if I continued my residence at the Hôtel Ritz and reported back to them on what I saw.

I was the perfect spy.

Fortunately, the forged release document from the zoo never came to light. After the majority of the women were transported to the detention camp in the spa town of Vittel in northeastern France, where I hear the food was better, the captain in charge was sent to the Eastern Front and never heard from again. The duke made certain the Nazis didn't touch me, though it made me uncomfortable knowing it was because of his connections to the notorious French Gestapo.

I have to admit I wasn't saddened when I heard about the mysterious death of Herr Geller by a Resistance fighter, his body found floating in the Seine. I'll never forget him working that damn crossword puzzle while he taunted me at the Ritz the night of my arrest.

I wasn't the only American in residence at the hotel and I know what Parisians said about me, calling me a collaborator, but Gertrud and I made quite a team. I dined in the hotel restaurant with SS officers and entertained the enemy at the château. It's amazing the intelligence I gathered when drunken Nazis came to have supper with me.

I worked undercover until Paris was liberated and then I was debriefed by the Allies. I intervened for the duke after the war, letting my contacts know he came on board and joined our Resistance cell and repented for his sins by gathering valuable intelligence, though Gertrud never forgave him for what happened to the girl found in the Seine.

And she never got over the loss of Hélène.

Last I heard she went back to Vienna to rebuild her beloved city, writing a book about her experiences in Paris during the war and using the profits to help refugees start over again.

No one knew I smuggled my handsome husband into my hotel room at the Ritz and hid him when he 'dropped in' to Paris on a mission. Yes, Max and I were married by the kindly priest he met on his way home from Spain, Father Armand, at Sacré-Cœur with Gertrud as our witness.

The floorboard creaks as I sneak back downstairs, reminding me Max promised to carry me over the threshold and up the stairs and into our bedroom the minute he arrives. He's set to muster out of the RAF any day and he'll be arriving in the States as soon as he can get on a ship.

His illustrated book which includes sketches that appeared in a London newspaper about the war in Spain is set to be released later this year. It's already receiving glowing reviews and he's fielding offers from several publishers for a series on his RAF experiences.

I'll never forget the first time those smoldering dark eyes caught me looking at him in the Paris café, making me think of a rogue painter from another time capturing me in his web, entwining my heart with silken threads so fine I never noticed, and so strong I couldn't break free if I wanted to. We intend to have that honeymoon we missed at the château near Paris, but it will be a working honeymoon. I want to set into motion my plan to turn it into a women's shelter with a medical clinic.

But first, I have another story to tell.

How the State Department granted me permission to travel to Berlin on a fact-finding mission earlier this year. I never put aside what Rachel said about her parents, never giving up hope the intelligence was wrong and they didn't commit suicide.

I had to find out for myself.

So I asked Uncle Archibald to pull some strings and I went to Berlin with a military attaché as my guide, a young Jewish sergeant from Brooklyn who escaped Germany before the war with his parents. I was devastated by what I saw. The city lay in ruins. Heaps of wood, trash piled up everywhere. Burned-out motorcars. Metal from tanks strewn about. A few Berliners riding bicycles... most walking or pulling wooden carts with goods and belongings. Lines of women using a relay system with buckets to clear out debris from bombed-out buildings. Children lost and without a home.

When we drove up to the music shop on Charlottenstrasse in the Army Jeep, I didn't know what I'd find. So many buildings were mere shells, rubble in the streets, but somehow the little shop was still there, bullet holes in the brick wall, broken pavements, but when I saw the white candle burning in the window and the tattered photograph Gertrud took of the Landau sisters and me sitting next to it, I couldn't contain myself.

Mutti.

She broke down sobbing when she saw me. Her hair was streaked with gray, her body thin, but her eyes never lost hope that someday her daughters would return. The Army sergeant helped me explain to her what happened to Rachel, Leah and Tovah, the lines on her face softening like smooth butter as the years drifted away, her eyes filling with tears as he spoke to her in German with her reading his lips and holding my hands.

When I told her in English she has a granddaughter, she understood and raised her eyes upward, mumbling a prayer.

By now we were in tears. Several moments passed, hugging each other, our hearts full, but there was still so much to talk about, how Mutti and Papa survived after the sisters left Berlin, how the suicide notes were a ruse Papa came up with and how Ulrich hid Mutti and Papa in the hidden room on the second floor Mutti used as an office. His wife never suspected since she hated the shop and refused to live here. She ran off with another man toward the end and Mutti has no idea what happened to her.

Then we took a moment to acknowledge the passing of Ulrich Mueller who was killed by an Allied bomb. Mutti lit another candle and said a prayer for the kindly man who saved their lives.

When I ask her what happened to Papa, she clasped her hands to her chest and tears ran down her cheeks, the love for her husband never waning.

After the war Papa's health failed... He died from pneumonia in late 1945 and is buried in the cemetery in the synagogue next to Mutti's parents with his favorite violin.

Once we had finished sharing our stories, Mutti packed a few precious items, including her crystal candy dish, eager to see her daughters again.

When we arrived in New York, Mutti and I took the train to Philadelphia. I didn't know how much I could tell Mother, but Uncle Archibald told me he debriefed her ahead of time, explaining as much as he could about my work with the OSS. What I've done will remain classified.

But not all of it.

The press got wind of my story, interviewed me in Berlin and came up with a dubious title for the article... *I survived the Nazi*

Occupation in Paris as told by a Philadelphia debutante. I avoided talking about my work with the Resistance. There are many others far braver than I who made the ultimate sacrifice and deserve the spotlight. But I was only too happy to elaborate on our work in forming and operating the *Kinder Air Transport* from Berlin to France (the only similar effort I know about was a flight ferrying children from Czechoslovakia to England in 1939).

I spoke freely and with passion about the Landau sisters and their parents' sacrifice to get them on that flight... and the others that followed. About Max... Gertrud... and Hélène. True heroes, all of them.

I choked up, reliving that exciting time in my life with deep satisfaction that I *did* make a difference during the war in many children's lives.

And now we're here.

I can hardly wait to see Rachel's face. She doesn't know we're coming since I wasn't sure when I'd get the legal entanglements completed. I had to jump through hoops to get Mutti approved as a refugee and since her daughters are already here, I got her a visa and we're working to get everyone permanent status. Having them live here at Lilac Hill clinched their case and Mutti's visa came though quicker than I thought possible.

I stop for a moment outside the library as I did so many years ago when this adventure began, when I embarked on the path to being a debutante. When I was too scared to face life.

Now I'm a daughter come home and a spy rolled into one. I stand, hypnotized by what I see. Three lovely young women playing Chopin with the warmth and surety of true *artistes*. Rachel on piano – she's twenty-three now. Leah on guitar – she's twenty. And Tovah on violin – she's seventeen.

And sitting next to her mother on the piano bench is little Jessy, three.

Clapping her hands and giggling.

'*Ist das meine Enkelin?*'

I turn and see Mutti behind me... and my mother, smiling widely. She heard the German woman was in the kitchen and wanted to meet this extraordinary woman who raised such lovely, talented daughters.

'Yes, Mutti, that's your granddaughter, Jessy,' I say, facing her so she can read my lips and using the endearment because I can't think of her any other way.

'*Sie ist so schön,*' she says with a heavy sigh. 'She's so beautiful.'

They say a child and a mother have a sixth sense, that a mother can distinguish her child's cry anywhere. Here on this summer day when the lilacs bloom in a purple so deep it vibrates, when the world is again at peace, it's the children... the daughters, who are so tuned in to their mother's voice, they stop playing at the same time. They stop and look at each other, not believing what they heard but not wanting to let go of the beautiful moment swimming in their minds.

Can it be? they ask one another, but it's Rachel whose faith never wavered, who let her heart rule instead of her reason, who turns to see us standing in the doorway.

'Mutti, *Mutti!*' she yells, and without asking *why, how* – because does it really matter at this moment? – Rachel and her sisters rush forward, crying, squealing with joy, embracing their mother with such warmth she's smothered with their hugs and kisses. She closes her eyes and breathes in the beauty of this moment. Even little Jessy knows Mutti is someone special when she grabs the hem of her grandmother's dress. Rachel picks her up and introduces her to her Bubbe... a moment only God could make happen.

We all start crying, even Mother. I've never seen my mother cry before. It's then she puts her arms around me.

'Welcome home, Kay,' she says with a catch in her voice. 'I'm so proud of you.'

My heart tightens. 'Oh, Mother, that's all I ever wanted to hear you say. I've missed you so much.'

'I've missed you, too,' she says, sniffling, then clears her throat, becoming once again the perfect Main Line hostess. 'Shall we go in and entertain our guests... together?'

I hug her tight. 'Yes, I'd like that.'

We walk arm in arm into the library, the laughter and tears making beautiful music that will live on for generations to come.

All that matters is, after all the heartache, the struggle to keep the world free and save those we love, we're safe here at Lilac Hill.

Rachel, her family, and me.

I can't wait for Max to arrive and see us all together. To think I had to leave here to find the joy that God brought to me when I lay in my husband's arms on a moonlit night, when the stars aligned for us and we reached out and grabbed the one we wanted. The one that shined the brightest.

And guided me home.

ACKNOWLEDGMENTS

Everybody has secrets. Things we don't talk about because they're too painful or we're embarrassed or we haven't come to grips on how they've affected our lives.

Writers have secrets, too. We let them fester in our minds and hearts forever, wanting to let go until the day comes when we can't hold them back any longer and we write down everything we've kept inside for a long time.

Well, not everything. We want to tell a good story, so not every detail or fact is important, but we let go and free emotions inside us that we've kept hidden for years.

I have a secret.

Like my heroine, Kay Alexander, in *The Orphans of Berlin*, I lost a baby on Christmas morning many years ago. A child who survived for twenty minutes. I remember it vividly and used those memories to write the Christmas scene, detailing the physical and emotional turmoil I experienced, beginning with that Christmas Eve when I went into premature labor and then the birth of my child the next morning.

I mention it because for years I was told to 'get over it', that I had to move on, so I pushed aside the raw emotions that tortured me that it was my fault. Thank goodness, mental health has changed and women can seek the help and resources they need if they face such a devastating trauma. I urge any woman finding herself in that position to do so.

It was that deep, emotional loss of a child that pushed me

forward when I wanted to write about the *Kindertransport*. For the parents of those Jewish children, it was losing a child in a different way, but the loss and gut-wrenching emptiness are similar. Imagine sending your child to a foreign country, not knowing if you'll ever see them again. So many parents didn't, since they were sent to concentration camps and didn't survive.

The British *Kindertransport* is well documented, but I've chosen to write about the French *Kindertransport* that took Jewish children from Germany and Austria to France by train. Approximately 10,000 Jewish children travelled to Great Britain on the *Kindertransport*, while numbers for France vary from 200 to 450 children.

The *Kinder Air Transport* that my heroine establishes from Berlin to Paris is fiction, though film footage exists of the *Kindertransport* taking Jewish children from Prague, Czechoslovakia to Great Britain by airplane in 1939.

In *The Orphans of Berlin*, my heroine, a woman who can't have children of her own, undertakes a life-changing, emotional journey where she finds peace and fulfillment in helping others and saving as many Jewish children as she can.

My journey to the publication of *The Orphans of Berlin* was not a lonely road. I had all the support and love I needed to make my story the best it can be.

Where would I be without my awesome editor, Nia Beynon? She believed in me from the beginning and we make quite a team. She always knows how to bring out the best in me and make my story shine. She's not just a great editor, but a classy lady, too.

My copyeditor, Candida Bradford, never fails to challenge me to make the story even better with her excellent observations and editing skills.

And my proofreader, Shirley Khan, performs a difficult job with expertise.

Also on Team Boldwood is digital marketing guru Claire Fenby, who works tirelessly to get our books to the readers with a creative flair that always impresses me. And marketing executive, Jenna Houston, who adds her talent to getting our books out there with timeliness and skill.

And of course, our fearless leader, Amanda Ridout, who guides us, her authors, with her magic wand.

Thank you all from the bottom of my heart.

And also to my readers for coming along with me on this difficult journey and allowing me to tell my stories about another time, another place that both fascinates me and inspires me. I hope it does for you, too. We draw courage from understanding the struggles others have faced so we may overcome our own.

Which is why every Christmas I say a special prayer for that little soul that found its way to heaven that morning so many years ago... and still shines their light on me.

ABOUT THE AUTHOR

Jina Bacarr is a US-based historical romance author of over 10 previous books. She has been a screenwriter, journalist and news reporter, but now writes full-time and lives in LA. Jina's novels have been sold in 9 territories.

Sign up to Jina Bacarr's mailing list here for news, competitions and updates on future books.

Visit Jina's website: https://jinabacarr.wordpress.com/

Follow Jina on social media:

f facebook.com/JinaBacarr.author

X x.com/JinaBacarr

O instagram.com/jinabacarr

BB bookbub.com/authors/jina-bacarr

♪ tiktok.com/@jinabacarrauthor

ALSO BY JINA BACARR

Her Lost Love

The Runaway Girl

The Resistance Girl

The Lost Girl in Paris

The Orphans of Berlin

Sisters at War

Letters from
the past

Discover page-turning
historical novels from
your favourite authors
and be transported
back in time

*Join our book club
Facebook group*

https://bit.ly/SixpenceGroup

*Sign up to our
newsletter*

https://bit.ly/LettersFrom
PastNews